ROBERT MURPHY

THE PEREGRINE FALCON 1963
THE POND 1964
THE GOLDEN EAGLE 1965

. . . and now his greatest nature novel

A CERTAIN ISLAND

"Both rewarding and enjoyable reading."
Denver Post

drawings by **JOHN PIMLOTT**

A CERTAIN ISLAND

Robert Murphy

AN AVON BOOK

AVON BOOKS
A division of
The Hearst Corporation
959 Eighth Avenue
New York, New York 10019

First Avon Printing, August, 1968

Cover illustration by Barry Driscoll

Printed in the U.S.A.

Howbeit we must be cast upon a certain island.

ACTS 27:26

The small expedition to Laysan Island with which this novel is concerned actually took place. The island can be found on the map at the location given, and the background of history and birdlife is true. But the characters and events set forth are imaginary. The young man who made the trip bears some outward resemblance to Alfred M. Bailey, who is now the Director of the Denver Museum of Natural History. Dr. Bailey was born in Iowa and several of his boyhood adventures suggested a few of the things that occur in the book, but that is all. Dr. Bailey is not Geordie nor were Geordie's problems his, any more than the other characters in the novel are the actual people who went to Laysan.

When I was first thinking of the book, I went to see Dr. Bailey. He and his family were most hospitable and generous in providing me with notes, diaries and museum publications, some of which are now out of print, containing Dr. Bailey's articles and pictures relative to the trip he had made so long ago. Without this help I doubt that the skeleton of A CERTAIN ISLAND would ever have been formed, and I am most grateful to them all.

Robert Murphy
Westtown, Pennsylvania

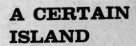

A CERTAIN
ISLAND

ONE

His name was George Sutton and they called him
Geordie; there was a Geordie in every generation because the family, being sober fellows and studious in the
main, held to a romantic and quixotic affection for a
remote ancestor named Geordie MacFarlane, "Old
Geordie," a Highland Scot who had lost his head because
of his enterprise with a claymore in support of Bonnie
Prince Charlie in the '45. There was a sort of wistfulness
in this affection, as though each succeeding generation
held the hope of another wild and reckless son who
would shake off the pale cast of thought, the family's

11

habit of carefully considering every decision, in the wholehearted pursuit of an immoderate illusion. None of them had ever admitted that if such a son appeared it would horrify them.

By the end of the 19th century there had been none and the prospect still wasn't very bright, for the family was established in Iowa by this time and was producing lawyers; as the century came near its end our Geordie appeared and he didn't seem a likely candidate either. A tall, thin, dark-haired boy with a slow, engaging grin, he was more interested in the wildlife of the prairie sloughs and along the muddy Iowa River than he was in Blackstone or anybody like him. Not that he was a poor student; his grades had always been good enough to encourage a lenient attitude on the part of his father, but the lenient time was about over.

"Here he is," his father said to his mother toward the end of that summer, "about to go into his first year of college, and he'd still rather sit in a swamp than in a library. Where does he get such tastes? When he was in grammar school it was understandable, and probably good for him. The exercise, and that sort of thing. And a certain amount of self-reliance as well. But, I must say . . ."

"He's been reading Darwin," his mother said. "I found the book under his bed."

His father snorted, a method of expressing himself that wasn't characteristic of him; he usually took a reasonable and even judicious tone. "That wretched man," he said with distaste. "If they'd shaved him he'd have looked more like a monkey than he did. Not that I think," he went on quickly, "that his theories are stupid. They are not. They have a good deal to recommend them, despite the uproar that they have caused. But Geordie will addle his brains with such stuff at his age. It's time he began to read a little law. I do think I've been quite patient with the boy, Lavinia, and it seems to me that it's high time we began to make him understand that his future will be ill-served by continuing to run the woods and little else."

There was a short silence in the high-ceilinged living-room. Lavinia Sutton, dark haired, with beautiful dark eyes in an oval face, had been sitting with her hands in her lap, looking at the Turkish carpet while her husband talked; she stood up, walked over to him, and put her hands on his shoulders. "Did you always want to be a lawyer, Alfred?" she asked. "From a little boy?"

"My father was a lawyer, and so was his father. I suppose it was natural that I wanted to be one."

"But did you really want to be one? Did you have a vocation, and burrow into your father's library before you went to that eastern college?"

She smiled at him, attempting to get a lighter tone into the discussion, for she had worried ever since the spring when his impatience had begun to show.

"Yes," he said, answering her question but not her smile. "Listening to my father talk about the law, I saw a sort of . . . of beauty in it, reasonable and orderly. What else is there here for him, Lavinia?" he asked, with great seriousness. "He'll never be a doctor; I'm sure he wouldn't be a good farmer or a storekeeper. If he keeps going as he is now, he'll end up like that dirty old Possum Boniface, who's always in my office to be got off some charge or other. *That* I will not have."

Lavinia Sutton fell back a step, and her hands dropped to her sides. "Oh, Alfred!" she said. "Surely you don't think . . . You can't be serious. Alfred, he's so young!"

"When I was his age . . ." he began, and stopped and made an unhappy gesture with one hand. "Maybe I've shown my impatience. I'm sorry. I'll try not to do it

again. Now I've got to go out and see Judge Meadows."
He kissed her, a little formally, turned, and started for
the hall. She watched him go, seeing the straight back,
the hair beginning to show a frost of gray, the carriage
that the town knew and respected; she knew that
Geordie respected him as well, perhaps too much, and
was therefore in his shadow. She sighed.

While Geordie's father was talking about Possum
Boniface, Geordie himself was sitting in a boat a few
miles away with Possum himself. How he had got there
was none of his own doing; he had been fishing from the
riverbank with his cane pole held by a forked stick,
stretched out in luxurious idleness in the sun and staring
dreamily at his cork when Possum had come along in his
scarred old boat, and backing it into the bank had in-
vited Geordie to join him.

"I could do with a mite of help, boy," Possum said.
"Climb in, and give me a hand."

"Sure," Geordie said. "Wait until I put my pole on
the bank."

He knew Possum and had often stopped by Possum's
shack a little further up the river for a word about where
the ducks might be or other such matters, for Possum was
always poking about and kept a sharp eye on the activities of what he called "the varmints." He was a hairy old
man, always grimy, who lived alone in a monumental
clutter. His horny feet were bare, as they always were
until frost, his unshaven chin was stained with tobacco
juice, and—to put a point on it—he smelled; he lived
out of a bottle and off the country and consequently
paid no attention to existing game laws or property lines,
but aside from this idiosyncrasy there was no evil in
him.

14

Geordie wrapped his line around the pole, hid the pole in the brush, and climbed aboard. He knew that Possum always had fish and hoped that the secret of this abundance might be revealed. He grinned at Possum, for Possum amused him; the old man's life was so different from the lives of the other people Geordie knew, so uncomplicated and empty of possessions that had to be eternally cared for, that he was a pleasant change occasionally. He wasn't a heroic figure, but he was free. "What's up?" Geordie asked.

"I need you to row," Possum said. "I aim to get a bait of fish." They changed places in the boat, and when Geordie had the oars Possum pointed to a backwater a hundred yards downstream with a stump sticking above the surface on the edge of it. "Row down there, and hang on to that stump."

Geordie eased the boat downstream, wondering how they were going to fish, for there weren't any poles or hand-lines visible. He didn't have to wonder long, for Possum reached under his seat, pulled out a box, and out of the box brought a stick of dynamite and broke it calmly in half. Geordie's jaw dropped a little; he had often heard of the spectacular effects of dynamite, and he knew that dynamiting fish was illegal. He was aware that he should put himself ashore and bow out at once, but the prospect was too exciting; he watched with a sort of horrified fascination as Possum put a cap and fuse on the dynamite, wrapped it and a stone in a piece of oiled paper, and tied everything up with a piece of fishing line from his pocket.

They had drifted past the stump by that time, and Geordie rowed back and took hold of it. Possum stood up, looked up and down the river to see if the coast was clear, struck a match on the seat of his pants, and touched it to the fuse. The fuse began to sizzle; Possum held the package for a moment and then threw it toward the backwater. A loop in the string caught on his thumb, and the dynamite swung around and fell into the boat.

Geordie's hair stood up and a paralysis seized him; he sat staring at the fuse, and couldn't have moved to save his life. Possum started to jump overboard, changed his mind, whirled about, and because his legs were crossed fell toward the dynamite. The boat rocked wildly; Possum's reaching hand fell two inches short, and he humped himself desperately along the floorboards, reached the dynamite, managed to half stand up, and threw the package toward the backwater. "Git!" he shouted, turning to Geordie. "Git!"

Geordie, hanging onto the heaving boat, was galvanized into action, and dug the oars desperately into the water. Possum scuttled forward and took the oars too and the pair of them pulled until their muscles cracked, splashing water all about. The boat began to move slowly; they got in about four strokes when the dynamite let go with a roar, concussion thumped the boat, and a column of water rose into the air. This frightened them so that they feathered the oars; Geordie fell backwards and Possum fell on top of him. The waves caused by the explosion almost capsized them, and after lying in terror for a moment they untangled themselves and sat up groggily.

The water was flattening out and a number of fish were belly up on the surface among fragments of trash from the bottom. They both stared at the scene for a moment, and then Possum pushed Geordie toward the bow, took the oars himself, and rowed into midstream. A long reach opened to the south, and at the far end of it they saw a boat. Possum muttered something to himself, straightened up to get a better look at it, and then bent to the oars and rowed rapidly to the point where he had picked Geordie up. He turned into shore, and Geordie scrambled out. Standing shakily on the bank, he exchanged a long look with Possum, who now seemed impatient to be gone.

"You going to collect the fish?" he asked.

"Heck with the fish," Possum said. A strange, greenish pallor had appeared on his unshaven face. "You can have 'em. I swallered my chaw, and I got to go home for my tonic." His jaw was shaking, and after abstractedly noting this Geordie watched him as he dug in the oars and made rapidly for a bend in the river and disappeared.

The boy sat down on the bank, drew a long breath, and blew it out again. He raised a hand to his own jaw, to see whether it was shaking like Possum's, couldn't find it was, and felt proud of himself. As he recalled the sequence of events fragmentary pictures of what he had seen as they scrambled about came to him, and then he began to laugh. He laughed immoderately, a little light-headed from relief, and when it was over he shook his head, looked up at the sky that he might never have seen again, and then lowered his head. There was a boat lying a few feet off the bank with a man sitting in it. It startled him so that he jumped; he hadn't heard it, or noticed it coming up.

The man was facing him, resting on his oars. He was a big man, well-muscled, bareheaded, dressed in khaki pants and shirt, with a square, sunburnt, unsmiling face; his gray eyes were like the eyes of a teacher who is trying to get to the bottom of some piece of classroom deviltry. Geordie stared at him, uneasy now and still startled by his sudden appearance.

"Did you see a boat with two people in it come by here, boy?" he asked.

"No, sir," Geordie said, and then recalled the other boat they had seen far down the reach. Maybe, he thought with a sinking feeling, it was the game warden. His throat tightened up, and he swallowed. He shook his head. "No, sir," he said again.

"Did you hear a noise?"

Geordie was a truthful boy, but he was frightened; he had heard many of his father's stories of malefactors being apprehended and going to jail, and he knew very well his father's feelings about them. He wanted to tell the truth and try to explain his innocence, but couldn't; all he could think of was his father's reaction if the man found him out and took him to his father's office. He was going to have to lie his way out of the situation. He swallowed again. "Yes, sir," he said. "I heard a noise. It was sort of like an explosion."

"H'm," the man said, and considered him. Then he said, suddenly: "You weren't in that boat?"

"No, sir," Geordie said, and felt himself beginning to shake. "I didn't see a boat."

"What's your name?"

"Geordie Sutton," Geordie said.

"Alfred Sutton's boy?"

"Yes, sir," Geordie said, and felt a trickle of perspiration begin to take its way down his back.

The man's eyebrows went up, and he nodded. There seemed to be a sudden relaxation of the tension in him, the feeling that he was about to pounce was lightened; the mysterious power of Alfred Sutton's name upon him was amazing. Geordie dared to take a full breath.

"What were you doing here, Geordie?" the man asked, in a tone that sounded almost friendly.

"I was fishing," Geordie said. "I'd just put my pole away." He was suddenly released from the immobility that had held him. "See?" he asked, and ran back to the brush where he had hid the pole. He got down on his knees and groped in the brush, his hands still shaking, and finally brought out the pole. "See?" he asked again, holding it up. "I was just going home."

"You were laughing like a loon."

"Yes, sir," Geordie said. "I . . ." No reason why he had been laughing like a loon came into his head, and he was sensible enough not to try to fumble about for one. "Yes, sir, I was."

The man looked at him for a long moment, nodded, and dipped the oars. Geordie watched him pull away, filled with a relief so intense that it was almost painful. The boat rounded the point and vanished. Geordie stared at the empty water for a few seconds, let out a long breath, and hid the pole again. He sat down beside it until the trembling in him stopped, stood up, and walked through the riverside brush to the narrow dirt road and got on his bicycle and headed home.

He was still a little light-headed with relief at having got off so lightly after his first brush with the law as he came into the familiar quiet, tree-lined streets with their well-spaced houses and stables in the rear, the lawns bright with early fall flowers in the flowerbeds, solid, staid, and respectable; in this reassuring atmosphere he began to settle down. His recent adventure, from the business with the dynamite to the encounter with the warden, began to seem improbable and far away, as though it had happened a long time ago and even to someone else, a story that he had heard and not been involved in himself.

He came to his own tree-lined driveway and turned in. The big wooden house, painted white, with a shingled cupola and a porte-cochere, was set well back from the street; there was a pretty little white stable behind it. The lawn beneath the trees was dappled with afternoon sunlight. It was a good house, one of the best in town, and rather impressive; it had been built by a real estate promoter who had made a good deal of money selling prairie farmland to immigrants from the East, land-hungry people who had heard of the richness of the prairie earth. Some of the land had been drained marshes that hadn't worked out very well for farming, and there had been litigation and other unpleasantness that had finally resulted in the promoter's moving away.

Geordie had been born in the house several years after his father had bought it, and his memories began with the big, high, airy rooms through which he still moved. His life in it had been pleasant, a typical Midwestern boyhood, provincial and easygoing, surrounded with plenty of open country, little conflict or big-city excitement, and with people from the University or the professions in the main. His father was regarded as the town's best lawyer, had a fine practice, and would probably end up as a judge. His bent was intellectual rather than physical; he had never been an outdoorsman and secretly thought (despite a number of his friends who seemed to enjoy outdoor life) that anyone who would arise in the middle of the night to go slopping around a duck marsh or march about to shoot wild birds much like chickens was somewhat of a fool.

He was proud of his intelligence and his position, and wanted his son to follow in his footsteps; it worried him that Geordie seemed to be headed for a life that would be fulfilled with an enterprise on the level of taxidermy or veterinary medicine—"horse doctoring"—or some similar messy business.

Geordie cycled through the porte-cochere and on to the stable where Laverty, the man of all work, was washing the Packard. Laverty, an old Irishman who looked a little like a monkey and had a fringe of ginger whiskers, was in a bad humor; he loved horses, the feel of good leather, and the delicate lines of fine coachwork, and always grew morose when he had to deal with the new-fangled devices that he called "machines." He looked up when Geordie appeared, spat on a fender to express his contempt of the car, and washed the spittle off with the hose. "Ah, now," he said. "The young frontiersman hisself. And what might you have been up to?"

Geordie almost told him, for Laverty in his better moments was full of tales of poaching in the old country and the new, but caught himself in time; he had found by bitter experience that a misguided word to Laverty found its way to Ingrid the cook and from there to his mother. "I've been fishing," he said.

"And where might the fish be? Do we all starve because Your Honor's after fallin' asleep by the river?"

"Do you think my name is Laverty?" asked Geordie, and ran around to the other side of the car before Laverty could turn the hose on him. He put the bicycle away, and watching his chance ran for the house; the nozzle turned his way, but the stream fell short.

Ingrid wasn't in the kitchen, and by the clock it was an hour until dinner; he went up the back stairs to his room. It was at the rear of the house, somewhat off by itself, a big, bright, corner room with four windows. There was an oval rag rug on the floor, Geordie had made bookcases that lined one wall, and there was a big, old desk of his father's with a green-shaded student's lamp, a muskrat's skull, a badly stuffed Wilson's phalarope, a pad, and a small Navajo pot full of pencils on it, a double bed covered with an India print, and three upholstered chairs. A double-barreled shotgun stood in a corner with a baseball bat, and the pictures around the walls were of birds and animals. Most of them were ani-

21

mals and birds of other countries—Africa, India, and the Arctic, places remote and mysterious; Geordie was a great reader of books about these places, and longed in an abstract way to visit them.

As he often did when he came into the room, he withdrew from the rest of the house, the people around him, and the things that he had been doing recently. He paused in the middle of the room and looked around, unseeing, for this was the place where he came to detach himself from his everyday life and, in effect, live the clouded life of the future.

This life, or the fantasies that made it up, weren't very specific, for he didn't know yet what he wanted to do. In his daydreams he wandered in far places, leading scientific expeditions into exotic jungles; sometimes he was being congratulated by presidents of learned societies for triumphs that he couldn't recall, and occasionally these men looked like his father. He was always pleased when they did, but in any case the visions would finally fade away and he would be in his room again, tingling and excited by the strangeness and color of them, but wondering for a time afterward what he had done to deserve the honors heaped upon him. Lately he had come to the point where the adventures weren't sufficient because of their inconclusiveness; he was beginning to realize in a hazy way that merely wandering about even in the most exotic situations didn't satisfy him.

For the past few months he had been groping about, trying various things; the stuffing of a few birds, which hadn't seemed to please his father very much, was one of them. He had even tried to write poetry, but it had all sounded so much like either *The Rubaiyat* or *The Idylls Of The King* (one he read in school, and the other he happened upon by himself) that he was discouraged by it. He wanted it to sound like himself, but when he sat down in front of a blank page and faced the question of what to say he couldn't find an answer and wound up echoing the others.

Today, when he got into this room where he was cut off from the outside world, in which just living was sufficient and the activity of living was satisfying, he wanted more than ever to find something that would give his inner life direction. This time his dissatisfaction was closer to the surface than it had ever been before. Perhaps the shaking up that the affair with Possum and then the game warden had given him was responsible, for he felt guilty about them even though he hadn't admitted it to himself, and this guilt made him more dissatisfied with his reveries than usual.

He stood looking at the phalarope. The light was waning in the room, and somehow the shadowed shape of the bird seemed to hold a clue to the future, a clue to an answer that wouldn't come clear. This feeling lasted but a moment; it popped into his head and was gone, a fugitive thing like a sound that one thinks he has heard but isn't sure, and it puzzled Geordie. How *could* it mean anything, especially about the future? He walked over and picked it up.

When it was in his hand, hard and dry, he began remembering. He had shot it in the spring, and as he recalled seeing the bird, one of three, falling into the grass of the marsh, the previous seasons of the year now passing began to come back to him.

TWO

The impetus to stuff the phalarope, which was the reason
why it had been shot, had come during the winter. It was
then that he had found an advertisement that had
caught his eye in one of the five-cent magazines that
circulated among the boys of the class. BE A TAXIDERMIST,
it said, in big, black letters. FIND FUN AND PROFIT IN THIS
FASCINATING HOBBY. There was a picture of a young man,
surrounded with mounted birds and animals in lifelike
poses, pointing them out to another young man who
seemed greatly impressed by the products of his skill and
industry. Geordie had never thought of stuffing any-

thing, for most of the time in his comings and goings he was surrounded by wildlife; the banks of the river and the marshes were lively with animals and nesting birds in the summer and vast numbers of migrating birds in the spring and fall. The great waterfowl migrations were still spectacular; they had not at that time been greatly reduced, and although market hunting was whittling down the clouds of ducks and shorebirds there were still immense numbers of them.

Seeing them alive and moving in great skeins across the sky, being out where they were and in the midst of them, had been enough for Geordie in the several winters that he had been allowed to go about and hunt. These had been mild winters, when he could get out; but the last winter, the one when the advertisement found him, had been a bad one. It closed in early with a series of storms, a lot of snow, and the howling, bitter cold such as only the prairie country can produce, and he had been held away from his usual trips. The hardy creatures that stayed in mild winters fled; they couldn't have been found even if he had been able to look for them.

He missed them, and he missed the trips. The long hours that he had formerly spent stalking a stray mallard or a pintail, trapping muskrats, hiding in a marsh for a possible shot, or exploring an island in the River had to be spent at home; snowball fights and what sledding could be had in a country where hills were low and infrequent weren't enough for him. It wasn't that he was antisocial; he got on well enough with other boys; it was just that he preferred, most of the time, to be out under the sky, out of town, among the birds and animals to watch and learn a little more about them. They were more interesting than people because they were more mysterious, forever changing with the seasons, infinite in their variety and curious in their actions, wary and hidden; and the vast sweep of the country had the same attraction to him that the vast sweep of the sea has to a sailor.

He missed all this so much in the short gloomy days when the wind buffeted the house that the advertisement caught him; if he couldn't be out where he wanted to be, this was a way to bring it home. He saw himself, like the man in the picture, surrounded with carefully mounted specimens. He picked up the magazine from the desk and went looking for his mother and found her in the kitchen with Ingrid, who was making pastry. Ingrid was a big, very fair, Danish girl; she had the tabletop covered with a great thin disc of dough and was buttering and folding and rolling it, and then doing these things again; the big warm kitchen was fragrant with the smell of spices and almonds and other things.

Geordie drew a deep breath and forgot the magazine for a moment. Sometimes, years later, in many strange corners of the world where the food was very bad and life was very uncomfortable, that wonderful fragrance would come to him for a moment and he would remember; possibly it was because it was connected with the advertisement that had been so important to him. Then he recalled the magazine again, and held it out. "Ma," he asked, "could I send the coupon?"

It seemed to Geordie that she looked at it for a long time, and her eyes narrowed a little as though she was thinking of something else. He began to feel very apprehensive, and then she nodded. "Why, yes, Geordie, if you want to. If you really want to. I'll do it for you, if you like."

The coupon brought more enticing literature, Geordie sent his money, and presently he had several books about taxidermy. They set forth the best way to skin birds and animals, how to treat the skins and mount them, how to make rugs and fur pieces, and listed supplies that were necessary. He paid little attention to the making of rugs and fur pieces but studied the rest with great seriousness and finally sent off for several tools and chemicals. He wanted to buy some glass eyes, but didn't know what to buy them for; that would have to wait until his subjects appeared. Now that he was ready to go to work there was nothing to work on, and finally he hunted up Laverty and found him in the harness room. Busy with a sponge and saddle soap, Laverty was feeling cheerful; there was a pot-bellied stove going full blast, and he was whistling "The Drummer Boy To The War Has Gone," working away on a harness with his sleeves rolled up.

"Ah, now," he said, pausing in his labors. "So it's something to stuff, is it? Belike you should be looking for a polar bear."

"They're a little big to start on," Geordie said, with a straight face.

"Not for a boyo with your insolence. They're not big enough."

"But Laverty, I've got to have something."

"There'll be plenty in the spring."

"I know, but I've got to practice before spring gets here."

"Ah, now."

"You can help me, if you will. Think, now."

Laverty grinned at him. "I could think better if I had a bun or two from the kitchen. That girl's been bakin' again."

"Will you really think of something if I snitch a pastry?"

"Buns and a little dram from His Worship's bottle. The one on the sideboard."

"Oh, no," Geordie said. The bottle was covered by a

law that he wouldn't break, a law as inflexible as those of the Medes and Persians. "I can't."

"I'm thinkin' of a cat," Laverty said. "What could be better than a cat? A great black beast, black as Belial and twice as nasty, with a tail on him would be better on a lion. Ah, think what you could do with him."

Geordie was thinking, and could hardly stand still at the prospect of it; a dramatic and marvelous vision filled his mind's eye. "Where would you get it, Laverty?"

"I might tell you and I might not, right this minute, but don't be after worryin'. If I had the dram—"

"No," Geordie said. "Two buns?"

"Maybe for two buns, then. But the girl can't know of it, or she'll be tellin' the Missus they were took for Laverty, and him with so little pleasure in his life."

"All right," Geordie said, and took off for the house. He went in the front door and drifted toward the kitchen, at once innocent and casual but taking advantage of any available cover. There was silence in the kitchen but he flowed around the corner of the coat closet and crept in among the coats; by moving them gently aside he could see most of the kitchen. It was empty, and he crept into it, found the pastries in the cabinet, and grasped two of them. Just then there were footsteps on the back stairs. His line of escape to either door was cut off, and after a swift, desperate look around he ran behind the stove, which was set out a little from the wall, and crouched down. Ingrid came into the kitchen, said something under her breath, and shut the cabinet door, which he had left open; then she sat down on the chair beside the kitchen table. Geordie's heart sank; it was hot and cramped behind the stove, and there was no telling how long he would be there.

Very soon he began to perspire, and his cramped muscles began to twitch. Ingrid sat on. Time drew out, and perspiration trickled down Geordie's hide and tickled him. Having hidden himself, he couldn't emerge now with some fabrication or other; he thought bitterly that if he hadn't panicked he could have asked Ingrid for the pastry for himself. She would have given them to him; she always did.

More time went on, and Geordie was in despair; just as he thought he would either have to die or crawl out and be in disgrace, the girl stood up and went upstairs again. He scuttled out from behind the stove, eased out the back door, and ran to the stable. His wet clothes stuck to him, and the cold made them clammy and dank. Laverty stretched out a hand and took the pastries. "It's blushing like a bride you are," he said, and sank his teeth into one of the pastries.

"I almost got caught. I had to hide behind the stove. I almost got cooked."

"Let that be a lesson to you," Laverty said callously, and chomped away with his eyes rolling.

He finished the pastries while Geordie stood fidgeting, wiped his mouth with the back of one hand, and sighed with satisfaction.

"Laverty?"

"So now you'll be wanting the cat. Well, you'll have it tomorrow."

"Tomorrow?" Geordie asked, vastly disappointed. "Can't I have it today? Where is it?"

"Ah, now, it's in a place and I'll have to get it. Tomorrow when you come home from school it'll be here. Get you gone, now. I have to finish the harness and fix the furnace and take the ashes out, my black curse on 'em. And then take the sleigh downtown for His Worship."

There was nothing for Geordie to do but accept the delay as patiently as he could, so he went back to the house and changed his clothes, wondering by what devious maneuvers Laverty was going to get the cat and why he had hidden behind the stove like a kid. Then he thought of glass eyes for the cat, wrote a letter to order them, and decided to ride downtown with Laverty to mail the letter. It was a delight to ride in the sleigh, warm under the buffalo robe, with the chilly wind in your face and the sleigh bells chiming.

THREE

Geordie's best friend and classmate, Spencer Torrance,
who lived in the next house but one to the Suttons, had
been kept abreast of developments in the matter of taxidermy, and Geordie told him next morning in school
about the cat. Spence had more interest in shooting creatures than in preserving their remains, but he was a good
companion and willing to take a hand in anything that
was new, so he came home from school with Geordie.
They didn't tarry on the way, and when they went into
the harness room the cat was lying on the table. They
recognized it at once and stared at it in dismay; huge

and black, with a white spot surrounding its left eye, it was the dearly beloved pet of Miss Cecily Enders, a redoubtable maiden lady who lived in the next block.

"Good Christmas!" Spence said. "It's Patch! Geordie, do you suppose he shot it?"

Words failed Geordie, for Miss Cecily was a disaster when something aroused her, and nothing in this world could have moved her more than the violent death of Patch. She doted upon Patch, she made a fool of herself over Patch; Patch filled her passionate and frustrated life. Geordie, staring horrified at the corpse, foresaw eventual discovery, Miss Cecily storming into the house like a ranting Fury, and his father (who walked very softly around her for much less than this) casting him into outer darkness. Laverty, that evil man, had betrayed him; he looked at Spence and opened his mouth but no words came out of it.

Spence recovered first. "Let's find Laverty," he said.

They ran out of the harness room into the stable to discover that the two matched grays weren't in their stalls; they ran across the yard and into the kitchen. Ingrid was writing a letter on the table, and looked up with a start when they burst through the door.

"Where's Laverty?" Geordie asked, in a quavering voice. "Ingrid, where's Laverty?"

"He takes your mother to a party. Soon he is back. There is trouble?" She stood up. "Something is not right?" As always, there was a tranquility about her, and it calmed Geordie; the feeling that everything was going along as usual took some of the panic out of him.

"We wanted to see him," he said. "We'll wait in the stable."

They went back to the stable again, and in a short time Laverty drove into the yard. He was rosy from the cold air, and cheerful; there was no hangdog look about him when he saw them, and instead of avoiding their eyes he saluted them with his whip. He pulled the grays up. "Why aren't you after skinnin' him?" he asked. "He's not thawed out, is it?"

Geordie looked at him, caught between a feeling of outrage and a dawning notion that he might have been a fool. "It's Patch!" he burst out finally. "You know it's Patch! How did you—"

"Sure and all it's Patch. Who else would it be? He died yesterday and she wants him stuffed." He began to unhitch the grays, turning his back on them.

"Oh," Geordie said, completely deflated. "Oh." He looked at Spence; Spence looked back at him, and grinned. Soon they were both laughing, and still laughing went into the harness room again.

Patch, as Laverty had suggested, had been frozen and wasn't sufficiently thawed yet to work upon. They moved the table closer to the potbellied stove and stood admiring the departed, turning him once in awhile to hasten his thawing. They heard the horses walking through the stable to their stalls and then Laverty joined them.

"Sure, and he's as big as an elephant," Laverty said, giving the corpse a poke. "It almost broke my back to carry him here."

"How did he get so big?" Spence asked. "He's the biggest cat I ever saw."

"Ah, she had him altered, the wicked creature," Laverty said, "and all the fine spirit in him went into growin'. That and all the calves' liver he ate and the feather cushions he sat on like a lord." Laverty rolled his eyes. "Get your knife, now. It think he's about ready."

Geordie felt the cat, nodded, and went to the house to get his tools. When he returned Laverty had gone off somewhere, and they set to work getting the skin off Patch; they had skinned muskrats and other animals and made a fair job of it. They spread the skin out and trimmed the fat from it, and then were faced with the question of what to do with the tail.

"The book says to skin it out," Spence said, thumbing through the pages.

"We'll never get it sewed up. I think I'll leave the bone in it."

"It'll smell."

"Oh, it'll dry out."

"Huh," Spence said, unconvinced. "Then it says to boil the skull."

"You get his head off," Geordie said. "I'll go get a pan from Ingrid." He went into the kitchen and came back with a small saucepan full of water; they put the cat's head into it and sat it on top of the potbellied stove. This done, they rubbed the recommended chemicals into the skin and tacked it up on the wall to dry. The saucepan began to boil.

"Want to go skating later?" Geordie asked, taking what was left of Patch and depositing it in the garbage can.

In the fullness of time, what with monumental labors, vexations, and compromises, the job was done. It had been a sort of secret enterprise accomplished in the harness room where Geordie's mother and father never came. This was just as well, for the room wasn't improved by the work; an odd and complicated odor now hung in it, and bits of wire, papier-mâché, wax, and whatnot were scattered all about. Laverty had always kept it very neat, but he had given up trying; he couldn't cope with it any longer, and was looking forward to the day when they would be finished and he could straighten up again. Unknown to Geordie he had made an arrangement with Miss Cecily to collect ten dollars when he delivered the finished work, but by the day Geordie stood back and announced that he could do no more Laverty had long since given up that pleasant prospect.

He stood beside the beaming boy, managing not to roar aloud at the creation whose resemblance to the departed Patch was purely coincidental. Patch's aldermanic figure was now more than slender, for the skin hadn't been stretched enough and wasn't well tanned; tanning was a process too complicated for them. His face was very lopsided and held an idiotic grin; he was walleyed, swaybacked, and lumpy, his hair stood up in places, and the untreated tail stuck out sideways at a right angle to his meager body as stiff and straight as a poker. Standing asprawl, as though about to collapse, on a carefully waxed board, he was a horrible parody of the world's most disreputable and underprivileged cat.

"You think she'll like him, Laverty?" Geordie asked proudly, blinded by the joy of creation. "Of course, his tail's a little stiff, but cats carry their tails that way sometimes."

Laverty turned away to gain control of himself, and then turned back. "Ah," he said. "So they do. I've often seen him do it."

Geordie grinned. "I think I'll put a cloth over him and give him an official unveiling when I get there," he said. "Maybe I'll even get her to reimburse me for expenses."

"Ah," Laverty said. "Don't you remember, now? She was to pay ten dollars for the work. I told you and you must have forgot. You were goin' to give me a bit of it for gettin' him and all."

Geordie looked at him and blinked. "I don't think you told me," he said mildly, and took it no further; money was incidental to him at the moment. "I'll go get the cloth, and take him now."

He went out and returned with a clean pillowcase which he draped over the cat. Then he picked him up. "I'll give you half," he said, as he left.

Bridget, the maid at Miss Cecily's, was an Irish girl and a party to Laverty's maneuvers; when she saw Geordie instead of Laverty bringing Patch home she suspected at once which way the wind was going to blow, and set about trying to temper it. "A good day to you, Mr. Geordie," she said. "Come into the parlor, now, and I'll get Miss Cecily for you. Could I have a bit of a look at him, the poor darlin'?"

"I don't think you'd better," Geordie said. "I want her to see it first."

"Ah, just a bit of a look, Mr. Geordie. It could be a secret between us."

"No," Geordie said. "Go and get her, Bridget."

Bridget saw he was determined, and gave up; she had made her try. She gave him a look that puzzled him and went out, and Geordie glanced about for the best place to stage his triumph. One end of the room was arranged as a "Turkish corner", with several floor lamps of pierced brass, a hookah on an inlaid taboret, beaded curtains at the French doors, a camel saddle, and a vaguely Oriental looking divan smothered under a profusion of draped scarves and pillows, and he decided that would be the place. He took the hookah off the taboret and placed it on the floor, put the covered cat in its place, turned on the lamps, and moved out into the middle of the room.

Presently Miss Cecily swept in, trailing yards of a frilly pink *peignoir* which contrasted oddly with her air of iron virtue. She was very tall and thin, and this was accentuated by an elaborate, high coiffure. She usually carried her jutting patrician nose high and looked down it to outstare everyone, but this afternoon she was almost simpering; she was at once ridiculous and formidable. Ordinarily Geordie would have gone a mile out of his way to avoid her, but today was different.

"Hello, Miss Cecily!" he said, and gave her his slow grin.

"Good afternoon, Geordie," she said. "Bridget tells me that you have brought our dear kitty home."

Her classification of Patch made Geordie stare for a moment, but he recovered quickly. "Yes, Ma'am," he said, and glanced toward the Turkish corner.

"Ah," she said, following his glance, "here he is, the dear one, in the place he loved the most. How clever, how sensitive of you, Geordie, to have guessed it! As he rested among the cushions he was like a great pasha, lordly and indolent but oh! so much the master of all he surveyed and its secrets! Let us look at him now, Geordie. I have been so impatient."

Geordie walked over, whisked off the pillowcase, and turned toward her. She stared; she took a step; her head came forward and there came over her face an expression of incredulity that changed swiftly to a look of outrage and horror. "Oh!" she exclaimed. "Oh, my darling!" Her voice went up and up. "What have they done to you? What have they *done?*" As Geordie stared at her, astounded, her face turned toward him; her eyes glared and her hair, apparently by itself, seemed to spring out like the writhing, snaky locks of Medusa. "Oh, you wicked, wicked boy!" She raised her hands and her fingers bent into claws as though she was going to rush over and take hold of him, and then she suddenly went off into shrieking hysterics.

Geordie had never seen a case of hysterics; the thought that she had suddenly gone out of her mind paralyzed him. He stood rooted, with the uproar washing over him.

Bridget came running in, caught him by the arm, and tugged him toward one of the French doors.

"Get you gone, for the love of Heaven! Get you gone, before she does you a mischief!" she implored, tugging at him. She picked up the cat, thrust it into his arms, and pushed him through the French door. He ran across the lawn as though fiends were after him, hugging the cat, followed by Miss Cecily's shrieks which were suddenly cut off as the door was slammed shut.

By the time Geordie reached home he had recovered enough to decide to take Patch up to his room and conceal him. He managed to do this without being seen, and hid the cat in his closet; after dinner that night he got it out, set it on the desk, and slumped down in the chair to look at it. Now that he had seen someone else's reaction to his work, and such a dramatic reaction at that, he began to see that he had been blinded by his own pride and enthusiasm. As he stared at the cat (and remembered Miss Cecily, a memory that would be with him for years) he began to see how bad it really was, and the longer he looked the worse it got. Finally he turned hot with shame, swung away, and stood up. There was a knock at the door.

"Geordie?" his mother's voice said. "Geordie?"

His first reaction was to hide the cat, but he realized the door was open and she would be able to see any move he made. "Yes, Ma?" he asked.

"May I come in?"

"Yes," he said, and stood waiting.

She came in; her eyes went to the cat, came back to him, and stayed on him. She wasn't going to mention Patch.

"Are you all right, Geordie? You were so quiet at dinner."

38

"I'm all right, Ma," Geordie said, and then, grateful to her for not pressing him, added: "I'm all right now." He was quiet for a moment. "I stuffed Miss Cecily's cat, and she didn't care for the job. There it is." He turned, and pointed at the perfectly obvious Patch.

She looked at Patch, and managed not to burst out laughing or make a slighting comment.

"I guess it's not very good," he said finally. "When she saw it, it nearly drove her out of her mind. I thought she'd gone crazy. Is she crazy, Ma?"

"She's not as well balanced as she could be, Geordie. She lives all alone, and hadn't anybody to love except Patch. It must be hard to be as lonely as she must be. Lonely people do strange things." She put her arm around him, and looked into his face. "Your first try?"

He nodded.

"Will you want to try some more?"

He nodded again. "I want to, Ma," he said. "With birds, I think. I don't know why I prefer this to law, but I do."

"Does that worry you, Geordie? Do you often think about it?"

"Sometimes," he said, and suddenly didn't feel like talking about it any more. When he really thought about it he wasn't completely sure; things got all mixed up. "I'll do better mounts than Patch."

"Of course you will," she smiled. "Keep him to remind you. Do good ones." She kissed him. "Good night," she said, and went out of the room.

He watched her go, and smiled after her. She had given him great comfort.

FOUR

Toward the end of winter the weather moderated, and the two boys could get out more. The chance of late storms was still too great for the parents of either of them to permit camping trips, so their expeditions were close to home and were daily ones. The country was bleak and cheerless and much of it was still under snow; there was little wildlife in evidence, but the animals left their tracks in the snow. These could be followed, and many of the events in the lives of their makers could be deciphered. The sudden end of a rabbit's wandering trail, a little blood, and the parallel marks of wingtips told them as plainly as though they had seen it that a horned owl had made a successful strike; small footprints and a shallow furrow showed them where a mink had dragged an unlucky muskrat to a place of concealment. They learned a good deal about the territories and routes of animals, and occasionally found the corpse of some creature whose life had been ended by the rigors of winter; following the trails showed them more than they could have found out in the softer seasons, when the vegetation was up and much was concealed.

On week-ends they were usually gone all day on these trips, wandering widely and carrying packs, for they had soon wearied of cold sandwiches and had decided to cook something at noon. Few people not in the last stages of starvation would have enjoyed their cuisine at first, but they improved. Of the two of them, Geordie became the better cook; he had always eaten well at home, and soon got tired of messy lunches. He spent some time with Ingrid, and the results showed it. His cooking wasn't elaborate, for he had no ambitions to be a chef, but it was sound and tasty.

After the ice went out they began to do a little trapping. It was for skins to sell to the fur buyer, not for specimens, for Geordie had lost his taste for stuffing animals after the debacle with Patch and hadn't got it back again. His interest, which had always rather favored birds, slowly swung more toward them as time went on. They had a stronger appeal to his imagination because of their freedom of movement. He read everything about them that he could get his hands on but still he wasn't satisfied. For these books were books of general circulation, somewhat sentimental and not very scientific. He never thought of the University library and its wider selection; if he thought of the University at all it was as a stuffier sort of high school, and it didn't occur to anyone to suggest it to him or to try to clear up his misapprehension.

Besides, he was busy. Having been housebound through the bad weather he had accumulated so much energy that he had to move about. The week-ends were too far apart to be completely satisfying, and as the days began to get longer he and Spence arose early and got out somewhere closer to home, before school. Their muskrat catch along the River north of town, and in the creeks emptying into it, was considerable; they went along without much incident until the morning when they caught the skunk.

Their muskrat traps were set in or near the water, with a wire attached to the trapchain so that the muskrats could dive for deeper water and drown themselves, but this time they knew from seventy yards away that a skunk had blundered into one of them and crawled up the bank, for it had been busily expressing its displeasure and the wind brought the smell to them. They stopped and looked at each other.

"Oh, my," Spence said. "What'll we do now? If we'd brought the rifle we could shoot him, but without it how will we get him out of the trap?"

"Maybe we could leave him until morning, and come back and shoot him then," Geordie said, but as soon as he said it he knew that he couldn't leave the animal in the trap all day and overnight. "We can't come back this afternoon. We've got assembly, and after that it'll be dark."

"Maybe we'd better look at him and see if we can figure something out."

They moved in closer, making faces that expressed distaste, to find that the skunk had moved around enough to beat down the snow; it was in a depression, and out of sight. They had to move closer still; they split up, so that

Spence could move in and peer down into the depression while Geordie made a noise on the other side to distract the victim's attention.

"Hey!" Spence said. "Hey, he's white! He's pure white!"

This was exciting news, for the fur buyer had offered a much higher price for white skunks; the trade prized them, for they were easier to dye or could be used as they were. Geordie forgot his caution, moved in too close, and was lightly sprayed. He fell back and Spence, excited in his turn, also got into the line of fire. They both were momentarily dismayed, but now that the damage was done and the prospect of riches was before them they had to go through with the enterprise.

"We got to get him," Spence said. "If we leave him, a hawk or a horned owl will eat him. We got to get him, Geordie."

"How?"

"With a long stick. Hit him on the head."

They separated and ran excitedly about, and then came back and began to belabor the skunk. This didn't seem to work very well; the unfortunate center of their attentions ran around at the end of the trapchain and desperately filled the air with its scent, a good deal of which ended up on their clothing. They were too excited to have thoughts of the cruelty of their method and were so inured to the smell by this time that they didn't notice it any longer; they moved closer to the doomed animal, took what it had to give, and finally did it in. They stood above it, winded, smelling to heaven, and triumphant, and then Geordie stooped and took it out of the trap. He put it into the bag that they carried with them, and they grinned happily at each other.

"Man, he was something. Maybe if we'd just teased him long enough he'd have run out of juice."

"It might have taken a long time," Spence said, and was suddenly struck with a thought. "You guess it's time for school?"

"School?" Geordie asked. "Good Heavens!" He looked at the sun. "We're late. Let's go."

Forgetting to set the trap again, they began to run. They ran and trotted most of the way to school, dangling the bag, stumbling and puffing; there were no students outside. Geordie hid the bag beneath one of the bushes in the yard, and they went into the building, along the corridor, and into their room.

The boys and girls were at their desks and there was a substitute teacher at the front, a man; they hadn't seen him before and their first swift impression of him was an unfavorable one. He was tall and thin, with a pale, thin face and a thin, pursed mouth; he stared at them with disapproval, but before he could speak the pupils nearest to Geordie and Spence clutched their noses and began to make extravagant gestures, and in the twinkling of an eye the class was in an uproar.

The teacher pounded on the desk to no avail, and then moved swiftly down the aisle; he looked as though he was going to take hold of them, but when he got near them he recoiled. His pale face turned scarlet, and he raised a lanky arm. "Out!" he said. "Out in the hall. Go!"

They went out, and he followed them. Standing over them, still scarlet and gasping for breath, he waved a hand around. "The idea! Disrupting the class with this . . . this mephitic stench, this horrible . . . Coming into my class in this . . . Young ruffians!" He stretched out a long arm for Geordie, and quickly withdrew it again. "Ruffian!" Further words failed him, and he stood shifting from one foot to the other, opening and closing his mouth.

Geordie had never been called a ruffian, and the strange gyrations of the teacher, without dignity or, so far as he could see, reason, were too much for him. "Yes, sir," he said. "Go to Hell."

The teacher froze, and stared at him; his color grew even higher. His eyes glared; his hands came up and he took a step forward, but once more the aura of skunk drove him back. "Insolence!" he exclaimed. "Obscene insolence as well! To the office! Come to the office at once!"

He took a wide half circle around them and started for the office in a rush. The two boys, confused and a little frightened now, looked at each other and followed him. He whisked through the anteroom and slammed the door, and they could hear his raised voice as he talked to the Principal. Presently he came out again, walked past them without a look, and vanished. Mr. Moore, the Principal, put his head out the door, looked mildly from one of them to the other, flinched, and said: "Meet me outside."

They went out and waited by the door, quiet and subdued, for Mr. Moore, the fountainhead of all authority, was an unknown quantity, mysterious and remote. He joined them, and got upwind. Rather chubby, calm and unruffled, he stood and looked at them for a moment; they could make nothing from his expression. "Now, then," he said finally. "How did you get so fragrant?"

"Sir?" Geordie asked, stalling.

"The smell," he said. "Did you put it on yourselves?"

"No, sir. We were trapping, and we caught a skunk."

"It's really strong, you know."

"Yes, sir," Spence said. "We were late, and so we came directly to class."

"I see. And then you told Mr. Jenks to go to Hell."

"Yes, sir," Geordie said. He looked down, twisted his toe into the ground, and looked up again. "He called us ruffians. We didn't *do* anything, Mr. Moore. We were late, that was all. We weren't behaving like ruffians."

"He's a city man," Mr. Moore said. "Perhaps he was overexcited. It's his first day here. Your teacher's been taken sick."

Geordie felt certain that Mr. Moore knew that their regular teacher would have acted differently.

"Well," Mr. Moore said. "I think you had better get home and clean yourselves up. Don't come back today. I'll have to talk to your fathers and see what we'll do. Off you go, now."

"Yes, sir," they said in chorus. "Thank you, Mr. Moore."

He waved at them, and they turned away. They collected the bag, and on the way home they agreed that Mr. Moore had been very reasonable, although they wished that he had seen fit to fix matters without bringing their fathers into it; neither of them looked forward to the unpleasant conferences that were sure to ensue.

"I guess," Spence said finally, "we do smell pretty bad. Do you think they're going to act the same way at home that everybody did at school?"

"We can go to our stable and get Laverty to bury our clothes, and wash before we go in the house. People are always talking about burying their clothes when a skunk gets them. Laverty can get us some clean clothes from the house."

"What'll we do about the skunk?"

"We'd better skin him now," Geordie said. "We can tack his hide up on the outside of the barn. Around at the back."

They started to skin the skunk beside the street, but an unknown lady of patrician appearance came along in a

46

gleaming electric brougham and stopped to watch them. Under her amazed regard they grew uneasy, and decided to finish the operation behind the stable.

Although Laverty had done his best, Geordie was still faintly redolent from his adventure when his father came in. His mother wasn't home; she had gone with a friend that day to the Amana Colonies twenty-five miles or so away and hadn't returned yet. She had wanted to buy a chair and the Germans at Amana, quiet, friendly people from Hesse who lived in a communal fashion, were such fine craftsmen that she visited them whenever she was looking for furniture. After finding out from Ingrid where his wife was, Alfred Sutton reluctantly decided not to wait for her. He called up the stairs, and Geordie came slowly down and found him in the living room. He was standing by a window, and obviously didn't relish the situation. To Geordie, quite conscious of sin but not really understanding all the uproar that had resulted from the simple trapping of a skunk, he seemed as always a little remote, a man of a different world from Geordie's where he had a mysterious power and everyone's respect.

"Hi, Dad," Geordie said.

"Hello, Geordie. Shall we sit down? I've had a talk with Mr. Moore."

"Yes, sir," Geordie said, and sat down on the davenport.

His father sat down next to him, raised his eyebrows almost imperceptibly, and moved a little further away. "Your teacher," he said, "will be ill for some time, and Mr. Jenks will probably finish out the term. In view of what has happened, I do not think that it would be to your advantage to remain in his class. I have made arrangements for you to finish the term at Prairie View Academy. You will not be punished."

"Yes, sir," Geordie said, thinking again of his father's power. Everything had been done; smoothly and invisibly there had been conferences with Mr. Moore and the head of Prairie View, punishment had been averted, and his life had been changed. "Yes, sir," he said again. "Will Spence go there too, Dad?"

"Yes," his father said. "I'm sure you will both do well there. Both Spence's father and I think that public school is best, but . . . From what I understand, you were justified in objecting to Mr. Jenks' treatment of you, but you were not justified in cursing him. There are other ways to object. One doesn't lose one's temper with a fool."

"Yes, sir. But, Dad, we were so surprised. He acted as though we had done it on purpose, he didn't give us time to explain. He called us ruffians, and I guess I got mad."

"I said that I thought you were justified, but that I wished you had used other means. I hope that you will recall this next time a situation of this sort develops."

"Yes, sir. I'll try."

"I hope so," Alfred Sutton said. He was silent for a moment, looking at the floor. Geordie sat quietly, wishing that he could go. Presently his father looked up. "You are almost college age, Geordie," he said. "You'll be going to college in the fall. Do you think now that the business with the polecat might have been a little juvenile?"

Geordie's heart sank, but he tried to explain. "He was white, Dad," he said. "They're worth a lot more when they're white, and we wanted to get him before an owl or something else did."

"Ah, yes," Alfred Sutton said, and although he tried to get interest into his voice Geordie knew it wasn't there.

He went on. "Your courses the first year will be general, but it's not at all too early to begin to think what you want to be. Have you ever considered the Army? Old Geordie was a soldier, you know."

"I know," Geordie said.

"You might consider West Point, or Annapolis," his father said. "They lead to good, professional careers, and I think I could manage an appointment." He stood up. "Think about them, Geordie," he said, and smiled. "I'll let you go now. Dinner will probably be a little late, with your mother at Amana, and you must have some studying to do. You will start at Prairie View tomorrow."

"Yes, sir," Geordie said, and left the room. As he climbed the stairs his depression deepened, for his father had been so measured and just about school and so obviously not interested at all in the skunk or anything that pertained to it. His tone when he had said "Ah, yes" had stopped anything that he, Geordie, had wanted to say.

FIVE

The two boys, after being more or less isolated as aliens
for a time at Prairie View Academy, were finally accepted by their companions just as signs of spring began
to appear in the land. The snow disappeared and the
thawing earth turned dark and muddy; roads became
quagmires for a time. The River rose in its season and
dropped again, a thin frost of green stole across the
world and burgeoned; the blue pasqueflowers, much like
crocuses, starred the prairie where it had not been
broken and changed by the plow and were followed by a
tide of other blossoms. Birds that had wintered in the

south began to appear in increasing numbers, some to journey further north and some to stay, and their voices took the place of the winter wind's. The dark and bitter season was over and in reluctant retreat.

After the roads became passable again and it was possible to move about freely, Geordie and Spence greased their traps, hung them up, divided the money they had made, and resumed their week-end expeditions. They were intoxicated by the return of life all about them and the warming air, the sunrises and sunsets over the vast reach of the prairies, and their freedom. They could camp overnight again, and looked forward to longer camps after school was out.

About the middle of April someone gave the city library a bird book that had an extended treatment of the Wilson's phalarope in it and the librarian, knowing of Geordie's interest, recommended it to him. He had seen phalaropes the previous year and found a nest or two, for a few of them nested in the vicinity, but he hadn't known very much about them. He had been unaware that the birds migrated to South America and that it was the male which made the nest and brooded the eggs, and that it was the female (or sometimes several of them) which pursued the male in the mating season. This was so unusual, being a reversal of the actions of other birds that he knew, that he was fascinated by it. The fact that the phalarope flew all the way to and from South America, through Central America and Mexico and the Mississippi Valley, was fascinating too; it seemed like such a small bird for all that flying, through jungles and mountains. It was the first bird about which he had been able to gather such complete information; it was a wonderful creature, and after learning so much about it he had to have one.

Ordinarily the two boys spent a good deal of time

along the River, or near it, for Geordie's father had bought him a rowboat the year before and they liked getting about in it; now they began to haunt the prairie sloughs, for the phalarope was a bird of the marshy meadows and could be expected to appear in them. The sloughs, oases of moisture in the dry, grassy prairies, contained a great number of birds; ducks nested near them, and there were always terns, blackbirds, coots, killdeers, and many other species gathered around them or in the air over them. Life was more concentrated about them than along the River, and there was always something to see. After exploring a number of them they finally picked one with a shallow pond covering six or seven acres in the middle of it, and pitched their tent among a few straggly trees on a rise that stood a few feet above the plain. The trees were swamp oaks five or six feet high and how they had got there was a mystery, for they were the only trees in all the wide view.

Someone must have planted them there and at first the boys thought that they had discovered a burial mound, for they had heard about the Mound Builders who had lived in Iowa before the Indians appeared. They didn't know that Mound Builders had always lived along the rivers and creeks, and the boys dug around with great enthusiasm in a search for artifacts. They didn't find any, because there were none, but for a long time afterward they liked to think that somewhere deep below their tent were mouldering bones and a little pottery placed there long ago by a vanishing race.

It was a little too early for the phalaropes when they first set up their camp, but the killdeers were there and they shot two of them with Spence's .22 rifle for Geordie to practice stuffing. The bullets didn't leave too much of the birds, but enough. The shotgun would have been better, but it is a noisy weapon, and they only wanted to use it once, to get a phalarope, lest there should be someone around who would hear it and make trouble for them. They also had slingshots, and they collected several blackbirds. Blackbirds were so commonplace as to be expendable and killing several of them didn't produce the same feeling of lawbreaking and sin as the killing of a more delicate and rarer bird.

They took the shotgun to the tent, each of them carrying half of it under his clothes, and hid it, wrapped up in greasy rags and oilcloth to protect it from the weather. They visited the blind every weekend, and then on a bright Sunday morning Spence stuck his head out of the tent just as three phalaropes flew past. They were females, close enough for him to see the cinnamon neck-stripe that males do not have.

"They're here!" he announced, pulling his head back inside and turning around. "Three of them just went by." Out went his head again; Geordie jumped out of his blankets and joined him.

Spence pointed; the three birds, flying together, swung a wide, fast circle and landed at the pond's edge, waded out until they were waterborne, and began to spin about to stir up the small organisms they fed upon. It was a characteristic phalarope gesture.

Geordie got the old binoculars and watched the birds, fascinated. They were pretty things, with their longish necks and bills and smooth feathers; that they had started to feed so quickly indicated that they had just come in from a long and mysterious journey. He had seen phalaropes many times before, but then they had been just birds to him; now they were the focus of an interest that had suddenly strengthened, for the book had revealed their uniqueness and by so doing had suggested how much there was to know of all other birds as well. He was so engrossed in watching them that Spence finally grew impatient and withdrew into the tent.

By now the phalaropes had finished their feeding and

returned to the shore, where they stood together at the edge of the water. Spence returned fully dressed and with the gun. They took it out of its wrappings and loaded it. The birds were well out of range, and they decided to see if they could walk up close enough to them for a shot. Geordie had the gun, and handed it to Spence.

"You shoot one," he said.

"You're a better shot than I am."

"I'd rather you did it," Geordie said. "I feel queasy about it now."

Spence stared at him. "You mean you're going to quit shooting?" he asked.

"I'm not going to quit shooting. It's just these particular birds."

Spence shook his head; this was all too much for him. He took the gun, and they walked around the edge of the pond. The birds flushed when they were still too far away for a shot, crossed the pond, and landed again.

"We'll never get close enough to them this way," Geordie said. "Why don't you stay here and crouch down, and I'll walk around."

Spence nodded, and Geordie went on. He got quite close to them this time before they flushed, uttering low, nasal, grunting sounds; they flew back across the pond again. He saw Spence rise when they neared him and fire; one of them went down, and he watched this with an emotion that was a strange mixture of regret and pleasure. He now had one to mount. When he reached Spence again, Spence handed him the bird. It wasn't quite dead; lying in his hand, beyond the effort of fluttering, it looked at him with dark and luminous eyes, gave a feeble shudder, and died. He stroked it and for a moment almost wept for this dainty far traveler so wilfully deprived of life. Then he went to the tent for bits of cotton to plug the shot wounds so that the feathers wouldn't be stained with blood. He was still in his pajamas.

The rest of that spring passed pleasantly and the summer, after school was out, was fine and free. The two boys weren't home a great deal; they spent most of their time camping in the marshes or along the River, and made a long float trip downstream, camping where the spirit moved them and stopping for as long as they pleased. They came back by train, with the boat in the baggage car, sunburned, scratched by briars and well bitten by the insects of the season, esteeming themselves as hardy adventurers and ready for some home cooking after a diet of mulligan stew and fish.

They had climbed river bluffs amid the ferns and wild grape and wandered over prairie not yet changed, with its golden coreopsis, white and purple prairie clover, yellow toadflax, and crepe-petalled primrose; they had made fine camps under the riverside trees and had plenty of time to watch the birds and animals about them. Their progress had been like that of the prairie rivers, wandering and slow; a sudden and violent summer hailstorm and several thundershowers had been the only thing to disturb their leisurely way. They spent much time swimming and jumped off all the bridges they came to, and the few people they met talked to them as though they were mature men on a sensible outing. Their memories were of golden dawns, warm, lively days, and long, quiet sunsets when feeding fish dimpled the water, owls awoke, and the creatures of the night began to stir beyond the firelight to go about their concerns.

One day they had an experience that they often

laughed about later, a thing that happened the day after they got back. It was very hot that day, and not feeling energetic enough to go very far they went swimming close to town with a few of their friends. They were all naked; standing on the shore to recover their breath after a tussle in the water, they were startled to hear a girl's voice calling: "Hoohoo!" They turned, to see a neighbor's twelve-year-old who had somehow wandered down to the river. They desperately tried to cover themselves with their hands, and before they collected themselves sufficiently to take refuge in the water heard her say: "Geordie Sutton, your hair's all wet. You'll sure catch it when you get home!"

SIX

Holding the phalarope, lost in recollection of the spring and summer that were gone, Geordie was recalled to the dim room by his mother's voice calling him from downstairs. He started violently and almost dropped the bird; he had been so completely immersed in his reverie that for a moment he didn't know where he was, and looked wildly around in an effort to identify his surroundings. His mother called again; this time there was a questioning note in her voice. This settled him down and the room became familiar again, familiar and solid and reassuring. He walked to the door and called back to her. "I'll be right down, Ma. I'm sorry."

He walked back to the desk and set the phalarope down in its accustomed place and suddenly, when his hand was empty of it, he began to cry. The flood of memories of the happy, carefree summer and the confusion and uncertainty about the future were too much for him. His hands grasped the edges of the desk and he rocked back and forth fighting against the tears.

Before he managed to get himself under control again there was a knock at the door. He dried his eyes, took a deep breath, and said: "Come in."

The door opened and Uncle Harry, Lavinia Sutton's brother, entered. He was a big, ruddy man, a dealer in grain and a duck hunter, a bachelor who often went to Chicago and the east and was therefore considered quite cosmopolitan. He was amused by this, and would infrequently drop hints about gay eastern girls to sustain it. The gay girls never saw him; he had a quiet arrangement in the town that suited him, and he spent his spare time away from shooting or business with several professors at the University or reading books of foreign travel. He was a quietly observant, sensitive fellow, fond of Geordie, and saw at once that Geordie was upset. "Hello, old boy," he said.

"Hi, Uncle Harry. I was just about to—"

"Don't hurry," Uncle Harry said. "I'll tell them to start eating, that you'll soon be down. I just thought that you might want to go to a lecture with me at the University this evening. Came up to ask you."

Geordie was grateful for this circumlocution and wanted to express his appreciation by accepting, but he was a bit dubious; he still felt shaken, and he thought of college lectures as stuffy. "Well . . ." he said.

"You'd be interested in it," Uncle Harry said. "It's about an island called Laysan, off in the Pacific somewhere. Has a lot of rare birds and things on it. Satterthwaite, the Biology man, was there last year and took some pictures he's going to show with the magic lantern."

"In the Pacific?" Geordie asked.

"Out near Hawaii. Volcanic island, I think."

Geordie looked at him, unconsciously nodding his head, for suddenly, in his mind's eye, he saw a lovely misty dark cone arising from the sea, hiding secret things that were new and strange. "A volcano?" he asked.

"I doubt it's a volcano now," Uncle Harry went on. "I think this is the top of an old one, just above the water. A nesting island for millions of birds. You'd better come."

"All right," Geordie said.

"Good. Wash your face and hands and come down when you're ready." He grinned and went out of the room.

Geordie stood for a moment smiling at the closed door. The emotional upheaval of a few minutes past had retreated into the back of his mind.

They moved into the living room after dessert, for Geordie's father liked to have a demitasse there, and as they sat about waiting to go to the lecture Uncle Harry told them a little about Dr. Satterthwaite, whom he called "Sat."

"Dr. Conover was at the University before Sat and did a great deal for the Museum collection. Sat's carried his work on awfully well. It's a very good university museum, and from what little Sat's said about his ideas for the future I gather that he has some that will make other museum people sit up and take notice. This Laysan Island he's talking about tonight is way off in the Pacific, out of the shipping lanes and deserted most of the time.

It's famous among biologists all over the world for the hundreds of thousands of sea birds that nest on it."

"It sounds very exotic," Geordie's mother said. "Why don't we all go? Wouldn't you like to hear him, Alfred?"

"I'd better stay here," Geordie's father said. "There's a brief or two I should look over, but the rest of you go along. Harry can drive the car. Geordie, go out to the stable and ask Laverty to bring it around."

Geordie nodded and went out to the stable and routed out Laverty, who came downstairs in his undershirt, muttering under his breath while he lit the big brass gas headlights, the oil tail light, and cranked the engine. They drove out under the porte-cochère; Laverty went back to the stable, and Geordie ran into the house to get his mother and Uncle Harry.

They started for the campus, which was near the river; before they reached it the quiet of the night was shattered by gongs and the clatter of galloping horses, and they pulled over and stopped to let a fire engine go by. The steam pumper was belching sparks, the driver leaned forward like a racer to hold his great plunging gray horses, and the whole splendid affair seemed to shake the earth as it roared past them and skidded around a corner further down the street. Geordie was still tingling with the excitement of it when they reached MacBride Hall, where the auditorium was, and parked the car.

"Let's hurry a little," Uncle Harry said, as they all got out of the car. "Maybe we can have a word with Sat before he begins. You know him, Geordie, I'm sure."

"No, sir," Geordie said.

"What? Hasn't your father . . . ?" He turned to his sister. "How's this, Vin? Haven't you or Alfred . . . ? I mean, with his interests, it seems very odd that he hasn't been at the house."

"Yes," Geordie's mother said. "Let's not go into it now, Harry."

"H'm. Well, all right. We'll try to fix it." He picked up the pace and they reached the auditorium and went in. The big room had a rather dusty, formal air and there were a number of people sitting in the seats, talking and waiting for the show to begin. In the center aisle, where the projector sat on a table, there was a lean, bald man talking to the projectionist, who gazed sadly at him and nodded occasionally. The lean man made quite a few gestures and talked rapidly, in little bursts; he seemed an intense fellow, and stabbed a finger at the other now and then to emphasize a point but grinned when he did it. A sort of lively good nature seemed to emanate from him despite his intensity, and Geordie felt drawn to him.

Uncle Harry marched up to him and laid a hand on his shoulder, and he turned around. He looked at Uncle Harry blankly for an instant, still thinking about what he had been saying to the projectionist, and then smiled broadly. "Hello, Harry. Good evening, Mrs. Sutton. Glad you could come. New territory for you, isn't it?"

"It is for Mrs. Sutton and Geordie, my nephew. You'll probably have to cope with him presently. We'd like to see you for a moment after the show, if you haven't anything better to do."

"Nothing to do. At least, nothing better." He shook hands with Geordie. "Seems to me I've heard about you from your uncle. Duck hunter, aren't you?" He stabbed the finger. "Know the marshes, h'm? You're just the man I've been looking for."

"Yes, sir," Geordie said, a little confused to have the finger stabbed at him and to be noticed so pleasantly. People of his father's generation were usually polite and a little distant, as though they were thinking of something else; the professor made him feel that he had quickly been accepted as an equal.

"We'll see you later, then," Uncle Harry said, and moved them both before him into seats.

Geordie sat down in a pleasant glow; as his mother and uncle began to talk together he fell to wondering why the professor, a learned man who had been all over the world, should be looking for a duck hunter who knew the marshes and for himself in particular. Although he had often moved about the campus he didn't know very much about the place; it had always seemed as remote from him as the City Hall or the Capitol in Washington.

Satterthwaite left the projectionist and walked up onto the stage. The audience grew quiet, and Satterthwaite clasped his hands in front of him and began to speak rather formally.

"My talk tonight," he began, "is about an island called Laysan, the summit of an old volcanic peak near the northern end of the Hawaiian Islands chain. This island became famous before the turn of the century for its remarkable nesting colonies of oceanic birds, which must have numbered a million, and for five other species that are unique to Laysan: a teal, a rail, a miller bird, a honey eater, and a finch. These species are unique because they evolved in an isolated environment.

"Dr. Conover, my predecessor here who many of you remember, and whom we have to thank for many specimens in our museum collection, went to Laysan nine years ago with an expedition from our University. He took a number of pictures, and an ornithologist with the party, Dr. Blandford, wrote an outstanding paper on the bird life. I am familiar with the pictures and the paper; ever since my first acquaintance with them I have longed to go to Laysan, and last year I had the opportunity."

He paused and grinned, as though he was pleased to have got through the introduction. He seemed to relax all at once; he unclasped his hands and stuck them into his pockets and took a few short steps back and forth. "It was a wonderful trip," he said, "and I'm glad I went when I did, for some very bad things are happening on the island.

"It was once remote and undisturbed, but around 1890 it was leased for twenty years to a guano company by the kingdom of Hawaii. The company manager was a German captain named Schlemmer, and around 1903 he introduced rabbits on Laysan to add to his food supply, for it was expensive to import provisions and fresh meat was hard to get. Maybe he had some idea of selling rabbit meat to the ships that came for the guano. At any rate, the rabbits began to increase, and having no natural enemies on the island they kept on increasing. By the time that Dr. Conover was there, nine years later, there were indications that they were destroying the vegetation, outrunning their food supply. When I was there last year this destruction had progressed, and a good deal of the vegetation that had once covered the island and stabilized the sand had been eaten. The petrels and shearwaters, which nested in burrows, were in many cases smothered when sand shifted over the burrow entrances in storms or high winds. In addition, many of the sailors from the guano ships had talked in various ports about the immense numbers of birds, and this brought feather-hunters, Japanese mostly, who killed hundreds of thousands of birds for their feathers, which they sold to the millinery trade.

"Of the two things, I think the well-intentioned introduction of the rabbits was the worst. It is a classic example of what happens when nature is interfered with, for an ecological balance that worked was destroyed. The feather-hunters were finally controlled when President Roosevelt, upon being told of their depredations, set aside the chain of islands as a wildlife refuge, but nothing has been done about the rabbits. They have continued to increase. The guano operation ceased in 1904, the last Japanese feather raid took place in 1909, but the rabbits are still there.

"That is a short history of what has happened on Laysan Island. Now we can have the pictures."

Several hands went up, but the lights began to go out and the hands went down again. "I will answer questions later," Dr. Satterthwaite said, and moved to the side of the screen.

The first picture appeared. It had been taken from the sea, and showed a flattish island beyond the surf, a shining beach beyond which low herbage could be seen, and a great number of birds in the air.

Geordie was a little disappointed to see the flatness of Laysan, for he had clung to a volcano in his mind, but as the pictures went on to show the house, sheds, and the tall tower that had all been built by the guano company, and then to show several palm trees, and then vast, almost unbelievable colonies of albatrosses, shearwaters, boobies, man-of-war birds and teal, little flightless rails, seals and huge turtles on the beach, he grew more and more fascinated. Satterthwaite kept up a running comment on the pictures, explaining them, and between his words and the pictures themselves a little world was built up, a remote, wonderful world full of strange birds and beasts that were extraordinarily tame because few of them had known men, a world of beautiful lonely beaches, lovely warm days, and sometimes wild storms. Geordie thought of camping on such a place and having it all to himself like Robinson Crusoe, of fishing to his heart's content, and watching the endless play of life about him.

He had never seen so many birds; he hadn't thought there were that many in the world. Satterthwaite had pictures of their strange courtship antics, their nests, and their habits; the pretty little honey eaters singing from the bushes, the finches perching on the shoulders of the expedition members, and great turtles turned over to be butchered for food. There were pictures of men collecting eggs, men swimming, fishing or working on bird skins, men walking through thousands of nesting sea-birds that seemed to pay no attention to them at all. When the show ended and the lights came on Geordie felt lost for a long moment; he had been so completely on the island that it was a great wrench to be brought back to the auditorium again.

Applause rippled around the auditorium, and he turned to see his mother and his uncle both smiling at him. As people began to get up to leave, a few of them gathered around Satterthwaite, who had come down from the stage. Uncle Harry got up and made his way to Satterthwaite too. They got their heads together for a moment, and a short, dark man came and joined them. The man and Uncle Harry moved off a step or two, and stood waiting. Presently all the people around Satterthwaite were answered, and the last one turned away. Then he, Uncle Harry and the dark man drew together and walked over to where Geordie and his mother were waiting.

"You liked Laysan, I hear," Satterthwaite said to Geordie.

"Yes, sir. I think it's wonderful. I'd love to go there."

"Well, we'll do the best we can at the moment. This is Dr. Black, the Director of our Museum, and he has something to show you."

Geordie shook hands with Dr. Black, who had a slight cast in one eye that gave him a faintly sinister air, or would have at any other time. "Yes," Dr. Black said.

65

"We would like to show you something. We'll go upstairs to the Museum, if you don't mind."

They went into the hall where Dr. Black turned on a few upstairs lights, climbed the staircase to the third floor, and followed Dr. Black and Satterthwaite into the Bird Hall. Their footsteps echoed hollowly in the empty hall; the cases glittered in the dim light. It was somewhat ghostly and strange; the shadowy cases were full of birds half seen, and Geordie wondered why he had never been in the Museum before. It was rather extraordinary that he had never made the effort to come here, but it was understandable; his father had never mentioned it, his mother hadn't thought of it, and his teacher at school hadn't been interested in natural history. The dim, tantalizing glimpses of all the birds as he walked along, added to the excitement that had been aroused in him by the lecture.

Dr. Black came to a door and unlocked it and turned on a dim light; they followed him around a semi-circular wall and through another door, and he turned on more lights. Geordie caught his breath, for he seemed to be standing under an open sky with scattered white clouds in it, on a sandy place, surrounded by real bushes and nesting and flying birds that he had seen on the screen a short while before during the lecture. All around, beyond the distant beach, was the sea, shading off into lovely colors and gleaming close to the shore with the whiteness of breaking waves. He was on Laysan; the illusion was perfect to his startled eyes.

"This cyclorama, this new departure in museum exhibits," Dr. Black said, "is entirely Dr. Satterthwaite's idea, quite original with him. We think it's wonderful."

"Really superb!" Uncle Harry said, and turning impulsively took Satterthwaite's hand and pumped it up and down.''Sat, it's marvelous. It will revolutionize museums everywhere. I congratulate you, I really do.''

Satterthwaite tried to look modest. ''Thanks, Harry. You're the first outsiders to see it. Don't say anything to anybody. We want to surprise people with it. We'll put a glass front on, and people can stand there and think they're on the Island.''

He went on talking, grinning with pride in his—and Dr. Black's—accomplishment, but Geordie had stopped listening to him and was engrossed in the surrounding details; the beautifully mounted flying birds suspended by thin wires, the perspective so skilfully done that it was difficult to tell where the actual objects left off and the painted background began, the rocks and bushes and different species of birds. There were even rabbits, which Dr. Satterthwaite had said were destroying the vegetation. Looking at all this and utterly fascinated with it, Geordie suddenly thought of his phalarope and instantly knew why he had stuffed it, blundering attempt though it was. This was what he wanted to do, this was the answer suddenly revealed, and he had a moment of giddiness to find it at last plainly before him. His place was going to be somewhere in the scheme of things that could bring such a wonderful group about.

A hand fell on his shoulder and he looked up, startled. Satterthwaite was standing beside him. ''How do you like it, my boy?'' he asked.

''It's the most wonderful thing I've ever seen!'' Geordie burst out.

''Perhaps you have the vocation, h'm?'' Satterthwaite nodded. ''You take a course with me, I think, and Dr. Black starts a course in museum techniques this coming semester. Between us we can soon find out, and so can you. It's a rewarding life, even if there's not much money in it.'' He grinned, and the finger shot out. ''The duck shooting season starts soon. Why don't we do some shooting together? Call me up, and we can plan something."

"Yes, sir!" Geordie said with delight. "I certainly will. Thank you very much."

Uncle Harry joined them. "Our friends have been very kind," he said, "and now we'd better let them go. Thank Dr. Black, Geordie."

Geordie went to thank Dr. Black, and soon they were all walking down the staircase. The three men were ahead; Geordie walked with his mother, almost like a somnambulist. She had seen his reaction to the cyclorama and heard what he and Satterthwaite had said to each other, and was disturbed that she had done nothing to give him the opportunity to know of such things sooner; all she had done had been to intercede between the boy and his father's impatience, and that hadn't been very much. She felt at the moment that she had failed her son, and hoped that she could make this failure up somehow. "Geordie," she said, "I'm sorry that I haven't done more to help you."

He turned and smiled at her; there was a sweetness in his smile that twisted her heart. "If you hadn't asked Uncle Harry to dinner we wouldn't be here," he said.

She nodded and smiled back at him. It was good of him to say that she had helped by asking Harry to dinner, but she wished he hadn't said it. It was the sort of thing that harassed men say to women when the women have done something that required no real planning or forethought.

SEVEN

"I have an inclination," Uncle Harry said, when they reached the car, "to treat everybody to ice cream."

"That would be nice," Lavinia Sutton said. "The sea air gave me an appetite."

Uncle Harry cranked the car and drove them downtown to the city's best bakery store, which had a room furnished with marble-topped tables and iron chairs. There he ordered ice cream and macaroons. The ice cream was famous for miles around, for the baker made it himself in a big freezer. Little was said until they had eaten half of their portions.

"I saw that bird on your desk when I was in your room this evening, Geordie," Uncle Harry said finally. "Where did you get it?"

"I stuffed it. Spence and I shot it in the spring."

"It looked very good," Uncle Harry said. "I didn't know you were a taxidermist. What sort of bird is it?"

"It's a Wilson's phalarope," Geordie said. "I found a book in the library about it. The male sits on the eggs."

"Poor fellow. But that's not the first bird you've stuffed, is it?"

"No, sir. I practiced on some others so I'd know what to do when I got the phalarope."

"I see," Uncle Harry said, and indeed he was able to understand a good deal. "How long has this been going on?"

"Since last winter, I guess. I read about the phalarope then, and after that I wanted one."

Geordie bent to finish the last of his ice cream, and Uncle Harry exchanged a look with his sister. It was a questioning look, as though to inquire whether she had known how long and steadfastly Geordie had held to his desire; she answered it with a slight negative shake of her head, and said: "I . . . we didn't really know, Harry."

"Well," Uncle Harry said, "we do now." He turned to Geordie. "I'm going to ask them to send you a card for the museum library," he said. "They've got much better books for your purpose, and you won't have to wait until college opens to begin reading them."

"That's something I'd appreciate very much."

Uncle Harry signaled for his check, paid it, and they went out and drove home. Alfred Sutton was still in the living room, with a card table in front of him covered with papers; he pushed it away and stood up. "Was it a good lecture, Geordie?" he asked.

"Yes, sir. It was about the best I ever heard. You

should have come, Dad. I wished you were there." He looked at his Uncle Harry, for they had promised not to tell about the cyclorama.

"Sat showed us a remarkable thing he's done," Uncle Harry said, "but we said we wouldn't mention it. You'll be able to see it soon, anyhow."

"I'll wait," Alfred Sutton said. "You'd better get to bed, now, Geordie."

"All right," Geordie said, and turned away. He stopped at the door. "Thank you an awful lot, Uncle Harry. I . . . For taking me, and for the card." He went out of the room, and they heard him climbing the stairs.

"The card?" Alfred Sutton asked.

"A card for the museum library. I'll get him one. It's a good three weeks before the term begins. Might as well give him a head start. I think it's rather remarkable that he was so steady in that business about his phalarope. He hasn't had much encouragement, you know."

"I know," Alfred Sutton said. "What was this about the phalarope?"

Uncle Harry told him; he listened closely, but with no change of expression. "It looks to me," Uncle Harry went on, "as though he has a very real inclination, Alfred, and that you've been too busy to notice it."

"It is difficult to know what a boy is doing or thinking most of the time," Alfred Sutton said. "The poet was quite right when he wrote that a boy's will is the wind's will."

He glanced at his wife, but she wasn't looking at him. Her head was bent, her glance was on the floor; she knew her husband's hopes and intentions for Geordie and suspected that her brother guessed them too now and was trying to plead Geordie's case in the only way he could. She couldn't be disloyal to her husband even though she disagreed with him, and at the same time she couldn't be disloyal to Geordie and the future he seemed to be finding for himself. She was in a nerve-racking predicament, and as the two men fenced with each other she felt that an iron band was inexorably tightening around her head and would soon crush it. She would have to leave, she couldn't listen to any more. "I think I had better go to bed," she said, looking up with the best smile she could manage. "Thank you, Harry, for the nice evening. Come again as soon as you can."

She left the room, and the two men watched her go.

"I suppose I should be going too," Uncle Harry said, deciding that he had said enough for the moment.

"Why not stay long enough for a game?" Alfred Sutton asked. "After we've finished you can take the car, bring it back in the morning, and we'll drop you on the way downtown."

"Well, all right. I'll get the board and the chessmen out while you gather your papers together. I really don't feel like going to bed quite yet."

After Geordie had gotten to his room and closed the door he felt his way to the desk, turned on the student's lamp, and sat down. He was suddenly very tired from all the events of the day and the emotional impact of those events upon him. The revelation of the way he wanted to spend his life, now that he was alone and undisturbed, completely occupied his mind; it made him a little light-headed, and filled him with an odd, rather disembodied sense of joy. He thought of the books he would be able to read when the card came, of the library that would lead him into the world he was so eager to enter, of being able to see the actual mechanics of museum work and possibly participate in them. Above all this, mistily superimposed upon it, were thoughts of expeditions to places wondrous and strange. In his exalted state he was like a newly-made knight at his vigil before his armor in the long, dark hours before starting out on his first quest.

Presently, overcome by weariness, he went to bed. The thoughts and visions and hopes swirling around in his head grew nebulous and confused, cleared, and grew nebulous again. Sleep took him, and as he slept he dreamed. His dream, like all dreams, was confused in its own logic but it related to a happy time in Geordie's life.

He was smaller and younger then, in those days, a boy in knickerbockers and a Norfolk jacket, with a long black stockings and a Buster Brown collar on his shirt, and he and his father were on a train. They had gotten on it after it had pulled into the depot behind the engine, a great, exciting, roaring iron monster wreathed in steam, shining with brass, clanging a bell and shaking the world. He had almost been afraid of it, and caught his father's hand. The engineer, a superior being high above them in his cab, raised a grimy paw in greeting and made them kin.

The journey to St. Louis was not a long one, but exciting because it was Geordie's first train ride. He had settled down by the time they reached the city, when excitement began anew. His first sight of the Mississippi and the great paddle wheel steamers, the bustle and traffic, and finally the Terminal Hotel kept his eyes wide and his head swiveling. They went into the dining room for lunch; against a background of gleaming linen, shining silver, and great chandeliers he saw his first Negroes, in fancy black suits. The sight of them stopped him at the door.

"Dad!" he said, in a stage whisper. "Dad! They're

black! What's the matter with them, Dad? Why have they turned black?"

Alfred Sutton smiled; he often smiled at Geordie in those days, or put a warm and reassuring arm around him. He put his arm around the boy now, and stooped to whisper to him. "They're Negroes, Geordie. All Negroes are black. They come from Africa, where the sun's very hot all the time. Perhaps they were slaves, or their fathers were. You've read about slaves, or heard people talk about them."

"Yes, sir. I guess I forgot," Geordie said, pretending that he had known about Negroes all the time. Nevertheless, for a little while he kept his father between himself and any black man who drew near them, until their first strangeness had worn off.

That evening his father took him to a show; after the few very amateurish theatricals he had seen the big theatre, the crowd and the music and the show itself, a road company's production of "The Chocolate Soldier," enthralled him so much that he had to crawl into his father's bed and talk about it all and ask questions until he fell asleep.

The next day they took a train for the west, for Geordie's father was going to Denver to look into a company in which he was thinking of investing some money. The sleeping car in which they traveled was another wonder, and by the time Geordie had investigated it to his own satisfaction, toured the train, and even talked at some length to several of the Negro porters the country was beginning to change and demand his attention. Watercourses became fewer, there were dry streambeds, the land grew more arid and the vegetation changed; occasionally they passed big prairie dog villages or saw a few antelope in the distance; presently, like clouds on the horizon, the Rockies began to take shape and as they grew closer gained solidity and thrust their great serrated peaks into the sky.

They were the first mountains that Geordie had ever seen, and he couldn't get enough of looking at them. Patched on the heights with snow, changing with every change of light, their vast rugged sweep, their shadowy canyons and bold shoulders and ridges somehow moved him almost to tears. He couldn't explain it, although he tried; his father tried to help him express himself and told great stories of pioneers, of mountain men, trappers, Indians, and seekers for gold. Alfred Sutton was a good storyteller; the warm simplicity of their relatonship and Geordie's interest and obvious admiration of his knowledge made him a better one. He filled the boy's head with wonderful tales, a thing for which there had never been a consistent opportunity in the busy, day-to-day life at home. Their companionship, so intimate and uninterrupted, made a magic circle around them that excluded all the usual distractions. By the time they got off the train in Denver, with the mountains so close and mysterious, hiding many wonders and colored by the bits of history he had learned, Geordie's affection and respect for his father was far greater than most men ever know from their sons.

This increased as the days went on. Geordie was introduced to the men Alfred Sutton had come to see. He sat quietly at their conferences, and it was very evident to him that his father was held in great respect and esteem; he had a presence that always set him a little apart. Geordie was very proud of this, but glad when the talks were over and he had his father to himself again and they could wander a little more before they started home.

They went to Colorado Springs, where Alfred Sutton rented a horse and surrey with a fringed top and a driver to take them out to the Garden of the Gods, and drove about among the great strange red sandstone formations that seemed to make of the place a different little world tucked in against the rise of the Front Range, and took the Moffat Road train around the Georgetown Loop.

This, to Geordie, was the best of all because it was in the wonderful mountains themselves. The endless evergreen forests, the white water of mountain streams, the spidery, scary trestles and the vast, ever-widening views as the train climbed upward was a source of endless fascination to a young flatlander. They climbed higher, to timberline where trees grew stunted and scattered and finally fell away and tiny, flowered plants took their place, into the snows of the summits where the air was thin and cold and it seemed that the whole world was spread below them.

They were among the evergreens again, on the way down, when the train stopped and two wild-looking, bearded men got on. They both carried lever-action rifles, and each had a wildcat skin thrown over his shoulder; they were the very stuff of Alfred Sutton's tales come to life, encountered in an atmosphere that had already strongly moved the boy. They made a tremendous impression upon him (an impression that remained long after it had drifted into the back of his conscious mind), and he caught his father by the arm. "They're trappers, Dad! They're trappers! I want to be a trapper in the mountains like them when I grow up."

Perhaps his perceptions were unusually acute at that moment, for somehow he was aware that his father had withdrawn from him, that their relationship was suddenly in abeyance. His father's expression hardened, and he shook his head. "You wouldn't like their life, Geordie. It's hard and dirty and poor. I think you'd rather be a lawyer, like your Dad."

Geordie recoiled, confused, but before he had time to collect his impressions his father moved swiftly to obliterate them. He smiled again and put an arm around the boy. "You're right," he said. "They're like Jim Bridger and the other mountain men. Aren't we lucky we've seen them? They're like the old times come back again."

Geordie nodded and smiled and snuggled into the encircling arm. The warmth was back again between them and he talked more about the two men; it was not until later, when they were back on the plain and the men had gone, that he half recalled the moment and felt bewildered and alone. This feeling came back to him several times after they got home, and deepened through the years in moments when he recalled the trip. He and his father never recaptured the wonderful closeness again, for there were distractions and other interests and people; Alfred Sutton often talked about the law and Geordie grew ever more interested in the outdoors. Imperceptibly they moved further apart. It was not an alienation but a subtle withdrawal on the part of Alfred Sutton, who probably didn't realize that he was withdrawing as his cherished wish seemed more and more unlikely of fulfillment.

As Geordie's dream moved toward its end he saw the two trappers again against the background of the heights, and then they began to fade. Before the men were quite blotted out, however, a darkness like the shadow of a cloud moved in front of them. The shifting vapor gathered into the form of his father and was outlined in a suffused and glowing light like that emanating from a heroic and beloved figure in an illustrated book of legends. In one hand he held the tablets of the law, which Geordie had seen pictured in the hand of Moses; he extended his free hand beseechingly in Geordie's direction and then he began to recede, to grow smaller and further away. Geordie half awoke and tried to follow him, but could not. He was bound in his place, and couldn't break his bonds. "Dad!" he shouted. "Dad! Don't go away! Wait! Wait for me!"

The two men downstairs heard him and jumped up, scattering the chessmen. They ran up the stairs. Lavinia Sutton, lying sleepless, leaped out of bed and ran toward his room. She reached him first, and had him in her arms when the men got there. He was still not fully awake, twitching as though still trying to follow the figure in his dream.

"It's all right, Geordie," the men at the door heard Lavinia Sutton say. "You were having a nightmare, but it's all right now."

"Dad was going away," he said, calmer as he awoke more fully. "I was dreaming of our trip to the mountains and the trappers on the train, and then he began to go away and I couldn't go with him."

Lavinia Sutton's hands stroked his back, and her look at the men seemed to ask them to go away and leave her with him. They glanced at each other and turned quietly away from the door to go down the stairs again. They didn't speak until they were in the living room.

"Gave me quite a turn," Alfred Sutton said. "It must have been the very devil of a nightmare, for he is old enough now not to be so upset by the usual thing."

"He seems to have felt that he was losing you, Alfred," Uncle Harry said, "You saw those trappers he mentioned on your Denver trip?"

"Yes. He was young then, he said he wanted to be a trapper in the mountains."

"I see," Uncle Harry said. "You must have tried to dissuade him then."

"I did, as a matter of fact. Extraordinary that he should recall all that now, and dream about it."

"Alfred," Uncle Harry said, "don't you see? It's . . . Ah, this is really none of my affair, but do you mind if I say something?" Alfred Sutton shook his head, and Uncle Harry went on. "It's vitally important to him, looking up to you as he does, to feel that he has your complete support if he chooses some other career than the law."

Alfred Sutton looked at the floor for a long moment after this was said, and finally raised his head again. "Harry," he said, "it's good of you to give me your thought on this, and there may be something in what you say. I don't quite agree with you that a life of stuffing things and all that will get him very far. He's young and doesn't realize this yet, but given time I think he will. The entire nation is getting away from this wide open spaces, backwoods sort of thing, developing, industrializing, growing up. I want the best for him, I don't want him left behind like an outdated frontiersman. No, I'll give him more time. He'll see it eventually."

Uncle Harry, realizing the futility of more talk, nodded. "Well," he said, "things seem to have quieted down upstairs, and I'd better be getting on."

"Take the car," Alfred Sutton said. "It was good of you to take them to the lecture. I'm sorry there was such an uproar at the end of it."

"We all enjoyed the lecture," Uncle Harry said. "Geordie, I think, enjoyed it most of all. Good night, Alfred." He nodded and went out the front door, thinking as he walked toward the car that he was all on Geordie's side now and would carry on a guerilla war with Alfred if he had to to help the boy in the direction he wanted to go.

EIGHT

Several evenings later Uncle Harry stopped by with the museum library card. Nothing was said about Geordie's nightmare after the lecture, for Geordie was rather ashamed of making such a scene at his age and didn't really understand why he had done it, and Uncle Harry carefully avoided any conversational gambit that might bring it up. He realized that the boy had been so strongly moved because he had already subconsciously chosen his way; he knew that Geordie wasn't going to have an easy time of it, that he would need support sooner or later, and he intended to lend a hand behind the scenes if and when the opportunity to do so presented itself. He would have to be careful, for he didn't want to alienate his brother-in-law and through him his sister. He didn't like the idea of meddling in the family's affairs, he admitted that Alfred's intentions were of the best, but he felt very strongly that Geordie had the right to choose his own career with a free mind and he hoped that something he might do would bring Alfred around.

The conversation among the four of them was general, and then the two men sat down to play a game of chess. It was too late to go to the library, so Geordie watched the game for awhile with mild interest and went to bed.

He and Spence had planned a trip for the next day, but he was so eager to get to the library that he went to Spence's house after breakfast and asked Spence to excuse him. "I'll go tomorrow if you want," he said. "But I really want to see the library and maybe get a book or two, now that I've got my card."

"You'd better go, I guess, then tomorrow we can go to Ringo's marsh and start building our blind. I can work on the decoys today. They need a little paint."

"You can come to the library with me, if you want."

"I don't think I will," Spence said. He enjoyed watching birds and shooting at some of them, but he didn't want to read about them. "You go ahead."

"All right. I'll get some nails while I'm downtown. We need more nails."

"We need some twine too. Get some of that. I'll see you tomorrow."

"See you tomorrow," Geordie said. He went home, got his bicycle, and rode to MacBride Hall. Instead of going to the library first he climbed to the third floor and went slowly through Mammal Hall and Bird Hall and looked carefully and long at the mounted specimens that he had only glimpsed in the dim light when Dr. Black and Dr.

Satterthwaite had taken them upstairs after the lecture. The museum had a very fine collection for that era; the life of the prairies was very well represented, and Stefansson and several other former students who had been to the Arctic or the tropics or to other parts of the United States had contributed to it, and Satterthwaite's predecessor, Conover, had both contributed to and organized it. Satterthwaite had carried on Conover's work and both of them had brought back specimens from Laysan. As he moved about, looking at all these things, Geordie began to realize the extent of the work and dedication that had gone into their collection and preservation and how important this was for the broadening of man's knowledge of his world. This hadn't occurred to him before because he had never thought of it in that light; what little collecting he had done had been intensely personal, as in the case of the phalarope; the several hours he spent in the museum broadened his outlook considerably.

Finally he went downstairs to the library. Because the fall term hadn't started yet there were only three people there beside the librarian, and he went over to her desk, introduced himself to her, and showed her his card. She was a middle-aged, bright-eyed woman, rather severe looking until she smiled.

"Why, you're Mr. Sutton," she said. "Dr. Satterthwaite said you might be in, and that you were interested in birds. Your uncle was here with him. It's nice that you can get acquainted with the library before the term starts. Can I help you?"

Geordie, secretly pleased to be called "Mr. Sutton" and placed by implication among serious people, gave her his slow grin. "Yes, ma'am," he said. "If you can show me how to find the bird books, I'd appreciate it."

"They're all under 'Ornithology' here," she said, and

got up and took him to the index files. She pulled out a drawer and took it to a table. "There. You can look through it and pick out what you want."

Geordie thanked her, sat down, and began to leaf through the file. He soon discovered that what Uncle Harry had said was true: here were riches far beyond what he had known before. There was so much that he was confused and didn't know what to choose; finally he took the drawer to the librarian's desk.

"I don't know what to start with," he said apologetically. "There's so much."

"You'll very probably be assigned basic and collateral reading when classes start, and they will suggest other things to you. But for now . . . Have you had any zoology, or avian physiology? No? That might be a good place to start." She went through the file, wrote several numbers down, and went with him to show him where to find the books. "Here's the physiology," she said, taking it down. It was a big book; he put it under his arm. She took down another. "This is a sort of introduction to zoology," she said. "You'll have it in your course, but it won't do any harm to look at it now." He took that one too. "You don't have to read them as carefully as though you were preparing for a test, but if you go through them you'll find a lot of interesting things. Read through them, and before you come back again I'll look up some other books for you to take out."

"I sure appreciate your trouble," Geordie said, very pleased to meet someone who was so helpful, and still a little startled that college wasn't, apparently, going to be as stuffy as he had imagined it.

"It's a pleasure to help anyone who is really interested. Dr. Satterthwaite will be in, and I'll ask him to recommend something."

Geordie smiled, thanked her again, and went out. By

the time he was outside he realized that he didn't even know her name. She was so different from the rather crabbed librarian he was used to, who seemed to find everything a chore, that she had confused him a little. In fact, the whole day so far had confused him a little and exhilarated him too, because it had made him feel a part of a serious and important enterprise rather than a boy whose inclination interested few people besides himself. He was so preoccupied thinking of this that he was half-way home before he remembered the nails and twine and had to go back for them.

He was so late that he missed his lunch, but Ingrid gave him some doughnuts and milk in the kitchen; then he went up to his room and spent the rest of the afternoon with the two books. He looked through the one on zoology first and decided to come back to it; he put it aside and curled up in one of the upholstered chairs with the other. There were many words in it that he didn't know; some he looked up in the dictionary and some he blundered over, guessing at the sense from the context. He went at it in a rush, like a hungry man bolting his food, knowing that he would read it again more carefully, but despite his haste he began to see how wonderfully birds were made for their function. He had known a little, but not much; the day of books that popularized such subjects had not yet come. He read on, fascinated.

The two boys finished working on their blind for the duck shooting season, and the fall term began at the University. Geordie managed to arrange most of his classes in the mornings, and so looked forward to several free afternoons a week when he could get out and wander about. Spence, who would be working toward an engineering degree, managed to hold out one afternoon a week besides Saturday, so they would in a measure be able to go together. The business of learning their way around, beginning classes, and settling into the routine of their new life occupied them for a time.

Geordie's favorite subject from the first was Biology, and Satterthwaite, who taught it, his favorite teacher. Other professors might occasionally have lapses into boredom but Satterthwaite had an unflagging enthusiasm for the science of life and its endless ramifications and mysteries. He was full of observations made on his various trips, and told many stories of his experiences. A number of these were hilarious, for he was a lively and inquisitive traveler without self-consciousness, and didn't mind laughing at himself over his misadventures. Lean and bald, restless, good-natured, talking in little bursts and occasionally stabbing out with a finger as Geordie had first seen him at the Laysan lecture, he led them on. Listening to him, Geordie was often very thankful that he had quietly held out for Biology when he and his father had gone over the curriculum and picked his subjects. "Biology?" his father had asked, without enthusiasm. "Are you quite sure?"

"Yes, sir. I'd like to take it."

"I understand it's rather messy, cutting up frogs and things. Why do you want to do that?"

"I want to know what makes them work," Geordie had said.

"Do you think you can come at the spirit or the life of the brain by watching a beating heart or examining a section of muscle? This seems to me to be trying to get at a mystery by cataloguing the mechanics."

This had been rather unfair, a tactic to confuse, but

Geordie had not been drawn by it. "Yes, sir. I guess it is, but I'd like to take it anyhow."

"If you wish, then. If it turns out to be unsatisfactory, you can change to something else next year."

As he worked on his zoology experiments Geordie often thought of his father's comment, and the more he learned of life processes the more wonderful the fact of life itself, beyond its mechanics, became to him. This was not the case with some of his fellow students, who were gradually turning into mechanists pure and simple, and there were many arguments in what they called 'bull sessions' outside of class. The mechanists were the more vocal and had concrete examples on their side with which they pelted the non-mechanists, who tended to go off into intangibles and lose themselves. Geordie would listen to these wrangles for a time, grin, and go off to the library; both sides got a good deal of mental exercise but neither ever convinced the other and he, Geordie, preferred to learn more about the habits and personalities of the birds and animals. The mechanists, he thought, would be laboratory men, researchers, who would make many valuable contributions which were greatly needed; he intended to become firmly based in laboratory techniques and then get out into the sun and air and perhaps discover not what a dietary deficiency or a parasite did to to a blue-winged teal but how and why it migrated.

Migration was particularly on his mind just then because he and Spence, on their days afield together, were seeing the beginning of it. As the leaves blazed in color and the countryside slowly changed from green toward the dry, dun monotone of winter the summer birds were leaving and the birds from further north were beginning to appear, some to pause a little and then leave, and some to stay. Goldenrod, and blue, white, and purple prairie asters (which have since that time largely disappeared with the original grasses), gave their color to the prairie; sunflowers had ripened their seeds and drew the seedeaters, and wild grape and crabapple bore their fruits along the river bluffs among the bright sumacs. Red-tailed hawks on the move drew their ellipses in the sky; blue-winged teal, early migrators, and an occasional boldly patterned avocet appeared in the marshes.

The two boys spent some pre-shooting season time in their blind, content to be lazily sitting in the pleasant autumn sun just watching the life about them. They were pleased to see that their marsh, which they had picked after a long survey of the marshes they knew, seemed to hold up in its attractiveness to birds. When they were pretty sure that they were going to have good shooting Geordie spoke to Dr. Satterthwaite.

"We've watched our marsh for a couple of week-ends," he said, "and it seems to be pretty good. You said at the Laysan lecture that you'd like to shoot with us."

"So I would, so I would. Nice of you to remember me, Geordie. Name your time and I'll be with you."

"You can come any time you want to," Geordie said. "After we show it to you, and how to get there, you could go whenever you wished. I've told Uncle Harry about it. I don't think anybody else knows about it."

"I'm already licking my chops," Dr. Satterthwaite said. "Incidentally, you'd better call me Doc out of class. I can foresee difficulty if you have to say: 'Dr. Satterthwaite, sir, there's a mallard approaching from the left.' Don't you agree?"

Geordie grinned. "Yes, sir."

"Can I give you a hand building the blind?"

"We've built it, and painted the decoys. All you have to do is come."

"Better and better. I'll always arrange to bring the lunches, then, when I come."

"Well," Geordie said, "I don't think you have to. I usually cook a little something."

Satterthwaite's look seemed to sharpen a little. "It will be a little hard to get used to all this luxury. Why did you turn into a cook?"

"I got tired of cold sandwiches, I guess, and then I watched Ingrid a couple of times. Ingrid's our cook."

"I hear from your uncle that she's a phenomenon. It will be great fun to shoot with you and Harry. I had a sort of running competition with him last year." The finger came out. "He beat me by five ducks. This year it'll be different."

"Could you come on opening day?" Geordie asked.

"Greater love hath no man," Satterthwaite said, "than to share the opening day with a friend. I'll have to give you a good term mark." He grinned. "I'll have to anyhow if you continue the good work. You're doing very well, you know." The finger transfixed him. "See that you don't slow down."

"No, sir," Geordie said, mightily pleased. "I won't."

"I know it's probably too soon to tell, but do you have any idea yet what you want to do? I guess it's inevitable as we learn more, but biology seems to be dividing into specialities. Have you any indication at all what you would like yours to be?"

Somehow it seemed to Geordie that there was some reason for the question beyond the interest that Satterthwaite had always shown in the plans and interests of his students. He didn't know what this reason could be, and couldn't guess. "I like birds best," he said, "but I don't think I'd like to do laboratory research on them. I'd rather be out where they are."

"An ornithologist, then, a field ornithologist. Good, very good. We'll see what kind of a cook you are."

He grinned again and managed to look mysterious; Geordie felt a stirring of excitement, for he was sure there was something behind all this. Perhaps it was a field trip, maybe into country he didn't know; he would love to take a field trip with Satterthwaite. His curiosity got the better of him. "Dr. Satterthwaite—"

"Doc."

"Doc, then. Do you have some reason for asking?"

"I should hope I had a reason for every question I asked," Satterthwaite said, and began to gather up his papers. "I've got to go. Stop in my office tomorrow afternoon and we'll make our shooting arrangements."

"All right," Geordie said, grinned, and went out of the room. He almost felt like skipping. Something was in the wind; something was surely in the wind.

NINE

The week-end before the season opened Geordie and
Spence made a trip to the marsh, to take the decoys and
a Dutch oven. Geordie, after conferring with Ingrid, decided that he would use it to make a fine stew, for Doc,
as he was trying to get into the habit of calling Satterthwaite, had put such a mysterious emphasis on cooking that he wanted to impress him. It was a heavy thing
to carry, and he hoped that lugging it along would turn
out to be worth the trouble.

"Good Christmas!" Spence had said, when he first saw
it. "You'll break your back with that thing. What do you
want to take it for?"

"I want to give Doc a real good lunch. He's got something up his sleeve. Besides, we can leave it there and use it again. They have another one here. I'll carry it."

"I'll carry it halfway," Spence said, "but the lunch better be good."

They set out in the brakecart; when they reached the point on the road opposite the marsh they could drive a way across the prairie, but the last half mile or so they had to walk. They were both tired of the Dutch oven by the time they got there, but were cheered by the number of ducks that took to the air as they approached.

"There are a lot of them using the marsh," Geordie said, with satisfaction. "It's going to be all right. It ought to get better as more of them come down."

They dropped their gear and made another trip to get all the decoys from the cart, and then put on their boots and took all the stuff they had brought out to the island where they had built the blind. It was a long, narrow island several hundred yards from shore, with some medium-height swamp oaks, sycamores, and other trees and a good deal of head-high brush on it; the blind was on the northern point with plenty of water in front of it. They put the decoys and the oven in the blind, and walked back sixty or seventy yards into the brush and gathered enough wood for a fire. Geordie's idea was to do the cooking there, away from the blind, among a few trees that would give some concealment. The brush would give them pretty good cover as they moved back and forth between the fire and the blind.

Because it couldn't be seen from any road and was unsuspected by most people, the little marsh, which wasn't more than twenty or thirty acres in extent, hadn't been shot or disturbed, so far as the boys knew, for a long time. No one who hadn't wandered widely over the country, as they had, would have known it was there, and they looked upon it as a secret place. It was shallow, with no stream flowing out of it to be followed up, and had a good growth of aquatic plants. Quite a few ducks nested on the island in the spring, and other birds, for the water surrounding it kept off weasels, wandering dogs, and other nest disturbers.

The two boys got through their chores and left as quickly as they could, so as not to scare any of the ducks they had flushed that might want to return for the night. They returned to Geordie's house where Spence spent the night.

The long-awaited morning finally came, and the two boys were shaken from sleep in the small hours by the alarm clock. They both staggered to the window and saw that it was very dark, overcast, and windy—a good day to keep ducks on the move. They sleepily congratulated each other, dressed, and went down to the kitchen, where Ingrid had left a bag holding the ingredients of a stew. By the time breakfast was ready they were wide awake. They had just finished eating when Uncle Harry and Doc came in, booted, bundled to the ears and bright-eyed with anticipation, to be followed shortly by Laverty, who was to drive them out and come back for them at the end of the day.

"God bless all here," he said, touching his forelock with exaggerated humility, "and may you be slaughtering a great lot of the poor ducks."

"It's nice to have your blessing," Uncle Harry said, grinning at him. "Can you keep up your good works and take a little of the chill off the day? It's too cold for this time of year."

"I'll try, sir, I'll try, but I can smell a bit of snow on the way, God forbid."

"Amen," Uncle Harry said, and looked at his watch. "It's time to go."

Geordie and Spence put on their boots and got their guns and shells, and Geordie picked up the bag; they all went out into the cold and windy dark, and climbed into the carriage. Laverty clucked to Uncle Harry's horse, and they set out. The carriage curtains were up and rattled in the wind; they pulled the buffalo robes up to their chins and snuggled into them. Geordie sat up front with Laverty, to direct him, and almost missed the turn-off point onto the prairie in the dark, but finally they reached the end of the ride and started on the walk after arranging with Laverty to check in the middle of the day to see if they wanted to leave then. The wind buffeted them and brought tears to their eyes, but a slowly mounting excitement kept them warm. There was a skim of ice on the water, and as it broke around them with a crackle there was a roar of wings and a great cackling as the sleeping ducks awoke and took off.

Fortunately the area before the blind had been in the wind's lee and the ducks had bunched there and kept the water open; it was a good omen. All four of them sloshed about and set out the decoys and then got into the blind out of the wind, to blow on their fingers and stamp their feet. Presently the first faint, suffused glow of sunrise appeared in the east and slowly began to spread, dyeing the overcast and setting the edges of the clouds on fire. They heard several ducks which they couldn't see return and splash down, talking to each other.

Geordie loved this hour of the day when he could watch the world emerge from night and open out toward the horizon; he loved the silence, the changing light, and life beginning to stir again. The sky was taking on more color and soon the ducks would begin to come in, but he tore himself away and went back into the brush to start the fire and put on the stew. There was a stirring in the brush as he went, a mink or a coon moving away from him to hole up for the day, and there was the dark and silent shadow against the paling sky of an owl on the move, glimpsed and gone. He started the fire, got some water in the oven, dumped the ingredients in, and set the oven on to cook. As he turned away to return four ducks came over him, their wings set, to swing into the decoys. They would be the first of the day, and he wouldn't be there; he stood and waited for the guns, but they didn't speak. Something had alerted the ducks, and they must have gone off. When he stepped into the blind again everybody was laughing.

"What happened?" he asked.

"We were all sitting down," Spence said. "Uncle Harry stood up for a look just as some ducks came in. He scared them, and they kept right on going."

"They didn't even pause to say good-bye," Uncle Harry said ruefully. "Just for that, I'll be sentinel."

He stood up in his corner of the blind to watch; the light grew stronger, and in a while Uncle Harry crouched down a little.

"Bunch coming," he said. "Keep low, and get set."

Excitement caught them all; they picked up their guns and their muscles tensed. They crouched, ready to jump up, trembling a little; they couldn't see, but could imagine, the ducks coming closer, closer . . .

"They're dropping," Uncle Harry whispered, reaching one hand out for his gun. "Dropping. They'll come in right in front. Eight or ten . . . Now!"

They all jumped up. Uncle Harry had timed it very well; the ducks, blue-winged teal, were just dropping their feet and backing their wings. Geordie picked out a drake and pulled the trigger, but nothing happened. The guns on each side of him opened up and several teal fell, and Geordie followed the flaring drake and pulled the rear trigger and nothing happened again except the click of the firing pin on an empty chamber as the flock scudded over them. In his preoccupation with the sunrise and the stew he had forgotten to load his gun. Disappointment and mortification turned him brick red; he sat down quickly, hoping to escape attention, but they were all looking at him with wide grins and nudging each other: they had all heard the last click.

"Very quiet gun you've got there," Uncle Harry said.

"Certainly is an improvement over these noisy things we shoot," Doc said. "Just a little click."

"Sort of a conservation measure."

"We'll have to tell people about it," Doc said, and they all laughed immoderately.

Geordie sat and took it, and finally even he began to grin. "I'll do better next time," he said, and loaded his gun. "I'll get the ducks." He waded out and picked up three ducks, and brought them in. In his absence they'd elected him watchman for his sins, and he changed places with Uncle Harry and stood with his head under the roof of the blind, back in the corner out of the wind.

It was full light now, or as light as it was going to be with the overcast, and there was still color in the sky; Geordie saw a marsh hawk beyond the water working its beat, rising and dropping on the wind. Four crows went by to the east, and then beyond them Geordie saw a single duck materialize against the gray sky. It was coming for them and he decided to get even with the other three by not saying anything and shooting it himself. The duck rapidly drew closer, began to swing away, saw the decoys, and swung toward them again. Geordie tensed, ready to grab his gun; there was an undertone of conversation beside him, and despite his concentration on the approaching duck he heard Doc say: ". . . and I've been in correspondence with the Biological Survey about a trip to shoot all the rabbits, and it is beginning to look as though something might . . ."

Laysan! he thought. *It's Laysan he's talking about! If he's going to Laysan he might be thinking of taking me!* The duck, a drake mallard, was almost in the decoys and setting itself to land; Geordie grabbed up his gun and shot at it. His concentration, however, had been so shattered by what he had heard that he missed it completely. It swung off the other end of the blind. Everybody jumped up and Doc, who was in that corner, swung and shot. It was a very long shot, but successful; the duck went down in a long glide and fell on the prairie beyond the edge of the marsh.

Everybody was looking at Geordie again, and Doc was grinning like the Cheshire cat. "I was going to get even with you all," Geordie said, to explain himself. "It was a single, and I thought I'd . . . I . . ."

"The vindictive type," Uncle Harry said and laughed. "Hoist with his own petard, he was." They were all laughing at him again, even Spence. "Well, my boy," Uncle Harry went on. "For the good of your soul, you can go get the duck. It will teach you to try to take a mean advantage of your trusting friends."

"Yes, sir," Geordie said. "I guess I'd better go get it. Spence, will you check the water in the stew, and build up the fire?"

Spence nodded, and Geordie crawled out of the blind and waded ashore. His head was full of wild surmises as he went, buffeted by the wind, and equally wild schemes as to how he could find out from Doc if there was any connection between the sentence he had heard in the blind and the questions Doc had asked him a week or so before. He was fully aware that there would be no real reason to take him, for he had nothing to offer. But still . . .

By the time he had reached the mallard, and settled down somewhat, he knew there was no way to ask Doc. It would not only be very presumptious, it would be stupid, for when he had tried it before he had gotten no real answer. He would just have to wait, and hope, and maybe he would see. He picked up the mallard, and as he turned toward the blind to start back he saw a flock of ducks come in and several splashes and then heard the rumble of the guns.

After a start that left something to be desired, Geordie's day began to improve. To his delight, he killed a duck that Doc had missed with both barrels, and then three others before the morning flights began to slow down. Everybody had done well, and they had had a fine time and collected a good bunch of ducks. They were all very happy with the little marsh, lonely and quiet as it was, with no one else anywhere in sight to disturb the ducks that were coming in. "Maybe we don't know how lucky we are," Doc said, in one of the lulls. "I have a notion that in a few years it's going to be very hard to find a modest little earthly paradise like this without owning miles of country. You two boys certainly did a fine job when you found it. I appreciate very much being let in on it."

"So do I," Uncle Harry said. "And I'm going to appreciate the lunch, for every once in awhile I get a drift of fragrance on the wind that makes my mouth water. Do we have to wait much longer? I had breakfast awfully early."

"It ought to be about ready now," Geordie said. He had been back to the fire several times, and when he had tasted the stew he had been very pleased with it. He and Spence now took the oven off the fire, put on the battered coffee pot, and brought the oven back to the blind swinging on a pole they carried between them. When the top was taken off a wonderful fragrance filled the blind, for Ingrid had helped Geordie add the spices. Doc and Uncle Harry exchanged happy glances. They handed out the tin plates and spoons, gave everybody a big hunk of bread, and fell to. After the first mouthful Doc sat chewing with his eyes on Geordie; there was an abstracted expression in them. Suddenly he blinked, his eyes focused again, he took another spoonful, and a wide smile appeared on his face. "Well, Harry," he said, "you told me, but you sold the boy short. Geordie, I'm your man. Any time you want to go shooting, just whistle." He thrust out the finger. "Or just look like you're going to."

"Yes, sir," Geordie said. He was very pleased, and more hopeful now that he might be chosen for whatever mysterious enterprise (for he was sure there was something) that Doc had in mind. "I like to shoot with you too. I get a nice chance to pick up a duck once in awhile."

"You do, do you? Harry, would you say that this rising generation fails a little in respect?"

"No," Uncle Harry said. "And stop worrying about your ego when your real worry's marksmanship. Eat your stew, man, before it freezes over."

Doc grinned and returned to his stew. After they had all finished they washed the spoons and plates and the oven, and sat outside near the blind drinking their coffee. Out of the wind and warmed by the splendid meal, they were content; a great and happy peace descended upon them.

"Laverty's coming back in a while, isn't he?" Uncle Harry asked presently.

"Yes; he is."

"Why don't we knock off and go with him? We have enough ducks, we don't want to shoot them all. If we get out now they won't be disturbed when they return, and that will make it better another day."

"Yes, sir, I think that would be fine."

"Agreed," Doc said. "Besides," he went on, pointing to the north, "it looks like snow over there. If—"

What he was going to say was never finished, for off in the distance, coming mellowly down the wind, there were the voices of geese. Like a family of groundhogs all trying to pop into the same burrow they scrambled wildly over each other getting back into the blind, sorted themselves out, and inched up their heads cautiously to peer through the reeds covering the front. Spence saw them first.

"Northwest!" he said. "They're turning! They've seen the marsh! they're coming!"

They scarcely breathed; the almost ecstatic excitement aroused in any hunter by approaching geese made them all tremble, but outwardly they were as still as stones. The big wedge, gabbling, swung into the wind, broke formation, and set their wings. The geese looked huge, and beautiful.

"One apiece," Uncle Harry said. "Now!"

Four geese fell, and with a great crying and beating of wings the rest swung and rose away on the wind. The four people in the blind pounded each other with exclamations of vast pleasure, and as he and Spence started out of the blind to pick up the geese Geordie saw the tiny figure of Laverty coming toward them far across the distant prairie. If he had come a few minutes earlier the geese would have swung away.

TEN

Doc had enjoyed the opening day so much, and was so
appreciative, that Geordie soon asked him to go again;
from this they fell into shooting together a good deal.
Their schedules were somewhat similar in free time, they
got along well together, and they both benefited. Geordie had wandered so widely that he knew a great deal
more of the country than a busy man could have found
out for himself, and this gave Doc better hunting; the
association was certainly good for Geordie. There might
have been a suspicion of an ulterior motive at first in his
cultivation of Doc; he was always on the alert to hear

more of Doc's plans and tried to ingratiate himself, but a genuine and increasing liking for the man soon took the place of this. It wouldn't have lasted on any other basis anyhow; Geordie was too honest for ulterior motives to hold him for long, and if he hadn't liked Doc he would soon have avoided him no matter what.

Sometimes they hunted prairie chickens or sharp-tailed grouse, but they spent more hours after ducks either in the marsh or along the river. Hidden in the blind or sitting quietly in the boat in the reeds along a bank of the river or one of the creeks or backwaters that opened into it they saw more. They were both endlessly interested in observing the actions and habits of wildlife and could be perfectly content to spend hours doing it; this made them even more agreeable to each other, and occasionally enabled them to pick up an unusual specimen for the Museum or one that had strayed from its usual range.

One day in the blind Geordie was on watch and caught out of the corner of his eye a pale, swift bird quartering past. He didn't recognize it, but reacted quickly; he grabbed his gun and shot. The bird fell, and when he retrieved it Doc identified it as a prairie falcon. "A partial albino," he said, "and well east of its range. It might be the first one recorded in Iowa. Very interesting. For some reason the Museum doesn't have one, and they'll be delighted to get it. If it is a first record, you'll be famous forever. Among a few people, that is. Incidentally, the museum course starts pretty soon. They've finally got the details straightened out. Are you still going to take it?"

"Yes, sir."

"I don't know whether I see you as a museum man or not. Like me, you like to waste too much time sitting in the bushes. Have you thought about that?"

"Yes. It's fun sitting in the bushes. Besides, we get a specimen once in awhile. If I'm going to be a naturalist I think I ought to take the course. I ought to know as much as I can. If I'm going to get specimens, I ought to know the best way to prepare them."

"That's sensible," Doc said, and stuck out the finger. "Why did you say 'If I'm going to be a naturalist'? Is there any doubt in your mind?"

Geordie was silent for a moment. "My father wants me to be a lawyer," he said finally, "and I . . . Well, he wants so much for me to be a lawyer. He's always wanted me to. He says that the country is developing so fast that sooner or later there won't be anything for naturalists to do. Do you believe that, Doc?"

Doc shook his head. "We haven't got very far," he said. "We believed in spontaneous generation until about forty years ago, we haven't known about viruses for more than eighteen or twenty. We don't even know very much about bird migration, which goes on around us all the time. The American Bird Banding Association, that might well give us very valuable information in a few years, was only organized two or three years ago. We've got a long way to go, and I think naturalists will be cutting trails for quite a time. Natural history, which is branching into all sorts of specialties, will tell us more and more about our world and life itself." He paused, and grinned. "I can't advise you what your life's work will be. You'll have to decide that for yourself. But don't think there won't be enough to do, well beyond your lifetime."

About a week later Uncle Harry was able to join them for the day. Geordie and Doc had used the blind two days before, and as they didn't like to use it too frequently they decided to shoot a backwater several miles down the river. A little way into its wandering course they rounded a corner and came upon Possum. Possum's back was toward them; he was leaning over the side of his boat, pulling at something. As Doc said later, he must have had eyes in the back of his head, for although they hadn't made a sound he ceased what he was doing, straightened up, and faced them with an air of surprise and innocence. He was as hairy and unkempt as ever, and his chin was brown with tobacco juice.

"Hi, boy," he said to Geordie, and gave a casual and all-inclusive nod. "You ever hear from that warden?"

Geordie stared at him, nonplussed; he didn't know what to say for a moment. He looked from one of his companions to the other, and found both their glances upon him. "No," he managed to say, finally. "No, I didn't." He lapsed into silence again, confused by Possum's treachery in airing the secret.

"That's good," Possum said. "That's real good." He picked up his oars. "Lost my tonic, and I ain't been able to find it. I got to git along. I been seein' ducks come in about a half mile back up yonder. You ought to git up there." He nodded again, bent to the oars, and was soon out of sight around the bend in the backwater.

Geordie bent to the oars too, anxious to be under way and to provide some distraction; Uncle Harry, who was also rowing, held off a few strokes and then began to row too. There was a silence in the boat. They moved out of the reach and presently got into the one that Possum had indicated; there wasn't a duck in sight. Both Geordie and Uncle Harry shipped their oars.

"He seemed mighty anxious to get us out of there," Uncle Harry said, "now that I think of it. Didn't you think so, Geordie?"

"Yes, sir," Geordie said unhappily. He was aware by

now that neither of them was going to question him directly but that they were both very curious. "I . . ." he said. "I don't know why he said what he did about the warden." Another silence greeted this, and Geordie saw that he was going to have to tell them. He blushed to the roots of his hair, and then stumbled through the story of Possum and the dynamite and the warden. "I thought he was just going fishing," he said. "And then after I got in the boat I couldn't get out. I thought the warden would tell my father, so I told him—the warden—that I hadn't seen him." He blushed again, and then felt greatly relieved that the story was out.

They were both smiling at him now, and Doc said: "The old ruffian's smarter than I thought he was. He was up to something, and decided that coming up with the warden business would distract us enough so that we wouldn't wonder about it or ask him what he was doing."

"I wonder what he was up to?" Uncle Harry asked. "He was pulling something up. What would he be doing that for, Sat?"

"I don't know, I can't . . . Wait a minute. I wonder if he has a sunken net in that reach, to catch ducks that might be searching around under water? I'll bet that was it, the old devil. Maybe he's thrown some corn in there, so that any ducks that dive for it would be caught and drown. By Christopher! Let's go back and see! If that's what he was doing, we can put him away for awhile."

This made Geordie unhappy once more. "Doc," he said. "Doc, if we get him arrested he'll go to my father to get him out. He always does. And if he tells about the warden . . ."

"Ah, me," Doc said. "Now you can see what evil courses can bring you to. Tangled webs, and all that."

"Besides," Uncle Harry said, "he probably went back

there as soon as we were out of sight and took up the net, if he has one. That's why he wanted to send us up here.''

"You seem to know his habits," Doc said. "Do you have a history of law-breaking and encounters with the warden too? Maybe it runs in the family."

"Everybody knows about Possum," Uncle Harry said. "He must be into me for twenty-five or thirty dollars. When he's really up against it, and can't find some law to break, he comes to me for a loan. His stories are so ingenious I always give him one."

Doc threw up his hands. "I'll say no more," he said. "We can't persecute this old friend of the family. He's got something on everybody. I'll go back to my ivory tower. Meantime, where can we get a few shots?"

"Maybe there would be some ducks up near the end of the backwater," Geordie said. "It's almost a mile, but there always used to be ducks there. There are a lot of muskrats there and they've thinned out the cattails enough so that the ducks like it."

"You're a naturalist already," Doc said. "Come back here and let me row awhile. You need a little peace and quiet to organize your conscience."

Geordie changed places with him, and they went on up the reach.

Geordie had been right; there were ducks at the head of the backwater, more came in occasionally, and they had a good afternoon. On the way out they stopped where they had encountered Possum and searched for signs of a net, but could find nothing.

Later, the two men dropped Geordie at his house, and after they had left there and were halfway to the University Satterthwaite said: "Harry, I think the Laysan trip is going to come off, and I'd like to take Geordie along."

"It would certainly be wonderful for Geordie, but why would you want him? He's no scientist yet."

"It's not really a very scientific trip. In view of what Conover and I both found on our trips I've got the Biological Survey thinking that it would be a good thing if a small party went out, shot all the rabbits, collected some more bird skins before some of the birds disappear, and make some observations. The most important thing is to get rid of the rabbits, if there's to be any of the island left. The Survey doesn't have the personnel to do it, but they want it done, and they can get us a little Government money and give us transportation."

"A pretty elaborate rabbit hunt," Uncle Harry said.

"Don't you see the—"

"I do see the importance of it," Uncle Harry said, "if we want to keep some unique species. I'm all for it. But where does Geordie come in?"

"There will only be four or five of us—ornithologists and such. There's usually a promising student or two to lend a hand with the incidental work—collecting, skinning, preserving skins, work around camp. Geordie would fit in fine. He's certainly a promising student, he's a good shot and—last but not least—he's a darn good cook. Have you ever spent a month or so on a deserted island with a poor cook?"

"I didn't realize you were such a sybarite," Uncle Harry said.

"Sybarite be hanged!" Satterthwaite said with some heat, and then laughed. "Stop pulling my leg. It's a question of survival. I've eaten enough bad food on these trips to choke a vulture, and I see a chance to avoid it this time."

They pulled up in front of Satterthwaite's house; Uncle Harry stopped the engine, but neither of them made a move to get out.

"The reason I'm discussing it with you," Satterthwaite said, "is this: do you think his family would let him go?"

"Why do you ask that?"

"Something he said. Something about his father wanting him to be a lawyer. It seemed to bother him, to make him unsure about what he ultimately wants to be. I'll be frank with you, Harry. If he's going to be a naturalist the trip would be very valuable to him; if he's not, it would just be a ride. It wouldn't be fair to some other kid who's going to be a naturalist to take Geordie just because he can cook."

Uncle Harry was silent for a moment. "I'll be frank with you too," he said finally. "There is a conflict. The boy wants more than anything else to be a naturalist. It's all he wants to be, and I don't know why my brother-in-law doesn't let him go his own way. Alfred keeps a little pressure on him a good deal of the time, and because he loves and respects Alfred he's stirred up quite a bit. I brought him to your Laysan lecture just to see if I could strengthen him in his effort to break away."

"You're with him, then."

"I'm with him all the way, although it's really none of my affair. I'm an intruder in a family matter."

"I think you're right, blast it. I'm with him too. I've seldom seen a kid I wanted so much to be a naturalist. He'd be wasted as a lawyer. Well, what will we do?"

"The question will have to be put to Alfred sooner or later," Uncle Harry said, "and as we aren't sure which way Alfred will jump, we'd better see if we can arrange the direction beforehand."

"I didn't realize you were such a Machiavellian type," Satterthwaite said. "Have you got some scheme all laid out?"

"Not yet, but I have a glimmer. I have a feeling that if

Geordie gets to Laysan his conflict will finally straighten out."

"It would help, I'm sure," Satterthwaite said. "But what's the glimmer? Can I take a hand in it?"

"Not yet. But something happened today that might be useful."

"I can't recall anything unusual happening, except that foul old reprobate. What was his name?"

"Possum."

"That's it. It has to do with Possum?"

"We'll see," Uncle Harry said.

"So. A pretty frail reed, I'd say, but any stick will do to beat a dog with." He bestirred himself. "It's my bed time," he said, and got out of the car. "It was a good day. Good night, Harry."

"Good night, Sat. Give the crank a twist on your way past the front of the car."

ELEVEN

As Geordie's classes started and he went about dissecting
his frogs steeped in formaldehyde and struggling with
taxonomy, the museum class began and he was soon in
the midst of the details of taxidermy, the making of fore-
grounds, and the elements of art as it served for back-
grounds and arrangement. Dr. Black, as he said himself,
was a very poor artist but a pretty good photographer,
and Geordie began to learn something about photography from him. He saw the importance of photography at
once, and was surprised that he hadn't been taking pictures for some time.

"I don't know why I didn't do it sooner," he said to Doc one day in his office. "Dr. Black doesn't have a picture of an Eskimo curlew, for instance, and now there don't seem to be any to take pictures of. I saw a few in the spring once, and I could have had a picture."

"I could have had pictures of them when a flock would cover a fifty acre field," Doc said, "and that wasn't so long ago either. Back around '93 or '94, I think it was, when I was in Kansas one April. I could have even had a picture of the last whooping crane nest in Iowa, back in '94, but who thought then that it would be the last one? I wasn't as big a fool as a lot of people were, thinking that these birds and animals would last forever at the rate they were being shot, but . . . besides, it was a cumbersome business to take pictures then."

"You took a lot on Laysan," Geordie said.

"I take a lot when I go somewhere else. I hardly ever take any around here. But now that you've got interested you ought to work at it. For practice, if nothing else. You're learning how to develop them too, I take it?"

"Yes, sir, I'm learning all I can," Geordie said, and added: "Sometime I may go somewhere too."

Doc's finger shot out. "Do you want to?"

"Anywhere. Anytime. I used to dream about going to Africa, or India."

"Where do you dream of going now?"

Geordie looked at him for a moment and then decided to say it, come what may. "I dream about going to Laysan."

Doc nodded, and considered him. "Why?" he asked finally, and the finger came out again.

Not many months ago Geordie, feeling the inferiority that all boys feel in the presence of their elders whether they admit it to themselves or not, would have stammered out something inadequate, but a change had been taking place within him. Recently, for the first time in his life, he had been accepted as an equal hunting with men; he had been able to take them to good places they wouldn't have found for themselves; and although he had been in college but a short time it had already opened up far wider horizons for him and given him a sense of purpose. He was, rather suddenly, more mature. The way he had stood up to his father about his choice of courses had been an early sign of this. "Why," he said, "I guess I'd like to go there for the same reason you wanted to go."

"Bravo," Satterthwaite said.

"I heard you say something to Uncle Harry in the blind about getting rid of the rabbits," Geordie said.

"H'm. So you've been laying for me ever since."

Geordie grinned. "Yes, sir."

Satterthwaite did not hide his pleasure. The more Geordie revealed himself the better Satterthwaite liked him; his only reservation now was whether the boy would eventually follow the course he had set out upon or whether, finally, he would be influenced by his father. Satterthwaite wondered whether he was attaching too much importance to this; any one of a number of fortuitous events could occur in the next few years to throw Geordie one way or another and all he had to base his reservation on was what Uncle Harry had told him, but he wanted somehow to assay Geordie's determination. He told himself that he was nit-picking at this juncture, but he had a troublesome feeling of responsibility toward some future scientist that he was unable to sidestep despite his liking for Geordie. He was wondering how to frame a question or two when the door opened and a man's head appeared around it like a head out of a Jack-in-the-box. It was a narrow head, with close-cropped red hair above a narrow, snub-nosed face with a thin mouth.

"Hi, Sat!" it said, and then saw Geordie. The eyes narrowed as though with dislike, and then widened again. "Sorry, I didn't know . . ."

"Come in, John," Satterthwaite said. "Come in."

The man came in. He was tall, and narrow like his face.

"Dr. Catton," Satterthwaite said. "Geordie Sutton, one of my students. A very good one, too."

Geordie ducked his head, smiling, uncertain whether to extend his hand. Dr. Catton settled this question; he nodded coolly and apparently dismissed Geordie from his mind.

"I was on my way north," he said to Satterthwaite, "and thought I'd stop in for a minute to see if the trip was still on the books and progressing."

Satterthwaite didn't reply for a moment; it was evident that he wasn't pleased with the other man's manner. He glanced at Geordie as though in apology and Geordie, seeing nothing but embarrassment for both Doc and himself if he stayed, took a step toward the door. "It was nice to meet you, sir," he said.

"Pleasure," Dr. Catton said, giving him a glance and dismissing him again.

"We'll finish our talk later, Geordie," Satterthwaite said. "We're shooting Wednesday afternoon, aren't we?"

"Yes, sir," Geordie said, and went out. As he walked toward his next class he thought rather unhappily about Catton. From what Catton had said, it had sounded as though he would be one of the party going to Laysan. The man had a nasty feel about him, something beyond Geordie's experience but disquieting; the narrowing of his eyes, for which there had been no reason because he didn't know Geordie, made the boy feel that Catton was full of an active hostility and maybe something more.

They decided to shoot the blind on Wednesday afternoon, and by the time they got there and were nicely settled the weather, which had been moderate for a few days, began to give signs of changing. Far to the northwest a dark bank of clouds began to roll up, and a cold wind began to blow. They didn't pay much attention to it, for small bunches of ducks began to come in and they were busy for awhile. Presently there was a lull in the flights, they sat down to get out of the wind, and Doc, who had been rather quiet all afternoon, cleared his throat.

"Meant to speak to you about the other day," he said. "I'm sorry about the way Catton acted."

"He didn't seem to like me very much," Geordie said.

"I don't think he likes anybody very much. He's a strange fellow, but some of his ornithological papers have been brilliant. Not that that makes it any easier to get along with him."

"Is he going to Laysan?"

"I'm afraid so," Doc said. "His university is putting up some of the money, and wants him to go along." He was silent for a long moment. "Geordie, are you going to be a naturalist, or a lawyer? I know it sounds like a silly question, for everything you do points in one direction. But I've talked with your Uncle Harry about this, and he tells me you're pulled both ways."

Geordie's face lit up with a big grin. "If you've talked to Uncle Harry you've thought of asking me to go," he said. "Oh, Doc, I want to more than . . ." He grew serious again as the import of Doc's question reached him. "I told you my father wanted me to be a lawyer. Maybe I ought to do what he says, but I want to be a naturalist. Doc . . . Doc, what should I do?"

Doc was looking at him, as he had once before, with an

abstracted, unfocused stare. Finally he shook his head, blinked, and his eyes focused again. "I'll take a chance," he said, as though to himself, and stuck his finger out. "I'm no wiser than anyone else," he said. "I try not to advise people, but I will go so far as to say this: I think the best thing, the happiest thing, is to do what you want to do. You'll have to work it out for yourself, but I'll help you if I can."

"Maybe Dad won't let me go," was all that Geordie said.

"Don't do anything about it," Doc said. "Leave it to Uncle Harry and me. And now that that's settled, let's get back to the business of the day." He stood up, moving out from under the roof of the blind. "Holy Christopher!" he exclaimed.

Geordie stood up quickly. It was snowing, the storm had moved in on them, and they had been so preoccupied that they hadn't noticed it. The flakes were coming down thickly, angled on the wind which had increased, and blotted out everything beyond a quarter of a mile or so. They had both experienced prairie blizzards a number of times, and were well aware of their dangers; the worst ones came up so swiftly and the snow was so blinding that farmers were sometimes caught between their houses and their barns and, unable to find their way, wandered about and froze to death.

They didn't waste time in talk and didn't take time to bring in the decoys. They gathered up their gear and their ducks and started for the shore. It had grown much colder suddenly and the water, which had been open in the main, was already beginning to grow slushy and thick and congeal around the bases of the reeds. A skim of ice was reaching out, and this slowed them. Doc almost lost his footing once, and if Geordie hadn't caught him would have gone down.

114

They reached the shore and with solid footing under them at last paused for a moment to get their breath, but they didn't stand long; the snow was thicker now and they quickly began to chill from the sweating they had done crossing the water. The wind whipped them and pushed them along; they were both grateful that they weren't facing it, or it and the snow would have blinded them. The going was bad enough without that for their horizon had closed in even more and was now down to a few yards. The storm had swallowed most of the afternoon light, and in the featureless grayness filled with snow they could see nothing; they could only keep the wind in the same quarter as it had been when they started.

It soon seemed to them that they had been walking for a long time, and they weren't sure where they were. In such a situation the mind stretches time out and begins to construct fears for itself. Could they possibly find the carriage, a tiny dot lost on the vast plain? They hadn't mentioned to anyone where they were going, but should they have stayed in the blind, where they had a little protection, and hope the storm would soon blow itself out? Had they been fools to leave, would they wander until they fell? They fought against these thoughts, and began to stumble occasionally. Presently they stopped, held up their ducks, nodded to each other and dropped the ducks. Then they clasped hands for reassurance.

Finally Geordie began to feel an uneasiness that was not connected with these thoughts in his mind; it strengthened and superimposed itself upon them. He didn't understand it at first; the storm battered at him and distracted him, but presently, as this uneasiness grew clearer, he realized that it was trying to tell him that their direction was wrong. It was a feeling, a sense of location, the mysterious sense that animals and a few

115

people possess; somehow he had developed it over the few impressionable years of his wanderings. It had guided him before, and now it was speaking to him again. He stopped and pulled Doc to a stop with him, and put his face close to Doc's.

"We're headed wrong!" he screamed above the wind, and pointed off almost at a right angle. "We ought to be going there!"

Doc stared at him. "Are you sure?" he screamed back. "The wind . . ."

"I think it's shifted! I *know* we ought to go that way!"

Doc stared at him a moment longer through the whirling snow, and then nodded. He could never say later why he had trusted Geordie's decision. "Thought had nothing to do with it," he would say. "I just knew in my guts that that kid somehow had it, that he was right."

Still holding hands, they turned and went on through the deepening snow. They were crossing the wind now, so the going was worse; they were blinded by the snow and the cold seemed to increase by the minute. Time drew out again and then, when hope began to fade into a numb, increasing weariness, they heard, upwind, the whinnying of the horse.

Neither of them thought at the moment that if their luck had taken them a few yards to the other side they couldn't have heard it for the wind; they stopped and hugged each other in gladness. Then they ran to the horse, took up the heavy hitching weight that had held it there, scooped out some of the snow that had blown in between the curtains of the carriage, climbed in, and gave the horse its head.

Wrapped in blankets in his bed, full of hot soup and with several hot water bags around him, Geordie hovered on the edge of sleep. His mother and father and

Doc, who was wrapped in a blanket and was staying for the night, stood looking down at him.

"Getting warm now?" his father asked.

"Yes, sir. I'm good and warm."

His mother leaned over and kissed him. "Good night, my darling. I'm so glad. Oh, I'm so glad."

Geordie put his arms around her neck and took her kiss, and she straightened up again, smiled at the men, and went out of the room. The two men looked at Geordie again. He had closed his eyes and his breathing had changed; he was already asleep.

"He got us to the carriage," Doc said. "I would never have found it. He's wonderfully at home in the out-of-doors."

"It seems a needlessly dangerous life, for small gain," Alfred Sutton said. "I will feel great relief when he finally decides to give it up."

"Would you let him go on an expedition with me?" Doc asked. "We usually take a student on these affairs, and I'd like very much to have Geordie."

"Indeed? Where does the expedition go?"

"Out to the Pacific," Doc said, "under the auspices of the Biological Survey."

"I appreciate your interest in Geordie," Alfred Sutton said, "but I am not at all sure that I would approve of his going so far. No reflection on you, of course."

Doc started to say something, and then decided not to. Alfred Sutton nodded to him, and went out of the room. Doc stood for a moment looking down at the boy, then reached out and stroked his forehead, very lightly, before turning out the light and leaving the room.

He left the next morning, before Geordie was awake, but the storm held for three days and increased in fury. If they had stayed in the blind, they would never have gotten out of it.

TWELVE

Several evenings later Doc stopped in at Uncle Harry's house and told him about the talk with Alfred Sutton. "I finally asked him the question directly," he said, "and he remarked that he doubted he'd approve Geordie's taking the trip. So, if you're still inclined for a bit of guerilla warfare, I suppose you'd better get started. There isn't too much time left."

"I've already gotten started," Uncle Harry said. "I thought he'd react that way. When did you get a chance to ask him?"

Doc had sketched in their homecoming, but had not

gone into any detail; now he did. "Geordie had already fallen asleep," he said, ending his story. "We were standing by his bed. Harry, there's no doubt the boy saved my life. I have a sense of obligation to him I'll never be able to fulfill. I'll break my neck to give him what he wants, and he wants to go. What is it you've done?"

Uncle Harry grinned. "I saw Moncrief, the warden, a few days ago and told him about our suspicions of Possum. He hid out in the marsh and caught Possum in the act, with a net. There's going to be a trial."

"I don't see—"

"I know you don't. You're too pure in heart, and too removed from the world in your ivory tower. To let you in on a grimy secret, I got Moncrief his job originally. I have my sticky little fingers in some of the politics hereabouts, although it's not generally evident. Moncrief knows exactly why I wanted Possum snared. I told him."

"You told him?" Doc asked, mystified. "What's that got to do with it?"

"At the right time, word will get around to Alfred that Geordie might be asked to testify about a former offense with dynamite."

Doc stared at his friend. "Glory be," he said finally. "I never suspected such depravity."

"I'll thank you to forget it."

"Yes," Doc said. "Indeed I will. But, you know, your maneuvers will have that boy in court, and the effect on him will . . ."

"Alfred won't have him in court. Alfred will have him safely out of the way. Probably as far out of the way as the middle of the Pacific Ocean," Uncle Harry said, and began to laugh at the expression on Doc's face.

The expression went from incredulity to a sort of outrage. "I don't believe it," Doc said finally. "Harry, you can't be serious. You're pulling my leg. Why, honest men wouldn't allow, or couldn't live under such a . . . such a . . ." Words failed him.

"My friend," Uncle Harry said, "I accepted long ago a state of affairs that you couldn't admit to yourself. The world isn't run by honest men; it's run by schemers and rascals, and honest men do allow it."

Doc shook his head. "I'll never admit it," he said. "But be that as it may, all of this will come to nothing. Everything hinges on the date of the trial, and I doubt very much if you can arrange that."

"Don't be too sure," Uncle Harry said.

"What? Don't tell me that you got the judge his job too."

"No," Uncle Harry said. "But he's an old friend, we went to school together, and he'll do it as a favor to me. I did explain some of the circumstances to him."

Doc threw up his hands, and got to his feet. "I'd better go," he said. "I'm glad you left me a little faith in the judiciary."

Uncle Harry stood up and went with him to the hat-rack in the hall, and helped him on with his coat. "Remember," he said, "not a word of this to anybody."

"Have no fear," Doc said. "Have no fear, you back-woods Machiavelli. I won't admit to anybody that I know you."

Geordie spent a few nervous days wondering what, if anything, was going on and trying to appear as though there was nothing unusual in his life. His mother judged his somewhat preoccupied air to be the result of his narrow escape in the blizzard and cosseted him out of gratitude that he was still alive; his father, after a week during which he showed more than ordinary affection, became preoccupied himself. Geordie could put only one interpretation on this, and the tension within him increased. Everyone in the house, even Ingrid, seemed to be walking around on tiptoe and he felt like a conspirator. Being by nature a frank and open boy, he didn't like the feeling in the least and was out of the house as much as possible.

He spent a good deal of time with Dr. Black, learning as many sidelights as he could about the skinning of birds and the preparation of their skins; he soaked up all he heard about the needs of a diorama maker in the matter of observations on the spot, and built several model dioramas himself. This last pointed out to him a number of things he wouldn't have thought of: little details of botany, and effective and accurate arrangement that would also please the eye.

Dr. Black, ordinarily a somewhat remote and lonely man (he admitted once that he usually asked the world "Why? Why?" when he got up in the morning) took a liking to him, and they often chatted like old friends together. They didn't mention the expedition, although Geordie thought that Dr. Black must know about it because he worked pretty closely with Doc and they seemed to get on well together. Geordie wondered about this reticence and finally, one day when he asked Dr. Black if he knew Catton, received a clear indication that life wasn't any more a matter of sweetness, light, and selfless cooperation in the academic world than it was in any other.

"Catton?" Dr. Black asked, with a sidewise look at Geordie. "Yes, I know him."

"Dr. Satterthwaite said he didn't think Dr. Catton liked anybody."

"What brought out that observation?"

"He didn't seem to like me when I met him, and I

asked Doc about him. That's what Doc—Dr. Satterth-waite—said."

"You can call Sat Doc to me, Geordie. We're all friends together. But you would be wise not to talk about one scientist to another, as a general rule. I regret to say that there are jealousies and a tendency toward backbiting in some of them. Dr. Catton is a powerful man in his field, and not always quite balanced when he thinks someone has crossed him. I sometimes wonder . . . But I had better take my own advice to you, and be discreet. Be careful if you have any relations with him. So much for that. You would be better employed looking for some chemical besides arsenic to use in treating skins than thinking about Catton. A number of good men have been killed when they grew careless in the use of arsenic. Never grow careless with it yourself."

"I try to remember every time I use it," Geordie said. "You told us about it when the class started, and that scared me enough to make me keep it in my mind." He grinned. "I guess I'd better go. Thank you for telling me."

Dr. Black smiled back at him and he went along to the Laysan diorama, to stand in front of it for a little while before he went home. He had been doing this occasion-ally for the last few days, for it was open to the public now and contemplation of it seemed to lessen the con-spiratorial feeling within him. As he looked beyond the birds and the vegetation at the blue Pacific in the back-ground, glistening white where the waves broke over the reef, he thought about the things he had heard of Catton and wondered what Dr. Black had been about to say and had decided not to. The words "not quite balanced" came back again, and Geordie wondered whether the unfinished phrase was to have been an extension of it, an even unhappier judgment. He suddenly felt a little chill run

122

up his back, as though he feared that the adventure he had looked forward to for so long and had hoped for so ardently was going to be made difficult or even be spoiled by the man he had met in Doc's office.

Doc had said that Catton was hard to get along with, but Dr. Black had gone further and upset him—not only about Catton but about many other scientists as well. Geordie in his innocence had held scientists as a class to be above the self-serving maneuverings of other men, and now he knew that they, or at least some of them, were not. Perhaps, he thought, his father, who knew the world, had been thinking of this all the time. A feeling of his own inadequacy and naiveté confused and depressed him, and he turned away from the diorama and started home.

Dinner was a quiet meal. Geordie had little to say and his father was still preoccupied; Lavinia Sutton tried to lighten the atmosphere but finally fell silent too, and after dinner was finished went off to a bridal shower for a neighbor's daughter. As soon as the door had closed after her Alfred Sutton said: "I'd like to talk to you for a few minutes, Geordie."

"Yes, sir."

"Let's go into the library," Alfred Sutton said.

They went into the library and Ingrid brought the coffee service in. Alfred Sutton poured himself a cup. "Would you like some too?" he asked.

"No, sir, I guess I won't have any."

Alfred Sutton, standing by the coffee table, put sugar into his cup and stirred it. It was evident that he was having a difficult time getting around to what he wanted to say. He picked up his cup, set it down again, took a few steps around the room, and then sat down. "The night you and Dr. Satterthwaite got home in the blizzard, he said that he would like to take you on an expedition that he's making shortly. Apparently this is occasionally done with promising students, and he seemed to think that you are a promising one."

"Yes, sir."

"That, at least, was pleasant to hear." He took a sip of coffee. "You've heard something of this expedition, I take it."

"Yes, sir, a little. It's to Laysan Island."

"Yes." He took another sip of coffee. "I've talked with Dr. Satterthwaite a bit more about it. It seems to be for the shooting of rabbits and some birds that appear to be becoming extinct. I assume that it can be justified scientifically . . ."

He let the sentence hang in the air, as though to imply that while the enterprise made sense to the scientists it made little to him. Geordie didn't say anything. He had been growing increasingly tense as his father circled the point, and by now had great difficulty sitting still. In the afternoon, standing before the cyclorama, he had almost wished he had never heard of Laysan; now he wanted with all his heart to go. Alfred Sutton finished his coffee, carefully put the cup down, and looked at Geordie; Geordie slide forward a little in his chair and moved his feet to conceal the trembling of his knees.

"I must say," Alfred Sutton went on, "that I am astonished at the way these scientists seem able to get about, especially upon such errands as this one. There have been several expeditions to this rather obscure and deserted Island. One would have thought that everything possible has been learned about it. But perhaps I didn't quite understand, from what Dr. Satterthwaite told me, the importance of going there again."

"It's the rabbits," Geordie said desperately. "They . . ."

He swallowed and fell silent; a feeling that he and his father were trying to communicate in different languages descended upon him. He suddenly seemed to be running a temperature; the palms of his hands grew damp with perspiration, and his clothes stuck to him. He began to feel a little giddy and then he heard, as though from a distance, his father speaking again.

"However, I have decided to let you go," Alfred Sutton said, and for an instant looked as though he had bitten into something very unpleasant.

There was a short silence, for it took a moment for Geordie to comprehend what had been said, and then he found himself on his feet without knowing how he had gotten there. "Dad!" he said. He couldn't seem to say more; his emotions were too much for him. He opened and closed his mouth several times and then managed to say: "Thank you, Dad. Thank you very much."

Despite the fact that he had given his permission only because of circumstances that he han't been able to change, Alfred Sutton was moved too; he began to extend his hand to put it on Geordie's shoulder, but because his own emotions were confused, and because he had always disliked any show of emotion, he withdrew it. They stood for a moment looking at each other and then Geordie suddenly moved close to him, kissed him on the cheek, and turned and walked quickly out of the room and up the stairs.

THIRTEEN

The next morning Geordie hurried to Doc's office and forgot to knock before he pushed open the door. Doc was sitting surrounded with papers, and looked up. "I can go!" Geordie said. "My father's going to let me go!"

Doc stood up, and they shook hands. "Geordie, I'm delighted. I'll have a list for you in a day or two of the things you're to take. You and I will be leaving two weeks from tomorrow. We'll meet the rest of the crowd in San Francisco and go to Honolulu on an Army transport. You'd better go see Black." He smiled. "Oh," he said, and stuck his finger out. "You may be the camp cook, and have to deal with turtles, fish, and whatever supplies they give us that will last ten weeks or so without refrigeration. It might be a good thing to have a conference with that Ingrid, and make up a list of spices and whatnot that you'll need. It will be a long swim to the nearest store."

"If you think I can cook well enough."

"No false modesty. You're a master chef, my boy. I still remember that stew on the opening day. In fact, that's what got me interested in you—that and the fact that you skin birds well. You'll work like the deuce, poor fellow."

"I sure worried about that stew. I wanted you to be impressed."

"You were scheming even then?"

"Yes, sir."

"It seems to run in the family," Doc said obscurely. "Well, off you go. I'll see you later."

Geordie went along to see Dr. Black, whom he found skinning a beautifully marked snowy owl.

"Thought I'd better attend to it myself," Dr. Black said, straightening up and putting his scalpel down. "It's the handsomest one I've ever seen. Came from up around the northern end of the state somewhere. You look pleased with yourself this morning."

"I'm going to Laysan," Geordie said. "My father told me last night I could go."

Dr. Black solemnly shook hands with him. "Congratulations," he said. "May it be the first of a lifetime of expeditions. I had heard that this was in the wind, but I didn't want to speak prematurely. I think that I'll give you a copy of the order for materials that should meet you in San Francisco. You can double check Sat. If he doesn't lose his list, that is."

"Does he lose lists?" Geordie asked, surprised; Doc had always seemed very efficient.

"He gets carried away watching the wildlife, and forgets things. He lost a camera last time he was there. Maybe you'll find it again, ruined by the spray. I wish you'd sort of keep an eye on him."

"I will," Geordie said, pleased. Doc's talk about the cooking, bird skinning, spices to be taken and whatnot, combined with these new responsibilities, were already making him feel a member of the expedition and showing him that he had a real place in it. "Can I help you with the owl?"

"If you have a little time. I've worked out a tricky new cut to get out the skulls of birds with big heads, and you might find it useful."

Geordie took off his jacket and rolled up his sleeves, Dr. Black picked up his scalpel again, and they bent over the owl.

The next two weeks were so full of excitement and the activities of preparation that Geordie hadn't much time to think over his talk with his father, the remarks he had heard about Catton, or anything else not having to do directly with the expedition. Of all these matters the one concerned with his father was most often at the edge of his thought and sometimes, just before he fell asleep at night, he recalled his father moving a hand toward him and then withdrawing it and his own feeling that they had been talking in different languages. This brought a melancholy upon him as he dropped off to sleep and once or twice he had a recurrence of the dream in which his father moved further and further away and finally vanished; he would recall it momentarily the next day with a feeling of sadness tinged with guilt, but he was so excited and busy that these things were pushed into the back of his mind. Sooner or later the time would come when he would have to cope with them, but it was not upon him yet.

Doc had arranged for his absence, and he had conferences with his professors to lay out the studying he was to do while he was away. There was a good deal of studying to be done, and he was glad that Christmas vacation would shorten the class time that he would lose. He also spent hours with Ingrid and his mother, and his calculations as to probable meals and quantities, based upon various mysterious ingredients such as turtles and birds' eggs, was a liberal education in mathematics in itself.

"Maybe I ought to be able to make some cookies too," he said to Ingrid, at one point.

"Ja, cookies would please. I show you."

"I think one or two kinds would be enough," his mother said, "and you should only make them about once a week. If you let them, they'll have you making cookies every other day. If they can all eat cookies the way you can, you'll need another ship to carry the materials."

"Maybe we'll all have to go on a diet,' Geordie said, as Ingrid began to gather together the ingredients for the cookies.

"I do hope you will," Lavinia Sutton said. "Your Uncle Harry says that there won't be a doctor there, and I'll worry about your getting sick the whole time you're gone."

Laverty had come in with an armful of wood for the stove while she was saying this; he stood and listened until she had finished. "Ah, now, Ma'am," he said. "Don't be after worryin'. He's never had a sick day in his life, and he'll stand fine against the heathen microbes in those parts. A lad as could get home from that blizzard, a new ax couldn't kill him." He put the wood down, and turned to Geordie. "Maybe you could be bringin' me home one of those hula skirts."

"For yourself, Laverty?" Lavinia Sutton asked.

"Not for myself, Ma'am, savin' your presence. I was thinkin'," he said, sidling toward the door, "of givin' it to Ingrid to wear on Swedish Flag Day."

He disappeared; Ingrid turned quickly to the wall cabinets, pretending she hadn't heard him, but a dark blush crept up the back of her neck.

At first it had seemed to Geordie that the day of departure would never come, and then suddenly it was upon him. He had little appetite for breakfast; his stomach didn't seem to belong to him. He hadn't slept well and now, thinking of the vast distances that would separate him for the first time from everything that was familiar and the people that he had known all his life, he had a sort of queasiness. His mother smiled at him frequently but was rather silent; his father ate his breakfast methodically, pushed his chair back a little, and leaned forward.

"I won't be going to the depot with you, Geordie," he said, "but your mother and your Uncle Harry will be there. I hope you will make the most of the trip. I'm sure that your observations, both of the people and of the work itself, will bring you to a decision about your future. You are fortunate in being able to go and judge whether that way of life will give you the satisfaction, both mentally and materially, that you would find elsewhere. You know I would like you with me, in the law; you've heard my opinion that our world here is changing and that the law will have an increasingly important place in it." He came to a stop, and stood up; Geordie stood up too. They shook hands.

Geordie, already involved in the emotions of his impending departure, was so moved by his father's careful attempt at summing-up that he couldn't say anything; he gripped his father's hand hard, trying to express his gratitude and affection.

"Good luck, boy," Alfred Sutton said. "Be careful." This time he put his hand on Geordie's shoulder, squeezed it, and walked out of the dining room.

They heard him in the hall putting on his coat, and then they heard the closing of the front door as he left the house. Geordie, who had sat down again and bowed his head, raised it and looked at his mother. She was wiping her eyes, and she smiled tremulously at him.

"I'm sorry, Geordie," she said. "I didn't mean to cry, at least until you were gone. But he loves you very much, and he's so afraid of being emotional, and he wants so much for you to do what he thinks is best."

"I know, Ma," Geordie said.

She was about to say: "He's so often right, he's given people so much advice that's turned out to be correct, that we should listen to him." But she did not; she had seen the effect of Satterthwaite's lecture on Geordie and watched him since that evening; she knew how he loved the outdoors, and how onerous the dry and confining procedures of the law would be to him. Alfred Sutton had given them all a good life and she had vast respect for his intelligence, but her intuition told her that this time he might be wrong. She said: "We'll have to leave pretty soon. Had you better make a final check, and say good-by to Ingrid?"

"Yes, ma'am," Geordie said, and went off on his rerands. The day took on a feeling of unreality. It seemed hardly any time before they were at the station, farewells were being said, and he was sitting by the window as the train gathered speed across the snowy world.

Doc went off somewhere and for awhile he sat alone,

staring out at the country he knew, still feeling the wrench of leaving and the pull of home. Then the country began to change and was new. It had no connection with his life, and this freed him. When Doc wandered back again and gave him a searching look, to know whether he was going to have a homesick boy on his hands for a time, Geordie said: "I guess we're really on our way at last, aren't we?"

"We are," Doc said. "We're really on our way."

FOURTEEN

The land gradually rose toward the backbone of the continent and continued to change. They came to the great wall of the Front Range, passed through it, and wound their way about westward through the mountains. Geordie was reminded of the two men with bobcat skins over their shoulders that he had seen so long ago on his trip with his father, and once more was moved by the peaks that thrust up into the sky, the shadowed canyons in which the white water streams were now covered with snow, and the snow-covered hanging forests of evergreens. They came out of the towering Wasatch Range into the deserts of the Great Basin, gradually left the snow behind for vast reaches of pale sand and pale, enduring vegetation and fantastically colored and jumbled rocks, and wound their way through snow again in the Sierra to descend into California's pleasant land.

Geordie was fascinated with it all; he was stuffed to bursting with impressions, and amazed by the variety and splendor of the part of America that he had seen. It seemed almost impossible to him that one country could be so vast and hold such differences, and when he considered that he had seen only a comparatively small segment it seemed more impossible still. The wonders of it made him want to see more, to move about and explore and know all of it; he didn't think he'd ever be satisfied until he did. He mentioned this to Doc as they neared San Francisco.

"It's a good start," Doc said. He had been enjoying Geordie's reactions. "But you'd better begin to think how to budget your time. There are half a dozen or so other continents that are going to need your attention sooner or later."

"You can kid me if you want," Geordie said, "but I'm going to try."

"If we weren't running so late because of the snow," Doc said, "I'd show you around San Francisco. Chinatown and all. But late as we are we'll have to get right to the ship, and it's too bad. They've done a great deal since the earthquake and the fire six years ago, and I can't think of a pleasanter town."

Geordie's impressions of San Francisco were hasty and confused, gathered between the railroad station and the ship: the white buildings and the steep hills, the busy waterfront and lovely bay. The ship had been wait-

134

ing for them, and they were no sooner in their cabin and unpacking than there was a knock at the door and as it opened a ruddy, weathered face topped with close-cropped gray hair appeared. The man's eyes were bright blue, and his cheeks bunched up and almost hid them when he smiled. "Hi, Sat," he said. "I was about to log you as a deserter. Good to have you aboard."

"I'm glad we made it," Doc said. "We ran all the way." They shook hands. "This is Geordie Sutton. I wrote you about him. Captain Maguire, Geordie. You don't have to salute. Just call him Cap."

Maguire stepped into the room and clasped Geordie's hand. "Nice to meet you, Geordie. From what Sat says about you I think we'll get along fine."

Geordie liked him at once. "Yes, sir," he said. "I think we will." He stood aside, looking at the big man, and let Doc and Maguire talk. He had been in the Navy, commanding destroyers, and was now retired; the Biological Survey had asked him to head the expedition, and Doc had told Geordie that he was just the man to keep the peace if scientific squabbles threatened to disrupt it. There was nothing very formal about the arrangement, Doc had said, but somebody had to be the final arbiter, and Maguire had been acceptable to everyone.

"Is Catton on board?" Doc asked.

"Been here for two days, but nobody's seen much of him. He gave me a hand the first morning he was here checking over the supplies. I haven't seen him since, but I take it he's here. We sail right after lunch. I'll let you finish unpacking, and see you at lunchtime."

He waved a hand and went out, and they finished stowing their clothes. Geordie pushed his bags under the lower bunk and straightened up. He hadn't thought of Catton for a time, but now that Catton's name had been mentioned the man was in his mind again, a sort of uncomfortable shadow. Geordie didn't want him there and was a little irritated at his own reaction, for he had seen Catton only once and it wasn't his habit to take such quick dislikes to anyone. He stood trying to puzzle it out, for his feeling was really more than a dislike; it was a sort of defensive hostility, and he had no reason to be hostile. He knew other people with bad manners, and didn't feel hostile toward them; he merely avoided them and thought no more about it.

"You look unhappy," Doc said, breaking in on his thought. "Something bothering you?"

Geordie decided not to go into it. "No, sir."

"Let's go take a walk around the ship."

"All right," Geordie said, glad to be distracted. "I'd like to. I've never been on a ship before."

They went on deck and wandered about until lunch was announced. They ate with the officers, and Catton wasn't there; Geordie said little, and listened to the others talk. Their talk was mostly of the sea and since many of their terms and references were unfamiliar to him he felt a little lost. Before lunch was finished there was a bustle that indicated they were getting under way, and Geordie excused himself and went out on deck to watch.

The lines were cast off and the ship began to tremble as her engines increased their revolutions; a widening strip of water appeared between her and the wharf. The whistle's bellow made Geordie jump; the bow swung, the engines settled to their working rhythm, and the ship gathered speed down the bay. The city, climbing its hills and pale in the sun, diminished astern and the ship began to rise and fall a little; Geordie, feeling really severed from the land for the first time in his life, was at once excited by the new experience and a little homesick for all the things he had always known and had learned how to cope with. Now everything was new and strange except the gulls riding the freshening breeze. As they approached the Golden Gate the motion of the ship increased, and after they had passed through it increased still more. An alarming queasiness moved in upon Geordie, and burgeoned into a dolorous nausea; his vision grew confused, and so did his sense of balance. His stomach turned traitor and cast up his lunch and finally, sweating, racked by his heaving interior, shamed and spastic, he clawed and staggered his way to his stateroom and hoped he would die.

It was two days before the sea flattened out and he lifted his head. Having always been healthy and untroubled by any ailments except very minor ones he wondered how he had survived such a fearful visitation, and was almost afraid to get out of bed lest he be smitten again. He felt drained and hollow as a drum, and a little light in the head. He watched the sunlight falling through the porthole for a time, wondering whether he dared to get up, and Doc came in.

"Well," Doc said. "You pulled through. I'm glad to see it. They were taking bets at the officers' table on the day of your demise."

Geordie smiled weakly. "I didn't think I'd make it," he said. "I remember you came in once in a while and held my head and covered me up. I sure felt awful. Does everybody get as sick as that?"

"One time or another. You'll probably be all right from now on. Are you going to join the human race again?"

"Do you think it would be all right?"

"I think so. I'll wait on the bow for you."

He went out, and Geordie got out of bed, dressed, and went up on deck. He was still a little light-headed, but when he came out on the foredeck into the sun he began to feel better. He walked to the bow, which was gently rising and falling, and joined Doc. The sharp stem parted the waves and turned up a bow-wave of gleaming white water; the Pacific stretched away limitless and calm. The salty air was just cool enough to be invigorating, and after a few deep breaths Geordie felt himself again. The homesickness that had descended upon him in the bay was gone, and at last he began to enjoy himself.

After a time Doc went off to talk to Maguire, and a little later a few porpoises appeared and played alongside the bow, keeping pace with the ship. Their maneuvers were so fluid and graceful, so plainly arising from a spirit of joyful play, that Geordie lost himself in watching them until Doc came back and tapped him on the shoulder.

"Time to eat," Doc said. "You must be ready."

Geordie turned reluctantly from the porpoises, and realized that he had never been so hungry in his life. "I guess I'm about starved to death," he said, "but the porpoises are so pretty I hate to leave them."

"You're really just beginning to live. It will be even better when we get to the island, but you'll miss it if you die now from starvation. Come along."

Aside from a storm that night the weather remained clear and tranquil, and now that Geordie had his sea legs he had a wonderful time. Catton, whom Geordie gathered was always sick when he was on the sea, stayed in his cabin; Doc and Cap were often conferring together, and Geordie was left more or less to his own devices. This suited him very well. He was all over the ship and made friends with everybody; he was usually on deck when the sun came up, and stayed there most of the day; he discovered flying fish and sharks, Leach's petrels, and had his first sight of black-footed albatrosses. Three of these great wanderers of the trackless ocean, with their seven foot wing-spread, appeared at dawn in the wake of the ship and showed him their consummate mastery of the air as they hovered and lifted and slid along the wavecrests on motionless wings. They had had a special significance ever since he had first read *The Rime Of The Ancient Mariner* in school, and he knew there were thousands of them on Laysan; he had read up on them in the University library. They were romantic birds to him, at home on the vast reaches of the western ocean; there were usually a few of them in sight for the rest of the trip, and he never tired of watching them.

The ship steamed on. Several days later they sighted the island of Molokai at sunset, and the next morning drew in under Diamond Head. A cloud clung to the crest, and the ancient, extinct volcanoes of Oahu, rising massively from the sea, were clothed in mossy green. The ship docked and old friends of Doc's and Maguire's greeted them with leis. Honolulu was a small town, easy-going and friendly in the soft, warm air, and among the palm trees and flowers, the bright colors and strange mixture of people, Geordie felt a long way from the snowy prairies where winter would hold the land for a long time yet.

It was all so different from the little college town that he had left he might have been a little homesick if he'd had time, but Cap wanted to get all their arrangements completed now that he was ashore. "If Geordie and I take our bags to the hotel and come back here to check the supplies as they're unloaded and moved over to the KITTIWAKE," he said to Doc, "you can wait for Catton to come ashore. You have to take charge of the feathers they took from the Japs two years ago and see that they're burned, and we might as well get that done." He shook his head. "They tell me they have eleven wagonloads. Those pirates must have killed a quarter of a million birds. We'll see you at the hotel about dinner time."

He and Geordie left with the bags, returned, and spent most of the afternoon checking their supplies as they were brought to the revenue cutter which would take them to Laysan. It was dirty work, and after they had finished they went for a swim. It was Geordie's first swim in salt water, and its buoyancy and the way the waves carried him up delighted him. They visited Doc's friends in the evening; the next day they saw a little of the island from a carriage, swam again in the clear water, went to the Aquarium, and were on KITTIWAKE by four o'clock.

At five the cutter cleared for Laysan, eight hundred miles to the northwest. She would pass many islands and shoals along the way, parts of the Leeward Islands chain that begin at Hawaii and extend to Midway and Ocean Islands at the end of the chain. They are the tops of an ancient volcanic mountain range that had been worn down by wind and weather and the sea and built upon by coral animals, older than the Hawaiian Islands and more eroded; most of them are surrounded by coral reefs and some of them are flat and stand only a few feet above the waves. They are lonely and remote, and only one of them, Necker Island, shows evidence of having been visited by Polynesian seafarers although they must have all been landed upon by these people at one time or another. Their very remoteness was what attracted the great legion of far-ranging seabirds to them to nest, for on them the birds were in large measure let alone.

KITTIWAKE would pause at several of them—Meeker Island, where the surf would be too rough for them to get ashore, and French Frigate Shoals, a few sand islands overshadowed by a precipitous rock whose pinnacle resembled a sailing ship. They would land on the sand island nearest the rock, but not stay very long because there were so few birds nesting.

FIFTEEN

They raised Laysan Island in the early afternoon, six days after leaving Honolulu, and as they closed it the air above the Island and the sea was full of birds. The deep blue water shaded off into pale green and aquamarine as it shoaled; a wind had come up within the last hour and the sea was very rough. The tall combers were breaking high and white, with long veils of wind-driven spray, on the reef and coral ledges and ochre-colored beach. Geordie, clinging to the rail between Doc and Cap, stared at the place that had been in his mind for so long. It had occupied his dreams and hopes and many of his waking hours, and now it was a reality. A red-tailed tropic bird, exotic and beautiful in its burnished plumage of pinkish white feathers, with a long tail that was red too, flying swiftly past close to the ship, seemed somehow in his mind to personify it.

The island was about two miles long and a mile wide, shaped like a bowl, and rose a little toward the center beyond the gleaming beach. Scanty underbrush covered the rising ground, and KITTIWAKE didn't rise high enough on the waves for him to see the lagoon that he knew was in the center. As they had approached it from the west after a wide half circle, he could see, small in the distance, the cottage where they would live, with two coconut palms in front of it and a hau tree on the side— the only trees on the island—the warehouses and the tower that had once been used as a lighthouse. The buildings had been constructed by the company that had taken the guano from the island years before. The ship was too far offshore to make out the birds on the beach, but there were great numbers of them in the air.

"The rabbits have eaten a lot more of it since I was here," Doc said gloomily. "It's beginning to look like a desert now."

A sailor came up and spoke to Cap and went off again. "Too late and too rough to land tonight," Cap said. "We're going to stand off and cruise a little until the morning. They don't want to chance dragging an anchor."

Geordie was itching to get ashore, but composed himself to wait; he knew that they would have to get through a passage in the coral in a lifeboat, and saw that they couldn't do it now. The wild water would swamp any boat without room to maneuver between the sharp coral heads, and no one could swim in such a place.

They stood by the rail until the island diminished astern, and went down to supper. They hadn't talked very much about the rabbits before, but now that they were about to land the animals were the main subject of their conversation. Doc was feeling depressed because of the changes that had taken place since he had been on Laysan before; even from the ship this change had been apparent.

"Doing away with the rabbits has got to be a holy crusade," he said, "and if anybody feels qualms about it I'll personally feed him to the frigate birds, in little pieces. We're not here to be sporting, we're here to undo a foolish act if we can, and it will be killing pure and simple, just like killing bacteria in an infected man. I don't know whether we got here in time to undo the damage or not."

"We'll know better tomorrow," Cap said, "and as soon as we get settled we'll get the rifles out. They'd better be carried at all times, everywhere we go."

"I think so too," Doc said. "The first month will be the most important. The rabbits will begin to get wary after awhile, and we'd better get as many as we can before that happens."

"What if they do get wary?" Cap asked. "Where will they hide? From what I could see this afternoon there aren't many places."

"The shearwaters and petrels dig burrows to lay their eggs in," Doc said, "and the rabbits will hide in them."

"Birds dig burrows? Come, now."

"They sure do," Doc said. "The shearwaters won't be nesting until May or thereabouts, but there will be petrels until Hades itself wouldn't hold 'em. You wait and see."

"I'll wait," Cap said. "Now I'm going to bed."

"Me too," Doc said. "We'll have to bestir ourselves tomorrow to get the stuff ashore and get settled. Going to turn in, Geordie?"

144

"I think I will. Pretty soon. Good night."

The two men said good night in return, and went to their cabins. Geordie went out on deck, found a dark corner out of the wind, and got his back into it to look at the stars for a little while. The ship rose and fell lazily, for a good deal of the wind had gone down with the sun. As his eyes grew accustomed to the darkness he began to see pale, flitting, dove-sized forms occasionally as they sped through the few bands of light from the ship. They looked like little ghosts and puzzled him for a short time until two of them dodged past making strange little squealing sounds, and then he remembered from his reading that petrels make such sounds and are nocturnal, hiding in their burrows by day and flying about at night. One of them startled him badly by suddenly appearing out of the darkness and hovering before his face with a thrumming of wings and sounds like a growling kitten; he threw both hands up and it slid off, leaving him to compose himself and finally laugh a little at his fright.

Even more than the tropic birds and the distant albatrosses he had seen in the afternoon it seemed a strange small spirit of the place where tomorrow he would go ashore into a remote little world that would be so different from the one he knew. A small shiver of anticipation went up his back and he had a moment of gratitude that he, of all the people in the world, was fortunate enough to have this adventure. Then he went off to bed.

They had anchored off the island when Doc awoke him, and he could hear the bustle of activity on deck. He dressed quickly, went to the salon and swallowed a hasty breakfast, and joined the others on deck. There was a cloud of birds over Laysan; the lifeboat was loaded for the first trip and the sailors were climbing in and taking their places at the oars, and at Doc's gesture he went over the side and got into the bow of the boat. Catton, looking pale and gaunt, came to the rail and was helped in next; he took a seat in the middle of the boat and stared unhappily at the floorboards, and Doc and Cap got aboard. The rest of the crew gathered on deck waved to them and they shoved off and the sailors bent to the oars.

It was a calm and pleasant ride until they got to the narrow opening in the reef, and then the boat began to pitch and there was white water all around them; Geordie thought several times that they would be capsized before they got through. He was kept busy hanging on, and they were all soaked with spray before they rode a wave in and grounded on the beach. Geordie jumped out and was the first ashore, which pleased him; he almost fell down before he adjusted to being on the solid earth again. The boat was pulled up a little higher on the beach and they began to unload it. Catton staggered a few yards higher on the beach, sat down, and was sick for the last time; Geordie had the grace to feel sorry for him.

When the boat was unloaded the sailors took it out again through the surf for another load, and for a moment Geordie stood and watched them, full of admiration for their skill, and then took his first look about. There was an air of decline, almost of barrenness about what he could see, for the grass was thin and patchy and the few low, scraggly bushes seemed to be dying, but he was too excited to notice it at first because it was so full of life. The beach, far to the north and south, was dotted with a multitude of big, dusky, black-footed albatrosses, as big as geese, wandering about, groaning, quacking, or screeching at each other, clapping their bills, or asleep; occasionally one would come in from the sea and land clumsily, sometimes pitching forward and falling over itself, and the birds that took off made long runs to get airborne. Many of them watched the men but showed no fear or apprehension; it was a little unsettling to see birds so tame and unconcerned. Gulls, terns, a few red-footed boobies, white Laysan albatrosses with dark backs and wings, and great frigate birds were in the air. Big birds were everywhere, wild birds that paid no attention to people; it was an astonishing and almost unbelievable sight. Of the terns the gray-backs were the most numerous and the noisiest; pretty and graceful, they swooped down on the people until they were almost head height before they swerved off.

Doc, who had been looking around too, turned to Geordie. "Quite a few birds left, huh?" he shouted, above the din.

"You told me, but I didn't imagine it would be like this," Geordie shouted back. "It's wonderful! All the birds of the ocean must be here!"

"This is only part of them. Let's begin to get the stuff carried up. They'll have another load in soon."

They picked up as much as they could carry and began to climb up the beach toward the buildings. Cap picked up a load and followed them. As they got into the thin grass and the portulaca they began to see rabbits, which seemed to be everywhere. The buildings, when they came to them, were lined along the foundations with rabbit holes, and rabbits were hopping about the thin, scattered grass around them. There was a honey eater, a little smaller than a robin and a brilliant vermilion in color, perched on a twig of the hau tree beside the house, and when it saw them it began to sing. Its song, so different from the raucous uproar of the sea birds, seemed like a welcome, and because of this the honey eaters were Geordie's favorite birds as long as he was on the island.

They stood for a moment smiling at it, and then dropped their loads and went into the cottage but didn't get much further than the door. The Japanese feather hunters who had raided the island two years before had lived in it and left it incredibly filthy, and the three of them spent the next hour cleaning out the worst of the trash. They left the door open and raised the windows to get the sea air through, and the honey eater which had welcomed them came in and hunted moths while they worked.

After they had gotten the cottage into fairly livable condition they turned to the cistern, which they intended to use to catch rainwater from the roof, and found that it was unusable. It was filled with the dessicated bodies of birds, for after cutting off their wings the Japanese had thrown them into the cistern; as they starved, and their body fat was used up, their skins didn't require cleaning. When KITTIWAKE, on patrol, had appeared and caught the raiders, the sailors hadn't thought to look into the cistern. Cap and Doc were dismayed at this discovery, for rain would be their only source of fresh water and they would have to find something else to store it in. They went to search about in the decaying warehouses. The first one, with one side blown away, held several thousand albatross wings; the next one had an old bathtub in it, and they cleaned this up and dragged it out under the eaves of the cottage where it would catch the rain.

Catton and several sailors came up with another load and they joined them on the return trip and spent the next several hours getting up their supplies from the beach. The rest of the day was spent in finishing the cleaning up of the cottage and getting their gear inside and arranged and fixing up the soundest of the warehouses as their workshop. Geordie set up the Army stove in a small building behind the cottage, stacked his supplies, and began to think about dinner. Cap and Doc came in with armloads of wood.

"We drew straws," Doc said. "We're the woodgatherers, and John is the dishwasher. I don't think he likes that very much, but it was an honest election. He won't have to wash any dishes tonight, for we haven't any water. I hope it rains. We've been working like the devil all day, so let's take a breather and a look at the estate."

Geordie had thought of climbing the tower for a view of the entire island when he had time and suggested that they do it, but when they got to the tower it was in such bad condition that they decided it would be too dangerous to climb. They spent a few minutes beside the cottage, looking west over the sea. There were dark clouds gathering far out, catching the rays of the declining sun around their edges, and holding the hope of a shower during the night; there were many birds in the air, and for a time the men were so engrossed in the view and their own thoughts that no one noticed that more rabbits seemed to be moving about now that evening was approaching.

Suddenly Cap snapped his fingers. "Rabbits!" he said. "I thought we came to shoot rabbits. Now's as good a time as any to start the crusade."

They went into the cottage and got rifles and several boxes of ammunition apiece, spread out in a line, and walked toward the southeast corner of the island. There were plenty of targets, and soon the rifles began to pop. As Doc had said, there was nothing sporting about it; yet if anyone had felt a distaste for this sort of execution it was soon dispelled by the melancholy state of the vegetation. They killed forty-five rabbits by the time the light grew so dim that they couldn't see their sights.

"Well," Cap said, as they walked back through the

twilight, "we've made a start, but it's a grimy sort of business."

"Grimy indeed," Doc said. "No fun at all. But unless we keep at it the place will be a desert pretty soon. I wish that Company manager had let well enough alone. As I read the notes of people who were here about ten years ago, this was a green and beautiful place. The damage has accelerated even since I was here last year."

Geordie walked quietly along with them, trying to picture in his mind Laysan as it used to be. The introduction of the rabbits had been an ignorant and wasteful business; for the rabbits, unless controlled, would eventually all starve, and in the destruction they had brought about exterminate several species of birds which existed nowhere else in the world.

They could see the first light go on in the cottage as Catton lit a lantern. "You're pretty quiet, Geordie," Doc said.

"I was thinking how stupid it was," Geordie said, "bringing in the rabbits."

"So you're a little depressed too," Cap said, "like I am. We weren't brought up to do this kind of shooting, although intellectually we know it has to be done. Well, we'll have to adjust to it, and quickly."

"If you recall, I tried to get around to this last night on the ship," Doc said.

"I remember," Geordie said, "but it didn't sink in then. It has now."

They had reached the cottage by this time, and went in and put the rifles away. Catton was lighting another lantern and paused to say: "Heard you shooting. How many?"

"Forty-five, I think," Doc said.

"I got fifteen. Pretty good start for the craziest rabbit hunt in history." He looked at Geordie. "When do the heroes eat?"

"Pretty soon," Geordie said. He lit his own lantern, and went out the door. He was thinking of Catton's look, which had been sardonic and seemed to imply that he didn't believe Geordie could cook anything fit to eat, but Geordie forgot this as he went around the corner of the house for there was a sound in the air like a wind blowing through trees. He stopped, puzzled, and suddenly there was a white-breasted petrel in front of his face that startled him as badly as the one on the ship had startled him. He ducked aside and the bird vanished; he turned the lantern up and saw many ghostly bodies flitting by. It was their crying that made the sound; there seemed to be hundreds of them. He ran around to his cookhouse and went inside and closed the door, for they gave him an eerie feeling and at the moment he wanted to get away from them. He started his fire, opened cans, and went to work. He was so busy that he didn't see another petrel fly in through the open window; as he stood stirring the stew in the saucepan it landed on his shoulder and he jumped as though he had been stung.

It left his shoulder but was soon back again, and he caught it gently, put it out the door, took off his shirt, and hung it over the window to keep any others out. He wanted to start off with a tasty meal, and the birds were too distracting. When he took the dinner around to the cottage door the moaning cries of the petrels were still going on, and he found the door shut and the windows curtained to keep them out.

"We didn't mean to exclude you," Doc said, as he backed in the door, "but this place was filling up with visitors."

"I know," Geordie said, "one tried to sit on my shoulder while I cooked, and I'm not used to birds in the kitchen. I'll be back as soon as I get my shirt."

When he returned they were eating enthusiastically, but paused long enough for comment.

151

"Now they believe me," Doc said.

"Sat made no mistake," Cap said. "If this is a fair sample, I'll stay."

Catton gave Geordie a sidewise look. "Not bad," he said grudgingly. "Not bad."

Geordie looked back at them, and decided he could afford a comment of his own. "It's just because you're so hungry," he said innocently. "You were seasick for so long."

The other two men bowed their heads to hide sudden smiles; Catton gave Geordie an inimical stare and began eating again. After a short silence conversation picked up again, but he didn't join it and left the table as soon as he was finished. Geordie wasn't pleased with his small triumph for very long; he soon began to wonder why he had gone out of his way to begin making an enemy when Catton's churlishness wasn't sufficient reason for it. Either Cap or Doc, in a like circumstance, would have laughed and acknowledged they'd got the worst of it; Catton seemed to take it as an insult and withdrew to nurse his grievance.

It had been an odd day. Catton was a puzzle. Geordie pushed his chair back, and as he did so the door blew open and a petrel walked in, climbed up his leg, clawed its way to his shoulder, and sat there calmly looking about.

It was a sleek and pretty bird about a foot long, with tubed nostrils, gray on the back, black on the nape, wings, and tail, with a white belly and forehead. Its tameness and unconcern in the midst of people were extraordinary.

Doc got up and shut the door. "Don't look so flabbergasted," he said to Geordie. "You'll get used to it."

SIXTEEN

The storm moved in and it rained most of the night; the bathtub was full in the morning and their water problems were taken care of for the time. Geordie was up early and watched the sun rise over the sea, making a bright path over the dark water and faintly coloring the spray on the reef. It looked as though they were going to have a beautiful day, and he hoped to be able to explore the island after the morning's work was done. Just as he was about to move off toward the kitchen a snow-white fairy tern, the most beautiful of sea birds, came in from the sea and hovered over him for a moment, so close that he could see its large dark eyes; it looked almost ethereal against the clear sky.

It flew off toward the south beach and he went into the house for a rifle before going to the kitchen, and while waiting for the fire to settle down walked behind the cookhouse and shot six rabbits. He was glad to find that he had somehow made the adjustment to such cold-blooded killing during the night, and wasn't depressed by it any more.

When he brought breakfast in there were half a dozen birds in the cottage—not petrels, which went back into their burrows when day came, but two miller birds, two Laysan finches, the honey eater, and the little gray-brown miller birds were flitting about after insects; the rail, a little pale olive-buff bird spotted with sienna and faint lilac gray, whose race had long since lost the ability to fly, was running about on the floor. None of them was paying the slightest attention to the people and as Geordie paused to look at them, seeing at one time four of the five birds that lived nowhere else in the world, one of the miller birds landed on Doc's head and sang its pretty song.

Geordie was enthralled by them; he stood holding his tray until the miller bird finished its song and took to the air again. "It's sort of like the Garden of Eden," he said. "It's a wonderful way to start the day."

"They've discovered us," Doc said. "They'll be here all the time now."

Geordie smiled with pleasure and put the tray down, and they fell to breakfast with the birds flitting about them. Cap announced the schedule for the day, and after breakfast was finished Catton went off with bad grace to wash the dishes and the rest of them went to work to finish the cleaning up of the house and the yard. Catton joined them after a time and they spent the rest of the morning

planting young coconut and eucalyptus trees that KIT-
TIWAKE had left for them, putting wire around them
to keep off the rabbits. They all had rifles with them,
and more rabbits were shot as they worked. Presently
Cap called them together.

"The Indians," he said, "put in fish with their corn
when they planted it, so we can bury a rabbit or two
under every little tree."

"Sort of poetic justice," Doc said. "They cut all the
young trees down, now they can help push them up
again. It will help with the sanitary problem, too. What
are we going to do with them when the trees are all
planted? We can't have hundreds of dead rabbits lying
around."

"We'll still have to bury them, or throw them into the
sea. Well, back to work."

They spread out again and shot and dug until lunch
time, which by common consent was a pick-up meal, and
then they rested awhile. Catton took the shotgun and
went off to do some collecting; the rest of them sat for a
time, loaded the cameras, and then went for a swim. The
water was clear and refreshing; it was Geordie's second
exposure to salt water, and he was even more delighted
than he had been in Honolulu by its buoyancy and the
pleasure of contending with the waves and being carried
effortlessly up on their soaring crests to see the island's
whole western shore and the congregation of gonies (for
he had already picked up this term for the albatrosses
from Doc) on the beach and in the air. Doc had said
something about exploring after lunch, but even with
that prospect before him he hated to end his swim.

Cap and Doc finally closed in upon him and chased
him out; they went up to the cottage, dressed, collected
the rifles and cameras, and set out. Cap decided to go up
the western shore; Doc and Geordie started south along

the beach among the black-footed albatrosses—black gonies—that were scattered about. It was still strange to Geordie to have birds calmly move off only a few steps and watch him go by. Many of them didn't move at all. One that they stopped in front of had apparently just laid its egg, and when they stooped before it the bird got up, bent over, and touched the egg with its beak as though to point with pride to what it had accomplished.

They took pictures of it and went on to the little fresh-water pond in the island's southwest corner. There was bunch grass in this vicinity and a few Laysan rails were running about in it; two ducks, dusky, with dark faces and white patches around their eyes, were swimming in the middle of the pond. They didn't fly and only moved a little further toward the far shore.

"They're awfully tame," Geordie said, and then recognized them. "They're Laysan teal! Now I've seen all five species of Laysan's birds! Doc, do you think that these are all that's left of them? They can't be down to two."

"I certainly hope not. There were less than a hundred when I was here before, and we were worried then. Even at that, they were the rarest duck in the world. But only two . . . I can't believe it. You'd better make a project of getting here frequently to see if you can see more."

"Yes, sir."

"John was intending to collect a pair or two, but I'll have to call him off that. We have a few skins back home, and we'll give him a couple of those."

"Last night, when I said something about his being seasick all the time he didn't like it. I guess I shouldn't have said it."

"You were certainly within your rights," Doc said, "but as closely associated as we are, and will be for six weeks or so, I think you'd better go easy with him. He was always a difficult fellow, and seemed to think he was better than anyone else and up on a little pedestal, but this time he's worse than usual. I don't think he's well, and being shaken up on the trip and not eating enough to keep a snake alive hasn't been good for him. Be patient, and offer to help him if the chance comes up. You'll probably be rebuffed, but just let it go."

"I'm sorry I talked back to him."

"Don't be sorry. Think no more about it."

They started to walk again, and came out on the wide south beach. The gray-backed terns were preparing to nest there soon, and there were legions of them; presently there would be more coming in from the sea. They swooped and dove at Doc and Geordie, tame and noisy; there were one or two pretty fairy terns among them, for they also liked that beach, and the two men moved through them as through a playful, living storm. A little further to the east, where the number of terns thinned out and the offshore reef ended, they came upon a sea turtle that must have weighed three hundred pounds. They hauled it out on the beach and grunted and heaved until they had turned it over on its back, where it lay waving its flippers.

"We'll come back later and collect some steaks," Doc said. "The tide's going out, and the old girl won't be able to get on her feet until it comes in again." He pointed north, up the beach. "There will be a lot of black gonies up there, but let's cut over to the lagoon now."

They started up the little rise behind the beach and as they got into the thin vegetation and scattered low scaevola brush they began to run into rabbits again. They were everywhere, seemingly as thick on the ground as the birds were in the air, and Doc and Geordie shot until their guns were almost too hot to hold and they had to stop for awhile.

A few more steps took them high enough to see the

lagoon. They were above the southeastern end of it; it was nearly two-thirds as long and a quarter as wide as the island. There was a wide portulaca flat on the western side, where great numbers of Laysan albatrosses, gleaming white with black wings were nested, for they liked the protected location; frigate birds were gathered about in what was left of the dying brush along the eastern side.

"They're not nest-building yet," Doc said. "But they'll start next month."

He had hardly finished speaking when there were protesting squawks from above and behind them, and they turned to see a big white bird with black-edged wings coming in from the sea with a frigate bird after it.

"Masked booby," Doc said. "Watch this."

The squawking booby was dodging about among the other birds in the air trying to evade the pursuer, but it couldn't fly fast enough; the frigate bird, as beautiful a flier as Geordie had ever seen, flew rings around it, headed it at every turn, and finally caught it by the tail with its beak and upended it. The booby disgorged several fish, and the frigate bird dove, picked them out of the air before they reached the ground, and flew off with them. Geordie had to laugh at the booby's disconsolate squawks as it turned out to sea again.

"Poor booby," he said. "That was a dirty trick."

"That's probably why they're called boobies," Doc said. "They let the frigates work them half to death and never fight back. Let's go show the frigates they aren't the lords of creation that they get to thinking they are."

They walked over to the low scaevola brush where the frigate birds were gathered. They were big and dark, with long, strongly hooked beaks. After watching the attack on the booby Geordie wasn't sure he wanted to get very close to them, but they were calm enough. Several of them had such large crops that they couldn't fly even if they'd wanted to, and Doc picked up a long stick from the ground and tapped one of them smartly with it. The bird opened its beak, disgorged its fish, spread its great seven-foot wings and got into the air.

"See," Doc said. "The fish are as good as new. Flying fish. Any time we want a fish dinner, that's one way to get it. I hope that was the bird that robbed the booby."

Geordie examined the fish and found them perfectly fresh, for they hadn't started to be digested yet; they were held in the crop and passed one by one as the stomach made room for them. "I'd like to try a couple," he said, and strung two of them on a stick to carry along.

They shot more rabbits, and then went around to the other side of the lagoon. The Laysan albatrosses, white gonies, were all over the portulaca flats, for they liked the locality, and rails were running around; the sandy margin of the lagoon was occupied by turnstones and plover, bristle-thighed curlew and red phalaropes, and the air all around was full of winged creatures. Their variety and numbers were an amazing thing to see, and Geordie was fascinated by it.

"I thought I'd never see so many birds as I saw when we landed," he said, "but that wasn't anything compared to this."

"Too many to see at once. You can spend a lot of time here, and get to know them one by one. Let's go on north and see if we can find Cap."

They started out, weaving a wandering course between the gonies, and Geordie got into an area where the portulaca was a little thinner and suddenly went into the ground up to his hips. He was on the edge of the nesting territory of the petrels and the sandy ground was honey-combed with their burrows; he was so busy looking all around that he hadn't noticed it. Doc stood and laughed at his struggles to get onto firm ground again, for every time he got one foot on apparently solid earth he broke through again. Several petrels clawed their way out of their demolished tunnels with him, and after a good deal of dusty rolling about he got back onto solid footing and watched where he was going thereafter.

"So that's where they go in the daytime," he said, when he got his breath back. "They've scared me at night, but I didn't expect they'd try to bury me during the day."

"You'll fall into their burrows once in awhile," Doc said. "Everybody does. You can't always be sure where they are, and you'll have your mind on something else and down you'll go. They'll start to lay pretty soon and be quieter at night, and then the shearwaters will get here and make even more noise. I must admit that birds that live in holes during the day and raise the devil at night seem very queer to me. I can't get used to it."

They went on, shooting rabbits along the way, and finally found Cap on the island's highest point near the northern beach. It was only about twenty-five feet high, but it gave a fine view over the sea where the surf was the most beautiful; Cap was sitting pensively on top of the little hill watching it, and started when they joined him.

"I had gotten to feeling that I was the only man here," he said. "Robinson Crusoe facing the empty sea. Ships practically never come this way. I doubt we'll see one while we're here, except KITTIWAKE when she stops back."

Geordie didn't know that KITTIWAKE was coming back. "She's coming here? he asked. "I thought she went home."

"She was going to Midway to have a look, and she'll stop in on her way back to Honolulu. But she won't stay more than an hour or so. After that we'll be marooned. Want to go home on her?"

"No, sir," Geordie said. "I like being marooned here."

"We might as well start back," Doc said. "We've got a

turtle turned over on the east side, and it will take a while to butcher it. Have you seen John?"

"He went by here an hour or two ago. I guess he's gone back to skin his bird."

As they started out Doc said: "Do you think we'd better ask him if he feels well enough to stay? I was saying to Geordie awhile ago that he didn't seem very well."

"He'd take it as a criticism," Cap said. "He doesn't seem well to me either, but maybe it was the trip. Anyhow, how do you ask him? He'll say for sure that we're trying to get rid of him, and steal all the glory."

Doc threw up his hands, and they went on around the beach to the east, passing the big colony of black gonies and the area of great boulders at the edge of the beach that Doc said harbored crayfish, and came to the turtle again. They were bloodied to the elbows when they'd finished, and took a swim to get clean once more before they cut around the edge of the lagoon to cross the island to the cottage with their steaks. When they were nearly home Geordie discovered that he was still carrying the flying fish that the frigate bird had contributed. They were dried out and seemed very unappetizing; Geordie decided that he would get more some other time, when he was coming straight back from the lagoon, and buried these in the sand. When they reached the cottage they all wrote down the number of rabbits they had shot on the board that Cap had hung up that morning. The total added up to one hundred eighty-six.

The turtle steaks were delicious, and even Catton complimented Geordie on them. "Really quite good, I must say."

"Thank you," Geordie said, surprised, and recalling Doc's advice added: "I'd like to help you skin some of the birds you collected today, if you want me to."

Catton's face took on a look of suspicion. "Why?" he

asked, and added: "In any event, I doubt you'd do it well enough."

Geordie, who had been standing by the table, dropped back a step, and Cap said mildly; "Come, John. The boy was only offering to help."

"I've never seen a boy yet who wanted to do any work out of the goodness of his heart, and I'd thank you not to catch me up on anything I might want to say."

Cap didn't reply, and Catton got up, took a lantern, and went out of the cottage. No one said anything for a short time, and Doc and Cap looked at each other with worried creases in their foreheads.

"There really is something wrong with him," Doc said finally. "He was always unpleasant, but now he seems to be feeling persecuted."

"I don't see how I can send him back," Cap said unhappily. "We've got nothing, really, to justify it except a nasty disposition. So far, anyhow. He'd raise hell, and then his University would get into it and draw yours in, and there'd be one of those academic scandals that would give the newspapers a field day. All our dirty linen would be washed in public."

Doc had prepared Geordie for Catton's rebuff, but no one had prepared him for the situation that seemed to be developing and the concern shown by both Doc and Cap startled him. Nor had he heard before, in such plain terms, an exposition of the effects and the power of academic politics. This startled him even more, and for a long moment he was brought back to his father and his father's doubts about the satisfactions of the life that had so engaged him.

Doc and Cap had moved closer together and were talking seriously in undertones, and he knew they preferred to be alone at the moment. Doc glanced up at him.

"I think I'll develop the pictures I took today," Geordie said.

Doc nodded and Geordie went off to his room to work on the pictures. He began to arrange his equipment, but his movements grew slower and finally ceased as he thought of his first full day on the island. Until a few moments ago he had been quite excited; now the excitement was gone and a feeling of depression had taken its place. He sighed, and deciding to do the pictures tomorrow he put the equipment away and went to bed.

SEVENTEEN

The sun was shining when Geordie awoke the next morning; he dressed, and when he went into the living room there were several miller birds, finches, and a single honey eater busily flitting about. It was such a cheerful scene, so lively and normal, that the air of gloom at bedtime the night before seemed far away. Doc was sitting at the table with a piece of paper before him, drawing what appeared to be a plan; a miller bird landed on his shoulder and began to sing, and he looked up and grinned.

"Merry Christmas!" he said.

Geordie stared at him. "What?" he asked.

"Merry Christmas!" Doc repeated. "Did you forget what day it is?"

"I guess I did for the moment," Geordie said. "It still doesn't seem like that time of year."

"Cap brought a bottle of wine along for Christmas dinner. We'll have to do something special."

"I ought to make a cake," Geordie said. "I would if I had enough eggs."

"We'll have plenty of eggs later, when the terns nest. They nest on the south beach and an unusually high tide always washes their eggs away. When they lay again all the eggs are fresh, but I wouldn't know how to find fresh eggs anywhere now. I guess we'll have to settle for more turtle steaks."

"They were good. I'll go around the island this morning and see if I can find a turtle."

"Do that," Doc said. "The rest of us are going to plant the rest of the trees. We'll excuse you."

Geordie went around to the kitchen, and in company with two rails that ran about his feet cooked breakfast; after it was eaten he started for the freshwater pond. The air was full of birds coming in from the sea, for they fed early upon the squid that left the surface a little after dawn. He shot ten rabbits on the way and found eight ducks on the pond. Three of them were mallards, and flew off; he was surprised to see them there, and they reminded him of home. The other five were Laysan teal. He was very pleased to know that there were at least three more of them, and they seemed so tame that he decided to see if he could get them closer, remembering from his reading that they were inquisitive birds and recalled a trick Possum had once showed him, to entice them closer. He lay down on his belly in the bunch grass with his camera in front of him, and waved his feet in the air.

The teal swam back and forth and craned their necks; soon they began to move in. They came closer and closer, while Geordie held his breath. When he finally took several pictures of them they were only a few feet away. He stood up and moved off, quite pleased with himself, for he doubted that anyone had ever been so close to them before. He could develop the pictures after dinner and they would be a fine Christmas present to Doc.

As he walked toward the south beach he fell to thinking of home again and the activities of the season, the presents and the Christmas tree and people coming in rosy from the cold and the house fragrant with Ingrid's cooking, and of his mother and father. For a long moment he felt very lonely for all the things that were so far away, and then he came into the great cloud of terns and was so engaged by their airy multitude that he cheered up again. He decided to make a day of it alone even if he did find a turtle quickly, and went on.

As luck would have it he found a medium-sized turtle before he had gone very far. He turned it over and butchered it because the tide was coming in, cut out his steaks, and carrying them up the crest of the beach buried them deep in the sand to be picked up again later. He had a pleasant swim to clean himself up and went along the beach until he came to a big nesting colony of black gonies. This was their favorite nesting beach, which they liked more than the lagoon. There were thousands of them gathered there, many sitting on eggs, others without eggs sitting or wandering about. They were noisy, as usual, and some of them were dozing with their heads on their backs. Geordie sat down several feet from one of them, which looked at him calmly with its dark eyes, and he thought of them all, after the young had grown large enough to learn to take care of themselves, wandering on their narrow seven-foot wings over the trackless ocean as far as the Aleutians and back to find their island again.

The life of the colony went on around him. Birds took off for the sea, running and flapping for long distances before they were airborne, and others came in; there wasn't much wind, and most of these made clumsy landings, sometimes pitching forward and falling all over themselves. When they did this they would get up, collect themselves, look rather embarrassed, and waddle off; beautiful in the air, they were quite awkward on land. Presently another bird came in and waddled over to the one Geordie was near. It was the other one of the pair, come to relieve its mate after several days at sea. They made a ceremony of the changeover, touching beaks and talking to each other. The one on the egg was reluctant to leave, putting its head down mournfully; it was finally gently pushed off by the other, waddled away, and took to the air. Now that it had finally given up the egg, it might not return for eighteen or twenty days, during which time the bird on the egg would neither eat nor drink.

Geordie had lost track of the time, but the sun was getting higher and he decided to move on and spend some time with the Laysan albatrosses and other birds before going back to the cottage. He stood up, and turning away from the beach climbed the slight rise toward the middle of the island. The stunted bushes began and there seemed to be rabbits under all of them; he started to shoot them again. The little flightless rails ran about, he had to be careful not to break through into the numerous petrel burrows, and high over his head the rakish frigate birds were soaring on the warming air; they usually robbed the boobies in the early mornings and late afternoons. He decided to visit their roosting section later, on the way back, to collect some flying fish as an extra course at dinner, and went on to the portulaca flats around the lagoon.

The Laysan albatrosses, which outnumbered the black-footed ones, were nested in droves on the western side of the lagoon. There was a flock of a hundred or so golden plover, which nested on the Alaskan tundra and spent the winter on Laysan, on the open beach near the water; they didn't trust him and flew at his approach, whistling their lonely cries. There were a few bristle-thighed curlews too, also northern nesters, birds with long, down-curved bills, that were tamer. He came among the albatrosses and sat down again.

Unlike the black gonies, which only made slight depressions in the sand, the white birds built up their nests a little. Occasionally one of them would reach out, pick up a beakful of sand, and then pat it into the low walls with the side of the beak. The one nearest Geordie had a few weatherbeaten old bones around it, all that remained of a bird or two that had been killed long ago by the feather hunters. Many of them napped, and the unmated wandered idly about; presently, thirty or forty yards away, two of them began to dance.

They drew close together with great solemnity, bowing and almost stamping their feet, and circled facing each other, continuing to bow. They fenced a little with their beaks, whetting them upon each other; one of them raised a wing and nibbled at the feathers beneath it. The other bird stood like a statue while this was going on, and snapped its long hooked beak five or six times. The first bird stopped its nibbling, pointed its beak at the sky, rose up on its toes, puffed itself up, and gave a long, ridiculous, nasal groan; the other snapped its beak loudly and repeatedly. They both paused for a moment and began to bow rapidly to each other again.

It seemed as though they were going to go through the performance again and Geordie remembered his camera. He got up and approached them for a picture, but they didn't want their picture taken; they broke off their dance and separated and wandered away. Geordie was

168

disappointed and waited for a time for another pair to begin, but none of them did; he finally decided that he would have to wait for another day. He threaded his way between them, pausing to pat one particularly benign-looking one, and continued around the north end of the lagoon to the frigate bird roost.

A number of these black pirates were sitting about on the stunted bushes and they looked at him calmly; Geordie was surprised to see several boobies nested on the ground immediately beneath them, and then decided that was the safest place for the boobies' young. The frigates couldn't get down through the bushes at them to pick the young boobies up when they hatched. Several of the frigates had big crops, and following Doc's procedure of the day before he found a stick and tapped them. As before, they regurgitated their fish, and Geordie collected a dozen good-sized ones, strung them on a stick, and walked back to the east beach and started along it for the cottage.

A fairy tern appeared above him and hovered, its wings translucent against the brilliant sky, the very picture of airiness and grace; then it dropped down in front of his face and hung staring at him with its big dark eyes, so close that he dropped his fish and raised his hand and caught it. It didn't struggle but lay quietly in his hand for a moment, a lovely bit of life, and as it rested there its mate came and hovered above Geordie's head and he let his captive go. He thought that they might be nested somewhere nearby, and decided that he would come back some day soon to see if he could find the nest.

He went along a little below the top of the ridge on the lagoon side, shooting rabbits as he went, recovered the turtle steaks, and cut around the end of the lagoon to the cottage. The surf on the reef and the changing colors of the ocean as the water deepened were beautiful. As he stood for a long moment looking out toward the empty

169

horizon he thought that this was the strangest Christmas he had ever spent.

Catton was busy skinning birds in the warehouse workshop as he passed it, having apparently been out collecting, and Doc came out of the cottage.

"We'll have a cake after all," he said. "I was out doing in a few bunnies and came across a goney that had just laid an egg, so I pushed her off and took it. It's in the kitchen."

"I hope it's good."

"It will be very good. I ate a few of them before. They're so big that you get tired of eating them, but it will be just right for a cake."

"I saw five teal," Geordie said, but didn't mention the picture.

"Two went over me a little while after you'd left, so there must be seven. That's a good deal better than it seemed at first."

"It sure is. I'd better get to the kitchen and start my cake."

"When you get things under control, come find me. We'll take a Christmas swim."

Christmas dinner went off very well with the exception of Cap's wine, which had gone sour.

"Too bad, too, after the chef has made such heroic efforts," Cap said ruefully. "I guess I should have averaged it, and brought two bottles. One of them might have been good. Well, we can't have everything, and we do have rabbits."

"We have two hundred and ninety-six less than we had when we got here," Doc said. "I was checking the board just before I sat down. That's good, but it's not

170

good enough. We'll have to bear down harder. Maybe we should eat a few of them."

Everyone looked so unenthusiastic at this that he discarded the idea. "I doubt I could eat one myself," he said. "But we will have to work harder at killing them."

"Yes," Cap said. "Everybody remember."

Catton spoke up. "While we're on the subject of shooting," he said, "I'd like permission to shoot a pair of Laysan teal. I seem to recall, Cap, that you forbade it. But we don't have a specimen, and the University—"

"I'm sorry, John, but I can't allow it. Only two have been seen so far, and it might mean their extinction."

Neither Geordie nor Doc said anything about the others they had seen, for they thought it would only stir Catton up needlessly; Catton scowled.

"They will probably die anyhow, and be lost," he said. "I think your attitude is rather silly."

He stared angrily at Cap, and Geordie, wanting to be out of the room if an unpleasant argument should develop, hastily excused himself and went to develop his pictures. As he worked he could hear the rumble of voices around the table, and then he heard Catton stamp angrily to his room. A silence followed; Geordie finally had his negatives done, and was very pleased with them. He waved them around to dry, and went back into the living room again.

"I have a Christmas present for you," he said, and gave the negatives of the teal to Doc. Doc held them up and squinted through them toward the light.

"These are really splendid," he said finally, and thrust out the finger; he hadn't done that for a long time. "If the teal vanish, as they well might, these will be the best pictures ever taken of them. Don't tell me if you don't want to, but how did you get so close?"

"I think I'll keep it a secret," Geordie said smiling. "It's a trick Possum showed me."

"Possum? Oh, that fellow in the marsh. He's certainly done well by you," Doc said, and then recalled that Geordie knew nothing of Uncle Harry's maneuverings. "You can tell him when you get home," he added hastily.

"The moon's almost full. Want to take a walk?"

"Yes, sir."

"Get your rifle and flashlight, and meet me out front."

The petrels were in the air in great numbers, their pale breasts glimmering as they flitted through the moonlight, their odd, low, growling notes rising and falling; sometimes one would hover close, and this would always be startling. They would appear in front of the face as though by magic, hang for a moment on flickering wings, and magically vanish, leaving the echo of their kitten-like growling in the ears.

"There must be thousands of them here," Doc said. "They're eerie little devils. It's like moving around through the spirits of the departed. I'm glad my conscience is clear."

With the pale birds flitting about them they cut across toward the southeastern beach. They came to a sandy area where the ground was honeycombed with petrel burrows, and to find their way through it without going in to their knees they used their flashlights occasionally. The flashlight beams picked up a number of burrows that had pairs of birds sitting together in their openings, and as Doc and Geordie drew close they would scramble out, sometimes blundering into the men's legs, growling, and vanish. The white tails of retreating rabbits moved off through the moonlight, and sometimes they could get close enough to shoot one; there was an occasional scurry of rails.

They came out on the beach north of the roosting

terns; the surf tossed its gleaming white crests high against the broken glitter of the dark ocean, and walking along the beach they were soon at the edge of the nesting black gonies. The dark birds dotted the pale sand; Doc and Geordie climbed a little above them, and as they stood looking out over them a pair approached each other not far from the water's edge, bowing, the preliminary of a dance. They were joined by several others. The thunder of the surf drowned out their groanings, but their posturing, in perfect unison, lighted by the moon and carried on against the backdrop of the breaking waves, was like an uncanny ballet.

When they finally broke off, another pair, a little further away, began to dance. Doc and Geordie were so intent upon watching the strange scene, at once eerie and enthralling, that they didn't notice the clouds racing in behind them and the rising wind. Soon the moon was swallowed up, the wind increased to gale force, and it began to rain, and almost immediately the rain turned into a roaring downpour that blotted out everything beyond a few yards away.

They shouted to each other, and stumbling out onto the beach again hurried south. The rain walled them in; their flashlights showed them little except the silvery surrounding raindrops and they stayed close to the edge of the water. On the south beach they lost it for a little and stumbled into some of the roosting terns, which rose wildly around them until they found the water's edge again. They went on, until they began to wonder if they hadn't passed the cottage, for the wind, coming from the west, blinded them with flying spray as well as rain. A lull came in the storm, and they saw the lights and stumbled up the little grade and went into the workshop and took off their dripping clothes.

They ran into the house for towels; Cap and Catton

had gone to bed and the only occupant of the living room was a finch asleep on the back of a chair. Its head appeared from under a wing; it regarded them drowsily, chirped once, tucked its head back again.

"Holy Poseidon!" Doc said, as he dried himself. "It was almost as bad as the blizzard that nearly killed us. We'd better take the rifles apart and dry and oil them. I've never been so wet, but it was worth it while it lasted."

"It sure was," Geordie said. "I was thinking this morning what a strange Christmas it was, but I hadn't seen anything yet. The petrels, and the albatrosses dancing in the moonlight . . . I'll never forget it the rest of my life."

"Amen," Doc said.

The rain began again with a roar, and they began to dismantle the rifles.

EIGHTEEN

It rained all night and all the next day; the heavy recurring showers marched across the sea and the sodden island, with intervals of lighter rain between them. The wind was cold and gusty, occasionally so high that spray from the ocean was flung against the house like hail, for the waves came far up the beach. By afternoon everyone except Catton, who had taken himself to the warehouse to work on skins and requested that they let him alone, was finished with his chores and at loose ends. Doc had completed the plan he was drawing, which he revealed to be for a pen for rails; he had decided to catch about a hundred of them and take them to Midway when they stopped there on the way home.

"It will be better to have them two places than one," he said. "If it happens that they don't survive here, maybe they'll manage to do it at Midway."

"Can't we catch some of the honey eaters and miller birds too?" Geordie asked.

"I don't think we could catch enough of them to make it worthwhile," Doc said. "If they just ran around like the rails we could chase them and catch them in nets, but, alas, they can fly. I doubt it would be any use transplanting a few of them. You need a good nucleus, what with the right sex ratios, the accidents of life, and so on." He began to wander around restlessly. "I think I'll put on raingear and take a walk. Anybody want to go?"

"I think I'll take a nap," Cap said. "It's too cold to get wet, and I never got enough sleep on destroyers."

"I'll go," Geordie said, and went to get his sou'wester.

They set out, heading for the lagoon. They had their rifles with them and shot some rabbits but not as many as they would have liked, for many of them had crawled into petrel burrows to get out of the rain. As they came over the height of land on the western side of the lagoon they began to find many of the petrel burrows blown shut, and several times they found petrels that had managed to get their heads out but nothing else; the sand held them captive, and most of them were exhausted and beaten by the weather.

"You see what's happened," Doc said. "There's been so much of the vegetation eaten up that there's not enough left to stabilize the sand any more. There's going to be a big loss of birds every time there's a bad wind."

They dug out the birds whose heads were showing when they came across them, and in walking about to do this broke through into burrows frequently; some of the

176

birds they dug out were too far gone to survive. They were wet and cold and covered with damp, sticky sand that itched by the time they could look over the lagoon. The rain had raised the water level considerably; many of the white goney nests had been built high enough to be just above it, but many more were awash and had been deserted. Eggs were floating about, many gonies were standing around disconsolately, having lost their nests, and there were a number of bristle-thighed curlews making the most of the calamity; they were busily eating eggs or carrying them off in their long bills.

"Glum sight," Doc said. "But we'll come back when the rain stops and collect some of the eggs, and blow them. I can always use them to trade with other museums which don't have them. I think I'm cold enough now to go back. How about you?"

"I am too," Geordie said. He was shivering, and ready to call it a day. "Do you think," he said, as they were walking back, "that it would be all right if I collected a few birds and prepared them for our museum? I know you brought a good collection of skins and eggs back when you were here before, but there must have been some things you didn't get."

"I think it would be a fine idea," Doc said. "We'll clear it with Cap, just as a matter of form, but I'm all for it. There are a number of species that move in and out of here that I didn't get, and they should be represented; maybe the taxonimists can make new subspecies out of them. We don't have too many skins of some of the birds here anyhow; we should send the National Museum a few more, and have a few extras ourselves. I'll make up a list of the ones we have enough of, and you can work on the rest. I'd rather you got them than I; I don't feel much like collecting on this trip, somehow. I'd rather just look and take notes and photographs. I'll have enough to do. We're going to take a goney census, I want to make a series of slides of blood films to see what the parasites are here, and so on. And shoot the cussed rabbits." He saw a rabbit, stopped, and shot it. "I don't know why I call them cussed rabbits. It's not their fault that they're wrecking the place. I always sort of admired rabbits, in a way. They're pretty defenseless, all predators live on them, but they've been around a long time and with everything against them have managed to survive. They're a successful species, but they've got no business being here. What's the total so far?"

"I looked as I came out," Geordie said. "What with the ones we've shot this afternoon it's about three hundred and fifty."

"Hardly scratches the surface. You saw what's been done to the petrels; presently it will be the honey eaters, the miller birds, and the rails, whose food supply will be gone. I think we'd better plan to make a special hunt every day, spreading out and marching the length of the island in addition to the offhand execution that we do."

"Yes, sir," Geordie said, remembering the sand-plugged petrel burrows and the birds they had dug out. "I think we'd better."

The next morning the sun was out again and they went back to the lagoon and waded around and collected eggs. The curlews had gotten there before them but they managed to get three dozen eggs. They drilled holes in both ends of each egg and blew the contents out. The little rails discovered what was going on and gathered around to eat the contents, running over their legs eagerly and squabbling with each other as they sat working on the sand.

A few evenings later, a little after sunset, KITTIWAKE appeared and stood off the island. It was too late for a landing, and as the sea was calm she anchored to await the morning. They packed the eggs, exposed film, and bird skins that Catton had prepared to go back on her. Before he went to bed Geordie walked around the cottage and looked at her lights riding well beyond the reef and thought of other times when the Japanese had appeared, probably to anchor in the same place, and come ashore to stay for awhile to slaughter thousands of birds for feathers for women's hats. It had been a wasteful and heartless business, and he could imagine the little men running about with their clubs along the eastern beach and the shores of the lagoon, smashing down the albatrosses on their nests and cutting off their wings, letting them lie beside their eggs to bleed to death.

He saw too the birds they had crippled and thrown into the cistern to crawl over each other and bleed and starve. He felt a little sick as he thought of it, and wondered how anyone, after watching the beautiful, gliding flight of an albatross or looking into its calm, dark eyes, could do such things. There were some creatures in the world, like the unfortunate rabbits, that had to be controlled; but the sea birds (including the lovely little fairy terns and any others that the raiders had been able to catch) harmed nothing. They were expressions of life in its infinite variety and beauty, and defenseless in their inexperience of the wasteful cruelty of men. Geordie discovered that his fists were clenched as he thought of those Japanese; he hated them, and was very glad that the men from KITTIWAKE had caught them and taken them in. They were not, however, the only offenders; many Americans had done things as reprehensible, slaughtering game for the market or just because it was there, emptying the plains of buffalo for their hides or their tongues.

179

Before Geordie turned away to go back into the cottage he determined that he would try, in some way before he was dead, to show them what dreadful things they were doing and get them to stop it. He didn't know, now, what he would do or how he would do it; but he was sure that it would come to him as he learned more.

The ship's boat brought the captain ashore the next morning; he spent an hour or so and left again, taking the material they had packed with him. Geordie had heard no more about the possibility of sending Catton back and when Catton went north on the island and the boat left without him it was evident that Cap had given up the idea. There wasn't, as Cap had said before, any real reason to do it except the nasty disposition, and in any event Catton hadn't made any scenes lately or caused any trouble. He did, certainly, seem to withdraw even more, but that was no reason to get rid of him.

The three of them watched KITTIWAKE weigh anchor and steam away and turned to the day's occupations. They had built up the fire again after breakfast to give KITTIWAKE's captain coffee, and as there was still a little life in the embers Geordie decided to make some cookies; so he built up the fire again. He worked with the rails and miller birds hunting around him and a honey eater singing from the roof, and when the cookies were finished he picked up his rifle and camera and went rabbit hunting.

He went eastward across the island and shot a large number of rabbits on the way, for they were out in force now that the sun had appeared again. The air was lively with birds and he turned northward when he reached the height of land above the lagoon; he stopped to watch a pair of frigate birds above the ocean. They were soaring very high in the air, black and rakish; when they soared their long forked tails were sometimes folded together to make points, and this, with their long, narrow, pointed wings, like somewhat flattened M's, added to their rakish appearance. They were superb fliers, admirably equipped for flight; Doc had told Geordie that their pectoral muscles made up about a quarter of their body weight and that their tails alone were controlled by seven pairs of strong muscles. Not even hurricanes, which drove such fine fliers as albatrosses down onto the beach, seemed to disturb them. Although it was a bit late in the morning for boobies to be coming back with fish they were waiting for one, and presently they saw it. They rolled over, backed their wings, and came down out of the sky like meteors; it was a thrilling thing to watch. Geordie unconsciously rose on his toes in the excitement of it. The booby couldn't have gotten away from one of them, much less two; they seemed to be everywhere about it at once, and made short work of its attempts to escape them. It disgorged its fish which the pair of them, seeming to merge in their swift maneuvers, picked out of the air.

Still tingling from the sight, Geordie went out onto the beach and turned north, between the nesting black gonies and the surf. He didn't stop to watch them this morning, for he had remembered the fairy tern and wanted to see if he could find its nest. When he came to the place where he had caught one of them several days before the bird appeared again over his head, so pale and translucent against the sky that it seemed almost like a ghost, a disembodied spirit with large dark eyes. As before it dropped down in front of him to stare at his face, grunting low, and he could have caught it again.

He turned up into the dying scaevola bushes and began to look about; suddenly he found the young one sitting on top of a piece of phosphate rock. It was a tiny, downy little thing, grayish brown, with a black patch on its head and two dark stripes on its back, with a short bluish bill and rather large, strongly clawed feet. It needed these claws, for fairy terns build no nest; they lay their eggs on a rock or the horizontal limb of a tree, and the young one has to cling to its precarious place from the time it is hatched.

Geordie, much engaged with it, sat down two or three feet away and unslung his camera. The nestling looked at him with interest but without fear, and he took several pictures of it. Just as he started to put his camera away one of the parents came in, accepted him without hesitation, and landed beside the chick. There were seven very small fish in its beak, held crosswise one after another, and Geordie hardly had time to wonder how the bird had managed to catch and carry them that way before the chick moved close and took the first one. The others were moved forward as the chick took the one at the tip of the beak; it was an extraordinary performance, and Geordie was so fascinated by it and by the sleek and gentle beauty of the old bird that he forgot to take more pictures. For a moment he was irritated at himself, and then realized that he would have many more opportunities. He waited until the old bird had flown off and got up and went south between the lagoon and the western beach.

His day's total of rabbits was fifty-one by the time he met Cap, who was also out shooting them, about halfway down the island. Cap had shot twenty-nine; they joined forces and zigzagged back and forth until they reached the cottage where they posted a grand total of ninety-six.

"Our best day, by far," Cap said. "We'll have to try to keep it at that level. You certainly did well today."

"Yes, sir. You know, it's a funny thing. I thought I was shooting a lot of them, and then after Doc and I dug out the petrels, when I saw what was happening to them because the rabbits have eaten so much of the vegetation, I seemed to shoot more."

"I know what you mean," Cap said. "I saw some of the petrels after the storm, and I seemed to shoot more rabbits too. Maybe we weren't doing as well as we could until we had an actual demonstration of the damage. We were dragging our feet a little, whether we realized it or not."

"I won't drag them any more," Geordie said.

"No. Neither will I. We'll take another march late in the afternoon."

They found Doc in the workshop, and all had some lunch. Geordie told Doc about the fairy tern's nest.

"I'll go back there with you in the morning," Doc said. "That bird's a little early, and probably the only one on the island with a chick. We'll both get pictures. I'd tell John about it, but he might want to take the chick. We'll just save this one for ourselves, and let it grow up." He grinned. "The tide will be all the way out in an hour or so. Why don't we go fishing on the reef?"

This sounded like a fine idea, and they all agreed. An hour later, wearing nothing but their shoes, they got into the small boat that KITTIWAKE had left them that morning and went out to the reef. The footing was not very dependable and when the higher waves came in they were up to their waists and had to watch their balance, but the fishing was good. Geordie was enjoying himself immensely when suddenly, after the crest of a wave had passed, he was gripped around one leg. Startled, he looked down. An octopus, a foot or two long, had come in on the wave and wrapped several of its tentacles around him. Swaying, gray, and rubbery, staring with its flat black eye, it filled him with a shocked, cold horror that momentarily paralyzed him; then, with a yell, he kicked it with his other foot. It discharged a cloud of ink, turned loose of him, and scudded off.

Doc and Cap both floundered toward him. By the time they got there he had recovered from his fright and was laughing a little shakily, somewhat embarrassed by the uproar he had made; the creature's sucking discs had left red welts on his leg.

"Are you all right?" Doc asked, coming up. "What was it?"

"An octopus," Geordie said. "It startled . . . it really scared the devil out of me. It wasn't big enough to do much harm, but it took hold and I looked down, and . . . Ugh! I guess I'll do my fishing from the boat, for the rest of this trip."

He shivered a little from the memory of that cold, impersonal eye, so alien and so different from the expressive eyes of birds and animals, but by the time Doc and Cap joined him in the boat again he was smiling about his adventure. They all laughed about it on the way to shore, cleaned their fish at the water's edge, and went up to the cottage. They had had a good afternoon and were feeling pleasantly tired and at peace with the world until they came around the corner of the house and found Catton on the porch. He put his hands on his hips and glowered at them; they all stopped and looked at him.

"Celebrating, eh?" he asked. His eyes narrowed.

"Celebrating what, John?" Cap asked. "Did you have a good day?"

"Oh, I had a fine day. Why wouldn't I? I had plenty of time to think about the fine trick you played on me."

"Trick?" Cap asked, in a puzzled voice. "What trick? What's on your mind, John?"

"Do you think I don't know you sent the Laysan teal skins back on the ship? Do you take me for a complete

184

ass? After forbidding . . . forbidding, I repeat, me from shooting those birds you got them yourselves, for your museum, and now you can laugh at me. Laugh, then. You won't do much laughing later."

There was a startled silence, and Cap and Doc stared flabbergasted at each other. Finally Doc said: "Nobody has shot teal or sent skins anywhere, John. Good heavens, man, where did you get that idea?"

"The teal weren't there when I came down today. I saw this . . . this kid," he said, pointing to Geordie, "a day or two ago, lying by the fresh water pool, waving his legs in the air to entice the teal into range. Oh," he went on, his voice rising, "I see it all. Ringing in this innocent looking little devil, thinking I wouldn't pay any attention to him."

"I was taking pictures," Geordie said.

Catton looked at him with such venom that he fell back a step. "Taking pictures!" Catton said. "Very likely!" His voice rose again, his face flushed, and he clenched his fists. "Taking pictures! Taking me for a—"

"Enough of that!" Cap rapped out, in a tone that must have made sailors quake in the past. "Stow that sort of talk, and come with me. We'll go to the pond right now."

He started off, and after glaring at his back for a moment Catton went after him. Geordie and Doc stood and watched them go.

"I'll be drawn and quartered," Doc said. "And the ship no sooner out of sight. So that's how you got so close to those teal."

"I didn't know he was anywhere around. I didn't see him. Doc, what's the matter with him?"

Doc shook his head. "I think we'd better keep sort of an eye on him from now on, but we can talk more about this with Cap."

"Yes, sir," Geordie said unhappily, for Catton's venomous look and the fact that Catton had been trailing him about and watching him, as well as the man's accusation that he had been brought along as an accomplice to underhand maneuvers, upset him a good deal. The accusation was so false as to be unbalanced, and Geordie had never had any dealings with unbalanced people; he didn't know how to estimate them or what they might do.

He and Doc sat on the front steps until Cap and Catton came back. Catton went into the house without looking at anyone; Cap sat down with them.

"There were five teal there," Cap said, "so I think we've got that business quieted down." He looked at Geordie for a moment, thoughtfully. "We'll have to . . ." he began, and broke off and turned to Doc. "I'd like to talk to you a little about all this later."

NINETEEN

In the morning, Doc and Geordie went off to the fairy tern's nest, to get more pictures. Geordie was rather silent; he had thought a good deal about Catton in the night, and had gotten nowhere. As they walked along the western beach Doc, who had been rather quiet too, finally broke the silence.

"Cap and I took a walk after you'd gone to your room," he said. "We're both disturbed about that affair yesterday, for John got you involved in it."

"He doesn't like me,' Geordie said. "He hasn't liked me from the first."

"I don't think you liked him either. You might think that you didn't like him because of the way he reacted to you, but you might have felt the same way if he'd been pleasant. For two people to dislike each other at sight isn't an extraordinary occurrence; it happens all the time, and no one else can explain it."

Geordie hadn't thought of this; it had never occurred to him, and he didn't know what to reply.

"He probably felt that," Doc went on, "but all this is beside the point, more or less. The point is that something has happened or is happening inside John's head, and changing him. I think he's on his way to a mental condition. I'm not a doctor; I don't know what it is or where it's liable to go; he ought to be under treatment, but that's not possible. We've got him on our hands, and we'll have to do the best we can. We'll have to watch him carefully and compare notes about what we see. He might get more . . . troublesome, and he might not. If he does we'll have to take care of it when we come to it. But he doesn't like Cap, who he thinks is not letting him do some things he wants to do, and he doesn't like you, and you'll have to be careful not to give him an opportunity to dislike you more. Keep an eye out and don't spend any more time than you have to by yourself. Have somebody else in sight if you can."

"I will," Geordie said. He had been thinking of the situation as very unpleasant but now, even though Doc had deliberately underplayed it, he realized that it might become dangerous. He was shocked and then angry that such a cloud had appeared over the island's fine, carefree life and would now continue to be there.

"It won't help any to be sore about it," Doc said, catching his expression. "That will just make it worse. Make up your mind to accept it and live with it."

"Yes," Geordie said, abashed, and by the time they

had walked the rest of the way to the tern's nesting place he was trying to make the adjustment.

He didn't make it that day; it didn't come easy for him, or all at once. For the next few evenings, as he lay in his cot before falling asleep, he struggled with it and learned some things about himself. It was difficult at first to accept Doc's remark that he might have been at fault too, with an unconscious but evident dislike of Catton; it had never occurred to him before to blame himself for the way people felt toward him. They had either liked or disliked him, and he had let it go at that. He began to see that this view was too simple and self-centered, and it was time he grew out of it. He had also fumed inwardly at being restricted even though the restriction was a comparatively mild one, and he realized that this was self-centered too. They would all be restricted; he wasn't the only one; and instead of withdrawing and letting Doc and Cap look out for him he should be looking out for them as well as himself.

As these things grew clearer to him he came to accept Catton as the others accepted him, and to lose his hostility; Catton was a sick man and it was silly to be mad at him. A few days later Cap gave him permission to collect a few of the birds that weren't permanent residents of the island, and the first one he shot was a gull the like of which he hadn't seen before. He didn't know what it was, and when he took it into the workshop, where Doc and Catton were working, Catton asked to see it. Geordie gave it to him.

"I think it's a Bonaparte's gull," he said, after he had examined it. "There's no previous record of one here." He held it, looking at it longingly.

Geordie realized that he wanted it badly; he glanced at Doc, who nodded slightly. "I'll give it to you, if you want it," he said.

Catton looked at him and blinked and looked again; Geordie could almost see him thinking, wondering what sort of trick was being played on him. There hadn't been an incident since the affair of the teal to arouse his suspicions, but he clung to them. "Why?" he asked finally.

"I think you want it very much," Geordie said, "and your collection's more important than mine."

"I'm glad somebody realizes that," Catton said. "I'll take it, only don't expect anything in return."

"I won't."

"And don't think that this will make me relax my vigilance," he said, and turned away to the skinning table.

Doc and Geordie went out, to go rabbit hunting.

"Well," Doc said, "you made a try. Don't remind him of it any time, though, or he'll be sure it was for some ulterior purpose." He shook his head, and added: "I was very pleased to see you offer it to him."

For a time Catton seemed a little better; he worked hard and kept to himself and found nothing to quarrel about. They all hoped that this would continue, but they watched him and tried to keep someone in view when they were moving around. They worked harder at shooting rabbits and by early January had killed close to twelve hundred of them, but despite this there seemed to be as many as before and the more intelligent ones among them were growing warier.

Their lives fell into a loose routine of rabbit hunting, photography, observation, a little collecting on Geordie's part, and swimming or fishing parties limited to the three of them in the afternoons when the weather was clear and warm enough. They did more fishing on the reef, and several times went out to collect good pieces of coral. Geordie began to hunt for shells on the beach, and gathered a collection, including some very fine cowries. The sooty terns appeared in greater numbers, and the noddies began to lay. More gonies came in off the sea, and after the storm, which had flooded out a number of nests, some of the albatrosses that hadn't suffered built their nests higher. Doc saw the first phalarope. The petrels were laying eggs or brooding eggs already laid and didn't fill the air any more at night.

Around the twenty-first of the month Doc reported that the first goney had hatched, and by the twenty-third there were a lot of young gonies. Geordie, who, when he wasn't shooting rabbits, had been spending a lot of time among the gonies, taking pictures of them and letting them nibble the buttons on his shirt cuffs, the bright screws on his tripod, and even his fingers, had to move off a little, especially from the black gonies. Now that the fuzzy, dark gray young were out of the eggs their parents, who had calmly allowed all sorts of liberties, became very belligerent. They would lunge out, snapping the hooked beaks that were capable of opening an artery, sometimes growing so excited that they would regurgitate their last meal; occasionally one would charge with extended wings, snapping as they came for him. They brooded the young for a few days, and for several weeks after that took turns shielding them from the hot midday sun. As the young grew older they began to move clumsily around a little, waiting for their parents to return, and Geordie often wondered how the old birds managed to pick them out of so many others. They were always hungry and would pester any adult bird for food, begging and wheezing; strange adults would often peck them viciously, but it didn't seem to discourage them. They were fed by regurgitation; their parents would stand over them, open their bills, and let the half-digested food drip into their waiting beaks.

Doc wanted to take an albatross census, and they divided the island into quarters and spent several days counting. When they were finished they built the pen for the rails. It would have been easy to start their captures with the ones that ran about the house, but none of them wanted to do that; they all liked the little birds around, and went further afield for them. The greatest number of them seemed to be around the lagoon, where they chased them with nets; it was a tiring and dusty business, for in the heat of the chase they would often break through into petrel burrows and flounder about up to their waists.

When Geordie had time between these enterprises and his cooking and rabbit hunting and general wandering about to watch the changing scene he did some collecting on his own and prepared the skins, for he wanted to give them to the University when he got home. There was a fairly constant population of migrant birds which spent the winter on Laysan: bristle-thighed curlews, Pacific golden plover, and European turnstones; others, such as phalaropes, sanderlings, black-bellied plover, and Siberian whimbrels wandered through the island chain, occasionally appearing and rare in any case. There was a romantic aura about them, for several made tremendous migrations from Siberia or Alaska to New Zealand and back again; besides that, they were wary and difficult to approach, unlike the sea birds and the birds of Laysan. Skill was required to get within range of them and to hit them, and it was exciting not only to find and identify them but to collect and prepare their skins.

Geordie patrolled the beaches and the lagoon with the shotgun when he had a chance in the hope of finding a rare specimen, but he didn't have the gun the day he saw a black-bellied plover on the shore of the lagoon; he had been rabbit hunting with his rifle, and they didn't often shoot rabbits with the shotgun. Doc had told him that this bird had never been recorded on Laysan, and it would be quite a feather in his cap if he could get it; he ran all the way back to the cottage for the gun, burst in through the door, and was startled to find Catton sitting sprawled on a chair with his head on the table. Catton sat up groggily; he was a bad color, and shaking, and had vomited several times.

"I'm sick," he mumbled. "I'm sick."

He let his head fall with a thump to the tabletop again. Geordie had a moment of panic, and then collected himself. He ran up to Catton and leaned over him. "Can I help you to bed?" he asked anxiously. "Do you want anything?"

"No, no," Catton said blearily. "Get Doc, get somebody."

Geordie stood in indecision for a moment, afraid to leave the man and afraid not to leave him for help; finally he decided to find either Doc or Cap and ran out of the house. There was no one in sight in any direction, and Geordie's heart sank; both Doc and Cap might be at the other end of the island. He decided that the best thing he could do would be to go toward the lagoon and get on the height of land around it, and trotted off in that direction. As luck would have it he was only halfway there when he saw them both come over the skyline; they had been at the lagoon and were coming home, and he shouted at them and put on speed. They began to hurry when they saw him running, and when he met them and told them about Catton they fell into a trot.

They were nearly at the cottage when Doc said: "There's no use of your coming in too, Geordie. Cap and I can take care of things."

"I saw a black-bellied plover," Geordie said. "I came back to get the gun and found him. If there's nothing I can do to help I think I'll go and get it."

"Yes," Doc said. "I'll hand you out the gun, and you take off." When he brought out the gun he looked concerned. "He hasn't any temperature," he said, "so it's not an infection of any sort. It can't be anything he ate, for we've all eaten the same food. The only thing I can think of is that he's got a dose of arsenic poisoning, and that's serious. He probably was already carrying some that he's been absorbing through his pores, and then eaten more by mistake or carelessness, and that's touched off a real attack. We'll try to wash him out and keep him quiet. Go ahead and get the plover if you can; you can give us a hand when you come back."

Geordie went off toward the lagoon, rather frightened by Doc's diagnosis, for he knew how dangerous arsenic poisoning could be. Catton knew too, but he had been working on a large number of skins and in his disturbed condition had probably been careless. He might die, and Geordie had never been so close to possible death before. He thought of everything around him—the sun, the wind, the island's overflowing life, the lovely shades of the ocean and the surf on the reef—being blotted out, and shuddered.

Several minutes later he was distracted from his thoughts by two red-tailed tropic birds that flew past him with their rapid, steady wingbeats, satiny white with a pale pinkish cast and striking red bills, playing together in the air. They were evidently courting, for in their swift, pigeon-like flight they milled about, dove, stalled, and even flew backwards, squawking, always maintaining an exact distance from each other. Once or twice the upper one, apparently the male, would bend his two long, red, spike-like tail feathers straight down to touch the bird below. They were so pretty and so extraordinary in their maneuvering that by the time they were gone Geordie had forgotten his thoughts of death.

He was delighted to have seen their airy dance, for he had heard about it and been afraid that he would not; there weren't many on Laysan, for they liked heavy cover to nest in, and the height of their nesting season was May or June. They were awkward on the ground and walked badly, but were wonderful in the air; not even the frigate, for all their superior flying, could bother them very much.

He went on, thinking about them and hoping that he would presently find a nest to photograph, and came to the lagoon. The young gonies were wandering or sitting on their tails with their feet in front of them and there was much activity among their parents; the plover was still in the same place but flew before Geordie got within range. He followed it almost to the northern end of the lagoon before he finally got a shot and killed it, and not wanting to go back right away kept on around the end of the lagoon until he came to the frigate's rookery.

A few of them were beginning to nest and the males, with long, green, iridescent scapular feathers, now had the big red sacs below their beaks inflated like footballs and were sitting on the bushes to guard the sticks that the females brought them, for they stole nesting material from each other when they could. The sacs were the male's chief attraction; when the female of his choice appeared over his head he would stand up and display them. They were, Geordie thought, a strange and somewhat ridiculous inducement and awkward to handle in the air, but the females seemed to be impressed by them. While Geordie watched, a female came down; the male rose up on the nest and leaned backwards and the female landed and imitated him. Facing each other, they raised their hooked beaks, spread their wings, and rolled their heads and their bodies. They gurgled and chuckled; the male's green scapulars rose like bristles, and both birds puffed themselves up, trembled, and finally mated on the nest.

Geordie turned away presently and started back. He hoped that now the frigates had started nesting he would be able to get pictures of their antics. To make better time he went out onto the beach. The tide was very low, lower than he had ever seen it, and he went out and poked about the boulders that were usually awash; in the deep pools around them he could see many big crayfish moving around but had no way to catch them; he thought of rigging up a long-handled net to be ready if the tide fell so low again. Further south he saw a flock of red phalaropes come in off the sea and head for the lagoon. All of the migrating birds should be increasing now, and more of the terns, both graybacks and noddies, should be coming in to nest. He turned over a big turtle on the beach near the end of the lagoon, and not having his knife with him cut across the island to get it and return.

Doc was sitting on the steps, with his rifle beside him; he'd been out shooting rabbits. "We've got him in bed," he said, to Geordie's inquiring look. "When we got him undressed we found his arms and legs all broken out. It's arsenical poisoning as sure as the devil. Cap's with him now; we're going to take turns."

"I'll take a turn too," Geordie said. "At least, I can holler if I need help or don't know what to do."

"No need for you to do it," Doc said. "I think we can keep you busy enough. Cap and I talked it over awhile ago. If John is laid up for long, or if he . . . doesn't make it, his collection will have to be filled. Cap can't skin a bird, and that will leave it up to you and me to collect and work up all the skins for John's university, the ones we want, and the ones for the National Museum. We have rails to catch, pictures to take, some sets of eggs to collect, and rabbits to shoot. I looked on the board awhile ago, and to date we've shot close to three thousand of them and they're getting wilder all the time, so our average will probably go down from now on. We're a long, long way from cleaning them out, and we've only got about five more weeks to go. I'll be out of circulation part of the time and Cap can help with the rabbits when he's free, but you can see that you'll be doing a lot of work. I'm sorry, Geordie. It won't be quite as leisurely for any of us as we thought it would."

"It's been pretty easy so far," Geordie said. "It's been sort of like a vacation, with plenty of time to look around. I don't mind working a lot harder, Doc. I'd like to do it. I hope I can fix the skins well enough."

"You'll do," Doc said. "Let's go out and shoot some more rabbits."

"I have a turtle on the east beach. I've got to go butcher him."

"Get your rifle and put the plover away," Doc said. "I'll go along."

When they returned they found Cap sitting on the steps, and he got up and walked toward them. They all stopped a few yards from the cottage.

"He's very sick," Cap said. "We didn't always have a doctor handy on destroyers, so I had to know a little medicine, and we'll just have to do the best we can. I've been thinking about the situation and I've decided it would be best if you, Geordie, stayed away from him. It would be unpleasant for you to help us nurse him, and unnecessary, and it might stir him up. From one or two things he's mumbled I take it he still thinks about that business of the teal once in awhile. He's pretty confused and I want to avoid confusing him more. You don't mind?''

''No, sir, I sure don't. I'd be glad to help, but I guess you're right that it's better I stay out of his sight. Doc's given me some work to do, anyhow.

''Good,'' Cap said.

TWENTY

The first thing Geordie did the next morning was to go through Catton's skins and eggs to see what he had collected, and to check over his lists to see how many specimens of everything he had intended to get. He was glad to see that the native birds, the honey eaters, miller birds, rails, and finches were about well enough represented already and not many more were needed, for he had never wanted to kill any of them. Their tameness, the pleasure they had given him around the cottage, and the fact that they might be on the edge of extinction had set them apart for him. He knew that they should be represented in several museums, especially if they might vanish from the earth, but that didn't make any difference; he just didn't want to collect them.

He was full of admiration for the skins that were there, for they were beautifully done; he hoped that some day he would be as expert as Catton. The man was universally disliked, and with good reason, but he was a master of his work; even lately, despite his disturbed condition, his work was faultless. It was depressing that he had always been so difficult, and more depressing still that he might die on this lonely island and his talents be lost.

Geordie turned away from this thought and tried to lay out a tentative schedule for himself. The basis of his days, he thought, would be to make rabbit patrols in the mornings and evenings with the rifle, and another for specimens with the shotgun in the middle of the day, for it was then that most birds were less active and liable to be resting where he could get at them. He would work on skins in the evenings after dinner. He knew that this would vary, and many times he would wish he had the shotgun when he had the rifle and the other way around, but that couldn't be helped. He should always have a camera with him, and there would be time on all the patrols to search for nests, watch the life about him, and so on. For a moment, harking back to Doc's advice to have someone always in view he wondered how he was going to do it; then he realized that this wasn't necessary any more, and felt pleasantly free.

Having gone over all this in his mind he decided to start off, for there was an air of gloomy apprehension about the cottage and he wanted to get away from it. He went in to get the rifle and the camera and found Doc finishing his breakfast; Doc had watched beside Catton part of the night, and slept late. "He's not good," Doc said. "I think I'll go with you, if you're going out."

They left in a somewhat subdued frame of mind, and headed for the freshwater pond; when they were nearly there Doc suddenly stopped. "Over there," he said, pointing. "Do you see it? It's behind the other albatross now, but it's an albino. We'd better get it. I've never seen one before."

They separated a little and moved toward the bird; it was Doc who shot it. It was a beautiful thing, and after Geordie had plugged the bullet hole with cotton they took it back to the warehouse, for they didn't want to leave it and it was too heavy to carry very far. After they had left it they went north, shooting rabbits as they went, cut around the northern end of the lagoon and looked in at the frigate bird rookery. A few of the males were on the nests.

"They've got eggs, all right," Doc said. "The males do most of the incubating. We might as well get a couple of sets now, while they're fresh and easy to handle."

"Maybe the eggs will be easy to handle, but how about the birds?" Geordie asked. Having watched the frigates' bold and piratical tactics in the air he wasn't at all sure that he wanted to get anywhere near their strong hooked beaks; it seemed to him that it would be safer to expose himself to a lunatic with a meat cleaver.

"Oh, they're all right," Doc said, and pushed himself into the scraggly bushes alongside of one. The bird looked at him, but didn't offer to demolish him; he ran his hand along the nest, eased it under the bird, and came out with the egg. He did the same with another one, while Geordie stood by apprehensively waiting for disaster. Doc came out of the bushes.

"Two are enough," he said. "They're usually very mild mannered, but a little uncertain. I was ready to dive at the first movement." He grinned. "The Polynesians used to use them like carrier pigeons," he said, as they walked off. "They'd tame young ones, take them off in canoes or whatever, and turn them loose when they wanted to send a message home. The blamed things would fly home and sit on their accustomed perch. They're pretty sedentary, as a matter of fact, although you wouldn't think it to watch them. They're perfectly happy to sit on a perch if they get fed once in a while. Seems strange for a bird that's so terrific in the air. Not even hurricanes seem to bother them. They can still sail around under perfect control when everything else has been driven down on a beach."

"I still don't think I'd do what you did."

"Well, maybe it would be just as well not to. If you ever want eggs, it would be better to get them at night. The birds go into a stupor then."

They shot rabbits all the way back to the cottage, and Geordie helped Doc blow the two frigate eggs and went out again with the shotgun. He shot a red-backed sandpiper, the first one they'd seen, and found a dead young Laysan albatross which he decided to take back and skin. He was halfway up the island by that time; the sky had begun to cloud over, and he decided to go back. He had enough to keep him busy for the evening, anyhow, and as a storm seemed to be coming up and the rising wind had a cold edge to it he didn't want to be caught out and soaked. By the time he reached the cottage the wind had risen to half a gale and was still increasing; the blowing sand was extremely unpleasant, and just as he reached the cottage the end warehouse, which they hadn't used because its condition was worse than the others, blew down.

After the storm had blown itself out they found that the toll of birds had been considerable; many young albatrosses had been smothered and covered or half covered by the shifting sand, the losses among the petrels was incalculable, for they had been caught in their burrows and covered up, and all of the ground nesting birds had suffered severely. It would have been worse if it had happened later when the Christmas Island shearwaters and more sooty and gray-backed terns were in, and Geordie mentioned this.

"Yes," Doc said, "you're right, but remember that this isn't the last blow we're going to have. The young gonies will be better able to stand another one later, but I doubt anything else will. When it's all said and done, it could be that the rabbits killed more birds than the feather hunters managed to kill. Let's take a walk around the island, and see what we can pick up. We haven't been very far yet."

He took a rifle and Geordie took the shotgun, and they started out around the south end of the island. A pair of mallards jumped off the freshwater pond and Geordie got them both. After he had retrieved them they both stood looking at the two ducks, of a species so numerous and familiar at home, and both their minds jumped back to the prairie marshes, the good times they had had there, and their families and friends so far away. There was a long moment of silence, which Doc finally broke.

"They make me a little homesick," he said, "but it won't last very long. I've spent so much time in so many places that I really don't have a home any more, and I suspect your life will be that way too." He smoothed the drake's feathers. "I don't know whether our interest in birds has made us like this, or the other way around. These birds might have come from Alaska or the Siberian side. Why didn't they just migrate south a little when winter came, and stay? Where have they been? What are they doing way out here? Do they interest us because they furnish endless speculation, or, like us, are they fiddle-footed and just want to see the world and do we feel drawn to them for that reason? If I knew the answers I'd know more about myself, for I think the mallards' basic reasons and mine are pretty much the same. I never was a mechanist, thank God." He paused, and shook his head. "I don't know why I went into all that, except that the fix John is in stirred me up."

"Is he better?" Geordie asked.

"He seems a little better," Doc said. "He does have a little palsy and occasional cramps, and pain in his arms and legs, and I hope he gets over that. We gave him emetics and we washed him out as well as we could after you found him, and we're keeping him warm and giving him a lot of water and some diluted milk of magnesia to help him get rid of the stuff. There's not much else we can do, except keep him away from arsenic from now on. I'm sure now that he already had a mild chronic case and then suddenly got too much somehow. He must have spilled it on a sandwich and not noticed that he did it, or something of the sort. In a day or two we can begin to feed him with stuff that's easy to digest. We'll just have to wait and see what happens."

"I feel as though I ought to be doing some of the nursing, that I ought to give you and Cap a hand. It doesn't seem right that I'm here and don't help."

"We've been over that," Doc said. "There's no use in going over it again. I think I'll take the ducks back and spell Cap for awhile. You go on, and when you get back we'll take a swim."

They parted, and Geordie went on. It seemed to him that a great many more gray-backed terns had come in from the sea, and he thought that soon they would nest. There were many more fairy terns, too, and they seemed to like the southern beach. The gray-backs were more numerous not far from the pond; they were pretty things with their black caps, the black lines through their eyes, and their pale underparts standing out against the blue sky. They were friendly and curious, and dove at him until he got away from the vicinity of the pond. A little above the beach he hunted around and found where two fairy terns were nested; he gently moved the birds and took their eggs, for Catton hadn't collected any. He knew he would have to collect several pairs of the terns sooner or later, but decided to wait.

He went on, cutting up toward the lagoon, and as they didn't have a surplus of shotgun ammunition he only shot at rabbits when he found several of them together. Near the lagoon he stumbled across a tropic bird's nest, under one of the scaevola bushes. Both birds were there, one of them on the egg and the other sitting closely beside. They didn't leave the nest but started a harsh screaming, and as he had to get another pair sooner or later he pulled them off and killed them both, and took the egg.

Collecting the migrants was like hunting birds at home, but this was somehow different. The island birds, tame and unwary, seemed more like friends than specimens and the tropic birds, both in themselves and in their flight, were beautiful. When the pressure he had applied to their breasts had stopped their hearts he stood holding them for a moment, as though waiting for his own reaction, and was surprised when he didn't have one. He had already subconsciously made the adjustment after Doc had told him to collect, realizing that the birds were needed as specimens and that science would put them to good use; they wouldn't be wasted.

He was pleased that he had arrived at this point, that he didn't feel as though he had betrayed or uselessly killed them, and went on. Around the shore of the lagoon there were a few dead young white gonies which had died since the storm; probably their parents had abandoned them. He picked up a couple of them and took them along, turning back toward the cottage because he thought that he and Doc had enough to handle with the things he was bringing in and the two mallards.

Geordie and Doc were kept very busy in the afternoons and evenings with their skinning and preparation of skins; the fact that they weren't nearly so expert as Catton drove them to taking extra pains, which meant extra time. This work, and the collecting they had to do, cut into their rabbit shooting, and although Catton's condition slowly improved to the point where they had to spend little time with him and Cap could lend a hand, their bags diminished. In addition to this the rabbits had gotten very wary. From record days in mid-January when they sometimes had killed two hundred or more rabbits they dropped down, on their worst days, to six or so, and for several weeks their average stood at about twenty-five a day. By the middle of February they had totaled about four thousand rabbits, which wasn't enough.

Presently Catton was well enough to be up and come to the table for meals, but he still had a slight palsy and it was distressing to watch the trembling of his hands. His legs hurt him, he often had headaches, and although he didn't say so he had trouble with his eyes. This was evident when he got into the bright sunlight, for he squinted and shielded his eyes. These manifestations were bad enough, but Cap said they would probably diminish with time; what concerned them more was his mental condition, which seemed to have deteriorated. He forgot things easily and occasionally fell into childish rages over trifles; this sort of thing threw a pall over their once pleasant meals and they always had to be ready to soothe him, but it was bearable so long as he stayed in the cottage or sat inertly on the steps. It was when he began to move about a little more that their troubles multiplied. His first appearance in the warehouse gave them an indication of the future.

Late one afternoon Geordie and Doc, who had been out shooting rabbits and catching rails, had also collected two fairy terns and brought them back to skin. They had put their rails into the pen and were at work on the terns, whose feathers came out very easily and consequently made them difficult to work on, when they heard footfalls with a curious flopping quality behind them. They knew at once it was Catton, for Cap was fishing and Catton still didn't have complete control of his extremities and dropped his feet flat; they glanced quickly at each other and stopped their work but didn't turn around.

The footfalls stopped immediately behind them and they could hear Catton's quick breathing. "Continue, continue," he said. "If you call that skinning a bird in Iowa, don't let me interrupt you."

Doc turned around. "Hello, John," he said, and Geordie could hear that he was being careful with the tone of his voice. "I know we're not very good, but we're doing the best we can. While you've been under the weather, we've been trying to fill out your collection."

"A labor of love, you might say," Catton remarked.

"In a way," Doc said. "You have a list to fill out, and maybe you won't have time now to do it all yourself. I know you'd have done the same for me, if I'd gotten into trouble."

"Would I?" Catton asked, and then there was a silence. Geordie sat, tense, and knew somehow that they were on the edge of a crisis; Catton would either accept what Doc had said or reject it, and if he did that it was impossible to predict what would happen. "Yes," he said finally. "Yes, I think I would help you. I'll help you now." His hand came down on Geordie's shoulder, and Geordie couldn't help a start. "Don't do that," Catton said, with the beginning of a roughness in his voice. "I'm not a leper. Move away."

Geordie very carefully slid out of his chair, and Catton sat down. He picked up a scalpel, and concentrated on the tern. He began to skin it, and despite the trembling of his hands the precision and delicacy of his work was remarkable.

Doc gave Geordie a sidewise look that seemed to indicate that Geordie should leave. "You don't need me now," Geordie said. "I'm going to shoot rabbits."

"Go shoot them," Catton said, without turning. "Earn your keep." As Geordie turned away he heard Catton say to Doc: "You can go too."

Geordie paused at the door; Doc slid out of his chair. "Good," he said. "I'll go shoot some too. Stay away from the arsenic, John. We need you too much.

He crossed to the door, and he and Geordie went out. After they had walked out of earshot of the warehouse Doc said: "Whew! I felt as though I was walking on eggs. I'll have to get that arsenic out of there when he's not around. Before he got into that, we usually knew what to look for from him, but now I don't think we do. It's going to be a little ticklish."

TWENTY ONE

Now they had a few days free from trouble, for Catton settled down to skinning birds, moving between the cottage and the warehouse and going nowhere else; he was quiet, withdrawn, and remote, as though they were all shadows to him. Doc or Cap would frequently make a quietly complimentary remark to him and he would look at them expressionlessly, his eyes rather blank and showing nothing. He ate what was put before him, frequently spilling his food because of his trembling. His mind seemed concentrated on the skinning of birds, and once in awhile they noticed that he would make the motions of skinning something when he thought that he wasn't observed; they were careful to avoid the appearance of watching him.

His apparent disinclination to go very far from the cottage and the fact that he was doing most of the skinning freed the rest of them from this chore and they were able to move about more, but either Doc or Cap arranged to look in on him frequently.

"I've moved the arsenic," Doc said, "so I don't think he'll get at it, but we don't want to leave him alone for too long. This concentration of his and the way he looks at you make me uncomfortable."

Geordie was away from the cottage as much as possible. He was very glad to be freed again, not only from Catton's depressing presence but because their time on the island was growing shorter. He had many birds to collect, and new birds were coming in. From the one or two masked booby nests that he had found earlier the total had now grown to thirty or so, mostly along the eastern side of the island. Two of the early eggs in one nest had hatched, producing ugly, naked, slate-colored creatures so voracious that probably only one would survive. Geordie got good pictures of them, and the older birds as well. They were heavy-bodied white birds with black wing edges and a black-bordered tail, and had always engaged him because their dark beaks and eyes and the black under their chins made it appear that their faces were thrust through white hoods. They were nested on the ground practically among the frigates that victimized them, which never failed to astonish Geordie, although he realized that the frigates couldn't get down through the bushes at the young, which they certainly would have eaten.

Christmas Island shearwaters, black, petrel-like birds that nested in burrows like the petrels, were beginning to come in, and Geordie collected a few of the early arrivals from under the bushes in the frigate bird colony. Like the petrels, the shearwaters weren't active during the day but flew about at night. Within a few days the eastern shore was full of them, and shortly after that they were all over the island. They wouldn't nest for several weeks, but as the colonies built up they became extraordinarily vocal, moaning, squawling like fighting cats, and flying about in the night.

They were followed by the first sooty terns, white-breasted birds that were dark above, with dark caps. They, also were largely nocturnal, appearing in the early mornings and late afternoons, noisy with their "wide-awake!" cries, flying about but not landing, apparently spending their days and nights at sea. Geordie shot the first two he saw, and brought them in.

"They never seem to sit down," he said to Doc.

"They'll sit down later, probably about the time we leave," Doc said. "They nest later, and I don't think we'll get any eggs. They're probably the most numerous birds here, when they all get together. They'll fly around and around, huge clouds of them, and go away and come back; and then one day one bird will come down and the rest will pour down after him like the snow falling in a blizzard, and then they'll nest. If they get here before we go you won't be able to hear yourself think."

"I'd like to see that," Geordie said.

"You'd remember it the rest of your life. There are so many of them that they look like a tornado whirling around. I think you'll have a chance to see it."

There were so many things to see, so many pictures to take, and so many specimens to collect that Geordie was constantly on the go. A good deal of the time he was with

Doc or Cap, for they had started their organized rabbit hunting again, but they couldn't bring their average up enough to suit them. Doc had found the first Laysan finch's nest with eggs in it, and the other small birds would probably nest soon; as they wanted a few eggs of each species they spent a good deal of time searching for them. Geordie noticed that the throat sacs of the male frigate birds had gone down, now that the eggs were laid and being incubated, and he missed them; they had been an exotic touch of color in a landscape that didn't have very much.

He spent much less time with the gonies now, for the old birds were at sea for longer periods and he had a collection of pictures of them; they had lost their novelty in any event. There were too many other birds to photograph and collect, as they came in, species by species, from the ocean. It seemed that they had arranged it among themselves not to nest all at once. He took more and more of an interest in photography, and as Doc had misplaced the other camera, just as Dr. Black said he would, he spent more and more time taking pictures.

"Maybe we could borrow Catton's camera," he said to Doc one day. "He brought one."

"He's hidden it somewhere, blast it. I hinted to him the other day I'd like to borrow it, and he just looked blank. You're doing fine, you're getting better all the time. You don't know how lucky you are that they invented something beside that ponderous big black box we had to haul around and always use a tripod with just a couple of years ago."

"I'd feel better if we had another one," Geordie said. "If anything happens to this one . . ."

"I don't want to stir John up," Doc said. "Every day that he's as quiet as he is now is a gift from heaven, and I keep on feeling that it won't last. He went off for a little while today. Cap said he went down to the freshwater pond, and sat there looking at the teal. He's got some sort of bee in his bonnet about them."

"Did he take a gun?" Geordie asked, suddenly feeling a hollow sensation in his stomach.

"No," Doc said. "Cap hurried back before he did, and hid them all. I'll show you where they are. Try not to let him see you with one."

"What does he think when we bring the dead birds in?" Geordie asked.

"I don't know. Maybe he doesn't think about it. We've had the arsenic away from him for some time now, and he doesn't seem to think of that. Want to go for a swim?"

"Yes," Geordie said. "I feel as though I haven't had a swim in a long time." He looked down over the sea, and saw that the tide was lower than it had been since they had come to the island. "The reef is almost all exposed. Doc, why don't we explore the reef?"

"Well, why not? We may not have another chance, and we've worked hard enough to take a few hours off. I'll pass the word to Cap. Maybe he'll come along too."

They had a fine time swimming and exploring the reef, and followed it until the tide began to come in again, finding a number of sea urchins and all sorts of interesting things. There were a great number of shells that they hadn't had a chance to collect before, beautiful cowries and many others, and they were well loaded down by the time they were ready to come out of the water. They had had such a pleasant afternoon and had felt so carefree that they were in high spirits when they got back to the cottage.

Catton wasn't around, and Cap decided to walk down toward the freshwater pond to look for him. Doc and

Geordie took two rifles from the hiding place and went north on the island between the height of land and the beach on the western side to shoot rabbits until it was time to prepare dinner. They had better luck than usual, which pleased them, and by the time they had gotten about as far as the northern end of the lagoon they were running short of ammunition.

"We'll have to get into the other box," Doc said. "I think I'll go back, and poison a few skins if Catton isn't back yet."

Geordie went with him for a way, and then decided to visit the lagoon. He wanted to see if any more shorebirds that they hadn't collected had come in during the day. He cut off to the east and began to climb the slope; the sun was dropping low and the sooty terns were in the air in whirling flocks. Their numbers had increased considerably and their "wide-awake!" cries seemed to come from every direction. Geordie paused and watched them for a time, and noticed several tropic birds as well; they had also increased in numbers within the last few days. One flew past not far from him with its quick and steady wingbeat, and the declining sun gave it a little added color. It was one of the most beautiful of the sea birds and he wished he knew it better, but he didn't think there would be very many of them on Laysan any more for they liked to nest in rather heavy cover and were such true wanderers of the ocean that they could move about until they found a place that suited them. He wondered how many birds had made a choice and moved away to other, more hospitable islands during the last few years as the vegetation on Laysan had declined and how many, like the petrels, had returned by instinct alone, only to be decimated by the drifting sand.

What degree of choice did birds have, how much of their choice was dictated by ancestral memory, instinct, and how did this vary by species? Perhaps they varied individually as much as people. Geordie suddenly recalled Doc's remark that the basic reason he and birds did some things was the same, and found that he was startled by it. Most of the talk he had ever heard had put people far above the rest of creation and separated them from it because, it was thought, people arrived at their decisions by a process of logic, while the animals were controlled by various instincts. He turned this over and over in his mind as he stood on the slope and realized that he had never quite believed it.

He remembered listening to the arguments of the young mechanists at the University and walking away from them to go to the library and learn about the habits and personalities of animals and then get into the sun and air. The sun and air had been the most important thing then, but now he was aware that he was here because of his feeling of kinship with the animals. This feeling, and the observations he had made because of it, had brought him close enough to them to realize that their reasons for doing things were the same as his own. Human motivation could be explained by animal behavior; if he could show people this, if he could make them realize it, it would help them to understand themselves. Maybe this had been his goal from the beginning and he hadn't realized it, but now he did. He had made a step. It wasn't a very big one and he had many more to make, but it was a beginning.

He came out of his abstraction and heard the cries of the terns again; the sun had dropped lower and they were beginning to go out to sea. He felt that he had grown a little; he straightened up and began to walk again. His head came over the top of the slope, and the first thing he saw was a figure down on the portulaca flats between himself and the lagoon, standing with one arm raised high among the albatrosses. It seemed to be posing, or making a speech; its attitude was so strange and unlikely that Geordie stopped at once and stared at it.

It was Catton. His shadow lay long before him among the white birds, which were largely ignoring him. Catton's arm dropped, his head fell forward for a moment; almost at once he raised it again, and threw both his arms up. He half turned, and Geordie could see his mouth opening and closing but couldn't hear what the man was saying.

A cold shiver ran up Geordie's back and for a moment he was unable to move; then a violent urge to escape freed him, and he turned and ran down the slope toward the sea. He was almost in the water before he stopped. He was panting and a sort of cold horror had hold of him; he was shivering, and with the vast empty circle of the sea before him he had never felt so alone. He stood a moment with his legs twitching as though they were, without his own volition, going to carry him on; he looked back to see if Catton had followed him, had seen his movement and come after him. The skyline was empty, and this calmed him.

He got hold of himself. After all, he hadn't been threatened; he had seen a madman making a speech to the unheeding birds. It had aroused a primal fear in him, it had been like a sudden confrontation with the powers of darkness, but that was past now. What should he do? The man needed help; should he go to Catton and lead him home? His quick reaction to that thought showed him that such a thing was impossible, that he couldn't do it. He started to run down the beach.

He was in sight of the cottage when he saw, in the distance, Doc and Cap hurrying up the slope toward the lagoon. He turned toward them, and then they saw him and stopped. He ran up to them, so out of breath that he was unable to talk, but Cap said: "Nod your head. Have you seen Catton?"

Geordie nodded, and pointed back the way he had come. He took several more sobbing breaths, and then could speak. "He's on the flats. He's preaching to the birds."

"He's what?"

Geordie's breath steadied. "He's making a speech to the birds." He showed them, using the wide gestures that Catton had used. "I came over the rise, my head did, and he was down on the flats. He scared me, and I ran down to the ocean, and then came here."

"Good Lord," Cap said, and looked at Doc. "I'll go get him. You two go back."

"I'll come along," Doc said. "You may need help. Geordie can—"

"No," Cap said. "It's got to be done this way. I understand this sort of thing better than you do." He raised a hand to them, and went off.

"Geordie," Doc said, "I've got to tell you something, and it might as well be now. Most of the arsenic's gone."

"Gone?" Geordie asked.

"I don't know when he did it," Doc said, "or how he found it, but when I dipped into it today, after I left you, I found that there was some arsenic on top but that the rest of it was sand."

Geordie stared at him.

"He's hidden it somewhere," Doc went on. "We'll have to throw away any food that's open, any food that can be contaminated. We'll do it right now. Come on."

Geordie followed him to the kitchen, with a gathering hollowness in his stomach as he realized that what Doc had really said was that they might all be poisoned; perhaps they had already eaten some of the arsenic. "Doc, do you think—" he began.

"No," Doc said. "It wasn't that way last night. Here. You take this and this and I'll carry the rest and we'll take it down to the beach."

He gave Geordie half an armful and they walked down to the sea and threw everything in. The backwash took it, and carried it out.

"Now," Doc said. "Leave nothing open or lying about and don't use anything except unopened cans or meat you've brought in yourself, and don't leave the kitchen unless somebody else is there. Maybe he just got some inexplicable notion to hide it and maybe it was more than that. I doubt we'll ever know, but now we're prepared for anything. Let's go back."

"All right," Geordie said. "What will we do now?"

"We'll play it by ear," Doc said, and they walked back to the cottage. As they came around the corner Cap and Catton were just coming in. They were walking together calmly enough; there was no evidence of trouble. Catton looked at them with no change of expression, and he and Cap went into the cottage.

Presently Cap came out again and joined them. "He's tired," Cap said. "He's gone to bed."

"Where did you find him?" Doc asked.

"Walking south on the flat, coming home. He even pointed out a redbacked sandpiper among some plover, and said there were only one or two records of it in this territory and hoped someone would collect it. He didn't seem to be interested in collecting it himself. That gave me a chance to say that I doubted we'd get enough specimens to fill out his list because the arsenic was running short."

"And?" Doc asked.

"He shook his head and said: 'Too bad, too bad.'" Cap was silent for a moment. "There's the question of the water. We'd better drink as little as possible until it rains again. Beginning now, we'll have to keep a watch on him all the time. Maybe we'll find out where the arsenic is. I've rigged a hidden string to his door to wake me if he leaves his room at night. Ah, me. It's only a couple of weeks until the ship comes back, and I hope we can keep things quiet until then."

"Amen," Doc said.

TWENTY TWO

A strange time began for them. It was at first, as Doc put it, like living on the slope of an uncertain volcano and being constantly prepared to spring into action. "Not that it's that simple," he went on. "When the volcano lets go you only have to jump and run. Here, if you have to jump, you don't know what's coming next."

This expressed the situation very well; a feeling of uncertainty and tension hung over them. They quickly fell into a routine of surveillance, spelling each other on a schedule, and for several days no one went very far away. Meals became somewhat of a problem, and weren't very tasty; wastage was greatly increased, and Geordie began to wonder if the supplies would hold out. Presently the tension relaxed a little, for Catton remained quiet and didn't go very far from the house; he skinned the few birds that were brought in and did little else but sit on the ground near the warehouse and look over the sea. Then a two-day stretch of bad weather kept them all from moving very far. It was rainy and cold, with high winds, and the burrowing birds suffered again; when it was over there were numerous dead petrels around, and the shearwaters were saved from a similar fate only because they had not yet started to nest.

After the storm was over Cap and Doc suggested that Geordie begin to move around again, checking in once in awhile to keep abreast of possible developments. "Cap and I will keep in touch with each other," Doc said. "There are still rabbits to be shot, the list isn't filling out yet, and there are always pictures. There's no need for all three of us to be here all the time. We'll try to sun-dry the skins and get them into something airtight when what's left of the arsenic gives out. We've got about four thousand rabbits to date. That's not nearly enough, and we'll do the best we can with our limitations. We'd better open the other box of ammunition."

They went into the warehouse and pried the top from the remaining case of ammunition, and Geordie took several boxes out. They felt curiously light, and he opened one of them. It was packed with blanks.

"They're blanks," he said, with a feeling of having been betrayed. "Doc, they've packed this one with blanks."

Doc stared at him, and began to root through the case. He pulled several boxes out from various parts of the case and opened them; they were all the same. He threw them down in a rage, and kicked them across the warehouse. It was the first time Geordie had ever seen him lose his temper.

"Damnation!" he said. "And again damnation! The stupid idiots must have felt the difference in weight and didn't bother to check. Oh . . ." He stood for a moment, until he was calm again. "Well," he said, "there it is. How many rounds do we have left?"

"Two hundred at the most, I guess," Geordie said, "if we rounded up all the boxes that are scattered around. Maybe Catton has some in his room somewhere, or in some of his clothes. Maybe a hundred more. We'll fail, then. We won't be able to do what we came to do."

"Yes," Doc said somberly, "we'll fail. Maybe we were meant to fail, maybe we would have failed anyhow. There are too many of them, they've got too wary, and we're too bedeviled. I said once I admired their capacity to survive, didn't I? I understand the case. I think the gods are with them, and always have been."

Geordie was too downcast to say anything, and for a long moment Doc was silent too.

"We'll do the best we can," he went on finally. "We'll cut them down until we run out of shells, and maybe we'll cut them down enough to give the vegetation a chance to come back in a measure. When we get home we'll see if we can't get the Government to send someone else out, some predator-control people, and clean them out. The only trouble is, it might take years before they do it. Bureaucrats move like glaciers, the Survey is never given enough money and has too many places to spend it; this is a remote place, unimportant to most people, unknown to them. It will be very difficult to get an appropriation, if they ever do get one. The chances are the survivors will increase again until the place is a complete desert of blowing sand, and the rabbits, the honey eaters, the rails and the miller birds will all starve together; the finches might survive because they'll eat anything, and most of the others will be diminished. You've seen what happens to the petrels and young gonies when the sand starts to blow. It will be far worse. One of the greatest nesting islands in the world will be wrecked."

He tossed up his hands. "I don't know. Maybe we were too optimistic to think we were going to shoot them all. We should have been prepared with additional measures so that if a contingency like John came up to take shooters out of circulation we would still have had traps, poison, whatnot. We should have had them anyhow. As to John, what could we do that we're not doing now? They may be able to do something for him if we get him home; if we had tied him up it might have put him into a state that would have wrecked that possibility. Cap and I talked about it, but we didn't get anywhere." He took a turn around the warehouse. "Well, you go ahead out. Shoot as many as you can, enjoy yourself, take pictures . . . Cap or I will probably join you later."

"Yes, sir," Geordie said. He got a rifle and the camera and started for the freshwater pond.

There was a good wind and the surf was high and beautiful as it broke over the reef but Geordie paid little attention to it; the blackest depression he had ever known had settled upon him. He loved the island and the things he had done and seen. And he had believed that they were going to save it. He saw now, in the light of what Doc said, that his enthusiasm had made him too naive. It was true that they hadn't been sufficiently prepared. He didn't know who was basically at fault, but that didn't make much difference now; what shook him was that men who knew far better than he what should have been done had been as naive as he. That was enough by itself, and then Catton had been piled on top of it. The feeling of apprehension that he generated, the overhanging expectation of trouble or even disaster, was constant and inescapable. He was quiet for the moment, but how much longer would he be? None of them could get away from this thought, and even the constant surveillance might relax for a moment at the wrong time.

Geordie's life had been spent among normal people; he had had no experience with an abnormality such as this, and because he had no key to it his imagination conjured up things that frightened him. Catton had never liked him, and several times lately he had caught Catton looking at him with narrowed eyes. What went on in his mind, why did he look like that?

He was approaching the freshwater pond by this time and soon he was in the midst of a great storm of sooty terns; their numbers had vastly increased in the last day or so. Their crying filled his ears and echoed inside his head, and their innumerable company wheeled around him like a whirlwind; they forced him out of his gloomy concentration. He couldn't maintain it in the midst of so much vivid, tumultuous energy, and he began to get outside himself again. When he passed the pond he saw five teal on it. One of them was separate from the others and looked puffed up and cold; he hoped that it wasn't sick or going to die. A little further on he came out on the south beach and saw that the gray-backed terns had started to nest.

There was a part of one colony that was sitting at the very edge of the water and some of the birds were hovering over it, and he realized as he watched that the wind was on shore and was driving the ocean over their nesting places. When he got a little closer he could see eggs rolling around in the backwash. The tide was almost at its high, and the thought came to him that other terns would nest there when the tide went out and he would be able to gather fresh, newly laid eggs. They could be a great help to their diminishing supplies. The urgent life around him, the sun and the wind, had taken hold of him. He took some pictures, and went along the beach. He walked to the northern point where the offshore wind was raising a splendid surf, and sat down and watched it for awhile. As he watched the great combers running in, cresting against the sky trailing plumes of spray, and crashing down in gleaming white, he thought for the first time in many days of home, and wondered what his father would have done in the matter of Catton.

He didn't want to go back to the cottage any sooner than he had to and decided to shoot rabbits until the tide was low again, when he could see if the terns had laid enough eggs to collect a dozen or so. He concentrated on the rabbits for several hours and managed to kill thirty-five of them. He finally decided he had better go back; Doc had asked him to check in occasionally. He cut across the island, and as he approached the cottage he could see Cap and Catton walking about. It was just about then that a rabbit jumped up in front of him, ran a little way toward the freshwater pond and stopped. It was a long shot, but he took it. The rabbit wasn't killed; it rolled over, got to its feet, and made a staggering run toward the two men. It was too shocked and hurt to see them and ran straight for them; it was almost upon them when it stopped. Geordie was running after it to finish it, and was close enough to see Catton start forward and put his foot on it.

He had apparently only stepped on its leg, and the unfortunate beast flopped about trying to escape him. It began to scream, sharp, piercing cries of pain and terror, and Catton began to kick at it with his other foot. He was clumsy about it, for the nervous involvement was still with him; it was a grotesque business, but what appalled Geordie was his expression of pleasure. He was enjoying the animal's distress and outcry, and he was not trying to kill it so much as to make it suffer more. Cap stood for a moment staring at him and then ran a few steps, picked up a stick, ran back, and whacked the animal on the head. It stopped struggling, Catton stepped off it reluctantly, and Cap took him by the arm and led him off toward the pond.

Geordie had stopped; he stood there, with the rabbit's screams still seeming to echo in his ears, and then saw Doc standing on the steps. They walked toward each other and met near the rabbit. Neither of them wanted to look at it.

"I wonder if he would like to have any of us in the same situation as the rabbit?" Doc said.

"Did you see his face?" Geordie asked.

"No," Doc said. "But I didn't have to. I'm not at all sure that Cap's string to his door is enough of a safeguard any more. Cap and I had better spell each other during the nights.

"I'll do it too." Geordie said. "I've been let off too much, so please don't tell me that I can't. I can stay awake a few hours, and give each of you more sleep."

"All right," Doc said. "I'll arrange things with Cap. If you hear anything at all while it's your turn, wake us both. Yell, do anything."

"Yes, sir. I guess I'd better do something about this rabbit in the meanwhile."

Geordie went to bury it before starting his preparations for dinner, for he wanted it out of sight.

TWENTY THREE

The days and nights passed in uneasy progression toward the time of KITTIWAKE's arrival, and as though in irony the weather grew even more delightful, cool and sunny; it was the beginning of the best time of year on Laysan. Thousands more sooty terns came in from the sea, and the shearwaters increased; their moanings could be heard anywhere during the hours of darkness. There were more tropic birds and fairy terns, and red-footed boobies began to nest. The gray-backed terns, as Geordie discovered, laid eggs with pink yolks; he never quite grew accustomed to pink omelettes, and wished mightily that he could make a pink cake.

During his watches in the night, when all was quiet except the shearwaters, the moans and squalls of these birds were like an accompaniment to his thoughts of protests and regret that their last days, which could have been so pleasant, were clouded by Catton's presence and affliction, by the tension of not knowing what he might do or when he might do it. Since the episode of the rabbit he had been calm enough, but it was an uneasy calmness; there seemed to be a waiting quality about it. Their lives and their work were circumscribed and limited by it and everything slowed down. They had trouble with some of their skins, for beetles got into them; meals were tasteless and lacking in variety. If any of them went anywhere it was with the feeling that they should soon be getting back, and the carefree companionship of their fishing, swimming, and exploration parties was gone.

Geordie kept busy reconstructing boxes from the old, broken boxes left by the Japanese hunters and packing them, collecting sand and grasses for Dr. Black and as many eggs and specimens as he could, and taking pictures and making notes on bird behavior. He spent as much time as he could shooting rabbits, and was joined by Cap and Doc as often as they were free. He finally found the other camera that Doc had lost on the ground below the nesting frigate birds, but the weather had pretty well finished it. He and Doc built a traveling pen for the rails, and he fished a little for the kitchen; at another very low tide he caught some crayfish with a long-handled net that he had devised, and they had a banquet. He dug out some shearwater and petrel eggs, for the petrels, which he thought had been pretty well wiped out by the blowing sand, once again seemed as thick as they had been originally.

In all these enterprises there was a pleasure tinged

with melancholy, so that sometimes they seemed to be made-work, a sort of marking time, for the joy had gone out of the adventure. The long-winged albatrosses coming in from the sea, the rakish, piratical, soaring frigates, the terns and tropic birds and all the other multitudinous winged life was still beautiful and endlessly interesting to watch, but his thoughts turned increasingly toward home and the mail that KITTIWAKE would bring him.

One day there was a little flock of red phalaropes on the beach, and he collected one of them. It was a female just coming into the bright breeding plumage, a trim, handsome little bird, of a species not well known because it spends most of its life far at sea, skimming the waves and coming down to float like a little gull at rest, migrating back to the lonely high Arctic to nest on the Alaskan tundra or in Siberia. It was a cousin to the Wilson's phalarope that he and Spence had shot, the one he had on his desk at home; and as he held it, there skirted on the edge of his mind, to be swiftly suppressed, the question of whether this was the life he really wanted after all.

In a day or two now KITTIWAKE was due, and their packing was about finished. The boxes of skins and skeletons, eggs and shells and other things they had gathered were in the dismantled workshop in the warehouse, ready to be taken to the ship. With what little ammunition they had left they shot rabbits. Geordie did more of this than anyone else, for Catton had become restless and Doc and Cap spent most of their time near him, or within hail of each other.

He roamed the island, intent on getting his last impressions of it, of fixing it all in his mind beyond any forgetting, although he knew he would never forget it. It would be in his mind forever, until the day he died: the sweep of the lagoon with its nesting flats dotted with albatrosses, the lovely fairy terns that came to hover before him like dark-eyed little disembodied spirits, the moaning of the shearwaters, the boundless sky and the boundless sea and the freedom they had had for awhile. He had a thick book of notes and a great many excellent pictures, but the color and movement and the things he had felt would be inside his mortal skull and he wanted them fixed and sure.

The morning of the day that KITTIWAKE was due the sea was rough and boisterous, breaking high on the reef; if she reached her anchorage off the island no boat would be able to make the passage. They looked for her occasionally but hadn't sighted her by lunch time, and thought the weather might have held her up. In the middle of the afternoon Geordie decided to pay a last visit to the freshwater pond, and picked up a rifle and went off. When he was near it a frigate bird that was soaring high above him slid down the air and skimmed the surface for a drink, rose on the wind and was whisked high again, black, rakish, and beautiful in its mastery of its element.

As he approached the margin of the pond Geordie saw a dark shape lying near the water, and coming up to it saw that it was a dead Laysan teal. It was probably the sick one he had noticed a few days ago; when he picked it up it was still slightly warm and limp, and had probably died within the hour. He was very sorry to see it dead, for now there were only six of them so far as he knew in all the world. At the same time he was delighted to get it; it was a treasure, for there were so few skins anywhere. He took it to the south beach, where he was able to collect twenty-three terns' eggs for supper, and turned back toward the cottage with the eggs inside his shirt.

He was so happy in his luck at finding the teal that he carried it by the legs for all to see. There was no one in the cottage and he went around to the back. Cap, Doc, and Catton were standing there, looking out to sea; KITTIWAKE had come over the horizon, and they were all looking at her. Doc turned, and Geordie held up the teal and said: "Lucky me! I found it dead."

Doc's face lighted up, and then quickly changed. His hand started to come up, to motion Geordie to silence or wave him away, but it was too late. Cap and Catton had heard Geordie speak, and they also turned. Catton stared at Geordie and at the teal, and then became very agitated.

"He shot it!" he exclaimed. "He shot it! He shot it, and all your wretched, cheating lies have come to nothing, for he brings it here for me to see! I knew it! Didn't I say? Now the ship comes in, there's no reason to wait, and now—"

His face contorted, he made a step forward, and Doc took him by one arm and Cap took him by the other. He struggled a moment and suddenly became still; hunched, hanging on the restraining arms, he looked like a trapped animal and showed his teeth.

"I didn't shoot it," Geordie said, appalled at his own foolishness. "I found it dead. It's been sick for a few days, I saw it away from the others . . ."

"It's limp, it's newly dead!" Catton said, and his voice rose almost to a screech. "Oh, liars! Oh, thieves!" He tried again to pull away, and once more gave up.

"Take it away," Doc said, and freed Geordie from the paralysis that had fallen upon him.

He ran around to the kitchen, took the eggs out of his shirt, found a sharp knife there, and ran on until he was over the crest of the rise around the lagoon. He didn't stop until he was on the flats, and dropped down. He was panting and shaking, the flats blurred on his sight, and his stomach seemed to be rising into his throat; he sat for a moment and then sprawled full length, with his head on his arms.

Presently, calmer now and filled with a sort of despairing regret at his own stupidity, he sat up again. He wondered what he should do and then thought that he would have to stay here, stay away from the cottage until the boat came in. He couldn't go back, he would have to leave Doc and Cap alone with Catton to do what they could with him now that he had aroused the man. He rocked to and fro in his distress, not knowing that he did it. "I should have known," he said. "Oh, I should have known." Then he saw the teal beside him and began to skin it, having trouble because of the trembling of his hands.

Some time later Doc found him there, sitting on the ground and staring at the teal skin in his lap. Doc sat down beside him, and put a hand on his shoulder.

"Geordie," he said. "Geordie, don't take it so hard, boy."

"Doc," he said miserably. "How could I have been such a fool?"

"Easy does it," Doc said. "We finally got a stiff shot of morphine into him, enough to knock out a horse, and he's sleeping now. I don't know whether they'll get through the reef tomorrow. We'll probably keep him under until the boat gets in. After that we'll have help, and he'll be so seasick he'll be no trouble anyhow. Come on, let's go back."

"I can't face Cap," Geordie said. "I'll never be able to face him again."

"Nonsense," Doc said heartily. "Cap holds nothing

against you. We understand thoroughly how excited you were about the teal. I'd probably have done the same thing."

"No, you're wiser than that. You'd never be that stupid, you never have been."

"Haven't I?" Doc said. "Come, get up, and let's go back. Were they tern eggs in your shirt? I'm ready for another omelette, and so are you."

When the sun went down the sea was still running high and a cloud bank lay on the western horizon; if it moved off, Cap thought, the wind and the sea might drop by morning and let the boat through the reef. "If it doesn't," he said, "the day after will probably be all right. I'll keep the needle handy, in any event, if we have to wait another day or so, but I think we'll keep watch tonight anyhow. Would you like the first one, Geordie?"

"Yes, sir," Geordie said. "I don't think I'll go to sleep very easily anyhow."

"You shouldn't feel bad," Cap said. "If you sinned at all, you made it up with that omelette. I didn't even mind the lack of salt. I'm going to sack out. Call Doc when your shift's over, and stop blaming yourself. Good night."

They said good night to him, and presently Doc went off to bed too. Geordie could hear him moving around as he undressed and he could hear the creak of the cot as he lay down on it. Quiet fell on the cottage. There was only one lamp burning now, low, and as it was a warm night Geordie presently got up and opened the door, which they had curtained to keep the petrels out. He could hear the shearwaters moaning, and after he had looked in quietly on Catton he sat down again; presently a petrel walked in the door. It walked across the floor, climbed up Geordie's leg, and sat on his knee looking at him. Then it moved up his thigh and started to scramble to his shoulder; he caught it gently, stroked it a little, and got up once more and tossed it outside into the air again.

Time passed slowly after that and Geordie, tired by the emotions and the events of the day, sat without thought, patiently waiting for his watch to be up. Finally it was, and he looked in on the sleeping Catton again, woke Doc, and went into his room. He was so tired by now that he dropped onto his cot without taking his clothes off, and was soon asleep.

Later he awoke with a start. It seemed to him that he had been dreaming, but he couldn't remember a dream; for a moment he lay listening, with a strange uneasiness. The house was quiet, but the uneasiness grew stronger, and after a moment he got up, quietly cracked his door, and looked into the living room. He had slept through Doc's turn and now Cap was on watch. Cap was sitting in a chair, facing Catton's door; he had turned up the light a little and was reading, and as Geordie looked he turned a page. He wasn't asleep. Geordie softly closed the door again, but now the uneasiness seemed stronger than ever, it ran along his nerves, and he went to the window next to the warehouse and moved the curtain aside and looked out.

For a moment he couldn't see anything in the darkness, and then he realized that there was a ghostly, disembodied, flickering sort of glow. His hair stood up, for at first he didn't connect it with anything and in his condition thought at first of some sort of supernatural manifestation; then he thought of fire. He dropped the curtain and moved quickly out into the living room, and Cap heard him and looked around.

"Cap!" he shouted. "Cap, something's happening out there!"

He didn't finish, because Cap stood up quickly and went to Catton's door. He opened it, and whirled around.

"He's gone!" he said. "Come on!"

They ran out of the house. There was no front on the warehouse, and as they came before it they could see the fire in the loose piles of dried grass they had gathered to stuff around boxes and things in their packing. It was already beginning to catch on the board walls.

"We'll have to get the boxes out," Cap said. "Get Doc."

Geordie ran into the cottage and through Doc's door and shook him awake. "Fire!" he said. "Fire in the warehouse!"

Doc jumped up and they ran out together. The fire was brighter now, and Cap had found a shovel and was throwing sand over the boxes and scattering the straw; the old dry planks of the wall were beginning to blaze. "The boxes!" Cap shouted at them. "Get the boxes out!"

Geordie and Doc ran into the fire, dodging the blazing straw and kicking it away, and began dragging the boxes out. They worked like madmen, dodging each other and Cap, now in the darkness and now in the firelight, gasping and tugging and stumbling about in their anxiety to save the boxes, and as Geordie ran back in from one of his trips he saw a figure suddenly appear and grapple with Cap and then he saw Doc running up and fell it with a blow.

"Get hold of him!" Doc shouted, and stooped to get his hands on the figure's head. Geordie ran up and felt around in the flickering light for the feet, and they lugged their burden out into the darkness and ran back.

This lost them the last two boxes, for while they were carrying Catton out the fire had progressed too much for them to go in again. They gave it up and withdrew a little and stood together, spent and gasping, sweating and begrimed and black like three infernal figures resting a moment from their demonic labors. The roof had caught fire, and the light from the mounting flames caught at the pale undersides of a few petrels that passed or hovered and seemed like minor demons flitting by.

"Pretty soon the house will begin to go too," Cap said. "We'd better save what we can out of it." He felt his pockets. "My needle," he said. "It's on the table. I'll get it and give him another shot. Stay with him until I get back, and then we'll get what we can out of the house." He turned and trotted off toward the cottage.

The sky began to pale, and in the wan, strengthening light they sat on the ground, leaning against boxes, and wearily contemplated the smoking ruins of the cottage and the warehouses. Soon the birds that took their prey at sea—the squid that came to the surface during the hours of darkness—would be off, to return after their hunting, and the day birds would begin to stir. Cap sat nodding a little way off beside Catton, over whose recumbent figure he had arranged a blanket. Half an hour earlier he had joined them for a few minutes and talked about Catton. "I don't know how he woke from the shot I gave him," he'd said, "or how he got out. I had to go out front for a minute or two, and maybe he crept out then and hid beside the door. It was pretty dark, but I thought I was watching all the time. I looked in on him just before I went . . . I'm sorry, but it doesn't make any difference now."

"None of it makes any difference now," Doc had said. "We could have tied him up or knocked him on the head and tossed him into the sea, but we're men of good will. How could we gauge him? He's lost in a maze we lack a map for, and I'm glad nothing worse happened. We've got most of the boxes, and that's the important thing. Don't blame yourself, man."

"Thanks for those kind words," Cap had said, and gone back to Catton again.

Geordie hadn't said anything. Cold and dispirited, worn out by the past day and the night, he had been wrapped in his own thoughts and depressed by the questions within him. He sat silent for awhile longer, shivering a little, ranging far back through the years and the things he had done and thought, and his efforts to find a way for himself; he thought of his father and how well Alfred Sutton had been able to control *his* life and how totally unable he seemed to control his own. He looked at the burned and smoking ruin in front of him and then around the island in the gathering light. It was flat and sandy, soon to be sandier still, a desert of blowing sand and a ruin itself, and revulsion filled him.

"Doc," he said. "Doc, I'm going to be a lawyer."

Doc turned a grimy face, and looked at him for a long moment. "So," he said quietly. "Go on."

"Doc, I love this life," Geordie said, beginning slowly, trying to say what was in his heart, for he owed Doc a great deal, "but there are too many things about it that can't be controlled. At almost every point the success of what we set out to do depended on someone else, and at almost every point they let us down. And now that we've failed it will probably take too many years, as you've said, for the bureaucrats to get around to doing anything so someone else can fix it. Doc, there are too many disinterested people that everything depends on for it to work. I don't think I could stand it, I'd finally get discouraged and give up, and then there would be nothing. It would be awful to know that you'd wasted your life."

He fell silent and looked at Doc beseechingly, as

though asking him to understand, and then dropped his glance to the sandy ground.

Doc didn't say anything for a time. "Yes," he began finally, in a quiet tone. "You've got it all there. It might even be worse than that. It certainly has this time, and it may be again. It's almost sure to be this way again, some-time or other."

He stopped and looked at Geordie's face, but it seemed closed and unresponsive to him. He wondered what to say next, or what to do. Ever since Geordie had found the carriage and saved his life in the blizzard he had watched and loved the boy like a son, and he knew that in Geordie's present mood he might make a decision that would waste his life. *Ah, the young,* he thought, *who would go through that again?*

Just then two honey eaters, obviously interested in each other, landed on the furthermost box and the slant-ing light gleamed on their brilliant vermilion feathers. Geordie had told him once that they were his favorite birds on the island. "Look," he said, and put his hand on Geordie's shoulder. "Look behind you."

Geordie turned and looked, and one of the birds began to sing. Geordie's eyes lighted up and his face changed; he looked quickly at Doc and smiled, and looked back again. "Oh, Doc," he said, "aren't they beautiful?"

"Beautiful," Doc said. "They'll go away in a minute and we'll go away soon, probably forever, and you can give them up. You'll give up the others too, all of them, and never think of them again except for an hour or two on Sunday afternoons on a short walk after dinner. There are so many beautiful things all over the earth, and a vast amount of good work to be done, but you'll have to give that up too."

"What?" Geordie asked. The honey eaters flew away,

flashing like little jewels in the sun, and he turned to Doc. He stared at his friend for a long moment, not really seeing him; he was looking into himself. Finally he shook his head as though to clear it. "No," he said. "I can't give it up. I can't ever give it up." He smiled.

Doc smiled back at him. "Good," he said, and let it go at that. "You know, I think the wind's dropping. In another hour or two they'll probably lower a boat."

Price showed no human emotion as he shoved Johansson out of the jailhouse. Johansson looked around, wondering why Price had let him out. Then it hit him. The street was empty, devoid of people.

No witnesses, a small voice cautioned him.

"You understand I can't just let you go," Price said. "Your next girl would be on my head, then, and the others after that. It can't go on."

Johansson turned to face the marshal. "I don't unnerstant," he lied. In fact, he understood all too well.

"I was distracted," Price explained, with an unsettling chill in his voice. "I let my guard down or forgot to lock the cell. Who knows how these things happen? Anyway, you decided to make a run for it."

Price drew his Colt and thumbed the hammer back. "So, run."

Johansson's face dropped. "You can't do zis!"

Price raised the pistol. "It's done."

Titles by Lyle Brandt

VENGEANCE GUN

LYLE BRANDT

BERKLEY BOOKS, NEW YORK

This is a work of fiction. Names, characters, places, and incidents either are the product of the author's imagination or are used fictitiously, and any resemblance to actual persons, living or dead, business establishments, events, or locales is entirely coincidental.

VENGEANCE GUN

A Berkley Book / published by arrangement with the author

PRINTING HISTORY
Berkley edition / July 2004

Copyright © 2004 by Michael Newton.
Cover design by Jill Boltin.
Interior text design by Julie Rogers.

For information address: The Berkley Publishing Group,
a division of Penguin Group (USA) Inc.,
375 Hudson Street, New York, New York 10014.

ISBN: 0-425-19383-7

BERKLEY®
Berkley Books are published by The Berkley Publishing Group,
a division of Penguin Group (USA) Inc.,
375 Hudson Street, New York, New York 10014.
BERKLEY and the "B" design
are trademarks belonging to Penguin Group (USA) Inc.

PRINTED IN THE UNITED STATES OF AMERICA

10 9 8 7 6 5 4 3 2 1

Rincon, Texas, was a played-out mining town. It was located seventy-odd miles northwest of New Harmony, squatting on the southern slope of the Davis Mountains, in Jeff Davis County. Its silver deposits had dried up years ago, leaving a handful of miners behind to scratch leftovers from the earth, dreaming about a mother lode they'd never find. A few of the diehards had turned their hands to raising scrawny cattle, stubbornly clinging to hope that Rincon would survive.

Matthew Price rode into town at sunset, from the south. He'd been three days on the trail, the first one leading him astray until he found a bartender in Marathon who remembered Oskar Johansson. The Swede was hard to miss at six feet five, with wavy white-blond hair and an accent so thick that he could've been fresh off the boat. Between cheap shots of red-eye, Johansson had told the bartender that he might try his luck in Rincon, mining silver.

Price couldn't be sure if the pointer was meant to mislead him, or if it was simply one more of Johansson's colossally stupid mistakes. The first had been raping a twelve-year-old girl. The second was thinking that he could outrun Matthew Price.

In another life, the crime would've disgusted Price without touching him personally. He might've joined a posse for the hell of it, if he had nothing else to do and if the sheriff didn't mind him pitching in, but tracking bad men had not been his job.

In those days, Price had saved his ammunition for jobs that put cash in his pocket—and for men who hunted him.

All that had changed in New Harmony, when he'd repaid a life-saving favor and made a stand for something larger, something more important than himself. The badge he now wore was part of it, a twist of fate he'd never have imagined in his wildest fever dreams. But mostly, Price acknowledged to himself, the change was due to Mary Hudson.

The doctor had saved his life in more ways than one.

And it was time to pay one more installment on that debt.

Price rode in past shops that might've been closed for the night or forever. He didn't know which. Didn't care. Rincon's slow drift into nothing was someone else's problem. Price had a fix on the saloon, urging his Appaloosa onward with a light flick of the reins, the barest pressure from his heels.

The Silverado had been stylish once, but it was on the decline now and fading fast. Its sign was barely legible, sun-bleached and weathered from bright crimson to a kind of Gila-monster pink, with bare wood showing through in scattered patches. Broad windows spilled lamplight into the street, but one of them was broken, wearing a crude wooden patch in the lower left-hand corner. The piano was badly out of tune, and Price marveled that anyone left in this rat hole could play it at all.

He dismounted, trusting the Appaloosa to stand on its own, and stepped onto the low wooden sidewalk, moving to one side of the bat-wing doors. Johansson stood out at one end of the bar, stoop-shouldered, in dour conversation with a shorter, darker man. The friend was bearded, with an unwashed face. Price couldn't see from where he stood if either man was armed, but he counted eleven other drinkers in the place, all packing iron.

Johansson wasn't drunk yet, from the look of him. Price estimated that he wouldn't leave the small town's only barroom for a while. There was time for one more brief delay.

Price scanned the street as darkness settled in, spotting the barbershop because it had a faint light showing through its window, maybe someone working in the back. Price walked the Appaloosa down that way and tied it to a hitching post outside the shop. The price of baths had been revised in paint of different shades until it settled at a dime. Throw in a shave, and Price could still get out for half a dollar.

The door was locked, and there was no immediate response to his first knock. He thought he saw a shadow moving in the doorway to the shop's back room, but that could be a trick of candlelight. Price tried again, and this time brought the ancient, long-faced barber out of hiding. He unlatched the door and opened it, eyes fixed on Price's badge for a moment before they found his face.

"Want something, Marshal?"

"A bath and a shave," Price replied.

"We're closed."

"Think one of you could open up, to make a dollar?"

The barber cut a sidelong glance toward his window, maybe wondering if his late visitor had missed the prices listed there. "You say a dollar?"

"For a bath and shave."

"I reckon we can handle that. Shave first?"

"Sounds good."

The barber locked them in and led Price to the small shop's single chair. Price doffed his hat and sat down, while the old man lit a lamp and mixed a cup of lather for his face. The wet towel that preceded it was hot enough to make Price think the shop had only closed within the past half hour or so. He sat and watched the dark street while the barber stropped his razor, then leaned back and closed his eyes.

Johansson might've found a drinking crony at the Silverado, but he hadn't been in Rincon long enough to make a decent friend, despite his outward charm and gift of gab. It had been different in New Harmony, the six weeks that he'd spent there, working at the livery.

Scene of the crime, Price thought, and wondered how the townsfolk could've been so wrong about Johansson. That was spilt milk now, of course, and Price himself had done no better when it came to seeing past the Swede's perpetually smiling mask. None of them recognized the creature lurking underneath, and now it was too late for April Ling.

But not too late to make Johansson pay.

Price wasn't sure what waited for the rapist in New Harmony. It wouldn't be a lynching rope, that much he knew, but there'd been no real crime to speak of in the five months he'd been marshal. He supposed they'd lock

Johansson up and send out for the circuit judge, or maybe ship him to the county seat for trial.

Unless Johansson made it simple and decided to resist arrest.

The shave was close and smooth, the bath just hot enough to cut a layer of clinging trail dust from his body. Price made sure his pistol rested on a stool beside the big claw-footed tub while he was bathing, never out of reach. He had no reason to expect an ambush, but he likewise had no reason to relax his guard.

When he was dressed again, with the barber paid and duly satisfied, Price left the shop and spent a moment on the sidewalk. It was full dark now, the Silverado's windows seeming lit with greater promise than they had possessed when he rode into town. It was illusory, but fantasies kept bartenders in business. One way or another, Price supposed Rincon's committed drinkers would be treated to a show this night.

The Appaloosa whinnied softly as Price took the reins in hand and led it slowly back toward the saloon.

"Anudder viskey here," Oskar Johansson told the barkeep.

"Make it two," his squat companion said.

The bearded man was Harley Gilson, an acquaintance of forty-eight hours or so. He shared Johansson's taste for whiskey, and had thus become the rough approximation of a friend. After the second round of drinks they'd shared, he had informed Johansson that there was no silver to be excavated from the earth within a hundred miles of Rincon, at the very least, and precious little else besides. It would've been a wasted trip, then, but at least he wasn't sitting in a jail cell in New Harmony.

Johansson didn't try to puzzle out what he had done to April Ling. It happened every now and then, when he was left alone with females of a certain tender age. There seemed to be no reason for it, but he'd given up trying to understand the urge after the third or fourth time he'd been driven to a lapse in judgment by the yearnings of his flesh. It kept him moving, out of Arkansas and Oklahoma, now across the width of Texas, but Johansson reckoned it was still a great big country, filled with opportunities.

He'd make a fresh start somewhere else, maybe in Arizona or New Mexico. If Gilson rode along with him, Johansson thought he'd have a better chance of being overlooked by any Texas lawmen he encountered, just in case the people of New Harmony had sounded an alarm.

The bartender poured shots of liquid fire for both men, waiting for their coins before he moved away. It was Johansson's turn to buy, Gilson saluting him before he drained his glass.

"You're a gentleman, Oskar."

"It's nudding."

"It's a favor that I won't forget," Gilson replied.

Johansson sipped his whiskey, nursing it. Gilson's appreciative mood might run out when the liquor did. It was as good a time as any to raise the subject of their traveling together for a bit, at least until they reached El Paso and Johansson could decide which direction he favored from there.

"I been tinking," he began—but then a voice somewhere behind him cut him off.

"Oskar Johansson."

That was trouble, even though he didn't recognize the voice. Johansson swiveled on his heel, one foot still planted on the brass bar rail. The belly gun tucked underneath his sheepskin jacket seemed to take on extra weight as he identified the speaker.

Matthew Price.

Johansson somehow found the strength to speak. "Marzhal. Vat brinks you here?"

"You need to ask?"

Johansson saw that Price had chosen his position well. The Silverado's other customers were all off to his right, Johansson's left, with no one sitting in the line of fire. Price stood at ease, looking refreshed despite what must have been a two- or three-day journey from New Harmony.

"Marshal, you say?" Gilson had stepped back from the bar and stood beside Johansson, facing Price. "Rincon ain't had no lawman for a year and something."

"That's a fact," somebody said from the far end of the bar.

Johansson felt a little better, knowing he had someone on his side. A little, but not much.

"I came for you, Oskar," Price said. "If somebody else wants a piece of it, that's all right, too."

"This gentleman's a friend of mine," said Gilson.

"None too choosy, are you?"

Gilson bristled. "What's that s'posed to mean?"

"It means your friend is wanted in New Harmony for raping a twelve-year-old girl. She nearly got away, but Oskar broke her arm and knocked her out cold before the rest of it."

The room was deathly still. Johansson felt the weight of hostile eyes, Gilson's among them.

"I mean to take him back for trial," Price told the silent barroom, "one way or another. Anybody wants to die helping a rapist, now's your chance."

Johansson knew he'd lost the room when Gilson edged

away from him. "None a my business," Gilson said, giving the marshal a wide berth as he maneuvered toward the door.

"Anybody else?" Price asked. Dead silence answered him. "Just you and me, Oskar. You want to try that Smith & Wesson?"

"I don't zink so."

"Set it on the bar, then. Use your left hand, nice and easy."

Johansson did as he was told. There was a chance they wouldn't hang him in New Harmony, but Price would surely kill him where he stood, without a second thought.

"Okay, Marzhal. I go vit you."

"Good choice," Price said. "I hope you didn't sell your horse to buy that whiskey. It's a long walk home."

The cat bumped Mary Hudson's elbow as she was about to scrape the contents of her plate back into the stew pot. She glanced at him, smiling, then set the bowl down on the counter.

"All right, then," she decided. "But you're getting fat."

The cat eyed her reproachfully, as if insulted, then set to work cleaning the bowl. Eyes closed in blissful concentration, he consumed the remnants of her lunch.

Time to go.

She had finished with her patients for the morning and had no appointments scheduled for the afternoon. In point of fact, New Harmony's residents rarely made appointments to see the town's only physician. They took fair health for granted, then came by unannounced at any hour of the day or night if some discomfort got the better of them. An average summer day was likely to include heatstroke, backache, assorted sprains and fractures, plus the occasional snakebite or scorpion sting. There'd been a heart stroke in April, and a burst appendix near the end of May.

Life and death on the prairie.

It was a far cry from city practice, where she had gone days, sometimes weeks, without seeing a patient. She'd searched long and hard for a place where her skills would be valued without regard to gender, and she'd found it in New Harmony.

Five months ago, she'd also found Matt Price.

He'd been her patient first, and not the most cooperative one at that, but she'd prevailed with some adjustments to her standard bedside manner and the rest, as someone said, was history. Their domestic arrangement would've caused a scandal most places, and it had raised some eyebrows even in New Harmony, but a community of outcasts was more prone to make allowances.

Besides, the town owed Price a debt that it could never quite repay.

She missed Matthew, now that he was gone to fetch Oskar Johansson. It was an ugly job, but unavoidable. Mary had no quarrel with the mission—she had treated April and had seen the damage that was done—but it took Price out of sight and out of reach. She'd grown accustomed to having him underfoot, or else down the street in the office the town had provided.

Most of all she missed him at the table during meals.

And in their bed.

"Not now," she muttered, and E.T. glanced up from scouring her bowl, then bent back to his work. He seemed to understand that humans sometimes held one-sided conversations with themselves and it was nothing to concern a cat.

The banking errand was a bit of busy work, devised as much to let her get outside and stretch her legs as to make sure she had sufficient money for the holiday weekend. There wasn't much to splurge on in New Harmony, but she was thinking of a new dress to inspire Matthew when he finally came home.

Something designed to wind up crumpled on the bedroom floor.

"Be good," she told the cat. "I'll be right back."

She didn't lock the door. Locking it was a habit she had broken sometime since arriving in New Harmony. She might return to find a patient sitting in her waiting room, but that's what waiting rooms were for. She was secure in the belief that none of them would rifle through her private things or let E.T. outside. If called upon to save her life by pointing to a thief in town, she would be lost.

The sidewalk's meager shade did nothing to relieve the day's oppressive heat. Across the street, Ardell Carver was running in the opposite direction, knees and elbows pumping. Mary wondered where he found the energy on a day like this, but didn't think to wonder what his errand was.

The urgency of youth.

At that age, every little thing was life-or-death.

The bank was on her side of Main Street, two blocks down. She saw a man outside the bank, slouching astride a sorrel mare. He held four other horses by their drooping reins and kept his face averted as she moved along the sidewalk. Dark hair spilled across his collar at the back, oily and lank.

She might have turned around right then, and so changed everything, but she had very nearly outgrown fear itself these past few months. A hint of apprehension nagged her as she reached the bank's front door, but she ignored it. Passing through, she heard the mounted stranger whistle at her back and knew, too late, that she had made a critical mistake.

The men who turned to face her as she entered all had pistols in their hands.

Lucius Carver was nearly finished with the next-to-last table. Like the others, it was twelve feet long and solid, though a dozen well-placed hammer strokes would break it down again and free the lumber up for other use. Twelve spacious tables had been ordered for the Independence Day festivities, but there'd be no place fit for storing them come Monday morning, and a frugal carpenter knew better than to waste supplies.

He wasn't *just* a carpenter, of course. From August through the end of May he was New Harmony's primary schoolteacher, a trade he'd acquired from his father and practiced at no small risk in Louisiana, before leading his family to Texas. There were no regrets on that score, now that all was said and done, but Carver still enjoyed diversity. It pleased him to create objects of value with his own two hands.

Sometimes he wished Ardell would show more interest in the building side of things, but children had a way of finding their own passions in life. Carver believed in guidance, and a firm hand when needed, but he didn't hold with forcing youngsters to pursue a family trade. The job a boy or man was forced to do might hold him for a while, but it would never touch his soul.

Not for the good, at least.

Carver was reaching for his plane, to smooth a few rough edges, when Ardell burst in upon him from the street. The courtyard where he worked was open-air, beside the livery, but fenced around with six-foot oaken planks. Ardell came through the gate as if shot from a cannon, wide-eyed, gasping to regain his wind.

"Daddy! You gotta come right now!"

"I'm working, son."

"Don't matter!"

Carver frowned. "It *doesn't* matter, I believe you meant to say. What's so important right this minute?"

"Strangers at the bank," Ardell gasped out, still wheezing from his run. "They're robbing it, I think."

Strangers? Robbing the bank?

Carver set down his plane. "What makes you think that, son?"

"They leave one out, holding the horses, and the rest of 'em goes in."

Carver ignored the lapse in grammar this time. He felt a sudden chill, the midday heat be damned.

"I warn you, boy, if this is some tomfoolery—"

"It's not! Come quick!"

The first gunshot was muffled, maybe fired indoors, but it was unmistakable.

"You stay right here, Ardell. Hear me? Don't step outside this fence, no matter what."

"But Daddy, I—"

"Don't make me tell you twice!"

"No, sir."

Carver was cautious, stepping through the gate, into the open street. His Winchester was back at home, the other end of town, and fetching it meant passing by the bank. He didn't plan to rush that move if he could help it. Not with bullets already in flight.

Strangers.

That stood to reason, since he knew no one in town would try to rob the bank. There'd been a time when lookouts watched the road and an alarm bell would've hailed approaching riders, but there'd been no call for such defenses in the months since Matthew Price had risked his life to foil a robber baron's brutal land-grab. April Ling aside, there'd been no crime worth mentioning around New Harmony in all that time. Their vigilance had withered on the vine.

Three blocks due south, he saw a mounted rider holding four more horses by their reins, all tangled in his left hand, with a pistol in his right. The bank's front door flew open seconds later, spilling other men onto the sidewalk. All four brandished guns, and two of them—one black, the other red-faced underneath a silly little hat—were holding flour sacks.

Our money, Carver thought with sudden anger. *There it goes.* He had to do something, but what?

"Hold up!" he shouted, jogging empty-handed down the sidewalk toward the bank, his voice the only weapon he possessed. "Stop, thief!"

Four of the five were mounted now. The slowest of them, idling there beside his horse as if he had nothing to fear, swiveled around to face Carver. Damned if he wasn't smiling, in the shade cast by his hat's wide brim. He raised his pistol casually, as if lifting a hand to greet a friend.

Carver leapt for the nearest doorway as the stranger fired. He heard the bullet sizzle past him, and the broad front window of the dry-goods store came crashing down in jagged sheets.

Jesus!

The other bandits started firing randomly along the street. Carver stayed huddled where he was, praying that Ardell had had the sense to follow orders this one time. If they rode his way, passing out of town, he'd be an easy target, but the greater risk lay in retreating under fire.

They chose the southern road instead. Carver could tell by the receding sound of shots and hoofbeats as they fled. He risked a glance around the corner, just as David Proud Elk ran into the street down range and blazed off three rounds from his Henry rifle.

Wasted.

Trembling, Carver emerged from cover and moved swiftly toward the bank.

Johansson stayed quiet for most of their journey together, which suited Price down to the ground. He was new at manhunting—or rather the part where he brought his man back sitting up in a saddle, instead of tied lengthwise across it—but it didn't seem to be such dreadful work. The worst part, Price supposed, would be imagining the crimes of those he escorted from place to place.

No problem there.

Since leaving home at twelve years old, Price had witnessed every kind of cruelty one human being could inflict upon another. Some of it was personal, some business, and too much of it appeared to have no reason whatsoever. Price had learned to think no more about the motives for a hostile action than he needed to predict an enemy's next move. In general, he didn't brood over the pain of others, and the ghosts who came to him in dreams were all his own.

Their last meal on the trail was eaten in the saddle, with a canteen passed between them afterward. Johansson didn't care for jerky, but he ate it anyway, keeping his strength up for whatever he found waiting in New Harmony.

An hour short of nightfall Saturday, Price had his first glimpse of home since he'd ridden out on Tuesday at the crack of dawn. A mere five days away, and yet he missed it more than any place he'd ever known. Price recognized it as a weakness, something enemies could use to break him down, but at the moment any thought of danger seemed remote.

Night overtook them on the flats, casting its shadow on ahead, but there were lights to guide them in New Harmony, and they were getting closer all the time. Johansson may have entertained some fleeting thought of breaking free, but he was wise enough to know that Price would blast him from his saddle without thinking twice. He'd taken fear into his counsel and delayed too long. Whatever waited for him now would be as inevitable as the next day's sunrise.

Cursing April Ling, Johansson followed Price the last five miles into New Harmony.

Price hadn't been expecting anything specific, but the town felt *wrong,* somehow. It was too quiet for a weekend, he decided, and there was none of the patriotic disarray he might've expected from yesterday's July Fourth celebration. The people he passed riding in were grim-faced, their number perhaps ten percent of what Price had learned to expect on a Saturday night.

He wondered if it was Johansson, the sight of him back in their midst, but that didn't make sense. It explained the long faces all right, but it didn't account for the near-empty streets. No one in town had known the day, much less the hour, when Price would return with his prisoner. And if they had, he imagined, there would've been more folks than usual lining the sidewalks to gawk at the monster.

No, Price reasoned. Something else was keeping them indoors, and he didn't like the feel of it at all.

Ignoring the cold lump of dread in his stomach, Price rode directly to his office with the two small cells in back. The front door wasn't locked. Price kept no guns or ammunition in the office, and there wasn't anything to steal except the desk that took two men to lift. There were no other prisoners in residence. The Swede would have the whole place to himself.

Price let the Swede tie up his horse, maybe the last time he'd be doing it—or much of anything else—in this life. He didn't try to muscle Johansson inside, the way some lawmen might have done. That kind of play was either acted out for show or from pure meanness, and Price saw no point in either. He had no audience to speak of, as it was, and he was already distracted by the town's depressing atmosphere.

The metal ring with two large keys hung on a peg behind his desk, well out of reach from either of the cells. Both cages were identical, so Price picked one at random, opened it, and locked the door again behind Johansson.

"Supper may be late," he told the Swede. "I'll see what I can do."

"I'm not zo hungry anyvay," Johansson said.

"My cooking, just as well."

He wouldn't ask Mary to feed the prisoner. She'd helped him out with several others, rowdy drunks and such, but Price wanted her nowhere near Johansson. Even granting that the Swede preferred his females twenty-odd years younger, Price wasn't sure he could vouch for his own self-control if Johansson's sickness got the better of him and he favored Mary with some lewd remark. Or if he touched her.

Price thought about it, going out, and paused this time to lock the office door. Word might've spread through town already that the Swede was back, and while Price trusted nearly all New Harmony's inhabitants to keep their wits about them, there was no sense tempting fate. A lock could make the difference between Price holding Johansson for the circuit judge and jailing one of his newfound friends on a manslaughter charge.

He pocketed the key and angled off across the street toward Mary's house. He was surprised to find the windows dark, a silence that was almost physically oppressive leaking from the house. His Mary wasn't much for turning in at dusk, unless she wanted something more than simple sleep. Price smiled at that, pictured her waiting for him in their bed upstairs—and fetched up cold, remembering that Mary shouldn't even know he had returned.

The door was locked. Behind it, scratching faintly, urgently, Price heard the cat.

"E.T.?"

This time he raised a fist, like any proper stranger, but a sound of footsteps hurrying behind him made Price turn.

"She isn't there, Matthew," Yolanda Carver said.

"All right. Where is she, then?"

"We need to talk," Lucius replied.

2

They sat Price down and told it to him straight, as it was best to do and therefore seldom done. There'd been five strangers, nondescript beyond the fact that three of them were white men, one was black, the fifth most likely Mexican. Survivors from the bank recalled the leader's Southern accent and the bowler hat worn by his second in command. They'd stolen seven thousand dollars, give or take.

And Mary Hudson's life.

The Carvers didn't try to sugarcoat it for him. Price had seen enough death in his time, dispensed enough of it to others, that they didn't need to coddle him. Yolanda felt an urge to help him, even so.

"I don't believe she suffered, Matthew. One shot, coming through the door. From the expression on her face, I doubt she even recognized the danger."

That was something, anyway, if it were true. Price had

seen fellows shot from ambush who had dropped without a whimper, no expression on their faces but an echo of surprise. He'd wondered, after seeing two or three of them that way, exactly *what* surprised them. Was it Death? A flare of pain before the end? A sense of spirit separating from the flesh?

After he'd stared into the vacant eyes of six or seven men, dead by his hand, Price gave up wondering. The question didn't seem to matter anymore.

"I want to see her," Price declared.

The Carvers traded solemn looks. "Oh, Matthew," said Yolanda, "I don't think that's such a good idea."

"I *need* to see her." Price was on his feet before he finished speaking, brushing past his hosts as they rose from the kitchen table, following. He glimpsed Ardell, their oldest, watching from the dark slash of a cracked door to his left. The boy, discovered, stepped back out of sight and softly closed the door.

It was full dark outside, still warm, but in another hour or so the temperature would drop as always in the desert, losing twenty to thirty degrees from the peak heat of midday. Price scarcely noticed as he moved along the sidewalk toward the undertaker's parlor, situated near the southern end of Main Street. He was vaguely conscious of the Carvers coming on behind him, and he knew in a detached way that the population of the sidewalk opposite had tripled since he stood at Mary's door. If he had scanned the faces following his progress, Price would have known every person present in the street, but he ignored them.

There was only one face that he longed to see, and he had come too late to make a difference there.

Price caught the undertaker in his shirtsleeves, a breach of decorum that left the man flustered and stammering.

The stutter had been overcome with difficulty as a child, but it came back to him in stressful moments. Thankfully, the undertaker—Richard Greaves, a name Price once suspected was contrived to fit his occupation—seldom found himself uneasy in the presence of the dead or the bereaved. He was a master in such situations, poised and in control.

Until this night.

Greaves didn't tell the marshal that his shop was closed to visitors. He didn't stand in Price's way or try to block the Carvers from pursuing him inside. The undertaker knew Death when he saw it, and he had the sense to stand aside.

"Where is she?" Price demanded.

"If you'd follow me . . ."

The work was done, and no great effort needed, if the truth be told. Yolanda Carver had not lied about the doctor's injury to spare her lover's feelings. One shot to her rib cage from the left, the entry wound almost concealed beneath her breast. The impact had been stunning; death was instantaneous, or nearly so.

It was the sort of death a gunfighter might wish for, in the moments when he didn't feel invincible.

Price stood beside the casket, lightly varnished pine, and waited while Greaves raised the lid on small brass hinges. Mary might have been asleep, hair brushed to frame her poor wan face. She hadn't been that pale in life, but something in the undertaker's art stopped short of making her the woman he had known.

Price removed his hat, embarrassed that he hadn't done so earlier. He felt as if she might sit up and scold him for the lapse in manners, and that foolish notion nearly made him put the hat back on. It was too late for scolding, though, and when he bent to kiss her in the casket, Mary's lips were cold.

His heart likewise, as Price straightened and turned to face the Carvers. "Start from scratch," he said. "I want to hear it all again."

On Sunday morning, when the breakfast dishes had been cleared away and they were nearly late for church, Yolanda Carver heard her husband ask, "What did you really think of Matt last night?"

"He's grieving, Lucius. What do you expect?"

"That's what concerns me," he replied.

"Meaning?"

"Just think about it, Yollie."

She'd been thinking hard about it until after midnight, when fatigue at last had laid claim to her and she had slept. She could recall no dreams, and that turned out to be a blessing in itself.

"You think he'll try to hunt them down," she said.

"Don't you? We made him take that badge—the town, I mean—and it's his job to track them, like he did Johansson. But he'd do it anyway this time."

"You're worried he won't bring them back alive?"

Lucius stepped closer to her, working on his tie, and dropped his voice to keep the children from overhearing him. "That's not exactly right," he said. "I think I'm worried that I don't believe he should."

Yolanda frowned, but part of her relaxed at hearing Lucius speak her secret thoughts aloud. "Maybe you're right," she said. "Maybe he shouldn't bring them back."

"Yollie!"

"All right, what of it?" she replied, almost defiantly.

"They're thieves and murderers, the kind of men who stole our home and killed your father in Louisiana. I remember how you felt back then."

"You talked me out of it, as I recall."

"I *begged* you out of it, my love. But those were different times, and you're a different man. You're not Matt Price, thank God."

"I don't believe I'm hearing this."

Yolanda wasn't sure if she heard disapproval or amazement in her husband's tone, but she stood fast. "Believe it, then. That trash opened the gates of Hell when they killed Mary. I, for one, will not be mourning when they get their just desserts."

"Nobody told me you were such a scrapper," Lucius answered, smiling.

"You've been knowing it for fifteen years, and then some," she reminded him.

He slipped an arm around her waist. "What say we send the children on to Sunday school and dawdle here a spell?"

Yolanda squeezed his hand, then stepped away. "You need a quick course in repentance, thinking such things on the Lord's day."

"All right, then," he muttered. "But help me do up this damned tie."

The preacher's name was Arley Burke. He was a young man, serving his first congregation, with huge shoes to fill. Replacing the late Joshua Bane had been no easy task, but most of New Harmony's Protestants thought Reverend Burke had potential. He wasn't there yet, but with luck he just might be a keeper.

His sermon that Sunday was titled "The Love That Forgives," and the one man in town who most needed to hear it was nowhere in sight. Yolanda Carver hadn't expected to see Price in church, his appearances there being almost as rare as hen's teeth. She could always hope, though.

She could always pray.

The preacher had chosen Luke 6:37 as his text: "Forgive, and ye shall be forgiven." He spoke from the heart about loss and the healing power of prayer, his voice trembling, nearly cracking when he brought it home to Dr. Hudson and the good she'd done for their community. They'd miss her terribly, he said—pause for a chorus of *Amens*—and it was natural to hate the men who'd killed her, but that feeling was a snare laid by Satan to trap the unwary, pulling them down to the level of killers and thieves. He backed it up with First John 3:15—*Whosoever hateth his brother is a murderer.*

Yolanda listened dutifully, but she was thinking of a different verse, this one from Genesis: "Whoso sheddeth man's blood, by man shall his blood be shed."

And she reckoned that counted for women, as well.

She had shocked Lucius that morning by speaking her mind, but he'd get over it. They might disagree—and she might change her mind by supper time—but for the moment, part of her wanted revenge.

Mary had been the first to welcome the Carvers in New Harmony. She'd hired Yolanda as her office nurse, three days a week, and thereby kept food on their table until Lucius could begin his teaching job.

But first and foremost, she had been a friend.

Yolanda couldn't hear the preacher now. She felt the tears spring to her eyes, and rummaged in her clutch bag for a handkerchief. Her fingers closed around it as the tall doors swung open and a shaft of sunlight blazed along the center aisle.

David Proud Elk stood in the doorway, letting his eyes

adjust to the shadows, scanning left and right for a familiar face. Seconds later, he rushed down the aisle and
dropped to one knee beside Lucius, down at the end of
their pew.

"You're needed at the jail," he hissed. "Right now!"

Oskar Johansson had been sleeping when the marshal
came for him. It had been something of a shock to find he
could sleep in jail, but his fatigue from traveling and late
nights wondering if he would hang for what he'd done to
April Ling had sandbagged him in the end. He'd tossed a
little on the cell's rude cot, apparently, and woke to find his
clothing twisted tighter on his body than it ought to be.

"It's time," Price told him, standing in the open doorway of Johansson's cell.

At first, the Swede thought he meant time for breakfast,
but there was no sweet smell of eggs and bacon in the air.
Glancing from Price's empty hands back toward his desk,
Johansson saw no breakfast tray.

Rising and tugging at his rumpled clothes, he asked the
marshal, "Time fur vat?"

"For you to go," Price said, and stepped aside to let Johansson pass.

A faint alarm bell sounded in the prisoner's mind. He
swiftly counted days and realized that it was Sunday morning. There would be no hearing on his case before Monday,
at the earliest, and only then if there'd been time to fetch
the circuit judge.

"Go vere?" he almost whispered.

"I've been thinking," Price replied obliquely, "and it
came to me that I can't trust you with the people here in
town. And more importantly, I can't trust *them* with *you*.

Temptation wears a body down. You have a lot to answer for, and with the mood they're in . . . who knows? They might do something they'll regret. They shouldn't have to live with that."

"I'm save vit you," Johansson said. "Ain't I?"

"No good," Price said. "I won't be here to watch you day and night. Come on, now. Shake a leg."

Reluctantly, Johansson left his cell. He didn't understand what Price was doing, why the marshal couldn't stay and guard him in the jailhouse, and it made him nervous.

"Are ve going somevere elze?"

"That's right."

"The coundy zeat?"

"Not quite. Go on outside."

There seemed to be no anger in the marshal's tone. Nothing at all, in fact, that echoed any human feeling whatsoever. That, Johansson realized, was what unnerved him most.

Outside, the morning was no more or less than he expected from July in Texas. God may have rested on the Sabbath, but the summer sun didn't follow His example. Main Street would be simmering by noon.

And where would Johansson be, then?

The street was empty. He imagined everyone in church, or else at home. There'd be no rush to open shops, no work at all to speak of in New Harmony, except for feeding horses at the livery.

No witnesses, a small voice cautioned him.

"You understand I can't just let you go," Price said. "Your next girl would be on my head then, and the others after that. It can't go on."

Johansson turned to face the marshal. "I don't unnerstant," he lied. In fact, he understood only too well.

"I was distracted," Price explained. "I let my guard down or forgot to lock the cell. Who knows how these things happen? Anyway, you made a run for it." Price drew his Colt and thumbed the hammer back. "So, run."

"You can't do zis!"

"It's done."

Johansson felt his bladder straining. "All your friends vill know it's murder!"

"They won't want to know. Somebody always has to do the dirty work. Besides, I won't—"

"Matthew!"

The voice came from behind Johansson, but he didn't dare to turn and seek its source. The Swede was frightened that his trembling legs would buckle if he took another step, and Price would kill him where he lay.

Two men ran up to join them, coming from the general direction of the Baptist church. Johansson recognized them both from passing on the street, though neither one had been a close acquaintance, much less a friend. It was the black man, Lucius Carver, who had called to Price by name.

"Matthew, you can't do this," he said now, breathless from his sprint.

"Go back to church," Price answered. "I'm just helping Oskar with his problem."

"That's the court's job," Carver said. "Not yours."

"My shit to shovel. You all wanted me to wear the badge."

"And it's supposed to stand for something," David Proud Elk interjected.

"Tell it to the lady down the street. Ask Greaves to let you in."

"That wasn't your fault, Matthew," Carver said.

"I'd say there's fault enough to go around," Price answered. "If I hadn't been off chasing Oskar, here, things might be different now."

"It's done, Matthew."

"Not yet. I need to see some men about a bank. But first—"

He raised the Colt until it leveled out, around chest-high. Johansson guessed the six or seven feet between them wouldn't slow the bullet down at all. He blinked when Carver stepped between them, blocking Price's aim.

"This isn't you," the teacher said.

Price held the six-gun steady for a moment, then lowered it and eased the hammer down. "You want him, he's all yours." To Proud Elk, then, the marshal said, "Are we still on, this afternoon?"

"I'll be there."

"Good."

They watched Price turn and move away, back toward the doctor's house. Johansson hadn't understood much of the conversation. Truth be told, he wasn't altogether sure why he was still alive.

"Tank you!" he told the other men. "You safe my live."

"It's best you don't remind me," Carver said, his face a bitter mask of ebony, and shoved Johansson roughly toward his cell.

The whole town came to Mary Hudson's funeral at one o'clock on Sunday afternoon. Price wore his trail clothes, guessing Mary wouldn't mind, but left his gun back at the house. He didn't need it at the cemetery, and Price thought it might've hurt her feelings.

There'd be opportunity enough over the next few days to give the Colt some exercise.

He stood and listened as the preacher rambled on about rewards in Heaven for the pains of life on Earth. Price didn't have much faith in gospel or the men who thumped it for a living. Some of them were parasites or tin-pot tyrants; others meant well, but the solace they held out to normal men and women finally came down to nothing more than empty words.

Mary had never been religious, but Price knew the ceremony was intended for her friends, to put their hearts and minds at ease. He looked around at tear-streaked faces, forced to wonder if it really helped, or if the whole thing was a waste of time.

"Amen."

That marked the end of it for Price. He wouldn't stay and see the hole filled in with dirt. He had too much to do.

Places to go.

People to kill.

But first, he had to tidy up the remnants of his life in town.

After the service, everyone moved in to share a word with Price, paying their respects and offering their sympathy. The men wanted to shake his hand or clap him on the shoulder, while their women mostly touched his sleeve and sniffled back their tears. The children fidgeted or stared, depending on their years. It made Price feel almost as if the funeral were his.

When it was done at last, the Carvers, all in Sunday best, trailed Price along the street to Mary's place. The children were as quiet as he'd ever seen them, Ardell watchful, Dempsey and Essie subdued by their brush with the trappings of death. The house still smelled of Mary, seeming to deny that she was gone. The cat met them inside and buffed their shoes with his orange fur, trying to herd them toward the kitchen. Price went for the living room, instead.

"We never talked about this," he began when they had settled into chairs. "She may have made arrangements for disposal of her things."

"It's not your worry now," Yolanda said.

"I know you have some training," Price replied.

"We'll get along."

"Someone will have to feed E.T."

"Matthew—"

"He needs a home. If you know someone wants a cat—"

"I'll take him," said Ardell. Both of his parents blinked, surprised.

"*We'll* take him." Essie beamed. "I'll help!"

"I bet you will," Price said. "He'll keep the mice out of your place, at least."

E.T. sat preening in a corner, carefully oblivious. A silent moment passed before Yolanda said, "Matthew, the Rangers ought to handle this."

"They ever get here, you can send them on behind me. They won't cross the border, though."

"Will you?" asked Lucius.

"When you think about it," Price replied, "it's just a line drawn on a map."

"You mean to do this by yourself?"

"Proud Elk's coming along to help me track them for a while."

"He has a boy to raise," Yolanda said.

"I know. He won't be gone that long."

"And if you find them?"

"When," he said, correcting her.

"What will you do?"

Price frowned and said, "What I do best."

Price carried his rifle and gear to the livery stable, arriving to find David Proud Elk there ahead of him, his gray mare saddled and ready for the road. If the scene at the jail had spooked Proud Elk, he didn't let it show.

"It's good weather for tracking," the Navajo said while Price was saddling his horse. "Light rain on Tuesday night, but nothing since. The trail they left is baked in solid now."

"You followed it how far, again?"

"Six miles or so, southeast from town. They made straight for the border, that was plain. I started thinking what might happen if I caught them. Leaving Louis all alone, I mean."

"You did the right thing, coming back," Price said. "Nobody's faulting you for that."

"You sure?"

Price changed the subject. "I appreciate you helping me this way."

"Least I could do." He hesitated, then pressed on. "She meant something to all of us, you know. That time Louis decided he should try to catch a diamondback bare-handed—"

"We should go," Price told him from the saddle. "I've already given them the best part of three days. It's all they get."

The Rio Grande lay twenty miles east of New Harmony, and Mexico beyond it. They'd been lucky so far not to get more border trash in town. Riding out, Price supposed the holdup or something like it had been inevitable, an ax waiting to fall. He couldn't change it now, but neither could he let it go.

Surrender wasn't in him, nor forgiveness.

Price had never been much of a tracker himself. He'd hunted men from time to time and found most of them in the end, but that meant asking questions, following behind his prey from one town to the next. It was a different game out in the wastelands, trailing strangers when he didn't know their names or destination. Still, the signs were plain enough when Proud Elk showed them to him, and Price paid attention, learning as he went along.

Five riders left a trail that he could follow, once he had the knack of it. If they split up, now, that would be another story. Price would have to make a choice, hope for the best. He only needed one, though, when he came right down to it.

One man alive and willing to give up the other four.

At one point, two hours out from New Harmony, Proud Elk showed Price the place where his quarry had stopped for a parley. He didn't know what they'd discussed, maybe where they were going, but it made no difference to Price since they'd ridden on together, toward the border. Mile after dry, sweaty mile they rode on, seeking the refuge Old Mexico offered.

The border meant safety. Beyond it, they couldn't be touched by the law.

The badge on his vest seemed to weigh more with each mile Price covered. He'd worn it for weeks, barely thinking about it at all once the novelty waned and he got used to seeing its glint in the mirror. It wasn't the tin star that changed him, or tried to. That had been Mary.

And Mary was gone.

It amazed Price to think that he'd gone for whole days, near the end, without wearing his gun. There'd been times he felt weightless, as if he might drift into space, but her love had secured him.

All gone, now.

The Colt on his hip was his anchor, its deadweight familiar, a part of his life Price had nearly let go for a while, then reclaimed. He'd been foolish to think it could ever be otherwise. This was his life, a long ride through the desert with death at the end.

At half past five o'clock, they topped a rise and saw the Rio Grande below them. The westering sun threw their shadows halfway to the river, across the last yards of American soil.

"They went over," said Proud Elk, as if there had been any doubt from the start.

"Thanks for coming this far," Price replied.

"You should think twice about this, Matt."

"I've thought twice, and then some."

"There's no more I can say, then?"

"That's right."

"Well, I need to get back."

"Yes, you do," Price agreed.

"You'll be missed."

Price regarded his friend with a smile. "You've confused me with Mary."

"No, sir."

"Well, I'm bound to do this, either way."

"Any word for the others?"

Price unpinned his star and handed it to Proud Elk. "You can tell them I resign."

"Good luck to you."

"I don't need luck," Price said. "Just time."

With that, he spurred his Appaloosa down the slope and toward the water's edge.

3

"The thing about your Mexicans," said Wiley Harpe, "is that they're basically a lazy people." As he spoke, Harpe checked the sun, verifying their southerly progress.

"I've heard the same thing said about *my* people," said Nolan. His glance slid toward Martinez, gauging distance, working out how far he'd have to bolt if the *bandito* drew on Harpe.

"Whoever said it was a liar," Harpe assured him. "Your Irish are drinkers, of course, but they'll get up and work the next morning regardless. With your Mexicans it's all *mañana*. Every time you turn around they're sleeping in the shade."

Nolan wished the colonel would shut up, but he'd been talking more or less nonstop since they had mounted up that morning. If it were anyone else, Nolan would've blamed the gab on nerves, but that excuse wouldn't cut it with Harpe. If the man had any nerves at all, Nolan had yet to see the proof of it.

Nolan decided that the colonel must be happy—or *relieved* might be a better choice of words. They'd lost time in Tierra Blanca, sating their appetites after the long ride from Texas; then Harpe's piebald mare had thrown a shoe five miles out of town and they'd had to turn back, wasting the best part of another day to see it fixed and regain their lost ground.

If it had been someone else's animal, Nolan's included, he guessed Harpe would've left him behind to fend for himself. Another time and place, Harpe might've tried to pull rank, demanding a replacement from one of his men, and to hell with any bloodshed it provoked. But the colonel was in a good mood since New Harmony—or as close as he came to one, anyway—and he'd given up cursing his luck an hour or so after they started back toward Tierra Blanca.

Now he was talking, and Nolan wasn't sure how much more he could stand.

"Comparing Mexicans to niggers, now—"

"What's that?"

Peck Hoskins had the sharpest eyes among them, even though his brain was on the shady side of dull. Nolan glanced back and saw the rangy Texan pointing up the trail, toward something well ahead of them. Even shading his eyes, Nolan couldn't make out any detail.

"Go check it," Harpe ordered, and Hoskins set off at a gallop, raising dust as fine as powder in his wake. The rest of them reined in and waited, staying out of pistol range in case it was some kind of trap.

Hoskins returned a moment later, cantering. The urgency had faded. "Just a coupla stiffs," he reported. "Already picked clean."

"Not a siesta, then?" Harpe asked, and winked at Nolan.

"Nossir," Hoskins answered. "Not unless they's sleepin' nekkid in the desert, each'un with a big hole in his head."

"We'll leave them to it, then," the colonel said, and clucked his mare back into motion.

Nolan checked the corpses as they passed. He thought they'd both been Mexican, but after several days' exposure to the sun and scavengers, he couldn't swear to it. No matter, anyhow. The dead men had been strangers, and their killers were most likely far away by now.

If not—

Nolan was shifting in his saddle, turning toward the nearest line of hills, when Harpe spoke from his left. "Forget about it. I said we'll leave them to it."

Nolan hated how the colonel sometimes seemed to read his mind. It spooked him, and it stole from Nolan any edge he might've hoped for if he ever had to face Harpe man-to-man, across a strip of killing ground.

"They kill each other all the time, I guess," Nolan said.

"Like anybody else," Harpe said. "One thing we have in common, anyway."

Nolan resigned himself to yet another numbing monologue, but Harpe lapsed into silence. For the best part of an hour there was nothing but the clip-clop of their horses' hooves and a relentless stench of death, now that the sun-baked corpses were upwind. Nolan ignored it, concentrating on the bleak horizon, calculating how long it would be before they reached another town.

The farm was a surprise. Nolan had thought the land too grim and unforgiving for a man to till, much less expect rewards for all that sweat. The house, off in the distance, was a long, low structure crafted from adobe, with a crooked chimney trailing smoke across the washed-out sky. They were upwind again, and couldn't smell whatever had been set upon the fire for supper.

"Looks as though they were expecting us," Harpe said. His smile was back, as cold and lifeless as the dead face of the moon.

Nolan imagined the sodbuster peering through one of his windows, down the barrel of a Winchester. A shooter with a fair eye and a steady hand could drop a rider at a hundred yards—which meant all five of them, before they reached the house.

"Might not be worth the trouble," he suggested, knowing in advance what Harpe would say.

The colonel proved him right.

"It's not *our* trouble," he replied.

Moroni Jackson's parents named him for the angel who had called on Joseph Smith and handed him the golden plates that had become the Book of Mormon, in September 1823. It was their bit of wishful thinking, giving him an angel's name, and there'd been moments in his thirty-seven years when it had been a burden, not unlike a millstone tied around his neck.

His name announced Moroni Jackson's faith to Gentiles everywhere he went. Three little syllables declared him as a Saint and marked him in the minds of unbelievers as an outcast, someone set apart. It didn't matter what they said about religious freedom in the States. A man who took his stand against the herd became an object of derision, singled out for scorn—or worse.

He should've found relief in Utah, where the Saints had

carved a desert empire for themselves, but conflict with the government in Washington had changed the old rules handed down by God, through Jackson's namesake. Plural marriage had been set aside by men who valued compromise and profit over principle. Jackson and other keepers of the faith had been confronted with a choice: to pick and choose among their wives and children, casting some out of the fold, or else to find another land where they could live in peace.

For Jackson, it had been no choice at all. He'd filled three wagons with his four wives, seven children, and their worldly goods, charting a rugged course to Mexico. Most of their animals had given up the ghost—and little Heber likewise, barely three years old—before they found a patch of desert no one else had claimed and put down roots. They'd eked a living from the arid land since then, raising a herd of scrawny cattle and a few sparse crops, dealing with border trash and red men as they came.

It wasn't paradise, by any means, but Jackson had another son to show for it, and just last week his youngest wife, Rebecca, had informed him she was in a family way.

Which made him all the more uneasy when the riders showed themselves.

His oldest boy, Brigham, had seen them first and come for Jackson, found him working in the south corral. Jackson had told the boy to fetch his Henry from the house, then stay inside, keeping the others out of sight. The first thing he had learned, living so far from anywhere, was to avoid flaunting the women when a stranger happened by.

Some appetites were better left unstimulated.

Jackson found a patch of shade along the east end of the house and waited. There were five men in the party, and he knew that if he meant to warn them off, he shouldn't wait

much longer. Fire a round or two well overhead, but in
their general direction, and they ought to get the message.
On the other hand, it might just rile them. They could fan
out and surround the place, pepper the house with rifle fire,
and keep his family pinned down. Come nightfall, with the
new moon barely showing, they could slip in closer for
the kill.

A time like this—and it had only happened twice before—Jackson wished he had older sons, or else a harder
heart. The last two times had been all right, prospectors
passing through in search of some new place to scratch the
soil and dream of gold, but this was *five* men all at once,
and while they worried him, he didn't have the stomach to
start shooting them without a call.

Fretting, he moved around to stand before the house
and called inside. "Sarah, fetch down my shotgun from the
mantel. Put it over by the stove. Naomi, check the Colt to
see it's loaded. Hide it somewhere within easy reach. The
rest of you, be quiet now. Don't show yourselves unless I
call you out."

It was the best Jackson could do to put his house in
order, with these strangers almost in the yard. The riders
hadn't slowed, approaching in a kind of wedge formation.
He could make out faces now, saw that the oldest of them
took the point. It startled Jackson when he saw that one of
the horsemen was black.

He went to meet them, moving well out from the house,
holding the lever-action Henry with his right hand on the
stock, his left arm crooked to support the long barrel. It had
been a tactical mistake, he reckoned, letting any of them
get this close, but there was nothing he could do to take
it back.

"Good day, sir!" called the leader. He was smiling fit to bust, by all appearances a happy sort.

"We don't get many strangers out this way," Jackson replied.

The forward rider didn't flinch. "We're all strangers," he said, "until we introduce ourselves and sit a spell."

"What brings you here?"

"It must be Providence," the stranger said. "Or maybe just the smell of that delicious stew."

Ezekiel Rogers wasn't altogether sure the Mormon, Jackson, would allow him in the house. He'd had some dealings with the Saints, years back in Arizona, and he recollected that they hadn't been too fond of colored folk. He was prepared to let it go without taking offense and bide his time—riding with Harpe these eighteen months had thickened up his skin where petty insults were concerned—but then Jackson had startled him by asking all of them inside.

It was his second critical mistake.

The first, as Rogers saw it, had been letting them get close enough to talk. Harpe had a silver tongue, when he was so inclined, and by the time his chosen prey saw through that Southern charm, it was too late. In Mr. Mormon's place, Rogers believed he would've started banging with that Henry right around the eighty-yard mark, taking down as many of the strangers as he could, before the others spooked and gave him moving targets.

Stepping across the threshold into semidarkness, Rogers had to wonder if the sodbuster was having second thoughts.

If not, he would be soon.

Inside, it seemed to Rogers that the house had been divided into four rooms, three for sleeping, and the one in which they stood for all the rest of daily life. He counted heads, four women and six—no, seven—children. The kids were roughly half and half for boys and girls, all wide-eyed and silent in the presence of five dusty strangers with guns on their hips. Their host was introducing everyone, but Rogers didn't pay attention to their given names.

It only made things harder, later on.

"We weren't expecting company," said Jackson, "but I think we've got enough to go around. Sarah?"

"I hope so, Mr. Jackson."

That struck Rogers funny, woman speaking to her husband that way, as if he were a neighbor or a peddler standing on her doorstep. He wondered if she dropped the "Mister" in the middle of the night, when they were bundled up in bed, and that set him wondering what she had under her brown gingham dress.

Not so fast.

While Harpe and Jackson made small talk, women busy at the stove and table, with the silent children looking on, Rogers studied the heart of their home. He noted pegs enough for two guns on the wall above the mantelpiece, and with the Henry still in Farmer Jackson's hand, that left another long gun unaccounted for. Rogers was looking for it, turning slowly in place and checking dark corners, when Jackson showed them to the table.

They might have stew enough to go around, but there was no surplus of chairs. Unless they ate in shifts, Rogers guessed five of the children would be sitting on the floor— but they surprised him again, fetching a smaller table from one of the bedrooms, bringing mismatched chairs and stools to go around it.

One big, happy family, Rogers thought, and plastered on his most engaging smile.

"Delicious, as expected," Harpe declared after he'd tried a spoonful of the thick beef stew.

Nolan and Hoskins bobbed their heads, Martinez grinning to reveal a sprig of something caught between his two front teeth.

"So tell us, Mr. . . . Harpe, was it?"

"It was, indeed."

"So tell us, Mr. Harpe," Jackson began again, "what brings you down from Texas?"

"We have business further south."

The answer left a lot to be desired. "What business would that be?" Jackson inquired.

"Our own, sir." Harpe immediately smiled to take the sting out of his words. "But since you've been so generous, I see no reason to be secretive."

Jackson sat waiting for a moment, then said, "Well?"

Harpe pushed back his metal plate and answered, "You might not believe it, looking at us in our present state, but we are missionaries."

Nolan blinked at that, and he wasn't the only one.

Jackson leaned forward, elbows planted on the table. "Missionaries?"

"Of a sort," Harpe said.

"What sort would that be, sir?"

Harpe drew his six-gun with a flourish, angling its muzzle toward the Mormon's face. "The sort," he replied, "who do unto others before they can do unto us."

When it was finished, Nolan sat outside the house in evening shade, passing a bottle back and forth with Rogers.

His people back East would've quailed at the sight of him sharing that way with a black man, but what did they know? Living all crushed in together in cramped flats, he reckoned that they were no better than white trash themselves.

He'd come a long way from Hell's Kitchen, but where had it gotten him? Nolan believed each man carried his own Hell around with him, hiding it most times, but offering glimpses to some of the people he met in his travels. The Jacksons had glimpsed Hell this evening, for sure.

"It's funny," Nolan said.

Rogers swallowed another jolt of whiskey, wiped his mouth, and passed the bottle back. "I didn't hear them laughing," he replied.

"Not *that*. I mean, that too, but in a bigger way."

"You're drunk," said Rogers.

"No, I'm not. You know I hold my liquor good as any man."

"Why aren't you making sense, then?"

"I'm just thinking."

Rogers smiled. "And that's your first mistake."

Nolan ignored him. "Don't you wonder sometimes how it happens? Here these people are, religious as the day is long, come all the way out here to be alone with God, and He sends us to visit them."

"He didn't send us anywhere," said Rogers. "We just came along, all right? Besides which, they were Mormons."

"Makes no difference."

"Tell that to my daddy, if you see him. He'll be the gospel-shouting bastard with a Bible in one hand an' a hickory switch in the other. Tell you all about Mormons and suchlike deceivers, he will. If you're smart, though, you'll plug him and go through his pockets before he gets started."

"My old man liked the belt," Nolan replied. "We didn't have a Bible that I recollect."

"Daddies are pretty much the same, I figure, either whipping on the sons or poking at the daughters. It's a wonder anybody turns out right."

"Like us, you mean?"

"We do all right."

"It was a close thing for a minute, there," Nolan replied.

"Close for Hoskins, anyway."

When it had started, after Harpe showed them his gun, the youngest of the Jackson women had produced a shotgun from behind the stove. Peck Hoskins was quick enough to nail her, but she'd winged him as she fell. Another couple inches to the left, and she'd have taken off his left arm at the shoulder.

It was bloody after that, with Nolan in the thick of it. Sipping the rotgut from his saddlebag, he made an effort to remember when such things had ceased to faze him, but he had no conscious memory of living any other way.

"Too bad she weren't a better shot," said Rogers. "We could split the cracker's share of what we picked up in New Harmony."

"That's something else. We can't go back to Texas now."

"Says who?"

"Just think about it."

"What, because Harpe shot that woman?"

"Right."

"You think she counts more than the deputy in Lubbock, or those squatters south of Midland? I don't recollect us leaving any calling cards around, and Texas is a *big* damn state. It's like a country."

"Still . . ."

"All right, then. If the Lone Star makes you nervous, try a piece of Arizona or New Mexico. Ride out to California for a spell, why don't you? Me, I aim to stay down here a while."

"How come?"

"You ain't had time or opportunity to notice yet, but there's a different take on gentlemen of color here in Mexico. Gringos have done them so much dirt, they don't appreciate a white skin like your folk above the line. A man like me, some money in his poke, could make a life down here."

"You're off to one fine start," Nolan replied.

"Mormons. Don't let it tax your mind."

I won't, thought Nolan. *That's the hell of it.*

"You think he meant it?" Nolan asked. "Will Harpe leave Hoskins back?"

"Hell, yes. You know the man. White trash can't ride, his ass gets left. Catch up or not, de cuhnel sho' doan giff a lick."

"Why do you do that?"

"What?"

"Start talking like some field hand every time the conversation comes around to Harpe."

Rogers retrieved the bottle, tilted it, and swallowed hard. "Because of what he was and what he is. Slave-driving man before the war, and Ku Klux in the Reconstruction time. You've heard his stories, same as I have."

Nolan felt the whiskey just enough to ask the question he'd been sitting on for months. "Why are you with him, then? Nobody's forcing you."

"Because he's hell on wheels, old son. He sees a job and gets it done. We haven't tangled yet because he knows I'm just the same. It's coming, though, you wait and see."

"You think so?"

"Trust me, Irish. And I *will* be ready for him, come that day."

"I warned him, didn't I? I told him, if he couldn't ride, he'd have to come along behind as best he could."

"You told him, fair enough," Nolan agreed.

"And what does he proceed to do," Harpe asked, "but drink himself into a stupor? There's no reasoning with that kind of pathetic specimen."

"Too bad that Mormon *señorita* didn't finish him," Martinez said. "Too bad we didn't do it."

"That's where we part company, my friend." Harpe's manners were immaculate, but there was nothing friendly in his tone. "It wasn't Peck's fault that the little bitch got lucky. In my estimation—and I still command this company, unless I'm very much mistaken—it was punishment enough to fine him for his tardiness."

"The *federales* catch him up," Martinez said, "he'll tell them who we are and where we're going, sure as shit."

"You underestimate him, Ruben. Peck may not be much in terms of thinking through a problem, but he hasn't seen the inside of a cell since he's been old enough to use a gun. Your Mexican police won't take him anywhere. Not breathing, anyway."

Martinez shrugged. "Bad news for us, though, if they do. He won't be happy when he finds that money gone."

"Fortunes of war," Harpe said. He knew exactly what the Mexican was getting at, thinking he ought to share the greenbacks lifted from their errant comrade's saddlebag. Harpe hadn't made his mind up on the matter yet, but he supposed he'd have to give them something, to avoid fighting all three of them at once.

Nothing on earth united brigands quite like greed.

Rogers was watching him. He *always* watched. Harpe understood the way a black man's mind worked, maybe better than Rogers himself. He hadn't spent all those years trading bucks and wenches out of Memphis without learning their ways. Rogers was crafty, almost as well educated as a white man of the better class, though where'd he gotten schooled was anybody's guess. Harpe didn't know and didn't care. It was enough for him to realize that he, himself, possessed God-given courage and intelligence the likes of which no black man could aspire to have.

It was his birthright and he wore it proudly, as he'd once worn Southern gray upon the battlefield.

That wasn't strictly true, of course.

He'd never been a regular, much less a colonel, but the trash he rode with these days didn't have to know the truth. It wouldn't matter to their tiny minds that Harpe had led a band of private guerrillas in the War Between the States, instead of fighting beside Stonewall Jackson. Some said Harpe's raiders made Bill Quantrill's troupe look like a bunch of sissies, and it didn't get much better than that.

"We ought to camp soon," Nolan said. "We should be far enough away if we get up and out tomorrow early."

"There's a stream, or used to be, about a mile ahead," Harpe told him.

Nolan made a small adjustment on his bowler hat, tipping it back a little, since there wasn't any need to shade his eyes. "You know," he said, "they may come after us. Could take a while, but when they find the Jacksons—"

"Who?"

"The Mormons."

"Oh."

"We left twelve bodies in that house."

"One in the yard," Harpe said, correcting him.

"I mean to say the law down here might not decide to let it go."

"You may be right, but *federales* seldom go to Agua Caliente."

"Why is that, exactly?" Nolan asked.

"You'll understand when you see it," Harpe told him. "In the meantime, let's just say that it's our kind of town."

4

Tierra Blanca took its name from bone-white salt flats west of town, stretching for miles beyond the range of naked eyes. Price skirted them, but couldn't miss the sun glare from the barren ground. It scorched the eyes, promising misery and death to anyone who passed that way. Far off to the southwest, a lazy whirlwind of vultures marked the last stop for some creature who had ignored the fair warning.

Price didn't rush his business in Tierra Blanca, even though a sense of urgency was riding him with vicious spurs. Life had a different rhythm there, below the Rio Grande. He had to walk a line, be casual, or risk entanglements that could derail his search entirely. Price had no reason to believe the men he sought were still in town, but they might well have friends who would alert them to a gringo asking questions, if he didn't play his cards exactly right.

The first thing any long-range traveler would do was take care of his animal. Price found the makeshift livery, a family operation from the look of it, and bargained for a price the way he was expected to. From there, it was a short walk past a silent, dried-out fountain in the village square to reach a two-story cantina that appeared to have no name. Small businesses around the square were mostly closed, whether from lack of trade or for siesta, Price couldn't decide. An old church blocked the south end of the street, positioned so that riders passing Tierra Blanca were compelled to make a choice, veer to the left or right to pass God's house. Price wondered if they'd planned it that way, or if some intrepid padre had built the church before there was a village and the rest were drawn to him.

What difference did it make?

It was cooler inside the cantina, and dark. It didn't seem to be a festive place, like some Price had discovered on the south side of the border. There was no guitar player, no dancing girl, but maybe they were hiding somewhere, waiting for the sun to disappear.

Price scanned the room, without a realistic hope of finding those he hunted. There were three committed drinkers in the place, all Mexicans and older than the men he sought. Each occupied a table by himself, with nothing but a dirty glass and a tequila jug for company. If there had been an Anglo in the mix, Price would've had to make a choice on how he should proceed, but he was spared that for the moment.

No good reason why they'd linger here.

Price had his story worked out in advance, rehearsed that morning on the long ride south. He had to make it natural, the kind of thing a wary bartender would swallow. Nothing fancy, just a simple tale of misadventure and

delay, a rendezvous that had slipped through his hands
from no fault of his own.

And if that didn't work, he'd find a more persuasive
way to ask the question.

Getting rough would be the last resort, because Price
wasn't absolutely sure the men he wanted had passed
through Tierra Blanca at all. If pressed, he would've called
it ninety-five percent, but there was still a chance he hadn't
learned his tracking lessons well enough between New
Harmony and where he'd said good-bye to David Proud
Elk. There'd been places on the trail where other riders
crossed his track, and Price couldn't have sworn that one or
more of those he sought hadn't joined forces with the new
arrivals, riding off east or west.

He couldn't swear, but south was still the best bet on the
table. If he lost it there, Price could go back and try the
other compass points, one at a time, until he got it right.
Patience might be a virtue of the saints, but certain sinners
had it, too.

For this job, Price had all the time he needed.

He had the rest of his life.

The bartender was copper-skinned, more Indian than
Mexican if Price was any judge. His hair was long and tied
back from the sharp wedge of his face. The old serape
draped across his chest did a poor job of hiding the pistol
tucked into his belt.

Price checked the stock behind the bar and said,
"*Cerveza, por favor.*"

The beer was warm, as he'd expected, but it cut the trail
dust well enough. Price finished half of it before he
launched into his fairy tale. His Spanish wasn't perfect, but
it covered what he had to say.

"I was supposed to meet some men three days ago," he

said. "I had some trouble on the way and just got in this afternoon. Still need to find them, if I can. They're drinkers, so I guess you might have seen them."

Wary, the bartender asked, "Gringos?"

Price let the insult slide. "Three gringos," he replied, "one older than the other two. Throw in a *negro* and a Mexican. Five, altogether."

The bartender considered it, refilled his glass, and pocketed the money Price laid on the bar. It was too much for beer, maybe enough for information.

"They were here," the barkeep said at last. "First time on Saturday."

"First time?"

"They drink, play cards, take girls upstairs. You want a girl?"

"No, *gracias*."

The barkeep shrugged. "Sunday, I see them go, but four, five hours later they come back. One of the horses needs a shoe. The loud one, *el viejo,* doesn't like paying extra to get it fixed on the Sabbath."

"He wouldn't," Price replied. "They got it done, though?"

"Done and gone."

"And that was Sunday?"

"Domingo, sí."

Just yesterday.

"I've missed them, then, for sure," Price said. "I don't suppose you saw which way they headed out?"

"You're friends rode south. Maybe you still have time to catch them, eh?"

Price smiled. "Maybe I do, at that."

•　　•　　•

Peck Hoskins hadn't seen his twenty-second birthday yet, but he had damn sure been around. He reckoned few men twice his age had seen or done the things he'd managed in twenty-one years and eight months—and the first ten years barely counted, before he'd run off from the place some called Home.

Hell would've been closer to the truth, the things his folks had put him through before he had enough and rode a boxcar out of Dickens in the middle of a cold November night, not looking back.

Call it eleven years and eight months, then, which made his roster of achievements even more remarkable. He'd killed nine men for sure, and shot three more who might've died, but Hoskins hadn't had the luxury to wait around and see. The last thirteen months or so, with Harpe, had been the best. They swung a wide loop and did what they damn pleased, when it pleased them.

Until last night, at least.

Hoskins remembered getting shot and paying back the bitch who gunned him. Even with the buckshot burning in his arm and shoulder, he'd been quick enough to take her down before the others started firing. Afterward, Harpe had grumbled that he'd shot the youngest of the full-growed women, like he had another choice and did it out of spite.

Not that it mattered, since his wound had kept him from sporting with the women who were still alive, regardless of their age. It had kept him on the sidelines with a bottle, drinking while the others had their fun, until the sobbing dwindled down to nothing and the lights went out. When Hoskins woke on Monday morning, with a throbbing head that matched the pulsing of his wounds, he'd found the others gone.

His money, too.

It was the first thing he'd discovered, when he found the strength to drag himself outside the reeking house of death. Hoskins supposed he didn't smell much better than the ones he left inside, but washing up could wait. He'd guessed, upon discovering the others had abandoned him, that they'd have run off with his money, too. And he'd been right.

Bastards.

They'd left his horse, at least, but Hoskins found he couldn't mount the bay and follow them. He tried it twice and slipped both times, the second fall painful enough that he blacked out and lost the best part of an hour, baking in the sun. Black flies had smelled his blood by then, and Hoskins had to rip the ruined left sleeve from his shirt, then bathe his wounds to keep the maggots out. He couldn't find a drop of alcohol in any of the whiskey bottles left behind, but he made do with water from the pump.

Binding the wounds one-handed was a chore, and then some. Hoskins cut strips from a petticoat he found inside the house, discarded in a corner, and secured the makeshift bandages with straight pins from a sewing kit. Most of the bleeding had subsided, but the pain was hanging in there and his arm was next to useless. Hoskins didn't think the bones were broken, but it wouldn't matter if he couldn't find a doctor and the damned thing got infected.

"Bastards!" Hoskins shouted it across the yard, making the cattle nervous in their pen.

Leaving him there to rot would've been Harpe's idea. The colonel had no truck with sentiment, and that was fine where strangers were concerned. But where was loyalty when it mattered? What was all that talk about comrades united in adversity?

Bullshit, is what it was.

"Old bastard hasn't seen the last of me," Hoskins advised the cattle. "There's a thing or two we need to talk about."

But not until he had the strength to ride.

How long would that be? Hoskins wasn't sure, but he supposed it would be helpful if he found something to eat. Not last night's stew, unless there was no other choice, but with a family the size of Farmer Jackson's, Hoskins guessed there must be ample food around the place. If necessary, he could always shoot one of the steers and cut himself a steak.

When he was fed and rested, Hoskins thought he'd drag one of the Mormon's chairs outside and use it as a stepladder to mount his bay. Should've done that the first time, he supposed, but pain and anger had confused him. Next time, anyway, he'd get it right.

He was about to go inside and check the pantry when his horse, still tied to the corral fence, gave a snort and shifted restlessly. Hoskins imagined it was thirsty, standing close enough to smell the water in a nearby trough but out of reach. He turned in that direction, then stopped short as something flickered in the corner of his eye.

He had to squint, shading his eyes, but there it was.

A solitary rider was approaching from the north.

"Ya'll need ta wait a spell," he told the bay. "We's havin' company."

There was something wrong with the farm. Price knew it from a mile away, although it took another hundred yards for him to put his finger on the problem.

Unnatural stillness.

It was far too quiet for a working farm on a Monday afternoon. Dead-quiet, in fact.

He reined the Appaloosa back to a walk and examined the layout. Cattle penned to the east of the house. Restless in their corral but not lowing for feed. A lone horse in the yard, saddled and ready for the trail.

Where was its rider?

Where in Hell was *anyone*?

He'd followed the bartender's directions from Tierra Blanca, keeping his mount headed south. An hour back, he'd spooked a flock of buzzards from their roadside meal, two corpses gone ripe in the sun, tender pickings. Price didn't know if the dead men were linked to his quest, but they had no secrets to share and he'd left the birds to feed in peace.

Now this.

He didn't want to think about what might be waiting for him up ahead, but there was no avoiding it. A farm this far from any town most likely meant a family. There'd be more work than one man could accomplish on his own, and too much solitary time for most to bear without companions.

Family would mean a woman, maybe children.

It meant playthings for the kind of men who'd left their bloody mark upon New Harmony.

Price didn't want to see inside that farmhouse, but he guessed there would be no avoiding it, unless the sodbuster came out and told Price to keep moving. That would be a victory of sorts, knowing the riders hadn't stopped to raise more hell, and maybe he could get some information if he didn't press too hard. Maybe someone inside the house had seen his quarry passing and could put him on the right track.

Maybe.

Price reached down for his Winchester, eased it from its saddle holster, and braced the rifle across the saddle before him. He scanned the spread for any sign of movement, either at the windows or beyond the house, but nothing stirred. Dark windows, damn it, with the shutters open. Anybody could be watching from inside there, and he wouldn't know until it was too late.

Get closer.

Price nudged the Appaloosa to a trot, gripping the reins in one hand and his rifle with the other. He had a choice of riding on directly toward the silent house, or veering off to one side. Changing course might throw a sniper off his mark, but he would also make a better target, cast in profile. Either was dangerous, but instinct told him he should keep on toward the house, closing the gap as rapidly as possible. If it was a mistake, he'd know it soon enough.

Dark windows, and he saw now that the door was standing open, too. He couldn't see a thing inside the house. The shadows huddled there defeated him.

Closer.

Around two hundred yards he slowed again, to check the windows, but it did no good. If he could shave another hundred off, he would be close enough to hail whoever might be still alive inside.

"Giddap, now!"

Price bent lower in his saddle as the Appaloosa found another burst of speed. The animal was grace personified, making the run seem effortless, as if the earth was spinning while the horse stood motionless.

Price didn't see the muzzle flash or hear the shot. Instead, he heard a grunting gust of wind escape the Appaloosa's lungs, before it pitched head-first into the dirt and sent him tumbling on ahead.

•   •   •

Peering through gun smoke, Hoskins worked the lever-action of Farmer Jackson's Henry repeater and waited to see the effect of his shot. He'd hit *something*, for damn sure, man and mount going down together in a swirling cloud of dust, but he couldn't be sure of his mark when shooting one-handed, with his borrowed weapon braced across a windowsill.

"C'mon, you bastard," he muttered. "Git up, if you're gittin'."

In truth, he couldn't see the fallen rider yet. The horse was down, its hind legs thrashing dirt, and that told Hoskins that he likely hadn't nailed its owner. Still, a fall like that could kill a man, with no help from a bullet. Break his neck, maybe, or snap his spine. Hoskins could walk out there and finish him, no sweat at all, as long as he was careful and—

The bullet missed his face by inches, spraying Hoskins with a burst of ragged splinters from the window frame. They missed his eye, but stung his cheek and jawline, drawing blood.

"God*damn!*"

He fired into the dust that hadn't settled yet, saw something man-sized charging through it, angling toward the cattle pen, east of the house.

Another bullet whispered past him, this time to his right. Hoskins fired twice more, jerking the shots—both wasted, he was sure of it—and dropped below the cover of the windowsill.

The Henry held a maximum of sixteen rounds. He hadn't checked to see if it was fully loaded, but if Farmer Jackson was a cautious man, Hoskins ought to have a dozen shots remaining, plus the Smith & Wesson on his hip. With one arm useless, he considered switching over to the pistol, but craved the rifle's stopping power.

"One clean shot," he told the scattered dead. "That's all I need."

But would he get it?

This was Harpe's fault, all of it. The colonel chose their targets, spewing all that military talk about surveillance and superior firepower, but they'd stumbled into shit this time, and Harpe had run out on him at the very moment Hoskins needed help. If that was leadership, Hoskins decided he would rather make a go of it alone.

As if he had a choice.

He edged up to the open door and tried to check out the corral, but only part of it was visible. He couldn't see a thing beyond the cattle, anyway, and shooting them would be a waste of ammunition. By the time he finished, his opponent could've circled back around the house, and Hoskins wouldn't even know it, with the gunfire ringing in his ears.

It suddenly occurred to Hoskins that he hadn't checked the other rooms for windows or another door. There'd been no time when they were sitting down to dinner; then the shooting had started and he'd taken leave of basic common sense from that point onward. Now, crouching beside the open door, he pictured his assailant creeping silently through one of the bedrooms behind him. Saw him crack one of the doors and ease a weapon through the aperture, aiming.

Jesus!

He lurched forward, saw no one but the dead, and drew no comfort from their stoic silence. Why should they care if he lived or died?

He had to check the other rooms, but if he left his place—

A floorboard creaked back there, or was it his imagination? Hoskins lunged to his feet with a curse and rushed the nearest bedroom door, dodging corpses that mocked him with glassy-eyed stares. With one hand useless, he kicked at the door and rushed through as it opened, sweeping the room with his rifle.

Nothing.

Check the others, then!

He stumbled backward through the bedroom doorway, moving toward the next in line. It stood ajar, no more than six or seven inches, but the dark gap frightened Hoskins. Angry and embarrassed, he bulled through into another silent room. Bunk beds for children who would never sleep in them again.

One room left.

Even before he crossed the threshold, Hoskins knew something was wrong. An unfamiliar shadow fell across the floor, across the huddled bodies. There was someone in the doorway, faceless with the sun behind him, watching.

Harpe's fault, Hoskins thought, and tried to raise his weapon, but he wasn't fast enough. The stranger shot him once and watched him fall.

"Blood's dark," Price said when he was sure the wounded man could hear him. "You know what that means, I guess."

Price had relieved the gunman of his Henry and the sidearm, then had slapped his face, not gently, until something sparked behind the murky eyes. The fallen shooter's lips moved, but he couldn't seem to find his voice.

"The bullet's in your liver," Price explained. "You've maybe got an hour, if you don't make any sudden moves."

"Doctor," the gunman said at last.

"I used to know one. That was in New Harmony."

It didn't seem to register. "Need help."

Price looked around the killing room. "You could ask these folks, I suppose."

"Pay you," the gunman offered.

"With the money from New Harmony, I guess."

He almost got it that time, frowning through the pain. "Who are you?"

"I'm the one you should've killed, instead of taking down my horse. I guess this spoiled your aim." Price nudged the shooter's wounded arm and was rewarded with a grimace.

"Hurts."

"I wouldn't be surprised."

"Help me." The stranger had a one-track mind.

"Before we get around to that," Price said, "I need some information."

Confusion vied with pain on the stranger's pale face. "What's that?"

"We can start with your name," Price replied. "Be like civilized folk."

"Hoskins."

That's one, Price thought. "All right. Now, four more names."

"Four more?"

"The ones you ride with."

Was that sudden anger, just behind the darting eyes? "They left me," Hoskins said.

"I'll settle up for you. Who are they?"

"Four."

"I know that much. Give me their names."

"They took my money."

"So, I guess you couldn't pay me after all."

"Killed these folks, too."

"The names."

"Colonel won't like it." Hoskins almost smiled.

"What colonel?"

"Harpe."

"He have a first name?"

"Wiley."

Price had never heard of him, which by itself meant nothing. "Wiley Harpe," he said. "I don't suppose he wears a bowler hat?"

"That's Nolan."

"Ah. First name?"

"Shame-us."

"What's that?"

"Irish."

Hoskins was drifting. Price needed to get the other names before he faded out completely. "Two more left," he prodded, leaning close.

"Rogers. The nigger."

"Given name?"

"Who cares?"

"One more."

"Martinez. Roo-Roo-*Roo*ben."

"Good. I just have one more question for you."

"Hurts now." Hoskins shifted on the floor and shuddered. The blood that glistened through his sodden shirt was nearly black.

"I'll help you with it in a minute," Price assured him. "First, you need to tell me where they're headed."

Hoskins blinked at him and said, "Hot water."

"Any kind you want. Just answer, first."

"Hot water. South."

Drifting, Price thought, and slapped him hard across the face. Hoskins let out a squeal, then dissolved into tears. "Hurts so bad!"

"Glad to hear it." Price rose, standing over the soon-to-be-dead man. "You won't mind me taking your horse, I imagine."

"Hot water!"

"There'll be plenty where you're going. Wait a spell."

Price looked around the slaughterhouse again, deciding that he didn't have the time or energy to plant so many corpses. Every moment that he wasted now, the four remaining bandits traveled further south. His main advantage, so far, was the fact they didn't know he was pursuing them.

They'd left Hoskins behind because he couldn't travel, Price supposed, and robbed him in the bargain. Why they'd left his horse behind was anybody's guess, but it would come in handy now.

"Don't run off now," Price told the dying man.

He took the other guns outside and left them on the doorstep, then walked back to where the Appaloosa lay in rusty-colored mud. A film of dust covered the horse's eyes. There was no more for Price to do except retrieve his gear and shift it to the bay.

It took him all of twenty minutes to retrieve his saddle and the rest, shifting the horse's bulk by inches as he slid the saddle out from underneath it. Price anticipated trouble with the bay, but it was easy, seeming not to care at all as he removed one saddle and replaced it with another, buckling the straps in place.

The cattle shifted in their pen nearby, hungry or frightened. Price opened the gate, stood back to let them bolt, but none of them emerged into the yard.

"Your choice," he said, and walked back to the house.

Hoskins was dead, eyes fixed upon the ceiling or some point beyond it, maybe staring at eternity.

"You got off easy, but the others won't," Price said.

The bay seemed almost grateful when he slipped its reins, mounted, and put the house behind them, heading south.

5

Price wasn't a one-horse man, but he'd ridden the Appaloosa so long that the bay felt strange now beneath him. It wasn't a bad horse—quite obedient, in fact, and glad to gallop—but it was *different*. It would take some getting used to.

I've got time, Price thought, and scowled at the shadow pacing beside him, horse and rider growing ever taller, leaning further eastward as the sun sank in the west. Its passing brought relief from the ungodly desert heat, but Price would've brought it back to noonday in a heartbeat, if he'd had the power. Yet another day was slipping through his fingers, and he couldn't hold it back no matter how he tried.

"It could be worse," he told the bay, and got a snort in answer.

It was true. Price hadn't thought he'd overtake the gang so soon, in fact had already prepared himself for the long haul. He'd pictured weeks or months of searching, braced himself for the frustration and the sneaking fear that he might never find the men he wanted. He could ride around in Mexico forever, killing every gunslinger he met, and still not find the ones who'd murdered Mary.

It was luck that he'd found their last stop, more luck that he'd found one of them alone, wounded and not the best shot in the world.

Still, close enough.

Each hour wasted felt like a betrayal of the debt he owed to Mary. Each mile traveled made Price question whether he could ever pay that debt in full.

Die trying, anyway.

If that was what it came to in the end, so be it.

Price had no other pressing demands on his time.

Hot water.

Hearing once again the outlaw's final ravings, Price could only wonder what had possessed him in those moments prior to death. Was it a hellish vision, or some plea to have his wounds washed clean? Could it by any stretch of the imagination point him to his destination.

"Crazy talk," he said, and had to smile at that, because there was enough of it to go around. A man talking to his horse in the middle of nowhere—*a strange horse, at that,* Price reminded himself—might be judged and found wanting by some.

"Lucky thing we're alone, you and me," he remarked to the bay.

It would be full dark within the hour, Price calculated, glancing at the western sky. Reluctantly, he started looking for a place to camp. Water was foremost in his mind, a smudge of trees with rocky hills stacked up behind them showing Price where he could likely find some with a minor deviation from his course. A half mile east, if that, and he could pick the trail up in the morning, at first light.

The bay agreed with him that there was water to be had somewhere around the stunted trees. Price gave the animal its head and let it take him to the nearly hidden spring that would draw men and animals from miles around. Maybe not the best place to camp after all, Price considered as he stood waiting for the horse to drink its fill. Someplace nearby, perhaps, if he could find—

The dust cloud warned him, well before the riders themselves became visible. A body of men, ten or twelve by the size of the plume they were raising, making steady progress from the south toward the spring.

How long before the point man would be close enough to see him?

Soon.

Price swung into the saddle, jerked the reins, and spurred the bay through spindly clustered trees to seek shelter among the stony hills nearby.

Lieutenant Maximo Ruiz Ortega wished his patrol could have ridden through the night to Tierra Blanca and shelter, instead of halting at the nameless spring to sleep another night beneath the stars, but the horses were too fatigued and thirsty to push on. He cared less for the men, who had been paid—not much, but still enough—to do as they were told.

Men were expendable and easily replaced.

A good horse took more time and care to train.

If he had only been a captain, thought Ruiz, this patrol of the wasteland would be left to someone else. He could relax in Ciudad Acuña or Monclova, idling at the barracks with a bevy of *putanas* at his beck and call, while someone else ate trail dust for breakfast, lunch, and dinner. He could file reports while some lieutenant and a band of wretched troopers chased Apaches, bandits, and assorted border trash all over the state of Coahuila.

But not until his next promotion, if and when it came.

Life was uncertain in the Federal Police. He could lead a dozen patrols through hostile territory without sighting an enemy, then ride into an ambush on some routine mission, what the gringos liked to call a milk run.

Out here, he was the law and court of last resort. The peasants feared and hated him because he was a *federale,* charged with tax collection in the spring, but he was not so much despised when Mescalero raiders swept through farms and villages, leaving destruction in their wake. His men depended on Ruiz to lead them safely home, even as they schemed behind his back to do as little work as possible. His captain . . . well, the bastard had it in for him. Why not admit the truth?

Ruiz wished he could turn back the clock, rewrite history to exclude the incident between himself and the captain's niece, but he was an officer, not a magician. The damage was done, and he might have felt better about it if she had been better in bed, perhaps a bit less scrawny when she shed her petticoats. Not worth the long patrols and other shit details with no relief in sight, but that was what he got for letting mescal get the better of him. He'd let the wrong head rule his actions for a night—not the first time, granted—and now he was paying the price.

But for how much longer?

Captain Sanchez was a vindictive *pendejo* with the memory of an elephant, curse him. Unless Sanchez resigned or was transferred, Ruiz might never escape from his shadow. In the meantime, all he could do was perform as expected and hope for a chance to distinguish himself, something spectacular without being lethal, to draw favorable attention from a patron higher up in the chain of command.

A major, perhaps, or a nice fat colonel.

Small chance of finding it out here, the lieutenant reminded himself as his squad reached the trees and the small, dribbling spring. It wasn't an oasis in the classic sense, but the spring never seemed to run dry, even in the midst of summer. The water had a faint mineral taste, but it had never sickened man or animal to the best of Ruiz's personal knowledge.

If it was good enough for horses, it would do for *federales.*

"We camp here," he said. "Sergeant Padilla, organize the men."

"Sí, jefe."

Another night in the desert, draping a lariat around himself by night to keep the snakes at bay, shaking his boots for scorpions at sunrise. There would be grit in the food—rice and beans for the third straight day, so that his men were flatulent and peevish, slouching in their saddles under the oppressive sun all day.

Tomorrow night, at least, they would be quartered at La Babia, before they started the long ride back to Saltillo. Nothing to show for it this time, in terms of bounty scalps or prisoners. The trip, like so much in Ruiz's life of late, had been a waste of time.

Dismounting, the lieutenant recalled his basic security procedures. "Vasquez! Ybarra! Ornelas! Scout the area while we pitch camp. Make sure we don't have any company."

The *federales* saluted and whipped their horses into motion, fanning out to search the grove of trees and nearby rocky ground. They would save their complaints until well out of earshot from the camp, which was all Ruiz expected from sweaty, underpaid privates. He didn't expect them to find anything, but Ruiz still had to go through the motions. The one time he let down his guard, there might be a dozen blood-thirsty Apaches crouched within a hundred feet of camp, waiting to kill him while he slept.

But not tonight, he thought.

With any luck at all, it wouldn't be tonight.

The search was halfhearted at best, but Price tracked the *federales* while they were at it, making sure they didn't come too close. He picked the high ground for a better view, wedged in between two slabs of granite thrust up from the earth as if a giant underground had tired of playing dominoes and cast his hand away from him with force enough to penetrate the soil and find daylight. Price's horse was tied below and out of sight, unless one of the scouts circled around the hill Price occupied.

He didn't plan to let them come that far.

Price wasn't wanted by the *federales,* but he knew their reputation well enough that he refused to bet his life on their observance of the legal niceties. There'd be no questions asked about a gringo drifter shot by nervous troops, assuming anyone remembered to report the incident at all. Anglos gambled with their lives just crossing the border, and some—like the men he was tracking—encouraged Mexican police to let guns do their talking.

Price preferred not to kill *federales* if he could avoid it, but he had no time to waste if they arrested him on a whim, no cash to spare for the standard *mordida* extorted from so many travelers as a matter of course. He was relieved, therefore, when the searchers turned back after galloping this way and that through the trees, stopping short of the crag where he lay and the low hills behind it. It was sloppy work, but it had saved their lives.

For now.

Price didn't plan to spend the night where he was. A cold camp was one thing, familiar from past experience, but he couldn't sleep so close to a troupe of potential enemies. Passing the night in their shadow meant losing the morning as well. He'd have to wait while they cooked breakfast, packed their gear, and hit the trail. Worse yet, if they returned the way they'd come, the southward road would be denied him altogether.

He would have to leave in darkness, when the riders settled into camp, and find his own rest somewhere on the trail. Riding straight through the night was out; Price was afraid to lame the bay or miss some sign of deviation from his quarry on the way. But he could put some ground between himself and the *federales* by moonlight, sleep without a fire, and push on again at first light, before the posse stirred.

As plans went, it was nothing to brag about, but it was the best Price could do in the circumstances.

He descended the crag in darkness, quieting the bay when it whinnied a greeting. They waited together until Price smelled food cooking, heard snatches of laughter wafted on a night breeze from the campers by the spring. When he was satisfied they wouldn't notice him, Price led his animal the long way around, walking a slow half mile to intersect the trail well south of the *federales'* campfire.

It was faster riding, but he still didn't push it, fearful of a crippling stumble on uneven ground. He concentrated on the moonlit track and counted minutes in his head, the one-one-thousand, two-one-thousand method of his childhood, when a pocket watch had been a treasure years beyond his reach. Price owned one now, but couldn't trust himself to read it by the faint light of a quarter moon. When he had counted off hours in the slow child's way, Price reined the bay off the road and found a dry gulch where the two of them could rest concealed, without alerting man or beast.

No fire tonight. No food but hardtack and jerky for his grumbling stomach, washed down with water from his freshly filled canteen. The horse made do with withered tufts of grass and offered no complaint.

Coyotes woke Price in the middle of the night, the Colt already in his hand before a conscious thought demanded it. He lay and listened to the eerie serenade, surprised the animals would bother for a moon so incomplete and altogether unremarkable. Price didn't understand what drove them to it, but he listened for a while and let the tuneless music lull him back to sleep.

A dream of Mary Hudson took him by surprise, his first since learning of her death. Price found himself in Mary's kitchen, watching from his old seat at the table while she worked on something at the stove. Her cat was underneath the table, polishing his boots with russet fur. All gone now, but it seemed so real that Price could smell the food cooking and feel tears of relief moist on his cheeks.

Mary turned from the stove to face him, smiling as she asked, "What's wrong?"

Price tried to answer, but he couldn't find his voice. Mary stood watching him for several moments, hopeful, then gave up and turned back to her work. His failure drove a spike of pain through Price's gut.

He pushed back from the table, startling the cat to flight. Price rose and moved to stand behind her, leaned in close to smell her hair. Mary smelled better than the meal she had prepared, no insult to the food. Her scent reminded Price of sunshine, flowers, and a hint of something sweeter yet, unnameable.

Price slipped his arms around her waist, needing to pull her close against him, but his hands passed through her, through the kettle she was stirring, on into the fire. He waited for the pain, no less than he deserved, but he was seemingly immune. He watched the bright flames lick around his fingers, leaving them unscathed, no Mary now between Price and the stove.

She whispered in his left ear, "You're too late."

Price spun to find her, fingers trailing painless smoke. Mary lay stretched out on the dining table, pale and solemn as she had been in her casket, at the undertaker's shop. Her soft voice, disembodied, said again, "Too late."

Without moving, Price found himself beside the table, staring down at her. He watched a scarlet blossom spread beneath the curve of her left breast. Price tried to cap the fountain with his hand, but Mary's blood scalded his palm where the fire had done nothing before. He shuddered with the pain but held his place, fingers steaming in crimson, until Mary opened her eyes.

And asked, "Where were you when I needed you, Matthew?"

Price managed not to scream, but when he jerked upright it made the bay shy back from him, startled. Price looked around, the dream fading, but still so real that he would not have been amazed to find the specter standing next to him.

Where were you when I needed you?

"Chasing the Swede," he said in self-defense.

The horse snorted derisively.

Price didn't care to take another chance on sleep. He felt no better for it, and could spend his time as well—better—preparing for the ride ahead.

How much farther? Price had no idea, but he would do his best to see it through. That meant keeping to himself as much as possible, avoiding trouble that wasn't his own. Until he found his quarry, he was just another gringo drifting aimlessly below the border, better left alone by folks with common sense.

Price shook out his blanket and rolled it up tight. He saddled the bay; still no protest, but he missed the Appaloosa's seeming eagerness. They had traveled far together and the horse had saved his life once, maybe without meaning to.

"Sorry I couldn't do the same," Price told the night.

The trouble with revenge, he knew from long experience, was that it never really did the trick. A man could kill his enemies, go on from there to kill their families and friends if he had time and energy enough—but in the end, what did he gain? The pain of loss that set him on the vengeance trail would still be there, gnawing its pound of flesh.

Price knew it, but he didn't care.

Killing the shooters from New Harmony wouldn't bring Mary back. It wouldn't make her rest more easily wherever she had gone, if there was anywhere to go.

Why bother, then?

Price knew that stopping them would head off more

atrocities, the likes of which he'd witnessed earlier, but that was secondary. He couldn't protect a world of strangers, even if he cared to try. The world beyond his reach would have to take care of itself.

Revenge meant paying back a debt, in this case, one that Price owed both to Mary and himself. *Where were you when I needed you?* she'd asked him in his dream, and there had been no satisfactory reply. He'd failed Mary and failed himself at the same time.

But Price was damned if he would fail a second time.

The moon was nearly down when Price broke camp, but there was light enough to mark his journey southward. Overhead, the sky was like a jet-black velvet curtain pierced by countless birdshot pellets, bleeding faint illumination from a lighted room beyond that Price could never reach.

And if he did, would he find Mary there?

He shrugged off the notion, concentrating on the ground in front of him. Price watched for pitfalls, rattlers whispering across the road, whatever might delay him in his quest. He didn't strain his eyes against the darkness, searching far ahead or off to either side, a fruitless exercise. Night had her secrets and she kept them well.

Price didn't push the bay. Having a horse shot out from under him was sobering; he didn't crave another spill just yet. Besides, his early start would place him closer to his prey.

Unless Price missed their trail in darkness.

Never mind.

He'd never gained a thing in life by worrying, and didn't plan to trifle with it now. The trail lay southward, and he would go on that way until he struck some evidence that he was in the wrong.

Dawn found him four miles south of where he'd camped, its first light cold and gray, with nothing to suggest what lay in store for desert travelers. The *federales,* well behind him, would be stirring in a bit, beginning breakfast rituals. Price had no reason to believe they would choose his direction, having passed that way the day before, but he would watch for dust along his back trail, just in case.

And if they found him, or he met another party on the way—then, what?

Decide that when it happens.

Another thirty minutes, and the sky flushed crimson in the east, fading to dusty rose above. The stars had bleached away to nothing. It would be full daylight within the hour, and Price would have to shed the jacket he'd put on against the early morning chill. Meanwhile, he took advantage of the light and urged the bay to a canter, making better time.

Price was vague on the geography for this part of Mexico. He knew the state was Coahuila, with its capital at Saltillo, a hundred miles or more to the southeast. Beyond that, all he knew for sure was desert and more desert, Zacatecas even farther south, and mountains that would force him eastward, toward the coast and Veracruz, if he traveled that far.

Price thought the outlaws would be foolish to head for Saltillo, where the *federales* had their garrison. Calling it foolish didn't rule it out, of course, but he imagined they had something else in mind. The leader, anyway.

The colonel, as the dead man called him.

Wiley Harpe.

Price didn't recognize the name, but what did that

mean? There were outlaws working both sides of the border whom he'd never heard of, maybe never would. This one—these five—had crossed his path by accident, the way a rabid dog might step out of the shadows and fasten himself on the leg of the first man he saw. There was no logic to it, no reason or rhyme.

All that mattered now to Price was finding Harpe and his companions, stopping them at some point down the road. There was no altruism in it from his point of view. They could've ridden on killing strangers forever, and Price would've gladly ignored them.

Except for Mary.

"Too late," Price told himself, and saw the horse's ears perk up.

He still didn't know Harpe from Adam, still had no feel for the man's wants and needs. Price couldn't predict where the stranger would lead him, or if he had anyplace special in mind after all. Suppose Harpe was riding without true direction, stopping to pillage and kill as the spirit moved him. What then?

At least he leaves a trail, Price thought, and found the notion didn't trouble him the way it would've when he still had Mary.

She was fading like the moon and stars—already gone, in fact, and never coming back. At least the sky lights would return with sundown, but the light Mary Hudson had brought to his life had been snuffed out, once and for all. Price missed the warmth she'd given him, nursing a cold and bitter hatred in its place.

Better than nothing, anyway.

It gave him all the reason he needed to live.

And when he'd finished with her killers . . .

Sudden gunfire crackled in the desert morning stillness,

somewhere up ahead of him, to the southwest. Price reined the bay in, listening, then spurred it on a new course when the sounds repeated.

Rifles.

They were distant yet, but unmistakable. Price guessed another mile or so would put him close enough to track the point of origin precisely. Close enough to count the shooters.

Close enough to see if one was black, and if another wore a bowler hat.

6

Spread-eagled on a granite slab, shaded—but barely—by another jutting upward to his left, the young Apache grimaced as a bullet struck the rocky face above him and deflected into space. A jagged shard of something, stone or metal, stung him through the threadbare trousers he had taken from the body of a whiskey peddler on the Rio Conchos, seven weeks before.

The wound was trivial, perhaps not even bleeding, but it told him that the scalp hunters could kill him where he lay, beyond their line of sight, if they got lucky with a ricochet. The bullet wouldn't have to find a vital organ, merely clip one of the arteries that pulsed beneath his skin and let his life run out in spurts across the sun-warmed stone.

They would do that, or maybe wait and starve him out, unless he killed them first.

The chance of that seemed slim. He'd counted six scalp

hunters in the party when the chase began, and only one of them had toppled from his horse, brain-shot by Little Hawk, before the others started firing back in earnest with their Winchester repeaters. Little Hawk had died a moment after firing his so-lucky shot, spilled from his pony with the long-dead whiskey peddler's frock coat flapping like a pair of broken wings.

Coyote Dancer made it almost to the granite pile before a bullet found him, shattering his arm and forcing him to drop his rifle. Still, he could've ridden on, but he'd turned back instead, drawing his knife left-handed, galloping into the guns with a defiant yelping cry. Another crash of gunfire smothered it, and Gray Wolf was alone.

It seemed to him that he would likely die that way.

Another bullet struck the granite face and shattered, followed by three more in rapid fire. Four guns accounted for, and now he had to think about the other one. Was he conserving ammunition, or had he been sent around to scale the crags and take Gray Wolf from behind while his companions pinned him down?

The young Apache scowled, embarrassed by his failure to anticipate the movements of his enemies. He knew enough of white men to expect a treacherous attack. Indeed, if the conditions were reversed, he would've done the same himself.

No mercy.

He had left his pony at the bottom of the granite pile when he dismounted, slapped its rump with the stock of his Springfield carbine to set it running without him. It wouldn't go far for now, but neither would it wait forever if he failed to reappear and call it to him.

The Apache's world was no fit place for sentiment.

Retreating while the bullets cracked and whined above

his head, some of them lancing him with shrapnel, Gray Wolf reached the limit of his shade. The scalp hunters had found his party shortly after dawn, bad luck, and even though the sun was barely three hands over the horizon, he could feel its heat. If he lay still much longer, there would be no shade, and then it wouldn't matter if the bullets from below found him or not. He had no water, and the sun would kill him if he gave it time.

It did not frighten Gray Wolf to imagine this as his last day of life. His scalp would bring a fair price in Durango, but he didn't care what happened to his body after he was dead. The elders of his tribe had been concerned with such things, teaching the traditions when they should've focused more on fighting skills, but Gray Wolf hadn't paid attention. When a man was dead, what did it matter if his corpse was buried, burned, or left to feed the desert scavengers?

What mattered was the toll of death and suffering inflicted on his enemies *before* he died. If the Great Spirit cared for anything, it must be that. A warrior would be welcome on the other side, while cowards were rejected.

Gray Wolf hoped that he could kill at least one of the scalp hunters before they took him down. Three would be better, and ideally he would like to kill them all. If it came down to even odds, he could play dead and lure the final enemy within his reach, then use his knife or even sink his teeth into the white man's throat.

Results were all that mattered in the end.

But they would kill him here, before he had that chance. Gray Wolf was nearly certain of it. Nearly certain, but he had to try in any case.

Setting his mind to it, he left the precious shrinking shade and went to face his enemies.

• • •

It was approaching nine o'clock, by Price's reckoning, before he found the hunting party. There were four of them that he could see right off, spread out in an extended skirmish line before a jumbled pile of granite slabs due west of where he sat atop a sandy rise. The four took turns with rifles, firing up into the rocks at something—someone—Price could not identify.

Distracted as they were, the hunters didn't see him closing in behind them. When he'd cut the gap in half, reduced it to a quarter mile or so, he took a folding spyglass from his saddlebag and scanned the battlefield.

There'd been no time to use the glass as he'd approached the farm, the day before, and it would not have let him peer inside the darkened house regardless. He could not have saved the Appaloosa with it, but it might do him some good this morning. It could tell him, maybe, if the shooters so preoccupied before him were the men he sought, or whether he should leave them to their sport and ride away.

Price framed each of the shooters with his glass, hoping for something that would tell him he had found the bandits from New Harmony. It took some time, studying each in turn and waiting for a head to turn, a face to be revealed in profile as they shouted back and forth to one another, plotting strategy. The first was Mexican, which gave him hope, but none of the remaining three was black. Wide brimmed sombreros, weather beaten as they were, would never be mistaken for a bowler hat.

"Damn it!"

Before he put the glass away, Price tracked across the rock face to its summit, fifty feet or so above the desert floor. He glimpsed a fleeting movement there and focused on it, waiting for the target to reveal itself. A lull in firing came, two of the riflemen reloading while their friends stood by and watched, before Price caught another hint of motion on the peak.

A young face framed by jet-black hair was there and gone, almost before he knew it. Price was left with an impression of a sharp nose, deep set eyes, and copper-colored skin. No doubt an Indian, which in this part of Mexico meant an Apache or a Navajo.

Price didn't ask himself what the young man had done to warrant death. In this land, when the races met, skin color was itself a crime and death the common penalty.

Not my business, Price thought. For all he knew, the cornered man could be a notorious raider, a new Geronimo. In any case, it wasn't Price's fight. These were not the men he sought. Their game was no business of his.

Price was packing the spyglass, preparing to leave, when one of the shooters called out from his place on the flats to their prey. "Listen up, boy!" he shouted. "We got you boxed in. You ain't goin' nowhere."

Price considered the claim. If it wasn't a bluff, it meant more than four shooters—at least one he hadn't seen yet, to seal off the back door.

And, so what?

"We can pin you up there till you starve," said the shooter, "and still get your hair. Come down now, and I promise we'll finish it quick."

Scalp hunters?

The Mexican government offered a hundred-peso bounty for each scalp removed from an Indian warrior, and Price understood that some hunters weren't overly cautious about who they killed in pursuit of the cash. He'd heard stories of gangs scalping women and children, raiding peaceful villages, and even scalping Mexicans to fatten up the pot from time to time.

It was a dirty business, but it wasn't his.

"You make us wait out here much longer," called the shooter from his resting place, "I guarantee it won't be quick. Maybe we'll take your whole damn skin, instead of just your hair. Might take all day and half the night."

Price frowned. He didn't want a piece of this. He had enough work set in front of him already, possibly a hopeless job. A detour wasn't merely time-consuming; it was dangerous. The scalp hunters might kill him before he had a chance to settle Mary Hudson's score.

And yet . . .

Some people were beneath contempt, but that didn't mean it was safe to ignore them. The men ranged before him were no better than those who'd killed Mary and the squatter family. Left to their own devices, they would doubtless keep on killing, either for profit or for the sheer hell of it.

"Not my fight," he muttered, scowling when the young bay snorted back at him. His shoulders slumped a little as he reached down for the Winchester.

"All right, we'll do it your way," Price replied, and flicked the reins to take them down the sandy slope.

Gray Wolf was pleasantly surprised when he saw four men crouched beside their horses on the desert floor in front of him. That meant the scalp hunters weren't as intelligent or crafty as he'd thought. Sending a single man around behind him wasn't wise, since there'd be no one to protect the climber when he was exposed, unable to defend himself. Still, it could work if Gray Wolf wasn't swift and steady when the killing moment came.

Retreating from the stony lip before the shooters had a chance to find their range, he turned and started crawling down the broad sloping expanse of granite. It was warm already, even through his clothes. Another hour, maybe less, and it would be uncomfortable to the touch. By noon he would be cooking like a piece of fatback in a skillet, with no water to assuage his thirst.

Gray Wolf dismissed the morbid thought. Unless he killed the scalp hunters, he would be dead by noon and all his troubles would be at an end. The prospect wasn't altogether frightening, but he resisted its allure.

A warrior's sacred duty was to slay his enemies.

Gray Wolf was honor-bound to do his part.

A choice confronted him when he was halfway down the sloping plane of rock. He could find cover to the left or right, but either hiding place restricted visibility to roughly half of the remaining granite pile below. A skillful climber coming from his blind side could be touching-close before Gray Wolf knew he was there, and that advantage could decide who lived or died this morning. Conversely, if Gray Wolf remained where he was, he could cover two thirds of the slope facing westward—but he had no cover from incoming fire.

Knowing that he could not afford to dawdle over the decision, Gray Wolf shifted to his left and found a shady niche that would protect his flank while he was waiting.

Waiting . . .

He began to wonder why the fifth man hadn't already arrived. Should he crawl out and try to glimpse a horse below, then calculate his adversary's path? Had he delayed too long and let the gringo scale his simple fortress unobserved? Was the scalp hunter peering at him even now, over his rifle sights?

Uncertainty made Gray Wolf restless. It seemed to make the heat worse, too. He wondered who among the Anglos had dreamed up the fantasy that red men didn't sweat or suffer from the desert sun. How could a people so bereft of simple knowledge steal a nation from his own?

There was no mystery to that, at least. Numbers had made the difference. Men and weapons by the thousands, with vast legions in reserve. For every adversary killed, a dozen sprang to take his place, while the Apaches dwindled to a fraction of their former strength.

It was a hopeless fight, but Gray Wolf couldn't quit because he knew the outcome in advance. It would be shameful, a dishonor to his ancestors and to himself.

And there was still a possibility that he might win this time. However slim it was, he had a fighting chance.

A scuffling sound brought Gray Wolf into the moment, clearing every other subject from his mind. He listened, frozen in a crouch, and heard the noise repeated from his left, downslope. As he had feared, he couldn't see the climber from his present hiding place. To make the kill, he must reveal himself.

So be it.

Gray Wolf edged into the open, careful not to let himself make any sounds that would betray him. He had not yet cocked the Springfield carbine, dreading its metallic warning that would instantly alert his human prey. That part could wait until he found a target and was ready for the kill.

Where had the noise come from?

Gray Wolf scanned the slab in front of him, saw move-

·ment—and mouthed a white man's curse as he picked out the fat chuckwalla scrabbling away in search of shade.

A voice behind him said, "Cussin' will send you straight to Hell, Injun."

There was no time to plan the move or calculate its consequences. Gray Wolf cocked the Springfield as he turned, throwing himself to his left in the same fluid motion. The carbine's heavy bullet struck granite a foot below where the scalp hunter knelt, ricocheted with a scream, and drilled the leather of one dusty boot.

It was the gunman's turn to scream. The impact spoiled his shot and pitched him from his place atop the rock. Panicked in a bid to break his fall, the wounded scalp hunter lost his rifle and struck the granite face with bruising force.

The white man was struggling to one knee, clutching at a pistol on his hip, when Gray Wolf leapt across the slab and clubbed him with the Springfield's walnut stock. The first blow staggered him; a second left him sprawled and writhing on the slab.

Gray Wolf knelt over him and drew his knife.

Price closed the gap between himself and the scalp hunters to an easy fifty yards before he reined in next to a saguaro cactus that was standing tall with arms raised to the sky in mute surrender. He remembered that the bay had not seemed gun-shy at his meeting with its former owner, but Price didn't want to take the chance. Dismounting, he took time to throw a loop of rein around one of the fat saguaro's bristly arms, then sat down in the narrow shade it cast.

Price turned in profile to his chosen target, braced his elbows on his upraised knees, and cocked the Winchester. The four scalp hunters still had no idea that company had come to call. A lull in firing told him they had lost their target, and he waited, swiveling the Winchester from one man to the next.

Deciding who should be the first to die.

It wouldn't be a showdown in the classic sense, but with the odds at four to one, Price wasn't feeling generous. Whatever got him through the confrontation in one piece would be the way to go.

Two shots rang out almost together from the rock pile. Price picked out the flat crack of a Henry, chasing something heavier. He didn't need to analyze it, as the four in front of him resumed their firing toward the rocks, providing all the auditory cover he could hope for.

Picking out the nearest of the four as his first mark, Price framed his rifle sights between the gunman's shoulder blades and then allowed an inch or so for windage. At the next barrage of shots, he fired, then pumped the rifle's lever action to eject hot brass and put a fresh round in the chamber, sharp eyes focused on his mark downrange. He watched the shooter jump as if someone had kicked him in the backside, then pitch forward on his face. Dying, the gunman scrabbled in the dirt a while and then lay still.

One down.

The three survivors concentrated on their shooting, sparing not a thought for one another. Price tracked down the line and chose the farthest from him as his second target, lining up the shot. This one was trickier, not only greater distance but an angling shot, his man almost in profile.

Price sat and waited for the kneeling scalp hunter to fire, so that his own shot was an echo of the other man's. His bullet found its mark, but didn't take the stranger down at once. Instead, the wounded sniper clapped a hand against his ribs and half-turned toward the source of his discomfort. Dark eyes barely visible between a wide-brimmed hat and scruffy beard sought out the enemy, swept past the point where Price was huddled in the cactus shade. The dying man removed his hand and studied crimson fingers for a moment, then raised it as if to hail the nearest of his comrades. Price was braced to fire again when the scalp hunter toppled over on his side.

The gunman closest to the last man shot paused with his weapon raised to fire and swiveled toward the fallen comrade on his right. Price wasn't sure what had alerted him, perhaps a noise of some kind or a flicker at the corner of his eye, but now he saw his friend was down and knew something was wrong. He spun to warn the other with a shout and Price moved with him, tracking to acquire his third target—the nearest scalp hunter still breathing, still oblivious to danger. Price released his pent up breath and squeezed the trigger gently, watched the shooter leap and wallow in the dust there as he fell.

Surprise can be a weapon, but it cuts both ways. Price was about to drop the last of the four shooters—taking in the shocked expression on his weathered face, the warning fallen lifeless from his lips—when suddenly his target gave a sideways leap and disappeared as if the earth had swallowed him.

Price blinked and held his rifle steady on the spot where number four had vanished while he assessed the situation. There must be a slope or gully that Price couldn't see from where he sat. With that in mind he waited, and his guess was proved correct a moment later, when the shooter popped up several yards from where he'd disappeared and fired a wild shot off in Price's general direction.

"Damn it!"

That one was a miss, but when the shooter tried again from yet another roost, his bullet gouged a woody bite from the saguaro six or seven feet above the ground. It was too close for comfort, telling Price he had to move or risk the next round drilling flesh.

He rose and stepped around the cactus. Maybe he would come back for the bay, and maybe not. He hoped he survived the next few minutes.

The last of the quartet was headed to Price's left, where five horses were tethered, popping up to fire at intervals as he proceeded in a southerly direction toward the waiting animals. Knowing that much, Price took a chance and broke from cover, running toward a point midway between the horses and the last place he had seen his adversary. It was risky, but Price guessed he had a better chance in motion than he would've sitting still and waiting for the rifleman to find his range.

He'd covered twenty yards of open ground before a movement to his right front told him the shooter had surfaced again. Price threw himself flat on the hard-baked ground as a shot rang out, the bullet whispering a word of death in passing. Awkwardly, Price turned and answered with a poor shot of his own, wasted, and watched his target drop back out of sight unscathed.

Where next?

He didn't know the gully's limits, didn't know if it ran straight on toward the horses, though it seemed the scalp hunter was doing fine so far. His enemy knew where Price was and he would be a fool to stay there, but the risk of standing up to run was no less real.

Price vaulted to his feet and ran, sparing a thought for the explosive sounds of gunfire that had echoed from the rock pile earlier. He wondered who'd prevailed in that contest, if he should look for reinforcements coming to assist his opposition, or if both combatants were now lying dead. The thought had barely crystallized when Price dismissed it, concentrating on the hard work of survival.

Near the forty-yard mark, almost halfway to the skittish horses, Price's enemy surprised him with another shot that grazed the dirt between his boots. Too close. Price didn't drop that time, but turned and answered with a hip shot, knowing that he didn't have a hope in hell of scoring on the run.

Still, it was good enough to put the shooter's head down and to buy a little time. Price used it veering to the right and picking up his pace, if that was possible with straining lungs about to burst. He saw the gully's lip a beat before he stepped off into space and plummeted to jarring impact with the earth some ten or twelve feet down.

Price had a vague impression of the gully running like a saber scar across the arid landscape, portions of its eastern bank providing footholds for a climber if he watched his step. He'd caught his adversary halfway down the slope, crouching and sliding down, with a surprised expression on his face.

Price fired and fired again, his elbow cracking painfully against the ground to work the rifle's lever action. Both shots missed, but they were close enough to keep his target moving, skittering downhill with one arm out for balance. As he reached the bottom of the gully, the scalp hunter winged a shot at Price. Another miss, but it spit sand and gravel in his face, spoiling his aim.

Price knew it couldn't last much longer at close quarters, both of them unloading so much lead. The first to score a wound would likely win it, with his enemy off balance, maybe stunned. Rolling, Price fired between his outstretched legs and saw his target sidestep, spinning like a dancer, seeming to anticipate his every move.

The scalp hunter's repeating rifle found him, lined up on his chest. Price knew he couldn't cock and fire the Winchester in time, with the hope of hitting anything. Disgusted with himself for letting Mary down again, he closed his eyes.

The shot was louder than it should've been, a different caliber entirely. Price opened his eyes in time to see the scalp hunter collapse, blood spilling from the shattered ruin of his face.

Atop the gully's western rim, the Indian he'd first seen on the granite pile was watching Price, a smoking Springfield carbine in his hands.

"Tell me, white man," he said, "why I should spare your life."

The white man studied Gray Wolf for a moment, then replied, "First thing that comes to mind would be your Springfield. It's a single-shot, and you already plugged my dancing partner over there."

Gray Wolf reached casually behind his back and drew the fifth scalp hunter's revolver from his belt. "And now?"

The white man made no move to reach his guns, but neither did he grovel, pleading for his life. "You want to kill me, that'll do it for you—if you're fast and sure enough. I might still catch a break, of course, and take you with me. Then again, I don't believe that's why you saved my life in the first place. I know it's not why I saved yours."

Gray Wolf considered that. It troubled him to owe a white man anything. "Why *did* you help?" he asked.

The white man rose without asking permission, started dusting off his clothes with no attempt to reach the pistol on his hip. "I grant you," he replied, "it's not the smartest thing I ever did. Let's say I didn't like the odds and let it go at that."

Gray Wolf saw something in the white man's eyes. "You are a hunter too," he said.

"Not their kind."

"How do I know that?"

"You have my word."

"A white man's word!"

"It's all I've got to offer you," the stranger answered. "You and yours need have no fear of me."

"Not if I kill you," Gray Wolf said.

"All right. If that's the way you want to go, let's get it done. We're burning daylight and I've got a long ride still ahead of me."

The white man's quiet self-assurance was unsettling. Gray Wolf should've felt more confident, his weapon already in hand, but there was something in the stranger's attitude that made him hesitate. Not fear, he told himself, but simple caution. Only fools rushed into battle without taking stock of their opponents, and they seldom lived to fight another day.

"If I don't kill you now," Gray Wolf declared, "my debt to you is paid."

The stranger visibly relaxed. "Suits me," he said. "I don't carry a ledger with me anyway."

The white man picked his rifle up left-handed from the dust, while Gray Wolf tucked the pistol back under his belt. He wore it to the front this time, for better speed, since he couldn't surprise the white man twice. He stood and watched the stranger scramble up the bank, awkward and sliding at the start, but keeping on until he reached the top.

"I claim the horses," Gray Wolf said.

"You're welcome to them. I don't guess the fifth man's coming back for his?"

"He thought to take me by surprise. It was his last mistake."

"No one to trail you home, then."

Gray Wolf might've answered that he had no home, as such, but he stood silent. It was never wise to share such information with a stranger, much less when his skin was white. It made him seem an easy target, vulnerable. Gray Wolf thought to turn the tables if he could.

"And where is home for you?" he asked.

The white man frowned. "Next place I camp," he said. "Right now, I'm headed south."

"Hunting."

"That's right."

"What sort of men?" Gray Wolf knew he was prying. It was risky, even foolish, but he felt a need to know something about the man who'd saved his scalp.

"Something like these," the white man said, and nodded toward the scattered bodies of the scalp hunters. "Two white, one Mexican, one black."

"I haven't seen them," Gray Wolf said.

"No matter. I'll catch up to them, unless I let myself get sidetracked once too often."

"You're not a lawman."

"No."

"And you're alone."

"Like you."

"No *federales*?"

"I've avoided them so far," the white man replied.

"Their headquarters is south."

"I'll try to work around them."

Gray Wolf found that he was running out of things to say. After the white man left him, he would search the scalp hunters for guns and ammunition, take their horses, and ride on—but where? He had no village, no more people who would welcome him as kin. The scalp hunters had killed his last two friends on earth. He'd grown accustomed in his life to loneliness, but there had always been *someone*. Coyote Dancer, Little Hawk . . .

Dead now.

"Where, to the south?" he asked.

"How's that?"

"The men you seek. Where did they go?"

The white man shrugged. "I didn't get a forwarding address, but they've been leaving bodies right along. They shouldn't be too hard to follow."

Something to the north caught Gray Wolf's eye. He turned in that direction, felt the white man turning with him, both staring across the flats where heat shimmered and made the cactus wriggle. Gray Wolf saw the dust and understood its meaning.

"We've got company," the white man announced. "Guess someone heard the party and they want to say hello."

Gray Wolf whistled between his teeth, a shrill note rising on the breeze. He didn't have to wonder if his pony would respond. A moment later he heard hoofbeats racing toward him from the west. The pony slowed as it approached, then stopped within arm's reach of where he stood.

"Still want the other five?" the white man asked.

"No time," Gray Wolf replied. He mounted in a single fluid motion, settling on the blanket that served him in place of a saddle.

"Right." The stranger turned his back, a sign of trust, and started jogging toward the point where Gray Wolf saw a bay horse tethered to a tall saguaro.

Gray Wolf sat where he was for another long moment, holding the pony's reins loosely in hand. He watched the band of riders drawing nearer, still not close enough for him to pick out individuals among them. Gray Wolf didn't know if they were *federales* or civilians, and he didn't care. In this land, any stranger he encountered was an enemy.

Except, perhaps, for one.

He wished the white man well, then wheeled his animal around and galloped off westward, raising trail dust of his own.

Price stowed his Winchester arid freed the bay's reins from the tall saguaro's crooked arm. He mounted, stared at the approaching riders for another heartbeat, and decided that the southern road was lost to him for now. He'd have to shake off his pursuers first, then find his way back to the road or choose another route heading the same direction. Once again, he cursed himself for being fool enough to stop and help a stranger on the way.

Spilt milk.

His unknown adversaries had the north-south road, which left Price with a choice of east or west. He made his choice impulsively, no reasoning behind it that made any sense. The bay was ready when he dug in with his heels, and Price hung on as it surged forward, running hard.

Westward.

The gully troubled him a bit, but not the bay. It could've been a line scratched in the sand, the way his animal leapt over it and landed on the other side without a stumble. It was flat ground after that, and he could see the young Apache leading by two hundred yards or so, riding as if the two of them were in a race for life itself.

Maybe we are, Price thought, and gave the bay its head. Tireless it seemed, closing the gap between itself and the Indian's pony. Price didn't glance back at the following riders just yet. He reckoned they'd stop to pick over the bodies, whoever they were, either looting or gathering clues. With any luck, they might be satisfied to confiscate the guns and horses, maybe take it as an unexpected windfall and forget about pursuing those responsible. If they gave chase, at least he'd have a decent lead.

Almost before he knew it, Price had cut the young Apache's lead in half. He had to think about it now, because he wasn't sure what to expect. *My debt to you is paid,* the Indian had said, but what did that mean? If he thought Price was pursuing him or showing others where he'd gone, would he rein up and use the Spencer? Price knew he was capable, and with the carbine he could strike while Price was too far away to strike back.

The problem was that Price had chosen his direction, and retreating now would hand him to the riders coming on behind. It wouldn't make him helpless, but their dust cloud told Price that he wouldn't like the odds.

Stick to it, then.

Price knew the young Apache couldn't hear him, coming up behind at speed, but something made him turn and look for just a second. Price had no time to interpret the expression on his face, but there was no move toward the Springfield carbine, braced across the pony's withers. By the time he'd closed the gap to forty yards, Price figured he wasn't about to be shot.

Twenty minutes into the race, he looked back and saw no trace of trail dust behind them. It told him the party of riders had stopped, picking over the dead and deciding what should be done next. The response, he supposed, would depend on who they were and what their errand was.

Federales were responsible for solving crimes in Mexico, but different members of the team approached that task in varied ways. Some were zealous to a fault, pursuing the most trivial violator to Hell and back, while others were for sale to the highest bidder, willing to ignore a wholesale massacre if the price was right. Most *federales,* in Price's experience, fell somewhere between the two extremes. They weren't averse to *mordida,* but they also kept an eye peeled for cases that could build their reputation, maybe boost them through the ranks.

Price wasn't sure exactly where scalp hunters rated on the victim list. The simple fact that they were Anglos wouldn't carry any weight, without a protest from the States—and that was so unlikely, Price decided he could rule it out. A team of *federales* might decide to let it go, then, or they might pursue the killers for a while and see what happened. If they chose the latter course, it could become a battle of attrition, with Mexico's murderous desert the only sure winner.

And what if they're not federales*?*

In that case, the possibilities were nearly endless. The riders could be bandits, cowboys, pilgrims, or a family en route to visit relatives. They could be Mexican or Anglo—any race but Indian, in fact, since they saw fit to travel openly through territory where a price was offered for a red man's scalp.

They could be scalp hunters, Price thought. Who was to

say the men he'd helped to kill were traveling alone? They might've been a scouting party, looking for a village their companions could attack by night taking its sleeping people unaware.

Friends of the dead would have a vested interest in avenging them, more so if they smelled bounty money on the wind. Scalp hunters were not bound by jurisdiction or whatever rules the *federales* followed when they felt like it. A hungry gang might follow Price the same way he was following his chosen prey.

Price reined his horse back to a walk and watched the Indian ride on without him for another thirty yards or so, before he realized he was alone. A backward glance led him to turn his pony back, reluctantly but coming all the same. His sharp eyes studied the horizon far and wide before he spoke.

"They still may follow," he reminded Price.

"I'm heading south, regardless. We can talk about it there, if they catch up."

The bronze warrior considered it. "I have no people to the south," he said at last. "I have no people anywhere."

"Sorry to hear it, but I guess that means you're free to go wherever you've a mind to."

"Free?" The young Apache frowned. "South, then, for now."

"You don't think it'll hurt your reputation, riding with a white man?"

"Who will know?"

"You've got a point," Price said, and offered his right hand. "Matt Price. I didn't catch your name."

•   •   •

They rode together through that day, with no sign of pursuers on their track. Gray Wolf was quiet for the most part,
and it suited Price. He had enough to think about already,
without small talk filling up his head.

The stop to help Gray Wolf and their "escape" from riders who'd apparently decided not to chase them had cost
Price the better part of half a day. His enemies were that
much farther down the road, pulling away from him—unless they'd stopped to spend time with another family. In
that case, Price knew he would likely miss them since he'd
deviated so far from the road. Missing that sign could send
him days or weeks out of his way, could mean he never
found the other four at all.

The sun had climbed past noon and they were chewing
jerky while they rode, when Gray Wolf spoke again. "You
mean to kill these men you seek," he said.

"First chance I get."

"They wounded you?"

"Not me," Price said. "Not wounded. There was someone close to me they killed."

"It is the same."

"And they stole money from my friends."

"You'll take the money back, when they are dead?"

The question took Price by surprise. "I haven't thought
about it," he replied.

"It's not important," Gray Wolf said. "You didn't ride
this far for coins and paper."

"No."

"In my eighth summer, soldiers killed my father. Three
years later, I was on a vision quest when scalp hunters at-
tacked my village. All were lost except Coyote Dancer,
Little Hawk, and Thunder Cloud. The *federales* hanged
Thunder Cloud at San Carlos last winter. Now I am alone."

Price swallowed the impulse to comfort Gray Wolf. There was nothing he could say to ease the young man's pain of loss, nor should there be. Each person dealt with grief and rage in his own way. Some wallowed in it and were paralyzed, while others ran amok. Too many found their answer in a bottle, while a few devoted the remainder of their lives to the pursuit of "higher callings."

Price would settle for revenge. Gray Wolf was free to find his own way through the barren land of hatred.

"How far will you ride south?" asked Gray Wolf when they'd gone another silent, sweaty mile.

"I don't know yet," Price answered. "The first thing I need to do is get back to the road. They're using it, or near enough. It worries me to think I'm missing them."

He told Gray Wolf about the family he'd found, the outlaw he'd eliminated. Gray Wolf listened without speaking while the story ran its course. "You've started to repay them, then," he said when Price was done. "You have the other names."

"For what they're worth," Price said. "They won't be leaving business cards around, just bodies. It was luck I found the last place they got busy. If I miss the next, they could be gone."

"They're riding south, you said."

"*He* said, but for how long? To Monterey or Veracruz? Why stop with Mexico? I could've lost their track already, and I'd never know the difference."

"No," Gray Wolf replied. "The Great Spirit would not allow it. There is balance to such things."

"Oh, really? How's that working out for you?" When Gray Wolf didn't answer, Price forged on. "It seems to me that balance doesn't count for much. The spirits either, when you think about it. If they give a damn—if they *exist*—why is a pack of animals like this allowed to wander free? Why are they even born?"

"Such things are not for me to say," Gray Wolf replied. "The spirits don't consult with men. If evil is not punished in this world, there is the next."

"I've heard that said," Price answered, "but it never made much sense to me. What good are gods and spirits, anyway, if all they do is sit around and watch things go from bad to worse?"

"The padres at San Carlos talk about free will," said Gray Wolf. "What they mean, I think, is freedom for the white man to do anything he wants."

Price had to smile at that. "Some white men, anyway. We have our share of Bible-thumpers who condemn their own."

"I think they twist the spirits' meaning," Gray Wolf said.

"You may be onto something there."

"Each person, I believe, must find a path and follow it. The spirits sometimes guide us, but we may not always understand their words."

"Makes sense."

"Do you believe," asked Gray Wolf, "that the person you have lost has found a better place?"

Price had been trying not to think about it, but he focused now. "I hope so," he replied.

"I hope so, too," the young Apache said.

All afternoon, Price kept expecting Gray Wolf to announce that he was leaving, but the two of them were still together when they camped at dusk. There had been no sign of pursuers all day long, and as he gathered firewood for the night, Price finally allowed himself to think they had escaped.

The fire would be a risk, but they could take turns watching through the night. They found a crater in the earth and camped down in the bottom of it, for concealment. It would only be a hazard in the case of a sudden flood, and cloudless skies told Price they would be sleeping dry that night.

Gray Wolf went out on foot before full dark, bearing a nearly empty water bag. When he returned an hour later, he brought water from a spring he'd found and two small rabbits freshly skinned. The horses drank from Price's hat and ate dry grass along the north side of the crater, while Price whittled spits and cooked the meat. It fairly melted in his mouth, a welcome change from jerky that was more like saddle leather with a dash of salt.

"I didn't hear you bring these down," Price said when they were nearly finished with the meal.

Gray Wolf produced a pair of sturdy sticks, bound cruciform and sharpened to a point at all four ends. By firelight, Price could see that two of those sharp points bore rusty stains.

"Less noise than shooting," Gray Wolf said. "Less damage to the meat."

"You throw it?"

Gray Wolf nodded. "Up to ten or fifteen paces."

Price refrained from asking whether the device was ever used to hunt two-legged game. He only had a bite or so of rabbit left, and didn't want to spoil the meal.

When they were finished and had pitched the bones well out from camp, Gray Wolf remarked, "Too bad the man you found couldn't say where the others went before he died."

"I asked him," Price replied, "but he was hurt before I got there. By the time I shot him, he was well past making any sense. I got the other names, and then he babbled on about hot water for a while, and that was it."

"Hot water?" Gray Wolf asked.

"Three times he said it," Price recalled.

"Maybe he did give up the rest."

"How's that?"

"Hot water," Gray Wolf answered. "Agua Caliente in the Spanish tongue. It is a town."

Price felt the short hairs bristling on his neck. "Which way?" he demanded.

"From here, southeast. Maybe three days."

"That close."

Price had prepared himself for an extended search, and his surprise encounter with a straggler from the gang had only reinforced his sense that Mary's killers would be difficult—perhaps impossible—to find. He'd seen the first as bait to keep him going, and determined that he wouldn't rest until the other four were dead—or he was. Now, it seemed to Price that he might have to look beyond the killing and decide what followed after it.

Not yet.

Before he planned another life, he had to locate Agua Caliente and discover if the men he sought were waiting there. If so, they still might prove too much for him. Price found he didn't mind that thought the way another man might have.

A man, perhaps, who hadn't witnessed so much death.

"Will they expect you?" Gray Wolf asked him.

"No. At least, I don't think so. They're cocky. That'll be the death of them."

"Such men deserve to die."

"It's not about deserving," Price responded. He had tried to put a noble face on it, but came up wanting. "I'm just paying back a debt."

"It is the same thing," Gray Wolf told him. "Who would pay this debt, if you did not?"

Price shrugged. "Let's wait and see if I can get it done."

Price tossed a coin to see who'd take first watch and lost on tails. While Gray Wolf huddled in his blanket, maybe dreaming, Price sat on the crater's rim and scanned the desert flats by moonlight, making sure the warrior's sleep was undisturbed. Despite the morning's battle and a long day's ride, he still felt energized, knowing that sleep would flee if he pursued it too aggressively.

Three days.

Price drifted, picturing the ride into a town he'd never seen. It had adobe buildings, sun-bleached like the desert, with their roofs made out of sod or terra-cotta tile. Maybe a fountain in the square, where new arrivals stopped and drank their fill before inquiring after strangers.

Agua Caliente.

Price felt foolish, knowing that he could've missed the town entirely if it hadn't been for Gray Wolf. He imagined scouring the wasteland for a month of Sundays, only learning of the town's existence when he finally grew desperate enough to read a map. He thought of finding it too late, after his enemies had tired of the place and dispersed beyond his reach, forever gone.

Not now. You're mine.

Or maybe he was theirs. Perhaps they owned a piece of him that Price could not retrieve, no matter how much blood he spilled. Maybe the emptiness he felt inside was permanent.

He sat and watched the stars wheel overhead, wishing

he knew the names of different constellations and the messages they were supposed to bear for humans down below. Price set no store by stargazing in daily life, but on a night like this all things seemed possible. He almost felt as if the distant sky lights could reveal his enemies, lead him unerringly to track them down and kill them one by one.

Or all together, if they wanted it that way.

The desert all around him was alive. Price heard the sliding, scuttling sounds of predators and scavengers about their nightly business, but they seemed to sense his presence and remained beyond the range of human sight. Part of survival in the wild was recognizing larger, stronger killers. Price supposed the night-hunters knew grim death by its sight or smell, and so left him alone.

He woke Gray Wolf an hour late, not touching him, but merely stepping close enough to cast a shadow by the moon's pale light. The ground was hard when Price lay down to sleep, but he was used to that. His dreams were bittersweet, and he awoke next morning to the first light of a blood-red dawn.

8

"It's feckin' hot out here," Seamus Nolan groused. He doffed the bowler hat to swipe a sleeve across his forehead, then replaced it, wishing he could swap it for the wide-brimmed hat Martinez wore.

"It's relative," replied Ezekiel Rogers. "I've felt worse."

"And where was that?" A part of Nolan hoped that hearing of a hotter and more miserable place would ease his misery somehow.

"The Mississippi Delta, Mr. Nolan. This is *dry* heat, not the muggy kind that smothers you so bad just sweating feels like work. You don't know heat until you've cleared a field of cotton in high summer, wearing chains."

"Maybe. But this is hot enough for me." He shifted in his saddle, trying for a better fit. There wasn't one. He changed the subject, telling Rogers, "I thought Hoskins might catch up to us before this."

"Did you?" Rogers smiled, just short of smirking.

Nolan didn't like that smile. "Why wouldn't he?"

Instead of answering, the black man said, "I didn't know the two of you were all that close."

"What's that supposed to mean?" Trail-weary as he was, Nolan wasn't entirely sure if he should take offense.

"Nothing." That smile. "You miss him, though."

"Don't you?"

"Redneck meant shit to me," Rogers replied, not smiling now. "I wouldn't give a nickel for his whole damn family."

Surprised by Rogers's vehemence, Nolan inquired, "What did he ever do to you?"

"You had to be there."

"Where?"

"Inside my skin." The smile was back. "Don't fret about it. Concentrate on getting through this bit without another hitch."

The more he thought about it, Nolan realized he didn't miss Peck Hoskins. It was more a sense of standing helpless, watching, while their group began to fall apart. Nolan supposed they needed every hand and weapon they could muster just to stay alive.

He tried again. "I only meant to say he knew where we were going."

"Now you got it," Rogers said.

"Got what?"

"The past tense. Hoskins *knew* which way we're going. Doesn't mean he'd be in any shape to follow."

"Why not? We only left him drunk."

"We left him drunk *and* shot *and* passed out cold," Rogers reminded him. "For all we know, he might've bled out in the middle of a whiskey dream."

"You think he's dead?"

"I *hope* so. Otherwise, he'll be one pissed-off redneck when he checks his saddlebag and finds that money gone."

"That wasn't us."

"Tell Hoskins that next time you see him."

Nolan figured he could deal with Hoskins if it came to that, trusting the shoulder wound to slow him down. "He doesn't worry me."

"I'm glad to hear it."

Still . . .

"You think somebody's found him?"

"Helped him out, you mean?"

"Whatever."

Rogers shrugged. "The Mormon wasn't big on neighbors. *Federales* might stop by, or an Apache hunting party. Either way, I'd say old Peck's shit out of luck."

"If it was *federales*," Nolan said, "they might get him to talk."

"Another reason you should hope he's dead."

Nolan considered it. Each mile they traveled took them farther into Mexico, farther from home. There might be hangmen waiting for him in the States, if they could catch him, but at least Nolan could speak the language there. He wouldn't stand out in a crowd if anyone came looking for him. Glancing at Rogers, he decided it could still be worse, but not by much.

"What's this, now?" Rogers asked.

Ahead of them, Harpe had his piebald mare stopped in the middle of the road. Martinez sat his chestnut stallion to the colonel's left, with ample room between the two of them. Nolan rode up beside Harpe, on the right, and raised a hand to shade his eyes.

"What is it, Colonel?"

"Wagons," Harpe replied. "I make it two or three."

Nolan could see them now, but damned if he could count the wagons. Maybe Harpe was guessing, but he wouldn't bet on it. The old man had been right before, at greater distances.

"How many men?"

"You give me too much credit, Seamus. We'll just have to go and see."

"It could be trouble."

"Not for us," Harpe said. "They're coming from the south. We haven't been there yet."

"Your call," Nolan replied.

"I call it opportunity, and it should never go to waste."

"If they outnumber us—"

"You worry too much, Seamus. If the odds aren't advantageous, for whatever reason, we ride on and nothing's lost. We have to pass them anyway. It can't do any harm to stop and jaw a spell."

No harm to who? thought Nolan, but he kept it to himself. The colonel had his mind made up, and no good ever came from bucking him. Nolan would go along and see what happened next, because he had no choice.

But he would also watch out for himself.

"Riders!"

Jesús Ornelas glanced up from his work, fingers smeared with axle grease as he prepared to mount the new wagon wheel. The old one had cracked on a stone that morning, but they'd nursed it for another six or seven miles before the rim separated and shattered the spokes. They had one spare, and any further setbacks might defeat them.

"How many?" he asked Margarita.

"Three," she replied. "No, four."

The children started babbling excitedly, before Roberto and Constanza hushed them. Jesús spared a glance for his brother as he stood, knees cracking painfully. Margarita stood beside the team, watching the northern road.

Four days from Paredón, and they'd been lucky until now. The broken wheel was bad enough, but strangers made it worse. If there was trouble, they could only use Roberto's wagon now. The eight of them would barely fit aboard without unloading it, and there'd be no time for that if the riders meant them harm.

No matter, thought Jesús. They couldn't outrun horsemen in the wagon, anyway.

"Roberto."

"Sí."

His brother was already moving toward the second wagon, where his rifle was concealed beneath the driver's seat. Jesús wiped his hands on a rag and stepped closer to Margarita, closer to his own small cache of weapons. It wasn't much—a single-barreled shotgun and an old revolver—but better than nothing.

He hoped so, at least.

The children, his three and Julio, stood with Roberto's wife Constanza on the far side of the wagon, watching wide-eyed as the riders made their slow approach. The two in front were gringos, Jesús saw now, with a Mexican behind them and a black man bringing up the rear.

All four were armed.

Another step brought Jesús to the wagon's forward wheel. The driver's seat was still a foot or so above his head. He guessed the weapons would've slipped to that side when the wagon wheel collapsed. It placed them

closer, but Jesús would still have to scale the left side of
the wagon and find them, reaching underneath the seat.
The move would leave his back exposed, together with his
family.

"Maybe they'll just ride on," said Margarita hopefully.

"Maybe." But Jesús wasn't counting on it. "Join Constanza and the children," he instructed her.

"Jesús—"

"Go now!"

The riders had drawn closer. While his wife retreated to
the far side of the wagon, Jesús mounted to the driver's
seat. He felt the leaning wagon shift beneath his weight,
not much, but still enough to be unsettling. He felt better
on the high seat, level with the riders now. Jesús glanced
down and saw the weapons, blanket-wrapped, below and
to his left.

Not yet.

Jesús heard his brother approaching behind him, from
the second wagon. Another moment and Roberto stood beside him, carrying the Winchester '73 that ranked foremost
among his prized possessions.

"Wait for me," Jesús instructed, lips barely moving.
"They may not mean us harm."

Roberto made a kind of snorting noise, but kept the rifle
down against his leg, its muzzle pointed toward the
ground.

At thirty yards the oldest of the riders called out to
Jesús, "Good day, *amigo*. You appear to have some trouble
there."

Jesús slumped lower on the wagon seat, his left hand
dangling closer to the hidden guns. "Is not so bad," he said.

"I beg to differ," said the gringo. "If you find yourself
afoot out here, you're in a lot of trouble."

"We fix it pretty soon."

"You don't need any help, then?" asked the stranger. "With the wheel . . . or anything?"

Jesús saw how the rider's gaze shifted toward Margarita and Constanza. Hidden as she was behind the wagon, he supposed the gringo couldn't tell Constanza was with child.

"No help," he echoed. *"Gracias."*

"Well, if you're sure. . . ."

The younger gringo, red-faced underneath a hat too small to shield him from the sun, said something Jesús couldn't hear, his voice dropped almost to a whisper. His companion smiled and tipped his hat. "Come on, boys," he commanded as he spurred his mare.

Jesús turned on the wagon seat to watch them go. It was an awkward posture, with his weapons further out of reach, but he refused to let the men out of his sight. Roberto tracked them, both hands on his Winchester and making no secret about it. There was something in the older gringo's attitude that telegraphed a warning, even though he hadn't made a hostile move.

At least, not yet.

Rogers was waiting for the signal, ready when it came. He read the colonel's posture, saw him stiffen as he poised himself to haul back on the reins and turn his mare around, already reaching for the big Colt on his hip.

And here goes nothing, Rogers thought.

He drew and fired across his saddle, toward the Mexican with the Winchester in his hands. It was a hasty shot and wasted, slapping hard against the wagon slats and raising dust.

"Goddamn it!"

Rogers cocked his six-gun for another try, but his target had already dropped and rolled under the wagon. He swung toward the other Mex and fired too late, as the wiry man ducked out of sight below the wagon seat.

He'll have a gun there, Rogers realized. He called, "Watch out!" to no one in particular as his companions opened fire.

The women were screaming and grabbing at children who scattered like quail at the first sound of gunshots. Rogers ignored them, concentrating on the two men who could kill him if he gave them half a chance.

As if in answer to his thought, the Mexican beneath the wagon fired a rifle shot. He didn't have much in the way of targets, mostly horses' legs, but if he dropped their animals the riders would be easy marks.

Rogers wheeled to his left, retreating toward the forward wagon's team. Passing the driver's seat, he saw his second target rising with a long gun shouldered, grim-faced in the shadow of his wide-brimmed hat. They fired together, Rogers missing for the third time while his gelding bolted from the sting of birdshot.

For a moment it was as if he'd joined the rodeo, bucking and jolting, nearly losing his Peacemaker as he clutched the saddle horn. One slip and he'd land sprawling in the dirt, maybe beneath the frightened gelding's slashing hooves. Gunfire behind him didn't help to calm the animals, but Rogers kept his seat somehow and calmed the gelding down enough to catch his breath.

"You sons of bitches askin' for it now!" he bellowed, hauling on the reins until they faced the action.

It was touch and go from where he sat, despite the odds. Martinez had gone back to check the second wagon or to find some cover. Either way, it had the same effect. Nolan and Harpe were grappling with their animals, returning fire while one Mexican tried to shoot their horses and his partner turned the air smoky around them with an ancient Navy Colt.

Rogers squeezed off his fourth shot of the battle, yet another miss, but it was close enough to make the shooter in the wagon turn and face him. Rogers fired again and winged him, saw the puff of dust and tattered fabric from a sleeve, but it didn't put the target down. Instead, the big Colt rose to meet him, bellowing, and Rogers heard the bullet whistle past him as he charged.

"God*damn* it!"

One shot left, and Rogers fired it on the gallop, saw his enemy slump backward with a grimace as the Colt went off again. This time, incredibly, the bullet clipped his reins and Rogers lost them, bending low across the gelding's withers as they galloped through the middle of the firefight, weapons hammering on either side of him.

It was a miracle that Harpe or Nolan didn't drop him, but he made it through somehow and stopped the gelding in another forty yards or so by dragging on a handful of its mane. It was hard to reach the dangling reins, but Rogers managed. By the time he turned around, Martinez had been blasted from his saddle and the Mexican's chestnut was running free.

Rogers holstered his empty pistol and reached down to draw his rifle from its scabbard. He levered a cartridge into the chamber and sighted downrange, past the closer wagon, waiting for the man who'd nearly killed him twice to show himself.

No hurry now, he thought. *We've got all day.*

And there he was, rising again with the long-barreled

shotgun in his hands. Rogers let him strike the pose, noting his stagger and the blotch of crimson underneath one arm, then shot him from the wagon seat and watched him fall.

"That's mine," he said. "You lazy bastards finish off the other one."

And so they did. With a flurry of gunfire, Harpe and Nolan routed the rifleman from his place beneath the wagon, bolting in a cloud of dust and gun smoke. He came up firing, but someone caught him with a bullet to the chest, then two more as he fell.

"All right, now," Rogers told the gelding as he put his Winchester away. "It looks like time for fun."

"I can't believe that *pinche cabrón* shot me off my horse," Ruben Martinez said.

"You're lucky it was only birdshot," Nolan told him.

"Lucky! Look at me and say that!"

Martinez stood with his shirt torn open and gaping, his torso bare and streaked with blood beneath it. Some of the blood came from small wounds like pinpricks that dotted his chest, while the rest clotted scratches across his flat stomach. The pinpricks were marks left by birdshot, fired from a range of twenty feet or so. The scratches had come later, and although they hurt him more, Martinez reckoned they were worth it.

"We've seen you, Ruben." Colonel Harpe spoke from the nearby wagon bed while buttoning his trousers. "If that Mex had sense enough to load a buckshot round, you'd be a dead man now."

Martinez recognized the truth of that, but he couldn't

resist complaining. "What about my shirt?" he said. "It's ruined, with the blood."

"Put on another one," Rogers suggested. He was sitting on the ground beside the second wagon, taking full advantage of its shade.

"Another one? What 'nother one?"

"Jaysus and saints preserve us," Nolan jeered. "We've got a one-shirt wonder here."

Martinez turned to face the Irishman, scowling. "You saying I don't smell good, maybe?"

"Not a bit of it, boy-o. We all admire your thrift, I'm sure."

"I don't stand by for being made a joke, gringo."

"No more of that!" the colonel snapped. "We've got a long ride yet ahead of us, and likely trials along the way."

"Tell this one he should mind his tongue," Martinez said. "Somebody like to clip it for him."

Nolan stood his ground, smiling, the fingers of his right hand wrapped around the curved butt of his Colt. "I guess this means the wedding's off."

Harpe vaulted from the wagon bed and moved to stand between them, thunder brewing in his face. "I told the both of you to stop this shit!" he growled. "You've had your goddamned exercise and that's an end to it, unless one of you wants to try his hand with me."

Nolan kept smiling, but his fingers broke their contact with the pistol. "No," he said, "I reckon not."

Martinez huffed and shook his head.

"All right, then," said the colonel. "If you need a shirt, look through the things these pilgrims left us. There's no telling what we'll find that could be useful later on."

Martinez turned his back on Nolan, moving toward the second wagon. This one had no bodies in it, and the contents were not stained with blood. He didn't need to see the women anymore. Instead, he would remember them as they had been in life, pleading for mercy that was nowhere to be found.

The shirts he found were all homemade, but they were clean and fit him well enough to pass a casual inspection. Mollified, Martinez claimed three for himself to spite the Irishman and stripped his old shirt off, wadding it up to dab the blood smears from his chest and stomach. As he dressed, Rogers and Nolan worked around the women in the first wagon, tossing their pots and pans into the dirt.

"No money?" Harpe demanded.

"Nothing yet," Nolan replied.

"I may have something here," said Rogers, opening a drawstring bag. Then: "Shit, it's just a rosary." He threw the cross and beads to join the cookware.

Martinez didn't trust a man who treated sacred objects with such disrespect. He'd robbed a church once, in his younger days, but afterward had regretted it, and was convinced the Holy Virgin had forgiven him his lapse in judgment. She forgave most anything, in fact, if the apology rang true.

Martinez hoped so, anyway.

"Well, Ruben," Harpe addressed him, "what about it?"

"Shirts," Martinez said.

"I see that, and I'm happy for you. What else have you found?"

He rummaged energetically through children's clothes and dresses, more cookware, a box of well worn tools. Martinez recognized the saw and hammer, but the other implements were strange to him.

"Nothing," he said at last.

"Damn it! Turn out their pockets, then. There must be something."

"Folk like these will travel light, Colonel," Rogers replied. "I'd say we got the only treasures they were carrying."

"Turn out those pockets anyway."

Martinez left them to it and climbed down to stow the spare shirts in his saddlebag. "Nine pesos," Nolan said at last. "That's it, for all of them together."

"Give it here," Harpe said, and waited for the Irishman to fill his palm with coins. The colonel shook them in his hand like dice and said, "Better than nothing, I suppose."

Martinez watched the old man standing in the middle of the road, beside a wagon full of death. It didn't seem to faze him. Nothing ever did. Sometimes Martinez thought Harpe wouldn't bat an eye if Satan rose up from the earth in front of him and asked him for the time of day.

There was another sort of fire in Harpe's eye now, as he stood squinting at the sun. "Let's ride," he ordered, pocketing the coins and moving toward his tethered mare. "We've got a fair piece yet to ride before we camp."

They stopped twelve miles south of the fresh killing ground, Harpe deciding that they'd traveled far enough to put some space between themselves and the crime. Dusk was falling when he spied a stand of scrawny trees, east of the road, and led his men to water with the self-assurance of an old-time dowser. The other three were quiet as they set up camp, and Harpe left them alone.

He had entertained them enough for one day.

Supper was beans and side meat taken from the wagons, just a trifle on the gamy side. Harpe calculated they would need more food before another day was out, but he wasn't afraid of starving on the trail. Bold men made their own luck, he'd decided long ago, before he had the right to truly call himself a man. That simple creed had seen him through the War Between the States and all that followed after it, unto the present day. It hadn't failed him yet, and Harpe wasn't afraid that it would let him down tomorrow.

"This meat's spoiled," said Rogers, poking at the slab of fatback on his metal plate.

"I've eaten worse," Nolan replied.

"And where was that?"

"Hell's Kitchen. Yuma. Here and there."

"There was a time, back in the war," Harpe said, "when this meal would've been mistaken for ambrosia."

"What's amborgia?" asked Martinez.

Harpe saw no percentage in correcting him. "Food of the gods, *amigo*. Jupiter and company enjoyed it on Olympus, so we're told."

The Mexican stared blankly at him, then went back to shoveling his beans.

Rogers scraped his pork into the fire and set his plate aside. "Colonel," he said, "I've often wondered how a well-bred, educated fellow like yourself came to the rootless life."

Harpe studied Rogers in the firelight, searching for a hint of sass that would demand he take offense, but Rogers kept his face straight and his manner humble. "Boy," he said at last, "you might say I'm a child of circumstance."

"How's that, *suh*?"

Harpe detected just a smidge of mockery that time, but let it go. "Since it's been preying on your mind, I'll tell you how it came about."

And so he did. Harpe sat and told them of his life before

the war, growing up on his daddy's plantation, the closest thing to royalty there was in Giles County, Tennessee. Life was sweet before that damned Abe Lincoln forced the South to pull up stakes and start a brand-new country. Even then they might have saved it, but the Yankees pushed and pushed until it came to killing and the rest was history.

"War changes a man," Harpe told them, winding down. "You see things, do things, then go home and find out it's not home anymore. You keep riding and next thing you know, here you are."

"That's a sad story, Colonel," said Rogers.

"I came out better than most," Harpe replied. "Damn Yankees didn't do your people any favors neither, boy. Our niggers had a home before the war, and steady work. They never had to think about tomorrow, where they'd sleep or where their next meal might be coming from."

"Or who'd whip their ass if they didn't work their asses off."

"Bullshit! My daddy never laid a hand or lash on any nigger who gave him a fair day's work. You're letting some damn fool in Washington piss on your head and tell you it's raining."

"You'd be forgetting, Colonel. I was there."

Harpe smiled across the fire. "I don't remember seeing you."

"My people did their fair day's work a good way south of Tennessee."

"Well, there you are. I'm not responsible for what you claim was done some other time and place."

Rogers displayed a vulpine smile. "You got me there, Colonel. Reckon I owes y'all an apology fo' bein' so ungrateful."

"Don't fret yourself about it," Harpe replied. "Ingratitude has always been a failing of the lesser races."

For a second there, he thought Rogers might make a move, the tension stretched between them like piano wire, but the moment passed them by. Rogers cracked another smile, using his field hand voice to say, "You is a caution, Colonel. Tha's a fact."

"I'm glad you think so, son," Harpe said. "And since we're all in such a jolly mood, I've got a little something in my saddlebag to help us sleep."

They passed the whiskey bottle twice around and finished it. The mood in camp had mellowed by the time Harpe drained the last few amber drops and pitched the bottle into outer darkness. Nolan drew first watch, while Rogers and Martinez crawled into their bed rolls.

Peace on earth, Harpe thought.

But he would sleep with one eye open, just in case.

9

Price smelled the battleground before he saw it.
There was no great trick to that, riding down-
wind of it, and he supposed Gray Wolf had caught the
scent before he did. Waiting, perhaps, to see if Price picked
up on it.

Price reined his horse to a standstill. "How long have
you been smelling that?" he asked.

The young Apache's shrug was eloquent. "Not long."

"Uh-huh."

It was mid-afternoon. They'd been three hours on the
road, since coming back to it from their detour. Price had
been watching out for trouble, but that didn't mean he'd
see it coming. In the wasteland a mirage sometimes
seemed real enough to touch, while enemies of flesh and
blood merged with the landscape and became invisible.
Before he traveled any farther, Price wanted to know what
lay ahead.

He took the spyglass from his saddlebag, extended it, and raised it to his eye.

"Two wagons," Gray Wolf told him. "Maybe three."

"It's two," Price said a moment later. And confirming it, as if there'd been a doubt left in his mind: "We've got some people dead."

"Not mine," Gray Wolf replied. "Not yours, I think."

"They're somebody's." Price put his glass away and urged the bay forward. He wasn't sure Gray Wolf would follow him, and didn't really care. The battle here was over and the dead had claimed the field. There was no danger, but there might be something he could learn.

About the killers, for example.

Maybe they were his, and maybe not. If so, perhaps they would've left him something. A forget-me-not. Perhaps a pointer to their destination.

Agua Caliente.

It was tantalizing, but he couldn't take it as the gospel, coming from a half dead stranger and translated by Gray Wolf. Price wanted more, but whether he would find it here, amongst the dead, was anybody's guess.

The smell of death got worse as Price drew nearer, but he'd long since grown accustomed to it. Sunbaked death was different than a drowning or a fire, but there was still a common quality about it, sickly sweet and cloying. There was no forgetting it, after the first time it was savored and identified. He'd heard it said that soldiers took the smell of killing to their graves, no matter how long they were out of uniform.

When he was halfway to the wagons, Price heard Gray Wolf coming on behind him, not exactly rushing it, but keeping pace. At fifty yards, Price reined the bay back to an easy trot, taking his time. He wouldn't draw the Colt without some proof of danger, but he did release its hammer thong. The small precaution didn't cost him anything, and Price felt better knowing he had shaved three quarters of a second off his draw.

This time the dead people were Mexicans, Price saw. The way it looked, one man had tumbled from the forward wagon's seat when he was shot. Another lay sprawled out beside that wagon, in the road. There were children, too, at least three in the dust. Price found the women only when he'd stopped beside the first wagon and looked into its bed. He wondered why the horses had been left alive and standing in their traces, then decided that the killers' malice might not reach beyond their own species.

Gray Wolf caught up to him as Price dismounted. After tying off his own reins to a wagon wheel, Price went to free the other horses. Gray Wolf watched him as if Price were in the midst of some arcane and unexpected ritual.

"No reason they should starve," Price said. "This way, at least they've got a chance."

Gray Wolf considered it, then steered his pony toward the second wagon. The abandoned horse made no attempt to shy away from him as he bent down to cut its traces with his knife and slip the harness from its head.

"This one is broken," he announced. "It does not run."

"Give it some time," Price answered. "It'll move when it gets thirsty."

"I should take it with me."

"Take both of them, if you want to."

"They don't look much good for riding."

"Maybe when they've had some food and rest," Price said.

"No time for rest, but I can eat them later." The Apache

saw Price watching him, and shrugged again. "You've never eaten horse meat?"

"Not that I recall."

"It isn't bad. Better than dog, at least."

"I'll have to take your word on that."

"White men have strange ideas sometimes."

Price stood beside the forward wagon, where he had a clear view of the killing ground. "You'll get no argument from me on that," he said.

Gray Wolf watched Price move among the dead and asked, "Were these killed by the men you seek?"

"It's likely, but I can't be sure."

"Not by Apaches," Gray Wolf told him.

"No," Price said. "Nor scalp hunters."

"Outlaws." He understood the white man's concept, though it had a different meaning for him. Gray Wolf had lived an outlaw's life from birth, condemned by his blood and the color of his skin.

"They went for the women," Price said, walking through it. "The others were just in the way."

Gray Wolf made no reply. He'd seen worse done by soldiers in Apache camps, while they were hunting so-called renegades. He wasn't sure if women suffered more than men in life and war, or if their suffering was simply of a different kind. The things he'd seen and felt all ran together in the end. They kept his hatred fresh.

"I ought to bury them," Price said.

"There are too many," Gray Wolf said. "It would take half the night."

"Still . . ."

"Have their spirits not moved on?"

Price studied Gray Wolf's face, his own eyes shaded by the flat brim of his hat. "Some folk would say so," he replied.

"They taught it at the mission school."

"All right."

"And if their spirits have moved on, what do the bodies matter?"

"It's a question of respect," Price said.

"You didn't know these people."

"No."

"Did you bury the others who were killed, before we met?"

Price frowned and shook his head.

"Because it would have cost you time and kept you from the killers," Gray Wolf said.

"That's right."

"What's different now?"

"Nothing. You're right."

Gray Wolf looked past him, to the north. "Besides," he said, "you won't have time."

Price turned to follow the direction of his gaze. Gray Wolf guessed that he couldn't see the riders yet, but still he asked, "How many?"

"As before," Gray Wolf replied. "Too many."

"Damn it!"

Gray Wolf couldn't have said if Price was disappointed by the interruption of his funeral plans or by the need to run again. The extra horses would be left behind now, he decided. Looking at them, Gray Wolf didn't think they could outrun a posse, even if they'd dragged their loaded wagons all the way from Jalisco. Dray horses were one thing, and runners were something else.

"I need more time," Price said.

"There is none."

"Right. You're right." Price stood his ground. "But I don't know which way they went from here."

Had he forgotten Agua Caliente? No. But Gray Wolf saw that Price was having doubts. "You work with what you have," he said. "What else is there?"

"Okay."

Though he agreed, Price still made no move toward his horse. Gray Wolf wondered if he would choose to stand and fight, knowing that it was hopeless. If so, he thought, the man would have to die alone. They'd ridden, for a time together, but they were not brothers. Gray Wolf wasn't even sure that they were friends.

In any case, his blood debt had been paid.

And still he asked Price, "Will you stay?"

Price glanced back at him, then faced northward, where the riders now were visible to white man's eyes. He shook his head. "There's nothing to be gained by that."

Gray Wolf had not expected the sensation of relief.

Price walked back to his horse, untied its reins, and mounted. "Do you care which way we go this time?" he asked.

The north-south road was lost to them again. "It must be west or east," Gray Wolf answered.

"We went west last time," Price reminded him.

"East, then."

Another solemn nod. "Suits me," the white man said.

They swung around the wagons filled with silent misery and left the road behind them in another moment, riding hard. Gray Wolf glanced back, hoping the trackers hadn't seen them, but his wishful thinking was in vain. Whether they carried a far-seeing glass like Price's, or they smelled the death in front of them and guessed the worst, he saw the distant horsemen veer off in pursuit.

"Faster!" he called to Price. "They're after us."

"It figures." With a cry, Price spurred his animal to greater speed.

Gray Wolf knew that his pony could outrun the bay with Price on board. He couldn't judge the horses that were chasing them, much less their riders, but he knew that it was foolhardy to underestimate an enemy. If it appeared they would be overtaken on the flats, Gray Wolf would use his springfield carbine, but for now he put his trust in speed and gloried in the fresh wind whipping through his hair.

Lieutenant Maximo Ruiz Ortega watched his men go charging off into the desert with Sergeant Padilla at their head. He had given the order for pursuit, but would not join the chase immediately. Rather, with the corporal and two privates left behind, he advanced to the south.

Toward the wagons and the dead.

Ruiz drew his pistol at forty yards out, barking an order at his small squad to remain alert. The stench of death should keep their eyes open, but he left nothing to chance. *Federale* recruits, sad to say, were not always the wisest of men.

At twenty yards Ruiz knew they were alone with the dead, but he still kept his pistol in hand for the comfort it gave him. Ruiz saw that the horses had been freed to wander off, but they had not gone far. It hardly mattered in the circumstances, since their one-time masters were beyond asserting any claims of ownership.

He counted five dead, men and children, as they neared

the wagons. One had broken down, he saw, and that had been the death of them. Ruiz knew there'd be women somewhere close, as well, but only found them when his horse shied from the wagon with the missing wheel. They lay together in the wagon bed, stripped naked to the unforgiving sun. The story of their final suffering was written on their flesh.

Ruiz bit back a surge of bile that threatened to embarrass him before his troops. He turned away from the tableau as if without concern for those who'd fallen, then saw the stricken faces of his men. The dead weren't Indians this time, or gringos. Underneath their dusty uniforms, his *federales* mostly came from peasant stock. These slaughtered could've been their parents, siblings, children.

They were furious and sickened, all at once.

"We'll catch the animals who did this," he assured them, even though he owed no promises to his subordinates. It didn't hurt to let them see his human side from time to time, as long as they were only fleeting glimpses and he never lost control. Rage was appropriate today, if carried with sufficient dignity.

"Lieutenant?" Like a child in school, the corporal raised his hand.

"There's no time for discussion now," Ruiz said. "We must catch up with the rest, before they go too far."

"I hope they do," the corporal said, remembering at the last second to add "sir."

"Too far ahead, I meant."

"Yes, sir."

But he had set Ruiz to thinking as they rode off to the east, chasing the dust raised by Sergeant Padilla's manhunters. It would be better, Ruiz thought, if they could take the animals alive.

Better for *him,* at least.

A *federale* officer had certain options when it came to handling felons captured on patrol. The strictly legal course of action called for prisoners to be disarmed and taken to the nearest garrison for trial. It sounded good on paper, but in practice it meant either ending a patrol the first time suspects were arrested, or else dragging them along—and feeding them—for the remainder of the trip.

Because that inconvenience troubled some commanders more than others, prisoners were sometimes killed while "resisting arrest" or trying to "escape." Mexican courts recognized La Ley de Fuga—the Law of Flight—which permitted officers to shoot a fleeing suspect, no matter how trivial his supposed crime. And if a few were hanged instead of shot, what harm was there in that?

But there was still a better way.

If he could bring the prisoners alive to Don Miguel Aristo de Montoya at La Strella, one day's journey to the east, there would be money in his pocket and the bastards would receive their fitting justice all the same. Better than if Ruiz had taken them to court, in fact, because he knew that Don Aristo would make sure they suffered for their crimes before they died.

Why not?

Ruiz spurred his stallion, clinging tightly to the reins. It was a race against Sergeant Padilla and the others now, before they overtook and killed the gunmen. There was no profit in corpses, but Ruiz couldn't complain unless he reached the scene in time.

"Rapido!" he hissed to his stallion. "Faster!"

The animal sensed his urgency, plunging forward with renewed effort, its hoofs pounding divots in the dry desert floor. Ruiz merely had to hang on, leaning into the wind as his men trailed behind him. Ahead, he glimpsed his troopers racing through a pall of dust.

"Hold on," he whispered, as much to the animal as to himself. "Just a little longer now. *Hold on!*"

Trust did not come easy to Gray Wolf. Bonds of trust were slowly forged and quickly severed in his world. And once those bonds were broken, they could never be repaired.

Gray Wolf had trusted Little Hawk and Coyote Dancer with his life, but now their lives were ended. He trusted his pony and his rifle, within limits.

And he trusted his own instinct.

It was instinct now that told Gray Wolf to separate himself from Matthew Price. Riding together as they were, with gunmen closing from behind, he knew they made better targets for their enemies than one man riding by himself. Why make it easier for those who meant to kill him, if there was a way to make their task more difficult?

Besides, his debt to Price was paid.

Gray Wolf considered warning Price before he made his move, then put the notion out of mind. Surprise was critical. Whatever happened in the next few moments could determine whether Gray Wolf lived or died.

Without a word or signal, then, he tugged the pony's reins and sent it wheeling off to the northeast, away from Price. A distant shout behind him told Gray Wolf his enemies were on alert, but he refused to turn and see if any of them followed him.

Not yet. It wasn't time.

He did glance at Price, and saw the white man riding on without him, to the east. Whether he was aware of Gray Wolf's deviation yet, the young Apache couldn't say. Price kept his head down, facing forward, concentrating on the ground in front of him.

It was the way to stay alive, and Gray Wolf followed his example. Bending low across his pony's withers to cut down on wind resistance, he spoke urgently, trusting the animal to understand. If they were overtaken, one or both of them would die. Should either manage to survive, it would be as a slave.

Gray Wolf wasn't sure how long his pony could run at full speed in such heat, but he knew the animal would not surrender while an ounce of strength remained. It would carry him until its proud heart burst and Death's weight pulled it down. Gray Wolf hoped that his enemies would quit the chase before that happened, but if they kept after him and he was forced to fight alone, on foot, so be it.

He would die with the same courage as the animal he rode, and those—if any—who survived to take his scalp would mourn the bitter taste of victory.

Gunshots rang out behind him, and Gray Wolf hunched closer to his pony, offering a smaller target. They were firing rifles, but the sound seemed *wrong* somehow. Another volley sounded, and he registered the fact that it was farther off. No matter how he strained his ears, Gray Wolf couldn't pick out the telltale sound of bullets whistling past him on the breeze.

He had no choice now but to risk a backward glance. Of those who had pursued him from the road, Gray Wolf saw only two still coming after him. The other four or five were chasing Price off to the east, and it was their gunfire that echoed far and wide across the wasteland.

Gray Wolf had a choice to make. He could ride on and hope the two men on his track would tire, give up the chase, or he could help them make that choice. Whatever

he decided, Gray Wolf knew there was no time for a pro-
longed debate.

The time to make his choice was now.

Cursing, he hauled back on the pony's reins and
brought it to a halt in swirling dust. Gray Wolf turned to
face his enemies, giving the gunmen their best target yet,
but only for an instant as he raised the Springfield carbine
to his shoulder.

They were still three hundred yards away, but closing
fast. It took more nerve to sit and wait for them than to go
riding off across the desert at top speed. His hands were
steady, as if Gray Wolf's life depended on them—which it
did. He cocked his rifle, waiting for the dust to settle and
his targets to come into range.

Closer . . .

Soon, now . . .

As soon as Gray Wolf's chosen target was within a
hundred yards, he fired. The heavy weapon kicked against
his shoulder, but Gray Wolf ignored it, busily reloading.
Only when he had a fresh round in the chamber did he look
to see if he had made the first shot count.

Downrange he saw a horse, confused and riderless,
running in circles on the arid flats. The dark form of its
fallen rider struggled in the dust, as if about to rise, and
then fell back again.

The second rider may have seen his comrade fall. In any
case, he recognized the danger to himself and tried to
wheel about while there was time.

Too late.

The Springfield bucked again, and this time Gray Wolf
saw his target lifted from the saddle on impact, tumbling to
earth as his animal bolted away. This one didn't move, but

lay slack in the dirt like a scarecrow cut down from its pole.

Gray Wolf paused for another moment, reloading the carbine, and watched Price leading the rest of the riders away. For an instant he considered riding after them, then realized it would be madness, tantamount to suicide.

My debt is paid, he told himself again.

And the gringo was on his own.

The second spray of rifle fire came closer than the first, making Price flinch, but his adversaries still had trouble with their aim. Price didn't know how long he had before they found the range, but at the present rate he guessed that one or more of them were bound to catch a lucky break before he could outrun them.

It was a waste of breath to curse them, so he concentrated on the track in front of him—or lack of one, to be more accurate. The bay was doing fine so far, running across the flats as if Hell was on its heels, but it was bound to tire or hit an obstacle at some point if the hunters didn't hit their target first.

Price couldn't fault Gray Wolf for going off alone. The ploy had worked, dividing their pursuers. It was just bad luck that a majority of them had stuck with Price. He didn't wish the young Apache any harm, but if he could've traded places at that moment, Price would happily have sent the posse's main force off to chase Gray Wolf and faced the stragglers with a bit more confidence.

The next gunshots Price heard came from the north, a fair way off, and had the sound of something heavier than what his enemies were packing. Gray Wolf's Springfield?

Price couldn't be sure, but if required to say, he would've guessed the Indian was no longer at risk from his pursuers.

That left four, by Price's count, although he couldn't guarantee the hasty census had been accurate. It didn't really matter, since there were enough of them to form a skirmish line and drop him with triangulated fire if Price should turn and challenge them collectively. His only hope was speed, and even with the bay's determination, Price knew he was running out of time.

He saw a range of mountains in the distance, but they were at least a day's ride out of reach. There might be something closer, boulders or a clump of stunted trees, but if there was, Price couldn't see it yet. And by the time he did, it would most likely be too late.

The bitterness he felt was focused on the men he'd followed south from Texas, leavened by the knowledge that they might elude him after all. With no belief in Hell to offer consolation, Price knew they would go unpunished— for the crimes that mattered, anyway—unless he saw to it himself.

And now that chance was slipping through his fingers like a rope of sand.

The horse could do no more, he realized. It had been running at top speed since they began the race, and it had nothing more to give. How long that pace could be sustained, Price didn't know. At some point they would fall together, and if he survived the tumble there'd be nothing left but blood and gun smoke at the end.

He wouldn't let the posse take him, that was certain. Price had seen the violence done by frightened and frustrated men, and he would not submit himself to that. Better to go down in a leaden storm than have his life protracted by a few more hours spent in screaming agony.

And maybe he could drop the bastards after all—or take them with him, anyway.

It would be something. Not the end he might've hoped for, but he'd never doubted how the final chapter of his grim life would be written. Only the specific details were obscure.

Price almost had his mind made up to turn and face his followers, when something struck the right side of his head with stunning force. The sudden pain had colors, blazing white shot through with streaks of red and gold.

As he began to fall, an old gunfighter's words came back to him. *You never hear the shot that kills you.*

Price had time to curse his fate before the sandy earth came up to meet him in a rush.

Lieutenant Ruiz stood over the gringo, surrounded by his men. He'd sent a corporal off to find the stragglers, but God only knows when they would return or if they would come back empty-handed.

In the meantime he had this one, battered and bloodied but clinging to life. Ruiz had thought the bandit was dead at first, and the idea set him raging until Sergeant Padilla corrected his mistake. Even now, in the aftermath of his tirade, the men eyed him curiously, wondering, why he should care if a miserable gringo lived or died.

"Count yourselves fortunate that this one lives," he said. Before one of the men could question him, Ruiz continued. "Don Miguel will be most pleased to have a gringo outlaw, I believe."

That answered any questions that his men might have and put the smiles back on their faces. Don Miguel Aristo de Montoya was renowned for his effusive hospitality. If he was pleased with their sacrificial offering, the *federales* could expect a feast to remember—and perhaps some portion of Aristo's generous reward.

Not too much, thought Ruiz, eyes taking in the greedy faces that surrounded him. *The lion's share is mine.*

He would remind them not to talk about it when they got back to Monclova, stressing what they knew already— that if Captain Sanchez learned of the transaction, he would pick their pockets and reserve a special punishment for anyone who tried to cheat him. Most of them despised Sanchez enough to screw him just on principle, but if there was a bit of money to be made, so much the better.

The gringo hadn't moved so far. Ruiz could barely see him breathing.

"I think he may die, sir," said Padilla.

"Hope he doesn't, Sergeant." Turning on the men, Ruiz asked, "Which of you shot him?"

The privates shifted. nervously, exchanging glances. One of them at last said, "Mondregon, sir."

Naturally. He was the corporal whom Ruiz had sent to track the others down, and thus was not there to defend himself. Ruiz assumed it was a lie, but there was nothing to be gained from arguing about it now. Sergeant Padilla simply shrugged when Ruiz looked to him for confirmation.

"Ola!" someone in the back row cried. "He's coming back!"

The squad turned as a single man to face the north, where a horseman was visible, headed their way. Ruiz assumed it was Mondregon returning, but he barked at the men anyway. "Stand ready! Form a double line!"

The *federales* did as they were told, the front rank kneeling so the men in back could fire over their heads.

Ruiz knew it was wasted effort, even if the rider wasn't
Mondregon, since no gunman could possibly defeat them
all. Still, he had learned that discipline was necessary if he
wanted to retain control.

"It's Mondregon," Sergeant Padilla told them when the
gap had closed to something like a hundred yards.

"All right," Ruiz replied. "Stand down."

They waited for the dusty rider to dismount, snap to attention, and salute. He offered no report, however, until
prodded by Ruiz. "Where are the others, Corporal?"

"Dead, sir. Both dead."

"What happened?"

"They were shot, sir. I think with a rifle. Long-range."

"And the man they were sent to bring back?" asked
Ruiz.

"There's no sign of him, sir."

Madré de Dios. "And you left them where they fell?"

The corporal blinked, scanning the ring of surly faces,
worried by the others watching him. "I couldn't catch the
horses, sir. I tried, but—"

Ruiz interrupted him. "Sergeant Padilla! Take a detail
and retrieve the bodies with their animals. The corporal
will be your guide."

"Yes, sir!" Padilla called four privates from the ranks
and led them toward the horses, Mondregon trailing behind them with his own.

"We ought to hang this one ourselves, sir," said a lanky
private named Tafoya.

Ruiz did not enjoy explaining orders to his men, but this
time there was no escaping it. "He'll still be just as dead if
Don Miguel does it, and we'll be better served."

"Yes, *sir.*"

Tafoya wasn't fool enough to sneer at his commander,

but his tone made Ruiz itch to slap the private's face. He brooked no insubordination from his men, and if Tafoya gave him any further guff, Ruiz would have to settle it decisively. For now, though, he was focused on the gringo lying at his feet.

"Where is his horse?" Ruiz asked no one in particular.

"It ran away, sir, when he fell," one of them answered.

"And you couldn't catch it?"

No answer this time, but the sound of shuffling boots.

A stupid question, Ruiz told himself. *The lazy bastards didn't even try.*

"Who has his pistol?" the lieutenant asked. An afterthought.

"Sergeant Padilla, sir."

It was Tafoya's voice again. Before Ruiz could turn on him, one of the others said, "Look, sir! The gringo's waking up."

Price felt as if the right side of his skull was pulverized. The pain required a grimace and a groan. He couldn't hide it from the *federales* standing over him, and in another moment they were hauling him erect. Rough-handed, one on either side of Price kept him from falling when they had him on his feet. They wouldn't let him raise a hand to wipe the fresh blood from his right eye, so he kept it closed.

The man in charge was speaking to him, but it took another moment for the buzzing of his voice to make sense in Price's throbbing head.

"You hear me, gringo?" the officer demanded, leaning close enough that Price could smell his sour breath. The hardware on his collar made him a lieutenant.

"Loud and clear," Price said.

"You'll pay for what you've done," said the lieutenant.

Price swallowed a rush of nausea and answered, "If you mean those pilgrims on the road, it wasn't me. I found them dead."

"Of course you did." There was a hungry edge to the lieutenant's smile. "And then you ran away because you're innocent."

Price couldn't argue that point, so he said, "Check out the bodies. From the state they're in, it's clear they died sometime this morning. I found them less than an hour ago. Your men were right behind me."

"You had no time with the women, then?" asked the lieutenant, goading him.

"It's not my style," Price answered.

"And my men?" the officer inquired. "Should I suppose you found them dead as well?"

Price craned his neck despite the pain, left eye examining the *federales* who surrounded him. "They look pretty healthy to me."

"I mean the two killed by your friend."

Price kept his bloody face blank. "I seem to be a little short of friends right now," he said.

"Indeed," said the lieutenant. "That might change if you would tell me where he's gone. If not . . ."

"Afraid I don't know who you mean."

The kidney punch would certainly have put him down, except for the two *federales* holding Price's arms. They had to struggle with his deadweight even so, until his legs remembered how to follow orders.

"I have no sense of humor," the lieutenant told him, "where the lives of my *compadres* are concerned. You'll tell me what I need to know before we're finished. This I promise you."

"You may as well get started then," Price said.

He braced himself as the lieutenant nodded, but instead of lighting into him, the men on either side of Price simply released his arms. He felt his legs buckle and couldn't keep himself from falling. When he hit the ground, a jolt of pain ripped through Price, starting from his wounded head and searing through him to his knees.

"You have some time to think about your choice," said the lieutenant, looming over him. Price noted that he stood to one side, so his shadow wouldn't shield Price from the sun.

They left him there, two men on guard, and went to tend their horses. Price tried to survey his situation without making any sudden moves. His Colt was gone, of course, his sheath knife likewise. Several yards away, Price saw his hat, blood-speckled, lying in the dirt. His horse was nowhere to be seen.

The *federales* obviously didn't have Gray Wolf.

That's something, anyway.

An hour or an aeon might've passed before Price heard more horses coming and his captors went to meet the new arrivals. Sitting up cost him another sickly swirl of pain, but it was worth it. Coming at them from the north, a group of riders led two horses bearing dead men, belly-down across their saddles. All of them wore *federale* uniforms.

Remembering the final shots he'd heard before a bullet found him, Price knew Gray Wolf hadn't missed his mark.

Where was he?

Gone. The young Apache didn't owe Price anything.

The *federales* took care with their two late friends, untying them and lowering their bodies to the ground. Price fought the dizziness and struggled to his feet as the lieutenant came back to him, this time with a shovel in his hand.

"Before we leave, gringo, you have a job to do." His shovel hit the ground at Price's feet. "Bury the men your cowardly *amigo* killed."

Price toed the sunbaked soil. "Could take a while," he said.

"You have all night," the *federale* told him with a smile.

Price passed out twice before he finished digging the two graves. A spattering of wetness on his face woke him each time, the acid smell of it enough to tell him they weren't wasting precious water. On the second time around, he caught one of the bluesuits grinning at him, buttoning his trousers, but it wasn't worth the beating he'd receive for lashing out at his tormentors with the shovel.

Dig, he told himself. *Just get it done.*

He finished with the second hole around mid-afternoon and wasted no time crawling out of it. Price didn't know what the lieutenant had in mind for him, but there was no point giving him ideas by lingering in a grave. Price moved a few yards off and sat down with the shovel close to his right hand.

A sergeant stood above him, yellow stripes on dusty sleeves. "You're not done yet, gringo," he said.

"Two dead men, two graves," Price answered.

"Two *empty* graves. Get up and bury them."

Price used the shovel as a crutch, rising unsteadily. The sergeant wasn't careful. Price could have gashed his throat and maybe reached his pistol by the time the others worked out what was happening.

And then?

He'd have six shots and nearly twice that many targets, each one of them armed. It would be worth the effort if he knew they planned to kill him, but the way it was, he couldn't say for sure. Price wasn't in a mood to throw his life away, if there was any chance of saving it.

He kept the shovel as he hobbled past the sergeant, only dropping it when he stooped to take the first corpse by the wrists. No one moved to help him, so he wasn't shy about dragging the body to graveside. In the process, he noted that Gray Wolf had scored a clean shot through the heart with his Springfield, likely dropping the *federale* before his target knew what hit him.

Price wished the young Apache luck. He was well out of this mess and hopefully wouldn't come back. There was no bond between them that called for a fresh sacrifice. It would've been foolish for Gray Wolf to tackle these odds, and whatever else he might be, Price didn't take the warrior for a fool.

Price rolled the corpse into its last resting place, taking care that it landed faceup. He wasn't sure it mattered, but that seemed to be a sticking point with most folks, as if burying a man facedown would somehow launch him on his way to Hell.

It made Price think about a shooter he'd once known in Abilene, Jack Sundberg. One night at the Long Branch, half a bottle down, he'd told the room he wanted to be buried facedown so the world could kiss his ass. It got a laugh, but when a posse shot the hell out of him two months later, he was buried just the same as everybody else, with blind eyes pointed at the sky.

Price dragged the second body over to its hole, then knelt to roll it in. This time he slipped, misjudged the distance—something—and the dead man landed on his side.

Price looked around and saw the other *federales* frowning at him, not sure if they really cared or simply wanted an excuse to have another go at him.

Price took the decision out of their hands, slipping down into the hole with the dead man and turning him over, arranging the body just so. This one had taken longer dying, with a bullet through one lung, but it was good enough to do the job. Long shots from horseback, in a hurry, and Gray Wolf was gone.

Price heard the *federales* moving toward him. This was when they'd do it, if they meant to leave him here. Price wasn't sure they'd want him buried with a member of their squad, but it would make no difference on his end. One bullet or a roaring fusillade just for the hell of it, it all came out the same.

He stood and waited, straddling the dusty corpse, watching the hostile faces that surrounded him. Price guessed it was as good a time and place to die as any he had seen. He thought again of Mary, wondering if there was any chance he'd see her on the other side, but reckoned they were bound for different places in the end, assuming there was anywhere to go.

"What are you waiting for, gringo?" the sergeant asked him. "We can't leave until you fill these holes."

"Where are we going?" Price inquired before he made a move.

The sergeant grinned at him. "You'll see," he answered. "I don't want to ruin the surprise."

Price rode one of the horses the dead men no longer needed, moving off to the southeast. The *federales* left his hands free, but his animal was tethered to the sergeant's saddle so he couldn't make a break for freedom. Not that it would do him any good, surrounded as he was, the only unarmed rider in the company.

Price went along because the only other choice was suicide, and while he lived there was at least a semblance of hope. He still had no idea where they were taking him, but their direction was at least partially south. Price was intensely conscious of the passing time, but there was nothing he could do to speed the game along.

He kept his eyes open and watched for landmarks on the way. They were already farther into Mexico than he had ever been, and if he saw a chance to run, it would be helpful to remember some of the terrain. Price didn't know where Agua Caliente was, in reference to their route of travel, but the sergeant scowled and told him to be quiet when he asked.

Just wait, he told himself. *You'll get a chance.*

Or maybe not.

Price wasn't any kind of legal scholar, but he knew a thing or two about the laws and courts of Mexico. The country had been ruled by France when Price was still in school, and they were ruled by the Napoleonic Code. In essence, that meant anyone accused of criminal activity was guilty until proven innocent, and Price suspected that his hopes of proving anything in court were nil. It would've been incriminating if the *federales* found him at the murder scene, but fleeing as he had put frosting on the cake.

Dead meat, he thought, and started calculating ways to keep himself from winding up in court.

The good news, he supposed, was that his captors hadn't killed him yet. It made no sense for them to let him live this long, unless they had a certain destination fixed in

mind. Price closed his eyes and tried to see a map of Mexico, imagining wherever they were taking him, but it
turned out to be a waste of time. For all he knew there
could be half-a-dozen towns within a long day's ride, and
any one of them might be the last place he would ever see.

Unless the *federales* dropped their guard.

Price couldn't count on it, but he would be prepared to
seize whatever opportunity they offered him. It wasn't
over yet, although he didn't have much call for optimism
at the moment.

Riding through that dreary afternoon, he nearly passed
out once again from heat and the incessant throbbing in his
skull. Price had been shot before, but never in the head.
This was a simple graze, as far as he could tell, but from
the steady beat of pain, he had to wonder if there might be
damage that he couldn't judge by simply poking at the
wound. His vision had been blurry when he first returned
to consciousness, but part of that was fresh blood in his
right eye, and the rest had cleared with time. Price guessed
that if he didn't die of sunstroke or fall off the horse and
break his neck, he should be fine.

At least until the *federales* killed him.

He thought about the charges they would file against
him. Murder certainly, and anything beyond that would be
window dressing, since they couldn't hang him twice. No
matter what he said in court, Price knew it wouldn't carry
any weight once the lieutenant had described the circumstances of his capture, how they'd had to shoot him from
the saddle as he fled the slaughter ground.

Hell, I'd *think I was guilty,* Price decided, *if I didn't
know the truth.*

And what good would the truth do him at trial?

Not much.

Price started thinking of escape then, working out the details in his mind. It would be easier before they reached a town and locked him up somewhere, but even then the odds were long against him. Maybe he could make it if the *federales* all got drunk and fell asleep, instead of standing watch that night, but something told him that it wouldn't play like that.

The hard way, then.

Like always.

Half an hour short of sundown, the lieutenant found a place that suited him for camping and he called a column to a halt. Price didn't argue when the sergeant told him to dismount. It wasn't time, he thought.

But maybe soon.

Later, Price wished he'd tried it while he had the chance. It was too late by then, of course. The *federales* made a kind of spicy stew for supper and supplied him with a plate, albeit grudgingly. Price spooned it with his fingers when they wouldn't let him have a spoon, but even so, it tasted better than the trail dust he'd been eating all day long.

He tried talking to the lieutenant while they ate, ignoring how the others glared at him around the campfire. "Will you tell me where we're going?" he began.

The officer considered it, then shrugged. "Why not? I doubt you'll recognize the name in any case."

"Try me," Price said.

"We're going to La Strella."

"Well, you're right. It's new to me."

"You've never heard of Don Miguel Aristo de Montoya, then?"

Price slowly shook his head, unwilling to revive the pain now that it had begun to fade a bit. "Can't say I have."

"You'll have the honor of an audience with him tomorrow," the lieutenant said.

"Is he the big noise in these parts?"

"You would be wise to show respect, gringo. This 'big noise,' as you say it, will decide whether you live or die."

Considering the circumstances and the look on the lieutenant's face, Price didn't think there was much doubt which way that vote would go. "So, he's a judge, then?"

The lieutenant blinked. "He is the don."

"The way I understand it, that's some kind of farmer," Price replied.

"A farmer!" The lieutenant glanced around to make sure everybody got the joke. "The don is much, much more than that. Aside from his *estancia*—some fifty thousand acres—he's a man of independent wealth and influence. He helps the people, manages affairs, and sometimes speaks for El Presidente himself."

"Must keep him busy," Price observed. "Unless I got it all ass-backwards, though, the last I heard you still had courts of law."

"Indeed we do," said the lieutenant. "The don, however, deals with special cases in a special way."

"I'm special now?" Price forced a smile to match the officer's. It gave his bruised, unshaven face a feral look. "You flatter me."

"Joke while you can, gringo. Tomorrow, at La Strella, you'll find less to smile about."

"I bet. It doesn't matter that you've got the wrong man, I suppose?"

That sent a wave of laughter rippling right around the

fire. The *federales* who spoke English had a good time with it, nudging one another in the ribs.

"I keep forgetting," the lieutenant said. "You're innocent."

"That's right. But if you want the men who left that mess along the road, I'll tell you where to find them."

The lieutenant's smile was mocking. "How would you know that, unless you're one of them?"

"Simple," Price said. "I followed them from Texas, where they robbed a bank and killed a friend of mine."

"You're hunting these *banditos,* then?"

Price nodded, almost certain that the explanation was a waste of time.

"Then you're a lawman?"

"Not today."

"Which means you have no warrants or credentials."

"Just the will to see it done."

Something in Price's tone made the lieutenant hesitate, frowning. "Who are these men?"

With nothing left to lose, Price spilled it all. "The leader's name is Wiley Harpe," he said. "The other three are named Rogers, Martinez, and Nolan. I'm not sure about their first names."

"Martinez is a very common name in Mexico," said the lieutenant.

"But the other three are Yanquis," Price replied. "Rogers is black."

"A *negro,* eh?"

"That's what I'm told."

The officer lifted an eyebrow at that. "You are *told*? Does this mean you are hunting men you've never seen, *Señor . . .*" He hesitated, then inquired, "What *is* your name, gringo?"

"Matt Price," he answered, confident it wouldn't mean a thing to anyone seated around the fire.

"And so you track these men you've never seen, because they killed a friend."

"That's it."

"And if you found them—then, what?" the lieutenant asked.

"I guess I'd have to wait and see what happened."

"Would you take them back for trial in Texas? Surely not. That's kidnapping."

"I hadn't thought it through that far," Price lied.

"Of course, I understand." The officer set down his empty plate. "You claim to know where these bad men are going?"

Price had already said too much to backtrack with a guessing game. "They're on their way to Agua Caliente," he replied. "I guess they could be there by now."

The lieutenant's smile lit up his face. "Congratulations, Señor Price. It takes a great deal to amuse me when I'm far from home. You have a storyteller's gift."

Price let his shoulders slump. It was a waste of time, as he had feared. "All right," he said. "Have it your way."

"I will," said the lieutenant. "Sergeant! Bring the rope and make this one secure, so we can sleep."

Price fought, but not for long. The rope was tight, its knots beyond his reach.

"Sleep well, gringo," said the lieutenant. "You can use the rest. Tomorrow you may try your luck with Don Miguel."

II

It was a long day's ride despite an early start. The *federales* rousted Price from fitful sleep before the sun had fully broken cover. Breakfast was a plate of last night's stew warmed over, after they untied him, several members of the squad watching his every move. Price didn't flinch beneath the scrutiny, but he was disappointed that they didn't let their guard down even when most people would be half asleep.

True daylight found them mounted and already under way, riding more or less into the sun as it rose. Price registered the course adjustment, but it didn't help him. It didn't matter how far he was forced away from Agua Caliente, if he couldn't shake his captors in the meantime.

Riding through that hot, dry morning, Price imagined what his enemies were doing. Not the ones who had him bagged, but those he'd traveled days and miles to kill for what they'd done to Mary. He imagined they had reached their destination and were settling in to have a high old time, drinking and whoring, maybe swapping stories of their travels with a few more like themselves. Price pictured walking in on them, saw their startled faces when they realized his business.

Would they fight or flee?

He reckoned Harpe would make a stand, but people could be funny sometimes, doing just the opposite of what might be expected. Take away the military title and he might be nothing but a drifter and a coward.

Maybe.

Thinking of the women Harpe and company had killed so far in Mexico, Price felt a moment of relief that Mary's ending had been relatively merciful. Imagining the bastards with her sent him to a dark place that he rarely visited these days. Not just a killing place where he felt cold as flint inside, but someplace where he gloried in it, wishing he could make the last grim moments of his enemies go on for hours.

If they didn't kill him first.

They'll have to get in line, Price thought.

Harpe's men weren't worried yet. Why should they be? They didn't know Matt Price existed, much less that he had followed them from Texas. And the way things looked right now, it wasn't anything that ought to cost them sleep. He'd been diverted from the hunt, and every mile Price traveled made it that much more unlikely that he'd ever come to grips with Mary's killers in this life.

And since it was the only life he had, Price reckoned he should try to use it well.

That resolution didn't help him shake the *federales,* though. They had him boxed, and even with a pair of Colts he would've been outgunned. That didn't mean Price planned to let them have their way, but he would have to draw another card or two and make the best hand of it that he could.

They took no break at midday, and the troopers didn't seem to mind. They had an air of expectation as the sun peaked and their shadows stretched in front of them, pointing the way to nightfall. Price had begun to wonder if the Mexican lieutenant's calculations were defective when a cry rang out and sent a ripple through the ranks.

"La Strella!" someone shouted, while the others sat up straighter in their saddles. The lieutenant didn't try to quiet them, apparently distracted by the chore of slapping trail dust from his uniform.

A mile or so ahead of them, a smudge on the horizon told Price they were coming up on trees or buildings, maybe both. He didn't have a picture of the layout in his mind, but Price had seen his share of Mexican *estancias* and knew the common pattern. There would be adobe walls, maybe some timbers in the mix, and red tile on the roof. The trees would be mesquite, unless they'd struck a well with the capacity to keep some other kind alive. In this part of the wasteland, he supposed it could go either way.

Outriders met them when they were a half mile from the compound. There were six of them, big hats shading their somber faces and repeating rifles in their hands. One of them questioned the lieutenant, but Price couldn't follow everything they said. There was a question of disturbing Don Miguel, but the lieutenant cocked a thumb at Price and got no further argument.

Riding in the last few hundred yards, Price took his time examining the spread. Besides the main house and a kind of barracks for the hands, he counted two large barns and half-a-dozen other outbuildings of varied size. Horses were penned in a corral built large enough to host a rodeo. There was no other livestock visible, but cattle on a ranch like this were often set at liberty to range miles away from home under the watchful eyes of trusted shooters. There could well be other pens or coops behind the house, beyond his line of sight.

When they were close enough to smell the kitchen's fragrance, the lieutenant fell back to a place beside his prisoner. "Be careful what you say to Don Miguel," he cautioned. "If you make a good impression, maybe he'll be merciful."

"Is that a fact?"

Smiling, the *federale* answered, "No, but you can always hope."

Lieutenant Ruiz let Don Miguel's *vaqueros* take their horses, detailing four of his men to accompany the animals and see them properly tended. With Sergeant Padilla and one of the corporals, Ruiz marched the gringo behind two armed guards to the house. Anticipation of reward did not entirely mask his apprehension at the other guards who came along behind with shotguns, cutting off that angle of retreat.

They entered Don Miguel's home from the rear, like servants, passing by the kitchen, where three cooks were busy with the evening meal. Ruiz could not surmise the menu from the glimpse afforded him, and while the smell entranced him, he had pressing business with the don. If he received a decent bounty, he could bargain for a transfer and promotion. With a vote of confidence from Don Miguel, success would be assured.

But if his gift was deemed unsatisfactory . . .

Ruiz shut down that train of thought before it carried him into despair. The guards delivered him to Don Miguel's vast living room and ranged themselves along the northern wall, where they could cover any unexpected action with their guns. The wooden floors were polished to a waxy shine that made Ruiz suspect fresh blood would bead and glisten on the boards.

The room had windows facing westward, toward the sunset, and a fireplace on the south wall large enough for a grown man to step inside. The stones were dark, as were the wooden beams that arched above Ruiz's head. Adobe walls kept out most of the heat, and let a tall cathedral ceiling catch the rest. Illuminated by strategic lamps and candles, the parlor reminded Ruiz of a cave.

Don Miguel Aristo de Montoya waited for them near the fireplace. He was seated on a dais, in a massive wooden chair that could've served some modest monarch as a throne. It nearly dwarfed him, though he was a man of average height and build, with arms thickened by labor in his younger days. The most impressive thing about him was the shock of wavy snow-white hair that framed his craggy, nut-brown face and matched his sculpted beard. A pale scar ran through one eyebrow, across his high forehead, and disappeared into his hair.

Ruiz knew all about that scar—or enough, at any rate, to fear the man who wore it. Don Miguel was not only a wealthy man of substance, owner of a huge estate; he was also a man with a mission, propelled by determination that some said verged on madness.

It would be six years in April since The Incident. Raiders from who knows where had struck a wedding party traveling between La Strella and Montclova, twenty

riders minimum, achieving near-complete surprise. Don
Miguel had killed two of the bandits himself and survived
the head wound that knocked him unconscious. Later,
when the pain and scorching sun revived him, the don
found his son-in law murdered with most of his riders and
the bride—his only child—missing. By the time he gathered reinforcements and gave chase, it was too late. The
bandits and the desert had had their way with her and left
a broken man behind.

Broken but not defeated.

Don Miguel had changed, but the disaster only made
him stronger. There were those who said it drove him mad,
but they would never say it to his face.

For five years Don Miguel had offered cash and other
bonuses for outlaws delivered to La Strella. *Federales*
were legally forbidden from accepting such rewards and
from participating in the exercise of vigilante justice, but
Ruiz was not the first who'd brought a captive to La
Strella. His examination of the crime scene had convinced
him that a hanging rope was insufficient punishment for
this gringo—and he could always use the money.

"Ah, Lieutenant," Don Miguel called from his throne.
"Come forward, please, and introduce our guest."

A shove set Price in motion toward the fireplace and the
dais set beside it. He was trying to decide what kind of
man erects a stage to sit on in his living room, but all that
he could think of was a lunatic who wanted to be king.

Bad news.

His escort stopped ten feet away from the dais and over-
sized chair. Its occupant regarded him with eyes so dark,
Price couldn't tell if they were brown or black. The

stranger's rigid posture made Price wonder if he'd been a military man, or if he wore some kind of spinal brace beneath his clothes. The outfit included a short jacket covered with beadwork, a dazzling white shirt beneath, and knee-high boots over dark leather pants.

All that he needed to complete the picture was a crown and sword.

Price half-expected his captors to kneel, but the lieutenant settled for a stiff bow from the waist. "Don Miguel," he declared, "I present this man to you for justice."

"Who is he?" the old man inquired.

"I can speak for myself," Price responded in passable Spanish.

"Then do so, by all means."

"My name's Matthew Price, and your boys here have made a mistake."

"Indeed?" There was something like amusement in Don Miguel's tone, but it didn't show up on his face.

"I found some people murdered on the highway west of here," Price said. "Your *federales* claim I did the killing, but they ought to know from looking at the bodies it was done a half day earlier, at least."

"These people, were they travelers?"

"Two families," interjected the lieutenant. "Their children were murdered, the women outraged."

Price saw the old man stiffen in his chair. "It was none of my doing," he said.

"He fled at our approach, Don Miguel," the lieutenant stated. "There was another with him who escaped after killing two of my men. Would an innocent man behave so?"

"I ran because your people have a certain reputation,"

Price replied. "They shoot first and forget about the questions. Ask your men if I drew down on them."

"You didn't have the opportunity, gringo!"

"Please, gentlemen." The would-be king spoke without raising his voice. "Señor Price, is it true your companion killed two officers?"

"Two were shot," Price admitted. "I couldn't say who did the shooting."

"And where has he gone?" asked Don Miguel.

"Beats me. I only met him on the road two days ago." Price knew how lame it sounded even as he spoke.

"You didn't ask his name?"

"He called himself Paco," Price lied. It wouldn't help him to denounce Gray Wolf, even if he had known the young Apache's whereabouts.

"I see. It's all a matter of coincidence."

"Not quite. I think I know the men who killed those people on the road."

"I'm listening," said Don Miguel.

Price told the story one more time, for all the good that it would do. New Harmony and Mary, following the killers south. He left out Hoskins and the other killings, judging that the *federales* had enough against him as it was. They couldn't hang him twice, but there was no point helping them tie the noose around his neck.

Don Miguel heard him out, his weathered face blank, dark eyes unblinking. When Price finished, he was silent for a moment, as if mulling what he'd heard. Beside Price, the lieutenant seemed about to speak, but something in the rancher's attitude dissuaded him. When Don Miguel began to speak at last, his voice was weary, almost pained.

"In other circumstances," he declared, "I might have been persuaded by your story. It is not unheard of for our *federales* to arrest the wrong man in a zealous moment. Please, Lieutenant, don't protest. You know I speak the truth."

The officer looked sheepish. He said something underneath his breath that could've been "Yes, sir."

"However," Don Miguel continued, "I do not believe a mistake has been made in this case. An innocent man may flee out of fear, but to kill two lawmen in the process? No, I don't think so."

"I told you already—"

"Your companion, *sí*. The mysterious Paco." Don Miguel shook his head almost sadly. "You should be truthful now, *Señor*. Your soul depends on it."

"I've told the truth," Price said. "I'll take my chances."

"As you wish." The old man nodded once, so that his beard almost appeared to blend with his white shirt. "I find you guilty of murder and worse," he declared. "Tomorrow at dawn you shall be purified by fire."

The rancho didn't have a dungeon, so they locked Price in a smokehouse built of stone, with no way in or out except a heavy door they barred from the outside. His escorts left him with a stubby candle and a box of matches, knowing he could do no harm. A narrow gap beneath the door admitted air and light until the sun went down, then only air. When supper didn't come, he settled down to pass the night as best he could.

The verdict had been no surprise. Price guessed the *federales* knew how Don Miguel would cast his vote before they made the trip. He wasn't sure what the old man had planned for sunrise, but he didn't like the sound of being purified by fire. That had a nasty ring to it—but at the moment there was nothing Price could do to change the plan.

And in the morning? What could he do then?

Not much, he thought, unless he found himself a weapon and a lucky break. But even then . . .

From what he'd seen so far, Price reckoned that Don Miguel had thirty-odd men on his payroll, at least. Assuming the *federales* stayed overnight, that made the odds against him better than forty to one. Price had no guns, no horse, no edge.

No hope.

That didn't mean he had to play along and make it easy for them, though. He'd always been a fighter, from the cradle up, and just because his case looked hopeless, Price was not about to yield and make the end a self-fulfilling prophecy.

Whoever came to fetch him in the morning could expect a scrap. If nothing else, he might drop one of them and grab a weapon. They would have to drop him cleanly then, instead of playing whatever sadistic game El Jéfe had in mind. It wasn't much, but if it was the best Price could accomplish, he would go for it.

And in the meantime—what?

Nothing, he thought. His guards had checked the smokehouse when they locked him in, leaving no knives or cleavers he could use the next morning when they came for him. The smokehouse hadn't been in use of late, as far as Price could tell. He wouldn't even have a side of beef or pork to hide behind and make the bastards work a little harder at removing him.

But he would have his fists and boots, his teeth and wits. Whoever came to fetch him in the morning would remember it until his dying day.

And that might be tomorrow, too, if they weren't careful.

Price had no fear of death per se. He'd played the final act out in his mind a hundred times, in different ways, none of them peaceable. Given a choice, he'd rather make it quick and clean, but nine times out of ten a dying man wasn't allowed to call the shots. This time, however, might just be a special case.

The worst of it was failing Mary. Price came back incessantly to that idea, twisting the knife. If he was out of time, so be it. But that didn't mean he had to meekly let his fate be settled by a stranger he had never seen before this day.

It was a shooter's lot, perhaps, living on borrowed time, but Price had work to do. And failing that, the least that he could do was raise some hell. He'd played the cards as they were dealt and he was busted. If the dealer wouldn't let him have another hand on credit, Price would do his best to spoil the whole damned game.

But something told him that his best wouldn't be good enough.

If raw will and determination were enough to save him, Price would've had nothing left to worry him. In fact, though, he was running out of time.

Price moved to check his pocket watch and found it gone. One of the *federales* must've lifted it after they shot him from his horse, while he was still unconscious. Under different circumstances, he'd have concentrated on a method of avenging both the theft and the insult, but they were minor irritations now.

He'd know when it was morning by the light beneath his door, or when the executioners came to retrieve him from his cell. If he couldn't stop them, couldn't get away somehow, he would be "purified by fire"—whatever that meant.

To Price, it sounded like a little taste of Hell.

The scrape of shovels and the solid sound of hammers woke Price in the gray hour before true dawn. He listened for a moment, then crawled over to the door and lay down with his left cheek pressed against the smokehouse floor, trying to peer out through the slit that was his only window on the outside world. He had a worm's-eye view of movement in the space between the big house and his cell, but Price couldn't have said what the early risers were doing if his life depended on it.

Which it might.

He edged back from the door, unsure if he could tell when they were coming for him by the sound of boots on sand and gravel. His prison muffled and distorted sounds. They could be right on top of Price before he knew it, and he didn't want the enemy to catch him lying down, face in the dirt.

There would be time enough for that when he was dead.

Price lit the stubby candle with his next to-last match and sat staring at the flame. He didn't waste time on another fruitless search of the smokehouse, since it had no secrets to reveal. Instead, Price held the candle close to his face and focused on its steady flame. He didn't want the outer light to blind him when his enemies came through the door, and even this poor light would help contract his pupils, thus eliminating hesitation when he had to move decisively.

Price hadn't worked out any kind of detailed strategy so far. He hoped to make his play outside the smokehouse, where at least he'd have some room to move, but that depended on his enemies. If they came in with ropes and tried to bind him prior to leading Price outside, he'd have to fight them on the spot.

Once he was bound, Price knew, he was as good as dead.

But if his captors carried guns . . .

His mind came back to Don Miguel's pronouncement of his sentence. Price still hadn't worked out what it meant, exactly, but he had the gist of it. The rancher meant to torture him with fire somehow, which made Price all the more intent on getting loose before somebody struck a match. If death was certain, if he had to choose between a bullet and a torch, Price wouldn't hesitate to face the guns.

Escape still beckoned to him, though, if he could only manage it. But how?

He'd been in tight places before—a brush with a lynch mob in Creed, Colorado; outnumbered and surrounded at Baker, in the Johnson County war—but there'd always been room to maneuver, something Price could turn to his own advantage. In Creed, he'd set fire to his own hotel and escaped in the confusion, passing as a member of the bucket brigade. At Baker, it came down to pure bloody business, killing shooters on the other side until the survivors gave up and went home.

Neither one of those plans would save him this time. The smokehouse wouldn't burn and his enemies *were* at home—most of them, anyway. They had Price at a disadvantage he might not be able to surmount, but he could try like hell.

For all the good that it would do.

Defeatism was fatal, Price realized, but it was sometimes hard to avoid. The numbers ranged against him,

Price's lack of weapons—there was only so much that an empty-handed man could do, regardless of his personal determination.

But he wasn't giving up.

Not yet.

Price made it forty minutes, more or less, between the time he woke and when he heard a scuffling just outside his door. The heavy bar was raised and set aside. A moment later pale light spilled into the smokehouse, causing Price to squint despite his preparation. Four men stood outside his cell, the *federale* lieutenant and three of Don Miguel's *vaqueros*. They all wore side arms, and the nearest stranger had a sawed-off shotgun aimed at Price's chest. The man behind him held a coil of blackened chain.

"It's time," the shotgunner declared.

"No breakfast?"

"You *are* the breakfast, gringo," said the young man with the chain. "We gonna cook you pretty soon."

Price noted the lieutenant wasn't joining in their merriment, but he had no time to consider what that meant, if anything.

"Maybe I'll wait for lunch," Price said.

The man in front lost his smile at that and let the muzzle of his weapon droop around knee-level. "Don Miguel wants you alive," he said, "but you don't need your legs."

Price shrugged and forced a smile. "You're such a gentleman, I can't refuse."

Eyes narrowed, Price stepped out into the pallid light of dawn. He saw the other *federales* watching from a point beside the house, setting themselves apart from members of the staff. Some fifty feet in front of Price, a sturdy wooden stake that wasn't there twelve hours earlier protruded from the earth, with deadwood and assorted scraps of lumber piled nearby. At once, Price understood the chain his escort had prepared in lieu of rope.

It wouldn't burn.

Don Miguel Aristo de Montoya stood beside the woodpile, waiting to receive his sacrifice. He was flanked by gunmen, but the old man didn't seem to notice them. He had eyes only for Price, watching the captive approach him and searching for fear in his eyes.

Don Miguel drew breath, opened his mouth to speak—and suddenly pitched forward as if mule-kicked from behind. He landed facedown in the dirt and shivered like a stranded fish. The echo of a rifle shot caught up to him a heartbeat later, and all hell broke loose.

Price acted without thinking through the move, knowing that any hesitation in that moment could be fatal. Spinning in his tracks, he grabbed the shotgun that was rising toward his head and twisted it with all the power of his upper body. At the same time, Price delivered an explosive kick to the *vaquero*'s groin that left him doubled over, bleating with the pain.

Price had the shotgun in the time it took to draw another breath. Beyond the retching shooter, the *vaquero* with the chain was smart enough to know he'd never reach his pistol by the time Price turned on him. He swung the chain instead, hurried but with the accuracy of a cowboy who'd been roping animals for years. The chain lashed out at Price's face—but he had dropped below its hissing line of flight.

He fired one barrel of the sawed-off shotgun, turning from his target even as the dying man took flight on wings of crimson mist. Price saw the *federale* officer retreating, running for his life back toward the house, and so he concentrated on the third *vaquero*. Even as Price turned in that direction, leveling the shotgun, his opponent reached the six-gun on his hip and yanked it from the holster.

He was almost fast enough.

The second shotgun blast tore through the gunman's rib cage like a hammer cleaving flimsy wooden slats. He went down in a kind of sloppy backward somersault, his pistol sailing from dead fingers as he fell.

Price swung the shotgun like a club and smashed its stock into the first *vaquero*'s face. The impact sent the man sprawling, Price on one knee at his side almost before the Mexican collapsed. The prostrate man wore twin Colts on a double gun belt. Price palmed one of them and cocked it, while his free hand went to work on the *vaquero*'s belt buckle.

Scanning the yard, Price saw the startled troop of *federales* scrambling for the nearest cover. Two of Don Miguel's employees crouched beside his body, as if shielding him from further harm. Some of the others were in motion, fleeing toward the house or outbuildings, watching for snipers as they ran. His personal bodyguards, seven or eight *vaqueros,* stood their ground and searched the area for targets.

In another second, they were focused on Matt Price.

He fired into their midst just as another unexpected rifle shot rang out, and two gunmen collapsed almost at the same instant. Those remaining knew that one of their companions had been cut down from behind, and it confused them. Several turned away from Price, seeking the sniper who had killed their friend and Don Miguel.

Price wasted no time searching for a phantom. He

squeezed off another shot, saw one of the *vaqueros* clutch
his side, and got the belt buckle unfastened on his second
try. Price rolled the inert shooter clear, scooped up his rig,
and threw the belt across one shoulder as he ran a zigzag
pattern toward the nearest barn.

Behind him, half-a-dozen guns were firing, and the
angry buzzing in his ears told Price that some of them were
aimed his way. Instead of wasting lead, he kept on running,
and in ten or fifteen seconds reached the barn. It wasn't
much in terms of cover, but at least it shielded Price from
shooters on the rear porch of the house.

As for the rest . . .

He saw two of them rushing him, hunched over rifles as
they ran. Price tracked them with the unfamiliar Colt and
fired as one of them slowed down to risk a shot. His .45
slug spun the human target through a jerky little two-step,
dropping him at twenty yards.

The other gunman knelt and fired a shot that wasn't
aimed, but still came close enough to make Price flinch.
Price thumbed his pistol's hammer back, and was about to
squeeze the trigger when somebody shot the rifleman and
dumped him sprawling in the dust.

Who *was* that?

Price didn't know and didn't care, as long as the distraction kept his enemies disorganized. And if his benefac-
tor thinned the crowd while he was at it, why, so much the
better.

Price broke cover, dodging toward the barn's only visible door. It was large, but swung easily open on well-oiled
hinges, shivering a little in his grip from the impact of bullets. Price ducked inside and crouched behind a tidy pile of
feed sacks, trusting them to shield him while his eye adjusted to the dim light in the barn.

It only took a moment, and he felt his spirits slump.

There were no horses in the barn, no animals of any kind. Price cursed the spacious, empty room. The only thing he'd done so far was to exchange his cramped cell for a larger one.

Not quite.

He had two pistols and approximately thirty extra cartridges. He'd shaved the odds, and had an unknown ally on the outside who was fighting even now.

Price wasn't finished yet.

His enemies might take him down, but they would have to buy their victory with blood.

Lieutenant Ruiz felt his men watching him as he crouched on the porch, pistol drawn, and surveyed the battleground in front of him. He couldn't tell what they were thinking, but it hardly mattered. Only his thoughts mattered now, if he could sort them out and find some exit from the chaos that surrounded him.

Ruiz had counted eight dead men so far, with Don Miguel among them. He had no idea whose shot had killed El Jéfe, whether one of his own men gone mad, or if it was some confederate of the gringo they were about to execute before the shooting started. Either way, the rifle fire was still ongoing, but Ruiz was more concerned about Matt Price, armed now and hiding in the barn. Worse yet, he feared how Captain Sanchez would react when word of this bloody fiasco reached his ears.

It won't make any difference if I'm dead, Ruiz considered, but the thought gave him no comfort. He could live with the embarrassment, even dismissal from the federal police, but only if he *lived*.

It had been risky bringing the gringo to Don Miguel without consulting Captain Sanchez first. He hadn't been paid yet, and now never would be, with Don Miguel dead in the yard. It had all been for nothing, Ruiz thought, unless—

He could still take Price back to Sanchez, of course. The captain wouldn't question why they'd killed the prisoner when he heard about Don Miguel's death. Ruiz could change the facts in his report to suit himself. His men and Don Miguel's *vaqueros* would support Ruiz, since the alternative was a confession to attempted murder. They couldn't hide behind El Jéfe now that he was dead. It would be each man for himself, and they would fall in line behind Ruiz.

The plan would only work, however, if they had Matt Price. Without his corpse for evidence, Captain Sanchez could still dismiss their story as a pack of lies and call for a court-martial on whatever charges he decided were appropriate. They might even be charged with killing Don Miguel, and while no judge in Mexico would burn them at the stake, the gallows was a prospect every bit as fearful to Lieutenant Maximo Ruiz Ortega.

"Listen, all of you!" Ruiz snapped at his men. "We have to flush the gringo from the barn."

"You're *loco*!" one of the young privates blurted out, then clapped a hand across his mouth too late to stop the words.

Ruiz dismissed him with a stony glare. "We can't go back to Captain Sanchez empty-handed after this," he said. "Your jobs depend on it. Maybe your lives."

And yours, they could've answered him, but no one spoke. They huddled on the porch and waited for Ruiz to spell out details of his plan.

"I've been inside that barn," he told them. "There's no entrance but the door you see. He's trapped and waiting for us now."

"Waiting with guns," someone muttered.

Ruiz made no effort to pick out the speaker before he replied. "We can take him. There are nine of us. We *must* take him. Sanchez will hold us to answer for Don Miguel's death, otherwise. Are you ready for that?"

Dead silence answered him, and the lieutenant knew he had them. There was nervous shifting in the ranks as each man checked his weapon, making sure he was prepared. Ruiz had no need to examine his revolver. It was fully loaded, and had never failed him in the past.

"Sergeant Padilla," he commanded, "you will lead the way."

The sergeant scowled at him, but didn't argue. Shifting his revolver nervously from hand to hand, Padilla issued orders to the men. "Constanzo and Madera, you're in front with me. Ybarra and Ornelas, circle to the left and cover us. Vasquez, Limaché, and Quintero, take the right and watch that door."

A muted chorus of agreement echoed from the troops.

"Will you be joining us, Lieutenant?" asked Padilla.

Anger lit a fire inside Ruiz. "Of course I will!"

"Be careful, then. We wouldn't want to lose you." With a parting sneer he rapped out, "Men! With me!"

When they were all in motion, sprinting toward the barn across a field of corpses, the lieutenant rose and followed after them.

Price saw the *federales* coming at a dead run from the house. A rifle shot dropped one of them as three were veering to his left, some kind of flanking movement, and the others faltered for a fraction of a second, then pushed on. He waited for them with a Colt in each hand and the borrowed gun belt buckled snug around his hips.

Price had eight targets and twelve shots before he was forced to reload. With luck, he just might pull it off.

And if he failed—well, it was better than the fire.

The rat-faced sergeant was leading, still twenty yards out from the barn when Price shot him in the chest. The *federale* dropped and rolled, a couple of the others nearly tripping over him before they got their balance back. Price took advantage of their confusion and hit a corporal on the run, then ducked back as the others returned fire. They peppered the barn with a wild fusillade, more angry than accurate.

Price kept his head down while bullets tore through the plank walls. He was cornered, and couldn't go out to confront his assailants without being shot from all sides. The good news was that it would be a quick death. The bad: Mary's killers would never pay for her murder.

Price couldn't accept that while any slight hope still remained. He examined the barn with an eye toward escape, and discovered a wall-mounted ladder that led to a hayloft above. It would give him the high ground, and maybe a chance to surprise his enemies. If nothing else, it would buy him some time.

Price holstered his weapons and climbed to the loft. There were hay bales enough to provide him with cover, but Price was more interested in the loft's loading bay. The double doors were open, and revealed a pulley system bolted to an overhanging beam, designed for hoisting heavy bales or other heavy cargo from the yard below. It was a standard rig, with both ends of the rope secured to a floor-mounted metal cleat.

Price guessed the hardware would support his weight, but that was only one third of the problem. If he jumped, he'd need to have the rope tied off at proper length, to keep himself from plummeting and winding up a fleshy sack of broken bones below. And even if he got the drop right, there were shooters waiting who might pick him off before he reached the ground.

It was dangerous, but it was still his only chance.

Price heard the *federales* muttering outside. They'd need a moment more to work up nerve for the assault, and he decided to make good use of the time. Price calculated distance from the loft's bay window to the ground, and tied off the rope a foot short of impact. He fashioned a noose from the free end, a slipknot to fit his left boot. Before he stepped into it, Price spent a moment reloading both pistols and cautiously scanning the yard.

It was then that he caught his first glimpse of Gray Wolf.

Price couldn't guess how he'd managed to do it, but the Apache had climbed up on Don Miguel's roof and lay prone on the tiles, lining up his next shot with the Springfield carbine.

A sudden surge of hope invigorated Price. He had a chance! Gray Wolf's appearance was a mystery, but Price wasn't about to look that gift horse in the mouth.

Gift horse . . .

Price did his best to focus on one problem at a time. He wouldn't need a horse unless he got out of the barn alive. If he accomplished that *and* made it to the pen without stopping a dozen slugs along the way, there would be time to think about his choice of mounts.

A few brief seconds, anyway.

Price heard the *federales* push their way into the barn. He couldn't tell how many made the rush, how many waited in the yard, but he was on the verge of finding out.

Instead of dueling with the point men, Price moved to the loft's open bay and slipped his left foot into the rope's running noose. He hoped it wouldn't snap his ankle when the slack ran out, but that was just a chance he'd have to take. Gripping the rope with his left hand, he palmed and cocked one of the six-guns with his right. Three awkward, loping strides and Price was through the window, plummeting to earth as if a gallows trap had opened underneath his feet.

Gray Wolf locked eyes with Matt Price for a moment, saw recognition on the white man's face, and then resumed searching the corpse-littered yard for new targets. He chose another of the *federales* clustered near the barn, because their uniforms were hateful symbols of the government that had destroyed his tribe.

It was an easy shot at forty yards, his bullet drilling through the target's back and bursting in a spray of scarlet from his chest. Two others cringed away, blood-spattered faces gaping as their friend collapsed.

Gray Wolf reloaded swiftly, almost without thinking. He had performed the simple movement countless times, and it was second nature to him now. He could reload the carbine in pitch-darkness, with his eyes closed, or while enemies were pouring deadly rifle fire in his direction.

So far that was not the case, but Gray Wolf knew it soon would be. He'd shot four men so far, including the apparent leader of the pack, and while his enemies were still disorganized and frightened, Gray Wolf realized some of them must be calculating angles, working out the source of gunfire. Any moment now he could be forced to change position, giving up his precious vantage point.

It had been relatively easy, slipping past the guards. Wealthy ranchers sometimes kept an army on retainer to protect their livestock, but they trusted one or two *vaqueros* to protect their homes by night. Gray Wolf had slipped past one watchman and cut the other's throat, tumbling his corpse into a well behind the house. He'd scaled a drain pipe to the roof in darkness and remained there overnight, until the sun revealed Matt Price and those who meant to burn him at the stake.

So much for "civilized" society.

The first shot from the yard shattered a tile three feet to Gray Wolf's left and stung him with the jagged shards. He spied the shooter crouched beside an outbuilding, and was preparing to return fire when Matt Price leaped from the barn's hayloft, clutching a rope in one hand and a pistol in the other. Gray Wolf saw him drop among the startled *federales,* rapid-firing into them before they could react effectively.

A second bullet from the yard came closer, and Gray Wolf returned his full attention to the enemy. The Mexican was rising, levering a fresh round into his Winchester's breech, when Gray Wolf shot him just above the belt buckle and put him down. It was a killing shot, but not immediately fatal, leaving the gunman to thrash and kick his life away.

But two more of the enemy had found him now, and their combined fire forced Gray Wolf into retreat. He scrabbled backward over tiles that had begun to draw heat from the sun. Loading his carbine on the move, he topped the low crest of the roof with bullets whispering around him, then made better time as he slid down the other side.

He reached the corner where he'd climbed the drainpipe earlier, and started down. A tile six inches from his elbow suddenly exploded to the echo of a gunshot from below. Gray Wolf glanced down in time to see a young *vaquero* cock his pistol for a second try.

Before his enemy could fire again, Gray Wolf released his hold and launched himself through space. His feet smashed into the *vaquero*'s face as the revolver spoke again, its muzzle flash scorching Gray Wolf's' trousers. He fell atop his adversary, hammering the Springfield's stock into the gunman's unprotected face.

Dead or alive, the Mexican no longer posed a threat. Gray Wolf scooped up his fallen pistol on the run, thankful to have it as two more *vaqueros* suddenly appeared before him, homing on the sounds of gunfire. They had come with weapons drawn, expecting enemies—but not a fierce Apache warrior, bare chested and bloodied, rushing toward them with his teeth bared in a snarl.

Surprise saved Gray Wolf's life. He shot the closer gunman with the liberated pistol, then fired his own carbine one-handed to finish the other. They fell side by side, leaving Gray Wolf to race for the spot where his pony was hidden nearby.

The drop jolted Price off his feet, two men down and two fumbling with guns as he rolled in the dust. He shot one of them from the ground, then kicked free of the rope and scrambled to his feet before the last could find his mark. No more than six feet lay between them as Price fired into the *federale*'s chest and dropped him where he stood.

The shooting brought their comrades rushing from the barn, confused and frightened. There were only three left, the lieutenant among them, and they came out firing aimlessly, filling the air with lead. Price hit the deck again and triggered four shots in as many seconds, firing for effect at point-blank range. His targets lurched and staggered, falling as the bullets found them and released them from the battle.

Rising, Price glanced up and saw no trace of Gray Wolf on the roof. Where had he gone? For that matter, where had he come from in the first place?

Never mind, damn it!

He had to find a horse and quickly, preferably one already saddled that would carry him without a fuss. There'd be no time for gentling down a rowdy animal while Don Miguel's *vaqueros* used him as a target in their shooting gallery.

Price rose and started for the pen, watching for enemies on every side. He'd traveled only a half-dozen strides when a riot of hoofbeats and shouting erupted behind him. Price turned to find Gray Wolf just rounding the southeast corner of the ranch house, with a gaggle of Don Miguel's men in pursuit. The Apache was riding his pony and leading a sturdy brown mare at full gallop. A glance showed Price that the mare was saddled, including a rifle of some kind tucked into a right-handed scabbard.

Price holstered his pistols and readied himself for the leap that might determine if he lived or died this morning. He was ready when the brown mare passed, and jumped to catch the saddle horn. Price missed the stirrup on his first attempt, dragging his feet for several yards until he caught it on the second try. He hauled himself into the saddle as they passed the horse corral, and Gray Wolf tossed him the reins with a flick of his wrist.

There was no time for questions as they raced away from Don Miguel's *estancia* with bullets whining after them. They should've made fair targets for a stationary rifleman, but maybe luck was with them, or the shooters were too shaken to hold steady on their mark. In any case, they cleared the house and outbuildings, riding southwest as if Satan himself was breathing hellfire down their necks.

At this speed, riding over open country, any slip could mean a fall fatal to man and horse alike. Price gave the mare her head, regardless, knowing that if they were overtaken there would be no question of survival. It was flee or fry, and Price would not be caged again.

Ten minutes later, Price glanced back and discovered they had company. It came as no surprise that Don Miguel's surviving men would follow, but he'd hoped they would be slower off the mark, taking more time to saddle up and hit the trail. Price counted eight riders before he gave it up and raised his voice to warn Gray Wolf.

"They're after us!" he called, hearing the rush of wind whip through his words.

Gray Wolf looked back and reined his pony from a gallop to a trot. Price overtook him as the trot slowed to a walk, and said, "I don't think we can lose them."

"No," Gray Wolf replied. "It's best to face them now."

"You mean it's a good day to die?" Price asked.

The young Apache frowned. "There's no such thing," he said. "But if we must die, so will they."

The two grim riders swung their mounts around to face the posse racing after them. Price drew the rifle from its scabbard, a well-maintained Winchester '73, and checked to verify that it was loaded.

"You made a good choice on the animal and gear," he told Gray Wolf.

The warrior shrugged. "It was the first I found."

"Okay." Price raised the Winchester and said, "Ready when you are."

"Soon."

Another thirty seconds passed before the Springfield carbine barked and sent a rider tumbling from his saddle far down range. Price fired and dropped another as the hunters started fanning out to save themselves. A couple of them were returning fire, but hastily, and they were next to go as Price and Gray Wolf found their range.

When six had fallen, the survivors turned and ran for home.

"They may come back with reinforcements," Price suggested, staring at their dust.

"We won't be here," said Gray Wolf.

"No."

"You're going on to Agua Caliente, then?"

"That's still the plan," Price said. "You want to ride along?"

"Today, maybe."

"That's how I take it," Price responded. "One day at a time."

13

"So how much farther is it?" Seamus Nolan asked, raising an arm to wipe sweat from his eyes. The midday sun was cooking him beneath his bowler hat, and he had barely enough water left in his canteen for one more decent swallow.

Harpe made a show of checking the sun and replied, "We'll be there before nightfall, no problem."

"I hope so," Nolan said.

Harpe cast a sneaky sidelong glance his way. "You never told me why you wear that hat."

"You never asked me," Nolan countered.

"All right, then. I'm asking now."

There were a thousand other things Nolan would rather have discussed, but Harpe had pinned him down. Reluctantly, he answered, "It's the only thing my father left me."

"Ah. And how'd he die?"

"I didn't say he died. For all I know, the bastard's still alive."

Harpe studied Nolan's face more closely then. "Just left you, did he?"

"Me, the mum, and my two sisters."

"How long back?"

"It'll be eighteen years come August."

"You still hate him for it," Harpe observed.

"Is there some reason why I shouldn't?"

"None that I can think of, but it strikes me as odd."

"How's that?" asked Nolan.

"Well, you've hated him for almost twenty years, and still you wear that stupid hat to keep his memory in front of you."

"That isn't why," Nolan objected.

"Oh?"

"First time I wore it, after he was gone, a couple of the other boys made fun of me."

"I would imagine so," the colonel said.

"I fought them, but they beat me down." Nolan could taste the filthy New York pavement even now. He saw it in his dreams.

"It happens," Harpe reflected.

"But I couldn't let it go. I looked them up one at a time and paid them back with interest."

"That's my boy."

"I'm not your boy."

"Figure of speech. Don't take it so to heart."

"Seems like no matter where I went, the next few years, somebody gave me shit about this hat. It's how I learned to fight." *And kill*, he nearly added, but restrained himself.

"And now? What is it you expect to prove?" Harpe asked.

"That I can see it through."

"You never found your old man, though."

"I never really tried," said Nolan.

"That's what you think."

Nolan almost asked the colonel what he meant by that, then let it go. His silence felt like a victory of sorts, though Harpe had gotten the last word once again. Not rising to his bait was something, though. For ten or fifteen minutes afterward, it helped Nolan forget about the broiling sun.

Almost.

The smart thing would've been to keep his mouth shut and conserve his energy, but Nolan felt a nagging urge to talk. "What are we doing after Agua Caliente?" he inquired.

"After?" Harpe's face wore an expression that suggested he had never thought beyond the town.

"You've got another job in mind, I guess."

"Not yet."

The answer startled Nolan. He had never known a moment since he started riding with the colonel when Harpe didn't have a plan on tap—more likely three or four. It struck Nolan as curious, even disturbing, that Harpe would've picked a town in Mexico at random, without having any reason or a later destination fixed in mind.

He didn't buy it for a minute.

"Just a thought," said Nolan, trying to sound casual. It did no good to press the colonel when a quiet mood came over him, as Nolan knew from personal experience. If Harpe had something in his craw, he'd spit it out when he was ready, not before.

And if he never got around to it, then what?

Nolan would have to work out the answer to that one himself, or maybe ask Rogers if he had a scheme they could share. Nolan had never been much of a planner, but this much he knew beyond doubt: The end of his trail didn't lie in some Mexican town where they'd never seen corned beef and cabbage.

Nolan didn't miss New York, but he would miss the States eventually. There was nothing to hold him south of the border, and if Harpe didn't have a fair reason for wanting to linger, they would soon be parting company.

That notion made him hesitate, wondering for a moment if the colonel would try to stop him from leaving. No reason on earth why he should, but Harpe got his mind in a strange twist sometimes and did things that made no earthly sense.

If it looked like he meant to stop Nolan, if it even *felt* that way without a sign or spoken word, the Irishman decided he would strike before Harpe had a chance to make his move. It was the only way to guarantee that he would have the upper hand.

But if his luck held, it would never come to that.

And if it did, all bets were off.

Price let the silence stretch between himself and Gray Wolf for an hour, riding southward. Then he said, "I still don't understand why you came back."

"You needed help," the young Apache said.

"No, seriously."

Gray Wolf thought about it for a moment, then replied, "You have a quest. Those men seemed to prevent you from pursuing what you seek."

"A lot of people don't get what they're looking for," Price said. "Most don't, in fact."

"I can't help everyone," said Gray Wolf, smiling.

"Good point," Price replied. "I should've known."

"Your quest is not like others," his companion said more soberly. "You seek nothing of value for yourself. No gold, no land. It is a debt of honor."

"It's revenge."

"They are the same," Gray Wolf declared. "You sacrifice your life for one who cannot even thank you in this world."

"I haven't sacrificed it yet," Price said.

"Where is your home? Your family? Where will you go if you survive your enemies?"

Price had no answers, and that knowledge left him with an aching hollow in his chest.

"You see now," Gray Wolf said. "A debt of honor may be paid, but it can never be erased."

"So, what was yours?" Price asked, hoping to shift the focus from himself.

"I told you of the scalp hunters who killed my people."

"All but you and three others," said Price.

"Coyote Dancer, Little Hawk, and Thunder Cloud. We came too late to die among our own, but we picked out the killers' tracks and followed them."

"How many were there?"

"Thirty-five."

"I wouldn't like those odds," Price said, reflecting that they'd faced the same or worse back at La Strella.

"When we found them, it was easy," Gray Wolf answered. "Killing one or two each night, mostly the ones they left on guard. They hunted us, and those who found us died as well. When most were dead, the last few tried to run. We hunted them like rabbits. I can hear them screaming still."

"And did it help?" Price asked.

"Help what?"

"The way you felt inside, having repaid your debt."

"Such debts are never truly paid," Gray Wolf replied.

"How's that?"

"Some debts involve a balance," the warrior explained. "You save my life, I save yours, and we are quits. Then I save yours again and you are once more in my debt."

"I'm not forgetting it," Price said.

"The other debt I speak of has no balance," Gray Wolf went on. "I failed my people by not helping them in time. Killing the scalp hunters did not erase that fact. I could confess it to the mission padres for a hundred years and find no absolution. It's the weight I carry to my grave."

"At least you're looking on the sunny side."

"Such matters are resolved in the next world," Gray Wolf explained.

"Those padres teach you that?" Price asked.

"The shaman of my village," Gray Wolf said. "Of course, he didn't know the scalp hunters were coming, so he may be wrong."

"I'd like to think it has an ending sometime," Price remarked.

"We all have endings, Matthew."

Right, Price thought. *And maybe mine's in Agua Caliente, if I ever get there.*

"Was it worth it?" he asked Gray Wolf. "Covering that debt you couldn't pay, I mean."

His trail companion shrugged. "I had no choice. But if you ask me whether I enjoyed the killing, I say yes."

"I don't want to enjoy it," Price replied.

Gray Wolf seemed honestly confused. "Why not? The men you seek deserve to die a thousand times."

"Don't get me wrong. I'll kill them if I get the chance,"

Price said. "But if I start to like it, I'm no better than they are."

Gray Wolf was silent for another moment. Then he said, "I think you have killed many men."

You've seen me kill a few, Price thought. He said, "More than my share, I guess."

"Did you feel anything with them?"

"Mostly relief that they went down instead of me. Anger, sometimes. Maybe a touch of satisfaction with a few."

"The worst of them."

"That's not for me to say."

"Who better?" Gray Wolf asked. "You killed them for a reason, did you not?"

"I thought so at the time."

"And now?"

Price mulled it over for a minute, then replied, "I killed them for a reason. Yes."

"It was their time. You were the instrument."

"Nobody's ever called me that before."

"When you have found the others, you will do what must be done."

"I guess we'll see," Price said.

There wasn't much to Agua Caliente at first glance. Ezekiel Rogers had seen smaller desert towns, but this one had a worn-out look that made him think the people might've pulled up stakes and left it to the lizards. For a moment he imagined Harpe had brought them to a ghost town; then his eyes picked out the dim lights flickering in several windows as the sun went down, and Rogers knew he was mistaken.

There was life in Agua Caliente yet.

And why did that put him on edge?

A quarter mile from town, he spurred his gelding up beside Harpe's piebald mare, the side away from Nolan. "Colonel," Rogers said, "I recollect you never told us how you chose this town particularly, after Texas."

"No. I never did."

Rogers got tired of waiting. "And the reason is . . . ?"

"I have a friend here," Harpe replied. "We've got some business to discuss. With any luck, it could make all of us rich men."

"What kind of business would that be?"

"The kind we're used to, only on a larger scale, for higher stakes. You'll hear the details soon enough."

Rogers decided not to press it, concentrating on the town before them as they covered the last hundred yards. A few people were out on the street now, as if the gang's approach had been telegraphed ahead and galvanized them somehow. Or maybe it was sundown, Rogers thought. The light fades and the night crawlers come out to play.

Come out to feed, more likely.

Rogers didn't like the turn his thoughts had taken. He was years beyond adherence to the superstition of his childhood. He'd spilled too much blood to fear the dead, even if they could get up and walk—which they couldn't, last time Rogers checked. These were nothing but regular townsfolk and peasants before him, and while they might well do him in if he gave them the chance, Rogers didn't plan on letting down his guard.

Not even for a moment.

He followed Harpe's lead as they entered the town, bypassing a livery stable and various shops—all closed now, with the coming of dusk—to rein up outside a two-story cantina on the east side of the street.

"I know the owner here," Harpe said. "He'll see the animals are taken care of while we get something to eat."

"And to *drink*," said Martinez.

"Lord knows I could use it," Nolan chimed in.

Rogers dismounted and tied his gelding to the hitching post in front of the cantina. Before they went inside, he took his saddlebags and rifle with him, just in case. Feeding the animals was one thing, but he didn't want the peasants messing with his Winchester or pawing through his things.

And if some kind of trouble waited for them in the tavern, he would have some extra firepower ready at hand.

Inside, the place resembled every other cantina Rogers had seen on this side of the border. It had no windows and no decoration to speak of, aside from an old bullfight poster whose colors had faded with time. The bar was standard size, with bottles shelved behind it. There were tables ranged around the murky room in no apparent pattern, flanked by wooden stools in place of chairs. Rogers counted a dozen drinkers in the place, most of them standing at the bar.

Harpe waved them toward a corner table, and walked over to the bar alone. The barkeep listened to him for a moment, nodding, then ducked into a back room, quickly returning with an older man in tow. The new arrival shook Harpe's hand without enthusiasm, making Rogers wonder if he'd count his fingers when the colonel turned him loose. They talked a while, more nodding, then the Mexican retreated to his hidey-hole.

"The animals are taken care of," Harpe announced as he rejoined them and sat down.

"I don't see anything to drink," Nolan groused.

"It'll be here. Have patience," the colonel replied.

"This town got any women in it?" asked Martinez.

"I wouldn't be surprised."

He'd barely spoken when a young woman approached their table, carrying a tray with four shot glasses and a bottle of tequila. Rogers guessed she was about sixteen years old and nicely ripened for her age. She wore a low-cut blouse and peasant skirt, ignoring the bedraggled men who eyed her cleavage while she poured their drinks.

"Something to eat, *Señors*?" she asked when all their glasses had been filled.

"What's good today?" Harpe asked, before Martinez had a chance to utter something rude.

With an enticing shrug, she said, "We have tamales, enchiladas, frijoles, and *carne asada*."

"Bring us all some of each, if you please," Harpe replied.

"*Sí, Señor.*"

She left them, moving toward the bar, and Nolan said, "So you were right. They *do* have women."

"One or two, at least," Harpe said.

"And what about your friend, Colonel?" asked Rogers, leaning forward with his elbows planted on the table. "Is he joining us for supper?"

"We'll just have to wait and see," Harpe answered with a cryptic smile. "The night's still young."

Price and Gray Wolf rode until the sky was nearly dark, then camped beside an upthrust slab of stone that let them build a fire without much fear of being spotted from the north. It figured that pursuers would've overtaken them by

that time, anyhow, but Price had taken all the reckless
chances that he cared to for one day.

The fire was just for warmth, since they had no fresh
meat or anything requiring flame to make it edible. The
saddlebags on Price's stolen horse gave up some pemmican, and Gray Wolf had his water bag, but it was too dark
by the time they camped for the Apache to go hunting with
his throwing sticks. The horses dined on cactus, green and
juicy after Gray Wolf peeled it for them, and Price thought
they might've had the better meal.

Price had avoided speaking of the next day's ride so far,
but it was time. Unless he lost his way or ran into another
ambush, he should be in Agua Caliente by the time the sun
went down again. For all Price knew, he could be dead by
then, but first he had to think about Gray Wolf.

"The town's due south from here, you said?" he asked.

Gray Wolf nodded. "We made good time today. You
should be there by nightfall, maybe sooner."

"And yourself?"

Chewing a strip of pemmican, Gray Wolf considered
Price's question. "If I go with you," he said at last, "I may
be forced to save your life again."

"I wouldn't want to cause you any strain."

Another nod. "I count you as my friend."

"I'm glad to hear it," Price acknowledged.

"But your enemies are not all mine."

"No reason why they should be."

"It is white man's business."

"That it is," Price answered.

"If I ride with you to Agua Caliente, you will only have
more trouble finding those you seek."

"I see your point."

Gray Wolf was right, Price knew. Few towns in Mexico

welcomed Apaches on their streets, whether they came in peace or not. Experience and standing policy encouraged anyone with the ability to kill stray Indians on sight. There'd be no questions asked beyond the daily rate for bounty scalps, and Price could write off any hope he had of taking his intended quarry by surprise.

It would be hard enough just finding them in Agua Caliente, without being spotted first. He didn't need the extra trouble that would come from riding into town with an Apache at his side.

"Where will you go?" he asked Gray Wolf.

A shrug. "Maybe I'll let the wind decide."

Price knew the feeling, drifting aimlessly. Testing the breeze could be as good a way as any when it came to choosing a new day's direction. "Well," he said, "I hope you find a quiet place."

"I think there is no place like that for us."

"You may be right. I'd like to find one, though."

"Maybe you will," said Gray Wolf, "after Agua Caliente."

Meaning what? Price almost asked him, but he didn't think the answer would be any consolation. Gray Wolf had been fighting hopeless battles all his life, and Price suspected that his only quiet place might be the grave. Some men like that looked forward to it, and while Gray Wolf didn't seem the type, Price thought he shouldn't look too closely, just in case.

A fatalistic attitude was one thing, but defeatism could slow a shooter's hand and get him killed.

"Why don't you get some sleep," Price said. "I'll take first watch."

"If you can stay awake."

"No problem there."

Despite the day he'd had, and the restless night before, Price wasn't sleepy. At the moment, the last thing on earth he wanted was to lie down on the ground and close his eyes. Mary was waiting for him in his dreams, and there was too much left unsaid between them.

Maybe in the next world.

Wide awake, he started piling fresh wood on the fire.

The prostitute in her teens was snoring softly, one arm thrown across Harpe's chest. The smell of liquor on her breath was strong enough to make his nose twitch, and the sounds she made were keeping him awake.

No, that was wrong.

The woman hadn't spoiled his sleep. Harpe blamed that on Lopez.

The bastard was supposed to be ready and waiting in Agua Caliente with plans for the job that would leave them both set for life. Harpe had sent Paco to fetch him first thing, but there was still no sign of Lopez, and the word came back that he could not be found.

Harpe lay and watched a cockroach make its way across the ceiling while the girl squirmed restlessly against him, caught up in a dream. The first wave of his anger had been dissipated in their coupling, but Harpe felt it building up again, the more he thought about Lopez.

If Lopez was gone, it meant that Harpe's retirement fund had vanished with him. If they couldn't pull the big job, there was nothing for it but to keep on doing smaller ones until his luck ran out and some lawman or vigilante caught him with a lucky bullet down the line. It wasn't what he'd planned, but Harpe had seen enough combat to know that schemes went wrong more often than they played out according to plan.

Still . . .

The thought of Lopez cheating him, recruiting someone else—likely a younger man—to do the job, infuriated Harpe. If that turned out to be the case, he wouldn't rest until he found Lopez and settled their account once and for all.

The girl's hand found Harpe's genitals and went to work, stroking. Harpe craned his neck to see her face by dim lamplight, but she was still asleep, still snoring. Didn't know who she was with and didn't care, as long as she got paid. It angered him, the way his flesh responded to her touch against his will. He couldn't hold the rage down there, where she was gripping him, but Harpe was damned if he would give it up that easily.

Snarling, he plucked her hand away and shifted on the sagging bed, rolling her over so that he could take her from behind. She'd drunk too much to wake immediately when Harpe entered her. It took him half-a-dozen thrusts before she came alive beneath him, squealing as she struggled to escape.

"Shut up, bitch!" he commanded, clamping one hand solidly behind her head, so that her cries were smothered by a pillow.

It was better for him when she fought, but still Harpe had to think about the women on the road to finish it. A last great heave, and she went limp beneath him as he spilled inside her. Drawing back, Harpe heard her thrash the pillow clear and draw a gasping breath.

That close, and she was lucky to be breathing.

"Get your shit together and get out of here," he told the sobbing girl. When she was slow to move, Harpe grabbed her by one ankle, dragged her from the narrow bed they'd shared, and dumped her on the floor.

Paco would hear the thump downstairs, but what of it? He wouldn't question Harpe, would never think of telling him to keep it down or any other goddamned thing. It was a weakness of his race that played to Harpe's advantage, and the colonel took advantage of it any time he could.

Lopez was stronger, more resilient, but he'd made a critical mistake if he imagined he could run a crooked game on Wiley Harpe and live to brag about it. He might be younger and a fair hand with a gun, but Harpe would see him dead before he took that kind of insult from a Mexican or anybody else.

The girl was gathering her scattered clothes from where they'd fallen on the floor as they undressed. Harpe didn't understand what she was muttering, and didn't give a damn. He kicked her in the naked backside for the hell of it, then slapped her for the pain she'd caused his toes.

"Get out, goddamn you, and be quick about it!"

Smiling for the first time as the door swung shut behind her, Harpe imagined Lopez squirming on the floor as boots hammered his ribs and groin. That wouldn't be the half of it, if he thought he could cheat the colonel.

He would be a long day dying if it came to that.

Or maybe he was simply laid up with a whore somewhere, himself. Maybe he'd be around tomorrow, to discuss the plan.

"You'd better be here, bastard!"

Having duly warned the empty room and spent his rage on helpless flesh, Harpe crawled back into bed and promptly fell asleep.

14

The fire had burned down to a layer of pale gray ash, the color of the morning sky, when Price woke Gray Wolf to another day.

"You were supposed to wake me," said the young Apache.

"I just did."

"You stood my watch."

"I had a lot to think about. Call it a small payment on that debt I owe you."

"You should sleep before you ride to Agua Caliente."

"There'll be time for that later."

Breakfast was pemmican revisited, reminding Price how much he missed ham and eggs, steak and potatoes. Even porridge would've been a welcome change, but that was part of living on the trail. With any luck, he might have time to eat a meal in Agua Caliente.

Or maybe not.

Price's stomach didn't concern him this morning. He didn't care if it griped and grumbled all day, as long as he had strength enough to reach his destination and complete his job.

After that, if he lived, Price could think about what happened next.

Gray Wolf had an Apache's inbred stoicism, taught from birth as a defense against a world of enemies who preyed on any weakness to destroy the remnants of his people. He would no more linger over long good-byes than he would try to cultivate a desert rose garden.

They clasped hands briefly and retreated to their separate animals. When they were mounted, Gray Wolf said, "One thing, Matthew."

"What's that?"

"When you have found the men you seek, remember why you hate them. Show no mercy."

"I'll remember," Price assured him. "And I'm not forgetting what I owe you, either."

"You can pay me back next time we meet," Gray Wolf replied.

Price nodded, played along with it, knowing the odds of that were slim. "Next time it is. Don't shoot me by mistake."

The warrior flashed a brilliant smile. "I never shoot a white man by mistake," he said.

With that, he reined his pony through a quarter turn and called it to a gallop from a standing start. Price sat and watched him travel westward until man and pony vanished in the morning haze.

Alone once more, Price started riding south.

He didn't know Gray Wolf's intended destination, wasn't sure if Gray Wolf knew it either, but they'd reached a final parting of the ways. Price guessed it would take something more than luck to make their paths cross yet again. Gray Wolf knew that, but still he hadn't called for any payment on the gift he'd given Price.

My life, Price thought, *for what it's worth.*

He focused on the ride ahead, uncertain how long it would be before he sighted Agua Caliente. Gray Wolf had expected him to reach the town before sunset, which could pose problems for a manhunter. Price had no reason to believe his enemies expected him—or anyone—to follow them, but there was still a chance they'd have some kind of lookout system to alert them if a gringo stranger came to town.

Nighttime was better, for concealment's sake, but it would also slow him down, and Price was running out of patience. He'd been too long on the road to welcome more delays, and the near-miss with Don Miguel had forcefully reminded him that he might fail to keep the promise he had made at Mary's grave.

Vengeance. Mary would've tried to talk him out of it, but this time she had no say in the matter. He placed no limit on the price of revenge, and was prepared to pay whatever might be necessary to achieve his goal.

It crossed his mind that Wiley Harpe and his companions might not understand that kind of dedication, but it made no difference. Price didn't really care if they knew why he'd come for them, although it might sweeten the showdown for him. If the opportunity arose, he'd tell them while they were alive to hear it. And if not, so what?

At some level, Price knew his taking down the bandits wouldn't mean a thing to Mary, even if there was an afterlife and she was conscious of his actions. Mary had already earned her peace by helping others while she was alive.

She didn't need his guns to fix a thing that wasn't broken in the first place.

Killing Harpe and his companions wouldn't be a treat for Mary, then. It was a gift from Matt Price to himself, a consolation prize for having failed her while she lived. Price couldn't make it up to Mary, but perhaps his sense of failure could be eased a bit.

Gray Wolf was right on that score. People sought revenge primarily to make themselves feel better in the wake of tragedy, the same way Bible-thumpers waived responsibility by claiming everything that happened to them was "God's will."

Gray Wolf was right about the other thing, as well. When Price found Mary's killers, there'd be no profit in treating them like human beings. He would need to cut them down as soon as he had verified his targets, or they'd do the same to him without a second thought.

Watching the sun climb higher in the sky, Price didn't think it would be difficult.

No mercy?

No problem.

A rat had burrowed into Seamus Nolan's skull while he was sleeping, waiting for the moment when he woke before it started gnawing on his brain. The throbbing pain evoked by any movement as he wallowed in his rented bed tied Nolan's stomach into knots. For something like the thousandth time, he swore off liquor with a vow to Jesus in His heaven.

And he knew it didn't mean a thing.

"Hair of the dog," he muttered, bolting upright in the bed despite the pain and nausea it cost him. Nolan scanned the floor and found an ancient chamber pot, lifting the chipped and yellowed porcelain receptacle into his lap. The smell that wafted from it to his nostrils told him he'd been busy sometime in the night, and that was all it took to tip him over, spewing out the acid remnants of his latest binge.

And just like always, Nolan felt immediate relief.

His head still throbbed, the rat still gnawed, and his mouth tasted as if he'd spent the night sucking a saddle blanket. He could stand without collapsing, though, and he finally got dressed without stumbling more than once or twice.

Nolan had stashed his poke inside his left boot, where he found the money undisturbed. He wasn't sure how much the whore had charged for last night's frolic, versus how much he'd spent on tequila, but it wasn't out of line. He still had money from the job in Texas, and if Harpe was right about his friend Lopez, they'd all have cash to burn before much longer.

If the taking of it didn't get them killed.

Nolan considered breakfast, but his stomach cringed from the idea of food. A beer or two would settle him, he reckoned, if the barkeep wasn't still in bed at this time of the day.

What time was that, exactly?

Nolan didn't have a watch, and there was no clock in the sparsely furnished room. Smelling the woman, her perfume, and what they'd done together in the darkness, Nolan crossed to fling the shutters wide and let the daylight in. It lanced his bleary eyes, but he withstood the extra pain, and felt himself a better man because of it.

What time? he asked himself again.

Judging from what he saw and heard outside—a slice of

filthy alley with the sunlight slanting down, a wagon rumbling down the nearby street—he guessed it was mid-morning, maybe eight or nine o'clock. Nolan was used to rising early on the trail, and even with the vicious hangover, it still felt good to catch up on his sleep.

He wondered if the others were awake and if they felt as bad as he did, after last night's cutting loose. It was traditional to celebrate the end of a long ride and dangers overcome, but Nolan's churning gut told him they hadn't seen the end of peril yet. Whatever Harpe was planning with this friend they'd never met, it would be doubly dangerous. The payoff of a lifetime, Harpe had called it, when a few shots of tequila had loosened up his tongue.

Nolan had learned one thing before he left Hell's Kitchen as a boy. That kind of money never came to anybody who was sitting on his hands and watching others do the dirty work. It had a price, and some who paid it didn't live to claim their just reward.

That's more for me, he thought, and tried a crooked smile on for size.

And then a sudden urge to flee came over him, like someone pouring ice-cold water down his back. He saw himself as plain as day, sneaking outside to find his horse before the others saw him, riding hell-for-leather out of Agua Caliente toward whatever compass point suited his fancy after he was on his way.

Nolan shuddered.

The moment passed.

He had nowhere to go and no one to accompany him if he abandoned Harpe. The colonel wouldn't track him if he left; Nolan already knew he didn't mean that much to Harpe. He'd be forgotten in a day or two and someone else would take his place.

The payoff of a lifetime would be lost.

"No feckin' way," he told the squalid room, and made his way downstairs.

Price saw the riders coming from a half mile out, north-bound on a collision course, and veered immediately from the road. His nearest cover was a stand of cactus and mesquite a hundred yards or so off to his left. Price reached it in seconds, dismounted, and led the mare into the thicket where they were concealed from the road.

Unless they'd already been seen.

Price didn't think so, since the riders sounded no alarm and didn't rush to intercept him. They were keeping to the road as far as he could tell, but he tied up the mare and drew his new Winchester from its scabbard just in case.

As the riders drew closer, Price recognized their uni-forms. More *federales*. They were making decent time without running their animals into the ground, and he won-dered if they had been called to La Strella. He'd seen no telegraph lines on the trip south, so far, but they might run further east, connecting towns he couldn't name. If word of the chaotic fight at Don Miguel's had spread, the hunters would be out in force.

Or maybe this was simply a routine patrol.

Price watched them pass, apparently unconscious of his presence on their flank. He counted twenty horsemen, one of them a paunchy officer who looked uncomfortable at the column's head. Price knew he couldn't take them all if they discovered him, but it seemed that they had missed him altogether.

Even so, he waited for the troop to dwindle out of sight, then slowly counted to a hundred for insurance. When he'd satisfied himself that none of them had doubled back to take him by surprise, Price put the Winchester away, untied the mare, and led her back to open ground. Instead of going straight back to the road, he set a course that took him parallel, and followed it due south for two more miles to put his mind at ease.

If they were hunting him, it could mean trouble all the way to Agua Caliente. Price had named his destination to the *federales* who had captured him, and then again to Don Miguel, but all of them were dead now. There'd been two or three *vaqueros* with the don when Price explained his mission, but he thought they might've fallen in the battle too.

He hoped so, anyway.

If even one of them survived and spilled his plans to the authorities, more *federales* could be waiting for him, standing between Price and the men he meant to kill. Would new opponents listen to his story more receptively, or had they been ordered to kill Don Miguel's assassins on sight?

Price couldn't take the chance, in either case. He didn't trust the law with Mary's killers, not in Texas or in Mexico. Eliminating them was *his* job, and he wouldn't pass it off to strangers, even if he thought they shared his dedication to a common result.

Price thought of Gray Wolf, heading west, and wondered if he'd meet more *federales* on the way. If so, it would be no risk the Apache hadn't faced before. And if they took him down, Price knew Gray Wolf would give a fair accounting of himself before he fell.

Price ate his last two strips of pemmican at noon, and split his water with the mare, letting the animal drink from his hat. It wasn't much, but it should keep them going until sundown if they didn't have to outrun any posses in the meantime.

"Slow and steady wins the race," he told the mare, remembering a childhood story of a turtle and a rabbit, something that his mother would've told him some night, when the old man wasn't in a funk from watching crops die in the field.

In Price's personal experience, slow sometimes won a gunfight if the other shooter couldn't aim for shit, but he had never seen it win a race. It was the same with nearly all the parables parents and preachers told to children. They had morals that worked well enough in church, but that were worthless in the world outside.

A man who turned the other cheek would get his head knocked off, most times. Pray for an enemy, and he would kill you on your knees. Do unto others worked all right for Price, as long as he could do it first and drop the other fellow.

It was a different kind of gospel, but it had kept Price alive until now.

He hoped that it would see him through the night.

"You have to try the hot springs while you're here, amigos. They are famous throughout all of Mexico."

"We didn't come from Texas for a bath, Lopez," Harpe said. "My friends would like to hear about the job, and they've been waiting since last night."

Ezekiel Rogers watched the porky stranger lean back in his chair away from Harpe, as if the colonel's breath was foul. Eladio Lopez kept smiling, but it slipped a notch and something dangerous came up behind his eyes. Rogers decided this was not a man he'd want standing behind him with a knife.

"Of course, amigo," Lopez said. "I was detained by circumstances I could not—"

"The job," Harpe prodded him.

"Muy bien." Lopez allowed his eyes to make a circuit of the table, lighting briefly on each face in turn as if assessing them for strength and weakness. "Colonel Harpe assures me that you all have certain skills of value to a man in my position."

"What position would that be, exactly?" Seamus Nolan asked.

Lopez leaned forward, lowering his voice. There was nobody else in the cantina at the moment, but he seemed to be a cautious man. "You know the pig Diaz who runs our country into ruin, *sí?*"

"We never met the man," Harpe said, "but we know who he is."

"Of course. The whole world knows of how he has raped and looted Mexico for thirteen years."

"Sounds like most any politician you could name," Rogers replied.

"No, no, amigo," Lopez answered. "With Porfirio Diaz, it's very different than you're used to in El Norte. He believes that all of Mexico is his by right, a gift from God. He sees the people as his slaves."

"Get on with it," Harpe said.

Lopez no longer smiled. "My people still resist him, after all this time, but we have no weapons to speak of, nothing that can match our enemies."

"We're not gunsmiths," said Nolan.

"No," Lopez replied. "I understand that you are thieves and killers, *sí?*"

None of them took offense at that, but Rogers thought he saw a problem. "You don't have in mind for us to kill this fellow you've been running down, by any chance?"

Lopez hooted with laughter over that. It took a moment for him to regain his self-control and wipe his eyes. "Forgive me, please, amigo. No, I certainly do not expect you to assassinate Diaz. You'd never get within a thousand yards of him. It's not your fault, but simply fact."

"So, what, then?" Rogers asked.

"The weapons that I spoke of," Lopez answered. "We have information on a shipment for the U.S. Army traveling through Texas two weeks from tomorrow. We have details of the route, how many guards will be aboard, and where the train will stop for water on the way."

"You want the guns," Ruben Martinez said.

"The guns," Lopez echoed. "The ammunition. All of it."

"Meaning we'd have to take the guards and crew," Rogers observed.

"A dozen Yankee soldiers," Harpe informed them. "Three targets each, together with a three- or four-man unarmed crew. We take them when the train stops, and it's done before you know it."

"How are we supposed to haul the guns?" asked Nolan.

"You will be supplied with transport," Lopez told him. "I assume that some of you know how to drive a wagon team."

"How much?" Rogers demanded, cutting to the bottom line.

"Ten thousand U.S. dollars if the shipment is complete," Lopez replied.

The sum made Rogers blink. "If you can put your hands

on that much money," he suggested, "you could buy the goddamned guns."

"We do not have the money yet," Lopez admitted.

"So, when *will* you have it?" Nolan pressed him.

"*You* will have it," said the Mexican.

"Say what?"

Lopez displayed a crafty smile. "The money's on the train as well. An Army payroll for the Texas garrison."

Rogers surveyed his three companions, and could not resist asking the question that he knew damn well was on at least two of their minds. "So tell me, Mr. Lopez," he inquired, "why shouldn't we just take the money for ourselves and leave the guns?"

"Of course it would occur to you," said Lopez. "You are only human, after all."

"That doesn't answer it."

"We'll bring the guns," Harpe said, "because I said we would. I gave my word."

It was an hour short of dusk when Price first glimpsed the town. There'd been no more patrols to dodge along the way, but he was feeling cautious, taking no unnecessary chances now that he had reached the last stage of his journey. There could still be *federales* waiting for him, tucked away in hiding, and he didn't plan to make the ambush easy for them if he could avoid it.

At a half mile out, Price stopped to rest the mare, dismounted, and got busy with his guns. He normally carried revolvers with the hammers resting on empty chambers for safety's sake, but Price topped off the Colts to their full complement of six rounds apiece, then checked to ensure that the Winchester was also fully loaded. That gave him twenty-seven shots before he had to fumble with loose cartridges, and Price hoped it would get the job done.

If not, there was a good chance that reloading wouldn't matter.

Price waited for dark, well away from the road. He watched for travelers and saw none passing either way, although his spyglass showed some movement in the town itself. His chosen lookout post precluded any clear view of the street, and in the time he spent watching, no gringo passed before the lens.

It made Price wonder if his enemies were even there, if they had passed this way at all. The gang member he'd killed days earlier could've been lying through his teeth, but there was only one way to find out. Price had to walk the streets himself, check the saloons and whorehouses, seeking four men he'd never seen before. They might stand out amongst the townsfolk, but the same was true of Price. His race and nationality spelled danger here, or anyway, the threat of it. There was a chance that Harpe and company had managed to befriend this town. They could be regulars, a group of valued patrons. What would happen then if Price rode in and tried to take them down?

What difference does it make? he asked himself.

Price had four targets on his list. He meant to kill them all if he had time and opportunity. Beyond that, he would take his chances. If the folks of Agua Caliente rose against him—well, it was as good a place to die as he had ever seen.

Price didn't want to visit them with death and grief, but anyone who tried to shield his enemies would be fair game.

At full dark, Price was mounted, slowly traveling a course to the southeast that would've taken him beyond

the town and back to open desert in another hour or so. He
didn't plan to go that far, however. When he'd left the road
a quarter mile behind him and the town lay to his right,
Price changed course once again, approaching from the
east. It might not be enough if they were watching for
him—*federales*, townsfolk, anyone at all—but Price had
spent enough time on preliminaries as it was.

He had his sights fixed on the main event.

Price took his time on the approach, no rushing that
would make him overlook a trap. It was a problem that he
didn't know the town and what was normal for it—certain
windows closed or open, dark or lighted; people teeming
on the street or tucked away indoors—but there was no
time for him to observe the native customs and become a
fixture in his own right.

It was now or never.

Everything came down to this one night, this hour, giving Price a sense that it had been his lifelong destination
from the start. He wondered if the other deaths had all been
leading up to this, but that assumed some kind of guiding
hand behind the scenes.

Price didn't buy it.

If there *was* a higher power and its hand had stolen
Mary from him, Price would make his stand alone, without
a whining plea for help. Trust was a favor to be earned, and
once betrayed, it was as good as dead.

Like Wiley Harpe. Like Nolan, Rogers, and Martinez.

It was strange to know their names but not the faces that
went with them. Price supposed he'd have no trouble picking out two gringos and a black man. If they had a Mexican companion when he found them, Price would kill him
too and hope it was the right one.

Better safe than sorry, and he'd come too far to flinch at any bloody deeds required of him.

Price found an alley, and the mare nosed into it with only modest urging. It was dark, but there were faint lights from the street ahead. Price found a place to tie the animal where he was confident somebody would discover it next morning, if he wasn't able to return, and left it with a fond touch as he went to find his prey.

15

Ezekiel Rogers polished off his fifth shot of tequila. He was frowning by the time he set the empty glass back on the table top. "So, Colonel," he began, "if you don't mind me asking, how'd you plan to split that money?"

Harpe had waited for the question, knowing one of them would ask it soon enough. Lopez had left them to discuss the matter in his absence, vanished upstairs with a whore to give them time.

"I'm keeping half because it's my deal and I've done the groundwork on my own," Harpe said. "You three split up the other half however you see fit."

He caught the shifty glances Nolan and Martinez cast at one another. Rogers, meanwhile, never broke his eye contact with Harpe.

"Five thousand split three ways, Colonel? You want us

to go up against the U.S. Army for sixteen hundred dollars apiece?"

"Not the Army, 'Zekiel," Harpe replied. "Some lazy guards who've made the trip a hundred times before without a hitch and won't expect surprises. Anyhow, when's the last time you took home sixteen hundred from a job?"

"Never, since I hooked up with this bunch," Rogers said. "Before that, I did fine."

"I guess it was a foolish move to quit your old job, then."

Rogers broke the staring contest long enough to pour himself another shot. "This is a risky job," he said. "You know it is. I'd like to hear why you're so anxious to go after it, Colonel."

"Ten thousand dollars," Harpe replied.

"That's five to you," Rogers corrected him. "I can't help thinking you've got something more lined up to make it worth your while."

How right you are, Harpe thought, keeping his face blank despite the urge to smile. He didn't owe a goddamned field hand any explanations, but Harpe knew he'd have to tell the three men something if he wanted them to make the long ride north and risk their lives to take the Army train.

"All right, you've caught me at it," he replied. The tone Harpe tried for was a mixture of sincerity and weariness. "I'm getting on in years, as you can plainly see. Cold winters don't appeal to me these days. I plan on staying down here when the mission is completed, maybe take it easy for a while. Lopez has friends who'll make it easy for me if they like the merchandise we're going to deliver."

It was an approximation of the truth, at least. Harpe saw no need to mention his arrangement with the peasant soldiers who were scheming night and day to overthrow Porfirio Diaz. So what if they'd agreed to pay him for his military expertise and counsel? Why should Rogers or the others care about a plan that held no promise for them?

"That's it?" Rogers was leaning forward, elbows on the table, glaring at him. "All of it?"

"What else did you imagine?" Harpe inquired.

"Oh, I don't know," said Rogers, slipping easily into the lazy drawl he used when he was feeling cocky. "Maybe I was thinking you'd worked out a plan to keep the whole ten thousand for yourself."

Harpe saw the other two perk up at that, eyes flicking back and forth between the black man and himself.

"That's foolish," Harpe replied—which wasn't quite the same as calling him a liar.

"Is it? You such bosom friends with *Meester* Lopez, who's to say you haven't made arrangements with his people to get rid of us, after we drop off the guns, and let you keep the whole damn pot?"

"One basic weakness of your average nigger," Harpe suggested, "is the way he lets imagination run away with him. Next thing, you'll want to ask a conjure woman if you oughta wear a chicken's foot around your neck for luck."

"You see, he's not denying any of it," Rogers said to Nolan and Martinez. "One of you go on and ask him if I'm wrong."

"No reason to believe in anything like that," said Seamus Nolan. Then he turned his face toward Harpe and asked, "Is there?"

"Course not," Harpe bluffed. "It's foolish nigger talk, that's all. Boy doesn't know when he's been handed something on a platter."

"It's the other hand that has me worried," Rogers countered. "Wouldn't be the first time some white bastard tried to stab me in the back."

Harpe pushed back from the table, chair legs scraping on the floor. "You need to mind your mouth, boy," he warned Rogers. "It could get you into trouble if you don't watch out."

Rogers had both hands beneath the table, out of sight, as he replied, "I'm watching, Colonel. What you got to show me, anyway?"

So this is how it falls apart, Harpe thought. His hand was on the curved grip of his holstered pistol when a shot rang out somewhere behind him. The tequila bottle shattered, spraying amber liquid everywhere, as Harpe lunged headlong for the floor.

Price knew the first shot was a waste almost before he pulled the trigger. Three of those who sat around the table dived for cover as he fired, while number four—the Mexican—slapped at his arm and toppled over backward with a startled cry of pain.

He'd come in through the rear of the cantina, slipping through a back door that was left unlocked for kitchen help and such. It was the second place he'd tried, after a quick look through the windows of a restaurant across the street, and halfway down the passage from the alley to the main room he had picked out voices speaking English. When he saw the four men seated at a table near the center of the room, Price knew he'd found his enemies.

The Winchester was at his shoulder, sights framed on the man he took for Wiley Harpe, when movement at the corner of his right eye told Price he'd been spotted by the bartender. He felt as much as he saw the Mexican duck to find a weapon stashed beneath the bar, and an involuntary flinch had made him pull the shot off center as the hammer fell.

Wasted.

He might have winged Martinez—if it *was* Martinez— but the way the man had fallen told Price that he wasn't badly injured, and the other three had suffered nothing worse than some tequila spattered on their clothes.

Damn it!

He turned to face the barkeep, levering the empty cartridge from his rifle as a fresh one took its place. It was his first clear view of the new target, rising from his crouch behind the bar to aim a double barreled shotgun from a range of roughly fifteen feet. Eyes narrowed under brows that met above his crooked nose, the Mexican was leaning into it. He wouldn't even have to aim.

Price shot him on the rise, his bullet drilling through the barkeep's upper chest left of the midline, spinning him off balance. It was enough to tilt the scattergun, so when both barrels roared together in the smoky room, the spray of buckshot tore into the wall a precious yard above where Price was crouching in the doorway.

Another shot exploded while the last exchange still echoed. This one was a pistol's sharp report, and Price ducked lower as a slug threw splinters from the door frame at his side. He pumped a shot in the direction of the upturned table, one more wasted as he scuttled to the near end of the bar and went to ground.

It angered Price to hear his targets moving, seeking new positions, when he couldn't bring them down. He was embarrassed and frustrated that he'd had Harpe in his sights and missed the killing shot that would've left them leaderless, shaving the odds to three on one. Three shots with only one clean hit was no great average, and he wasn't even sure the bartender was dead.

A voice called out to Price. "You're making a mistake, friend."

"Not if one of you is Wiley Harpe," he answered.

There was momentary silence after that, not even scuffling sounds of movement as the outlaws thought it over. Maybe they were flashing hand signs back and forth. Price couldn't tell and didn't care. If they were fool enough to rush him, he would drop them. Even if they killed him, he would hold on long enough to see the bastards dead.

"How do you know my name?" the same voice asked, at last.

"I got it from the one you left behind."

"How's that?" Their spokesman seemed confused. One of the others shifted as he spoke, edging a bit to Price's right. They didn't have him covered yet.

Price played the game, waiting. "You left him at a farm to keep the dead folks company, five days ago."

"Hoskins!" another voice chimed in.

"Shut up!" Harpe ordered. Then, to Price: "He told you where to find us, too, I guess?"

"That's right." More shuffling movements as he spoke. Price tried to see them in his mind, work out their plan, but it was lost to him.

"Why are you dogging us?" Harpe asked.

"You left a mess in Texas, at New Harmony. I'm here to settle the account."

"Are you a lawman, friend? I mean, if so, you've strayed a trifle far afield."

Nobody laughed at Harpe's poor joke.

"I used to be," Price said, "but don't let that concern you. I don't plan to take you back."

"We understand each other, then." Harpe almost sounded pleased until he raised his voice and shouted, "Now!"

Instead of rushing him, the outlaws made a mad dash for the stairs located at the south end of the room. They ran behind a screen of gunsmoke, fanning wild shots from their pistols, more to spoil their adversary's aim than in the hope of dropping him. Price ducked and dodged the bullets as they flew around him, peppering the walls and dusting him with granules of adobe.

He returned fire, too. Three shots from floor level at blurred legs on the run. It was a desperate bid, but he got lucky with the last shooter in line. A splash of scarlet marked the hit and told Price he had scored.

While running footsteps thundered overhead, Price rose and went to find the gunman who had fallen on the stairs.

The rifle bullet struck Ezekiel Rogers in mid-stride, punched through his thigh, and dropped him on the stairs. He started slipping backward, gasping from the pain, but caught himself before the slide became a tumble. He could feel the warm blood soaking through his pants as if he'd wet himself.

It was a bad place to be hit, but when he forced the wounded leg to move, Rogers could tell the femur wasn't broken. There were no great, rhythmic spurts of blood to mark a severed artery. Still bad, but not the worst—unless he let it keep him down until the shooter came for him.

New Harmony, for Christ's sake.

It had sounded like an easy job, and played that way while they were in the middle of it, but he hadn't known the holdup would come back to bite them on the ass. Who

was this shooter, anyway, that he would track them all that
way for taking down a small-town bank?

The woman. Shit!

That made it personal, a killing grudge, with Rogers
stuck on the receiving end this time.

A scuffling sound of movement in the room below him
motivated Rogers to attack the stairs with new resolve. He
crawled instead of running, grasping with his free hand,
digging with his elbows, pushing with his good leg while the
risers gouged his chest. He glanced back, half-expecting to
behold the nameless gunman lining up his final shot, but
Providence or something else had purchased him a little
time. He reached the landing, dragged himself over the last
step, and lay panting while he caught his breath.

Tie off that bleeder, damn it!

Rogers felt his mind begin to drift, and recognized the
symptoms of a body slipping into shock. He had to stanch
the blood flow from his wound and keep his wits about
him if he wanted to survive.

Did he?

Hell, yes.

Rogers glimpsed furtive movement at the bottom of the
stairs, and fired a pistol shot in that direction, blasting
splinters from the banister. The absence of immediate return fire made him wonder if the image had been conjured
by his failing brain—until a rifle slug drilled through the
wooden floor, six inches from his hip.

"Jesus!"

He rolled away and scrabbled lizardlike across the landing, trailing blood behind him. Narrow corridors led off
left and right, five rooms to either side. Rogers looked for
the others, but he couldn't see them.

Yellow bastards!

Another bullet through the floorboards made his mind
up for him. Humping to the left, he found a safer place to
pause and stripped off his belt, wrapping it around his
bloody thigh above the wound. Tying it off, Rogers experienced a moment's dizziness, but fought it down and
clung to consciousness.

If he passed out, he was as good as dead.

Get up!

It was a struggle, but he made it to his feet, bracing his
back against the grimy wall. Leaving a trail of blood behind him, Rogers lurched along the hallway, looking for a
place to hide.

Price knew it could be death to rush the stairs, but every
moment wasted gave his enemies more time to burrow in,
or maybe slip out through a second-story window. He was
stalling at the risk of letting them escape.

He'd used up eight of the Winchester's fifteen shots, but
Price had plenty left to finish off four men, with two of
them already hit. Emerging from the dead space underneath the stairs, Price edged around until he had a clear
view of the landing overhead.

Nothing.

The bloody drag marks verified his first impression of
the slowest runner's wound. It was a solid hit, but still
might not prove fatal.

Price meant to correct that oversight.

He started slowly up the stairs, Winchester cocked and
ready, testing each step for a sound that might betray him
to a shooter waiting just around the corner, out of sight.
When he was halfway up, a door opened and closed somewhere above him, but he couldn't place the sound.

Price reached the landing, noting more blood there, around the point where he'd fired through the floor. There should be more of it, maybe a body, if he'd scored a second hit. Tracking the line of fire, Price saw where both slugs had drilled wasp holes in the ceiling.

Never mind.

It was a gamble and he'd lost. That didn't mean he couldn't get it right next time around.

The blood trail led to Price's left, but he delayed pursuing it. The hallway ran in both directions, serving rooms that he assumed were rented out for sex or sleeping, as the case might be. The men he hunted were hidden behind one or more of those doors, no doubt ready to kill Price on sight.

Or had some of them already escaped?

Scouting the place, he'd seen that there were windows on the second floor, but none at ground level, as if the builder had forgotten them and then corrected his mistake as he worked closer to the sky. Call it a ten- or twelve-foot drop, no fatal obstacle to anyone intent on getting out in haste. For all he knew, there might even be ropes or ladders in the rooms to make it easier in case of fire, although he'd seen none mounted on the walls outside.

The drab cantina's upper floor was sparsely lighted by a kerosene lamp on the landing and another on a table at the far end of each hallway. Price was tempted just to shoot the lamps and watch the place burn down, but he couldn't be sure who else was huddled in the upstairs rooms, waiting out the sounds of battle before they emerged. Fire played no favorites, and his own recent brush with a foretaste of Hell stayed Price's hand.

He'd search the place room by room, if that was what it

took to find Mary's killers. At least the blood trail on the
filthy strip of carpet to his left gave Price a starting point.

It was a risky proposition, though. If he bypassed the
three doors that stood between himself and the end of the
blood trail, any one of them might hide an enemy prepared
to shoot him in the back. Conversely, if he checked the
other rooms before proceeding to the one where he was
certain one of Mary's killers had concealed himself, he
could be wasting further time, and any noise he made
along the way would put his wounded adversary on alert.

The mental image of exploding lamps was looking better by the minute.

No.

He'd play it smart and check the rooms as he proceeded, even if he found the doors locked and was forced
to kick his way inside. Price thought there was at least a
fifty-fifty chance the racket would unnerve his enemy, instead of bracing him to fight. The risk was there regardless,
unless blood loss had rendered the man unconscious, and
the edge Price would achieve by creeping toward the
fourth door down seemed marginal at best.

Get on with it.

He stepped into the left-hand hallway, and had almost
reached the first door when a stumbling footstep sounded
on the stairs behind him.

Seamus Nolan hadn't made it with the others to the tavern's second floor. He'd tried, but wasn't fast enough, and
when the shooter started blasting back at them from somewhere near the bar, his nerve had broken. Veering off while
Harpe and his companions raced upstairs, the Irishman had
spied an open door beneath the staircase, ducked inside,

and closed it after him, praying that the gunman hadn't seen him.

It turned out to be a rancid-smelling storage space, festooned with cobwebs that suggested it was rarely used. They tickled Nolan's face, and something wriggled down inside his collar, but he kept himself from crying out or slapping at it with a force of will.

Damn spiders wouldn't kill him, but the shooter was another story altogether.

Nolan huddled in the musty dark, his pistol gripped two-handed, cocked and pointed at the door. It wouldn't help him if the stranger started firing through the panel, but if Mr. Texas came to check the closet, he was in for a surprise.

He didn't, though.

Nolan could hear him moving just outside the closet door, but when another pair of rifle shots rang out, no bullets pierced the door. God only knows what *that* meant, but he stood his ground and waited, trembling and ashamed of it, but too damn scared to risk a peek outside.

Another moment and he heard the shooter moving off, then slowly walking up the stairs. Nolan tried to imagine what the bastard looked like, but his mind was blank. When his opponent's cautious footsteps were directly overhead, Nolan lifted his weapon, aiming at the closet's ceiling, cobwebs draped around his hands. He almost fired, but then a gritty rain of dust came down and left him gasping as he swiped it from his eyes.

"Bastard!"

Appalled at having spoken, Nolan clapped a hand across his mouth too late. He froze, waiting to hear the gunman change directions, coming back to kill him, but it didn't happen. Instead, footsteps mounted to the upstairs landing, pausing there.

Nolan saw his chance and seized it, slowly opening the closet door. He peered outside, dreading a trap, but there was no one left in the cantina's main room. Stepping clear, Nolan swept the room with his six-gun, ready to fire at the first sign of trouble, but no one challenged him.

He had a clear run to the door from where he stood, but any sniper at the top of the stairs would be able to drop him. Nolan hesitated, listening, but no sound issued from above to tell him whether it was clear or if the gunman was waiting for targets to surface.

Stand or run?

There was danger in waiting too long, Nolan realized. The Texas gunman might double back, change his mind about hunting Harpe and the others from room to room, and Nolan would be caught flat-footed. He should flee into the night while there was time, and get the hell away from Agua Caliente with his skin intact. If Harpe survived the night, he could find someone else to help him rob the Army train.

And yet . . .

It struck Nolan as cowardly to run and leave the others to their fate. Granted, they weren't exactly friends—he hadn't grieved a minute over Hoskins—but it wasn't Nolan's way to run from anything resembling an even match.

This time, the odds were four to one against their enemy. What were they frightened of?

Dying, Nolan thought, and mouthed a silent curse as he turned away from the cantina's exit. Instead of running for it, he made his slow way to the foot of the staircase and studied the landing.

Empty.

Nolan was about to take his first step when he saw the bloodstains on the stairs. Somebody had been hit, and badly, from the look of it. It hadn't been the stranger, since the blood trail started on the staircase and there'd been no gunplay once the stranger had started climbing.

Harpe? Rogers? Martinez?

Nolan almost turned away then, but the small voice in his head kept nagging him to be a man and take the shooter down. He pushed the bowler hat back on his head and started slowly up the stairs.

Not slow enough, though.

Halfway up, he stumbled without rhyme or reason to it, no danger of falling as he caught himself, but it seemed loud enough to wake the dead. He wondered if the shooter on the second floor had heard it, and his answer came a heartbeat later, with the sound of rapid footsteps drawing nearer.

Nolan could've rushed the landing then, but that meant more noise, and he couldn't aim for shit while he was running. Better to stand still and—

Nolan saw a shadow at the corner of the landing and squeezed off a hasty shot that scored the wall. Panicked, he fired again to keep the shooter's head down, wishing now that he'd retreated from the tavern while he had the chance.

No time.

Thumbing the pistol's hammer back, he used both shaky hands to brace it for another shot, but never found his mark. Just then, a crouching figure swung around the corner with a rifle shouldered and a slug ripped into Seamus Nolan's chest.

Dumbfounded at the way his luck had turned, the Irishman fell backward, tumbling down the bloodstained stairs.

16

Price tracked the bandit as he fell, ready to fire again if necessary, but his adversary landed in a boneless sprawl, pistol and bowler hat sailing in opposite directions on impact.

And that left three.

He turned back toward the blood-streaked hallway on his left, prepared to start the search anew. His quarry in the fourth room hadn't moved, but there were still three doors to check before Price reached him.

One step at a time.

He moved toward the first door, noting the number 6 painted around eye level, faded red on plain unvarnished wood. Whoever owned the place, he hadn't wasted any pesos on decor.

Price listened at the door as best he could, afraid to press his ear against the panel on the off chance that one of his enemies might have a gun aimed at the other side. A shooter still might drop him when he tried the door, but there was no point making it a giveaway.

Price crouched beside the door and reached out for the knob. It wobbled in his hand, then turned and let him push the door inward. Price braced himself for gunfire, but it didn't come.

Wary, he peered around the door frame, checking out the room. There was an unmade bed, a narrow table with a washbasin atop it, and a coat hook on the wall. Price saw no closet, and the window facing him was shut, latched tight from the inside.

He rose and glanced both ways along the hall.

Nothing.

The second door was number 7, telling Price that numbers 1 through 5 were in the other wing. He stood before it, poised to move, but hesitated as his ears picked out a snuffling noise. It sounded like a woman crying, but he wasn't sure—until he heard the impact of an open palm on flesh.

The woman squealed in protest, sobbing out a curse in Spanish. Price used the distraction to kick in the door, pushing through in a crouch. He'd barely cleared the threshold when a pistol flashed and hot lead whined beside his ear.

The Mexican he'd winged downstairs was grappling with a nearly naked woman on the sagging bed, trying to silence her, when Price burst in to interrupt. At the sight of his pursuer, the bandit had cranked off a wild shot, then rolled from the bed and dragged the woman after him. She screamed, and Price heard further sounds of struggle on the far side of the bed.

He might've risked a shot along the floor, but dingy bedding screened his view and any lead he threw in that direction placed the woman's life at risk. Price didn't know if he could save her from the man who held her captive, but he wouldn't take her down himself if he could help it.

After several moments grappling on the floor behind the bed, the Mexican called out to Price, "You want this woman, gringo?"

"Not today," Price answered. He was rolling even as the pistol spoke from hiding, drab sheets billowing to let the bullet pass. It struck the wall somewhere behind him, wasted.

"Better luck next time, Martinez," Price called out, goading the shooter.

"How you know my name?" the bandit asked him, still invisible.

"Come out here and we'll talk about it," Price replied.

"Hokay, gringo. You want to talk, we talk."

Martinez struggled to his feet, the woman pinned in front of him. He had one arm around her waist and kept his pistol's muzzle pressed against her neck. She'd lost what little clothing she'd been wearing in their struggle on the floor.

Price found the sight of her as stimulating as a bucket of cold water in the face.

"Le's talk, gringo," Martinez said, leering across the woman's shoulder.

"Now I see how tough you are," Price told him over rifle sights, "I've changed my mind."

He shot Martinez through the left eye at a range of ten feet, slamming him against the wall beside the room's lone window. The dead gunman's grip was tight enough to take. the woman with him when he fell, but she broke free of him an instant later, wailing as she fled past Price and out into the hall.

Price checked Martinez, making sure one shot had done the job, then followed her. Emerging from the room, he glimpsed a furtive movement to his right, and turned in time to see the black man he had glimpsed downstairs, aiming a pistol from the doorway where the blood trail stopped.

Price ducked and heard a bullet whisper overhead, riding the echo of a shot. He rapid fired two rounds along the wall and missed both times, as his intended target drew back out of sight. Behind him, brittle sounds of breaking glass were followed by a hungry whooshing noise.

Price glanced back toward the landing, where a lamp had stood seconds before. The table that supported it was now ablaze, legs planted in a pool of liquid fire, while flames shot up along the wall and licked the ceiling black.

His exit from the hallway would be cut off soon.

Price let it go and turned back toward his prey.

Rogers wasn't sure what had possessed him, stepping out to try his luck with the stranger that way, but he'd missed the shot and now he was caught like a rat in a trap.

I was already trapped, he reminded himself, but it had a hollow ring. Before, at least, there'd been some tiny doubt as to whether the shooter would find him before someone else intervened. Now Rogers was next on the list, and he'd shown the gunman exactly where to find him.

So, why wasn't he kicking in the door?

And what on earth was that *smell*?

A second later Rogers recognized the scent of wood smoke and a thrill of panic raced along his spine. *Sweet Jesus!* Was the place *on fire* now? Could his plight get any worse?

Maybe.

At least his leg no longer pained him. It was cold and numb below the makeshift tourniquet, forcing Rogers to hop or hobble like a peg-leg pirate when he walked, but fear provided all the energy he needed.

On the other hand, he had nowhere left to go.

The shooter would be right outside his door by now, ready to pounce the moment Rogers showed himself. Hunkered behind the bed, he strained his ears for sounds of movement in the corridor outside, but nothing came to him. The walls were thin enough to shoot through, but he didn't want to waste his last three shots and let the stranger catch him helpless, in the middle of reloading.

Wait it out.

The stranger had no better view of Rogers now than Rogers had of him. The door was closed between them, and he'd have to cross that threshold if he meant to make a killing. Rogers simply had to hold his pistol steady on the doorway and be ready when it happened.

Just like that.

Unless the goddamned place burned down around him, first.

A sudden rush of clomping footsteps past the door made Rogers fire without thinking, a reflex he couldn't control. His bullet drilled the door almost dead center, dim light beaming through the hole, but he heard nothing to suggest he'd dropped the shooter.

Two rounds left before his Colt was empty, now.

Rogers considered why the stranger would've rushed on past his door that way, with no attempt to come inside. If there had been connecting doors between the rooms, Rogers would've suspected he was looking for another angle of attack, but all the rooms were self-contained. The

Texan might slip in next door and try his luck at shooting through the wall, but Rogers didn't think he'd have much luck.

So, what the hell . . . ?

A sudden crashing blow against the door took Rogers by surprise. He almost loosed another shot as it flew open, but he caught himself in time, seeing the empty doorway.

"Come on in," he taunted, hating the involuntary tremor in his voice. "We'll sit a spell and talk this over."

"No, thanks."

As he spoke, the stranger pitched some object through the open doorway. It was something Rogers knew he ought to recognize, but the survival impulse took control and made him fire again while it was in midair. Grim recognition hit him even as his bullet struck the tumbling lamp and it exploded into flame.

The blazing kerosene was everywhere—on walls and ceiling, etching brilliant patterns on the floor, amidst the tangled bedding inches from his face. Rogers lurched to his feet, still covering the doorway with his pistol, and hop-hobbled toward the room's single window.

Heights had never been a friend to him, but he preferred a twelve foot drop in darkness to the threat of being shot or cooked alive.

Rogers glanced over toward the window, judging distance, and his adversary took advantage of the moment, squeezing off a shot that struck his wounded leg and brought him down. Rogers fell heavily and lost his pistol as he rolled across a patch of burning kerosene. The flames latched onto him, eating his shirt and vest, racing to taste his flesh.

Rolling and thrashing on the floor, Rogers saw his opponent watching from the doorway. The sight made him determined not to scream.

Struggling to hands and blistered knees, then to his feet, Ezekiel Rogers turned his back on Texas and rushed head-long toward the window, plunging through it into flame-streaked darkness as he fell.

Price watched the curtains smoke and shrivel for a moment, then retreated from the room as flames advanced to meet him. Turning to face the stairs, he found the first fire well advanced, framing the exit from the corridor he occupied.

Still one more room to check before he moved on to the other wing.

Price crossed the hall with no pretense of stealth and kicked the door that had been numbered 10. Firelight showed him an empty room, but he entered and looked behind the bed to satisfy himself that nothing had been overlooked, no shooters left behind.

Outside, the smoke was starting to become a problem. It obscured his vision and made breathing difficult. As Price approached the crackling wall of fire, he wondered who'd be waiting for him on the other side.

Instead of pondering the problem, Price leapt through the flames and landed crouching on the other side. No gunshots greeted him, and after glancing briefly at the empty room below, he moved to sweep the five remaining rooms on the second floor.

Price was about to try his luck with number 5 when another door opened, the farthest one down on his right. A well-dressed Mexican emerged, grinning beneath a wide-brimmed hat. He carried three pistols—one on each hip,

together with a small one tucked behind his belt buckle—
but made no move to reach them yet.

"Gringo!" he called to Price. "What's all this crazy
business, eh?"

"Nothing to do with you," Price said, "unless you're
here with Wiley Harpe."

The Mexican uttered a whooping laugh at that, showing
gold teeth. "You want to play with my amigo? We have
work to do, gringo. I need him."

"You can find somebody else," suggested Price.

"Someone I trust enough to do this job for me? I don't
think so."

"Who am I talking to?" Price asked.

"I am Eladio Lopez. You know my name?"

"Can't say I do."

"That hurts my feelings, gringo. You should leave this
place, before I take offense."

"That's not about to happen," Price replied.

"Hokay. I thought maybe you were a reasonable man,
gringo. It's my mistake."

Lopez was faster than Price had expected. Even watching him, waiting for it, the draw was a blur. He pulled two
guns at once and fired from the hip without aiming. It was
close even so, the slugs cleaving air at chest level and siz-
zling past.

If Price had been standing erect, either shot could've
dropped him before he could fire—but he wasn't. The
crouch saved his life, and he dropped all the way to the
floor as Lopez cocked his pistols again. He was fast and
determined, but no longer laughing as Price found his
mark with the Winchester's sights.

Three guns went off almost in unison, with Price's shot
an instant ahead. His bullet struck Lopez an inch below

and to the left of the Mexican's silver belt buckle, burning through to find an exit at the back. Even so, wounded, staggering, Lopez came close to killing him. One pistol bullet struck the floor a hand's width to the left of Price; the other nicked his hat brim and went on to chip his right boot heel.

Price cocked the Winchester again and fired its last round at his staggering opponent. This shot struck Lopez a foot above the other entry wound and knocked him down. He lost both pistols in the fall, but that still left the belly gun. Price drew his right hand Colt before he rose to face his enemy.

Lopez was done, not dead, but fading fast. The second shot had pierced a lung, and he was choking on the blood. Price watched his hands, and bent to ask, "Where's Harpe?"

"You want him?" Lopez forced a bloody smile. "Find him yourself, *chingado*."

"Suit yourself." Price holstered his Colt and plucked the small revolver from his dying enemy's belt, breaking its cylinder and spilling the cartridges into his hand. He dropped the empty gun and tossed the shells behind him, toward the stairs.

As he was turning from Lopez, Price saw the Mexican's eyelids flicker, his gaze shifting beyond Price toward one of the rooms on his left. Price turned in time to see a blur of movement there, and threw himself prostrate as gunfire echoed in the hallway.

Wiley Harpe had waited in the dark for death to find him, listening to shouts and shooting from the other wing of the whorehouse until his nerves were drawn as taut as newly strung barbed wire. He'd planned to spring from hiding and confront his enemy—or better yet, to shoot him in the back—but then Lopez had intervened and given him some extra time. The Mexican had failed to kill his adversary, though, and now Harpe realized the job was his.

If he could get it done.

Surprise was still the key, in single combat as on any battlefield where he had led troops in the War Between the States. The only sin Harpe recognized in any fight was losing, and he didn't plan to lose this one.

The stranger had already ruined any dreams Harpe had of settling down in Mexico with the proceeds from one last robbery. For that alone, Harpe owed the bastard pain beyond all measure, and he meant to pay that debt in full.

But he was also frightened half to death.

It galled Harpe to admit it, but the stranger had him spooked almost beyond the capability of framing a coherent thought. His mind was racing, but its output was a jumble of disjointed images, most of them grim and bloody, none inspiring confidence. Harpe knew his own abilities, but this shooter had polished off his men and Lopez, too, as if they had been whelps still wet behind the ears.

Harpe saw his chance—or, rather, *heard* it—when the shooting ended and the man from Texas tried to question Lopez. Harpe took the muffled muttering outside his room to mean the Mexican was down. Cracking the door, he saw the stranger standing with his back turned, tall and spare, a perfect target.

Trusting in the hinges not to squeal, Harpe pushed the door open another foot and raised his six-gun. He'd already cocked it while he waited for the enemy to find him, so the noise wouldn't betray him now.

Unable to resist a parting glance at Lopez, even when

he should've fired immediately and been done with it, Harpe saw the Mexican glance from his killer's face toward where Harpe stood with weapon poised. The staring eyes and bloody smile cost Harpe a precious second, and he knew the stranger saw it, too, because in that same instant he was moving, pivoting to draw a pistol, diving for the floor.

Harpe fired, too late. He missed the lunging gunman by a foot or more, and heard his bullet smack the wall beyond where Lopez lay.

Jesus!

Harpe bolted from the doorway as the stranger fired. He felt the bullet pluck his shirtsleeve, but it missed his flesh. Fleeing, he fired another shot behind him, just to spoil the stranger's aim.

In front of Harpe, the landing and the upper portion of the staircase were engulfed in flames, smoke hovering against the ceiling like a thundercloud. Harpe plunged into the fire without a second thought, knowing that certain death awaited him unless he made it to the street.

The fire licked at his clothing, singed Harpe's brows, and crisped the fine hair on his arms. Gasping, he reached the stairs and launched himself through still more flame, until the world slipped out from under him and he went tumbling down.

The corpse of Seamus Nolan broke his fall. Harpe stared into the dead face of the Irishman, then saw his Colt Peacemaker lying on the barroom floor nearby. Scooping it up, a gun in each hand now, Harpe seized the moment that might be his last and bolted for the door.

•   •   •

Price drew and fired a hasty shot at Harpe as Harpe was bolting down the stairs, but Harpe found cover in the drifting smoke and made it to the open floor below. Price tried again before his target reached the door, and saw Harpe flinch, but couldn't tell if he was hit or merely spooked. Another moment and the bandit was outside, lost in the darkness.

"Damn it!"

Price glanced toward the stairs, swarming with flames, and thought he'd try the simple drop instead. He put the smoking Colt back in its holster, braced one hand against the banister, and vaulted it, plunging twelve feet to land atop a small table. It buckled from his weight and spilled Price to the floor, but he recovered swiftly. Springing to his feet, he checked the room for living enemies, then raced to follow Harpe.

The outlaw had a lead, and wasn't wasting it by hanging back to ambush Price. It would've been a relatively easy shot, Price stepping from the lighted room onto a darkened street, but Harpe was nowhere to be seen. Instead of muzzle flashes, there was only darkness and the distant howling of a dog.

The few lights Price had seen while riding into Agua Caliente must've been extinguished when the shooting started. He was literally in the dark, crouching beside the door to the cantina, listening for footsteps in the night.

Where would Harpe go?

Price guessed the answer would depend on whether he was hiding now or trying to get out of town. Escape required a horse, and Price had spied the livery stable during his reconnaissance. It stood a long block from the tavern, to his right, but if his quarry wasn't there, Price would be giving Harpe more time to find a hiding place and lay a trap.

Choices.

Price started for the stable, since it was the only other landmark he'd identified so far and searching door-to-door for Harpe would take all night and well into tomorrow.

If the locals didn't kill him first.

Price guessed that some of them were watching him, although he couldn't prove it. There was nothing obvious— no curtains flickering or shadows slipping into alleys—but he felt eyes tracking him as he moved cautiously along the street. It could be Harpe. he reasoned, but in that case there'd be shooting if he came too close.

Price wondered if the residents of Agua Caliente would defend their gringo visitor. They'd shown no inclination toward it so far, if he discounted the bartender and the two-gun shooter who had introduced himself in the bordello. Neither one of them had been a serious surprise—one fighting for the place that paid his bills, the other for a crime partner—and Price surmised that neither represented Agua Caliente's citizens at large.

Still, there were towns in Mexico, as Price knew very well, where outlaws were not only tolerated, but welcomed, sheltered, and protected. Agua Caliente wasn't on his short list of such sanctuaries, but that didn't mean its people weren't corrupt or capable of killing. Price kept that thought foremost in his mind as he proceeded, guns drawn, toward the stable.

When he was halfway there, a shadow *did* move, stepping from a doorway on the far side of the street. Price swung in that direction, dropping to a crouch, but held his fire when he made out the figure of a slender Mexican with empty hands raised overhead. Slowly, the stranger lowered his left hand until his index pointed in the same direction Price was headed, to the livery.

So much for loyalty, Price thought.

Unless it was a trap.

For all he knew, the whole town could've gathered at the stable, waiting to surprise him in a rush with guns, pitchforks, and axes, anything that came to hand. In that event, depending on the numbers, Price knew they could likely overwhelm him, even tear him limb from limb.

But he would take some of them with him in that case.

And he could wait for Harpe in Hell.

An alley on his right yawned dark and silent, but no enemies emerged to challenge Price as he passed by. Behind him, there was no trace of the Mexican who'd shown him where to go. A few more paces brought him to the stable, and he put his left-hand gun away to try the door.

It opened at his touch.

Price slipped inside, as quietly as possible, and hoped it would be good enough.

It wasn't.

Price had barely crossed the threshold when a muzzle flash lit up the darkness and a bullet blazed a track across his ribs.

17

"You still alive, Texas?"

Harpe waited for an answer from the darkness, but the stranger made no sound. Did that mean he was lying dead or wounded near the stable entrance, or was it a sign he'd gone to ground and meant to let a pistol do his talking for him when the time was right?

Harpe couldn't answer that one, but he gave the tricky bastard credit for his quick reflexes. Blood still trickled from the shallow graze across his left bicep, where the stranger had winged him as Harpe made his run for the cantina's exit. It could've been worse, but it troubled him knowing that he'd come *that* close to a hole on Boot Hill.

"It's fine with me if you don't want to talk," Harpe told the shadows. "We can finish up our business anytime you're ready."

From his left, a spot Harpe hadn't counted on, a gunshot flared and spayed his face with splinters from the wooden slats that shielded him. A horse shied in the dark behind him, kicking at the narrow confines of its stall.

His horse?

Harpe didn't know or care right now. He wasn't getting out of there until he killed the Texas shooter, anyway.

Harpe swallowed the impulse to trade shots with his adversary in the dark. He would be wasting ammunition, and the muzzle flashes would betray him to the enemy. Better to wait and see if his pursuer made an error that would tip the balance in Harpe's favor, sometime soon.

And if he didn't, then what?

Harpe still had the best part of the night before him, but if sunrise found them in a standoff, it would be more difficult to hide from his assailant. Daylight was his enemy, as much as Mr. Texas cutting off his access to the street and freedom.

"That was close," he taunted, "but not good enough."

The stranger didn't speak. If he was moving, looking for a better vantage point, he must possess the grace and patience of a stalking cat.

All right, Harpe thought. *Let's see if I can shake you up a little.* Groping blindly on the floor around him, fingers questing silently, he found a crooked nail. It wasn't much, but maybe it would serve him. Rearing back, he pitched it with his left hand, toward the stable's entrance, willing it to strike some object that would amplify the noise of impact.

Harpe grinned fiercely as the nail struck metal and rebounded with a hollow *clang,* his finger tensing on the six-gun's trigger, but the shooter didn't fall for it.

Bastard!

Slowly, with utmost caution, Harpe began to crawl across the stable's central strip of open floor to reach the stall directly opposite his hiding place. He cringed at the exposure, muscles tensed to take the impact of a bullet hurtling from the shadows, but the gunman either missed his move or else decided not to risk a shot without a clear-cut target.

When he'd wriggled into cover on the far side of the aisle, Harpe paused to wonder what he'd gained. A new perspective on the battleground, perhaps—but would it help him spot and kill his enemy?

We'll see.

One thing was certain. He'd decided not to waste his breath on any further conversation that would help the shooter find him in the dark. Let the hunter work for it and see if he had what it took to survive.

For his part, Wiley Harpe was a longtime survivor who didn't plan on dying this evening. Anything the stranger wanted, he would have to take by force.

Where is *he?*

Harpe had no idea, but there'd been time for him to fix the stable's layout in his mind before his enemy arrived. There were ten stalls on each side of the center aisle, but only five were occupied—all five behind the point where Harpe was hidden, in the sixth stall on the right. The shooter was somewhere in front of him, between Harpe's cover and the door. That gave him ten stalls and some space around the entryway in which to hide.

Let's shave that down a bit, Harpe told himself.

Taking his time, avoiding any careless sound, he crept out of the stall and slipped into the next one, moving two yards closer to the stable's door.

•   •   •

Price grimaced as the hand he'd pressed against his ribs showed dark blood on its palm and fingertips. It was a flesh wound, nothing serious, but still it radiated pain each time he moved more than a fraction of an inch.

Lucky he's not a better shot, Price thought, before remembering his own poor marks in that regard. So far, he'd fired five shots at Wiley Harpe and couldn't even swear he'd grazed the target.

Harpe was slick, all right, but he was also trapped.

He wouldn't reach the street while Price was still alive.

Knock wood, Price thought, but didn't risk the noise.

He'd changed positions after firing at the outlaw's voice, to spoil Harpe's aim, and the old trick of lobbing a rock or whatever it was hadn't duped him into revealing himself. Unless Price missed his guess, Harpe would be on the move before much longer, angling for a shot to let him finish it. Price didn't plan to make it easy on him, even though the stable's layout limited his range of movement.

There were only two ways Harpe could reach him, in the last analysis, and Price ruled out the noisy, awkward route of climbing over the partitions separating the individual stalls. That meant he had to use the central aisle if he advanced, or else hang back and wait for Price to seek him out.

Which would it be?

Price didn't know the man he'd come to kill, but he had known the *type* throughout his life, and they were seldom known for patience. Harpe wouldn't like the waiting. It would gnaw at him and make him wonder if his last chance for escape was slipping through his fingers while he huddled in the dark. And he most definitely wouldn't want the sun to catch him penned up in the stable.

No.

The bandit would try *something,* but predicting his exact move was beyond Price's ability. It still came down to waiting for the move, unless he found a way to force Harpe's hand.

But how?

Price thought of burning down the livery, but he didn't want to hurt the stabled horses, and he also knew the first flare of a match would light him up for Harpe to pour on everything he had.

No good.

Maneuvers in the dark were risky, prone to making accidental noises that could draw fire from the enemy, but staying rooted in one place could also get him killed. The frightened horses in their stalls were making noise enough to cover him, if Price was careful, but he knew one careless slip could mean his death.

So what?

If he could take this last one with him—Harpe, the leader of the gang—his long ride and the deaths along the way wouldn't have been in vain.

It came to Price in that instant that he still didn't know which member of the gang had murdered Mary Hudson. And as quickly as the thought took hold, he realized it didn't matter. They were all the same, had acted with a single mind in that crime and in countless others. All their hands were bloody, and the punishment deserved by one applied to all.

Price didn't stop to think where that left him, in terms of guilt. He was too busy crawling toward the nearest empty stall, timing his movements so the horse sounds from the far end of the stable covered them.

Or so he hoped.

The joke would be on him if Harpe was waiting in the

very stall he'd chosen, crouching in the shadows with his pistol cocked and ready for a point blank shot to Price's head.

There's only one way to find out, Price told himself, and crept on slowly, slowly toward the stall.

Harpe nearly missed the noise, so focused was he on his own advance and the compelling need to make no sound. Because he needed to be quiet, every noise that reached his ears was supernaturally amplified, down to the whisper of cloth against his flesh. Never mind the inevitable scraping of his boots against the floorboards, which sounded like a rasp on hardwood to his nervous ears.

And so he nearly missed it—but not quite.

Amidst the general cacophony, Harpe heard a subtle shifting noise, off to his left. It wasn't the restless stamping and neighing of horses, for damn sure. And it wasn't any noise he'd made himself, because it reached his ears as he was poised to move, still frozen in an attitude of worried listening, not even drawing breath.

It might've been his pulse pounding, except that when he heard the noise, his heart had skipped a beat.

So close!

Harpe slowly turned his head, frightened his vertebrae might creak and give his enemy a target in the darkness. Moonlight hardly breached the stable, just a slash that spilled in through the doorway, and a dread of fire meant no lanterns were left behind at night. Still, after hiding in the dark so long, Harpe had begun to notice—to imagine?—that the shadows were not seamless velvet-black. There were degrees of darkness, shadings that betrayed objects and animals, perhaps movement.

Or maybe it was only in his mind.

Harpe raised his six-gun, moving with arthritic speed. The pistol was already cocked. There'd be no warning for his enemy before the muzzle flash and echo of the shot. If Harpe could only make it count, his troubles would be over—for the moment, anyway. He could ride out of Agua Caliente, take his time about returning to the States and sizing up another job. Recruit a few good hands, and—

First things first.

Harpe waited, trembling in his immobility, until the shadow he had chosen as his target seemed to move. It was one stall ahead of him and on the far side of the aisle, where Mr. Texas might be lurking if he planned to catch Harpe creeping up on him.

Might be.

Might not.

An error now could be his last, but Harpe was sick of waiting. It was time to take a chance and see what happened next.

The colonel held his breath, hardly a change, and closed his eyes before he squeezed the trigger. There was no sense being blinded by the muzzle flare, when he might need another shot to finish it.

The Colt's explosion set the horses kicking in their stalls again. Harpe hoped his piebald mare wouldn't be injured, but he'd swap it for another animal if need be, once he verified his enemy was dead.

The echoes of his shot were still reverberating when a pair of six-guns answered, rapid-firing from the shadows where his slug had gone. Harpe saw he'd picked the right stall, but he had no time for celebration as the bullets cracked and sang around him. Five shots in a rush, with two distinct and separate muzzle blasts.

Not dead, for damned sure.

Harpe retreated to the stall he'd left a moment earlier, firing a wild shot as he slithered backward.

Wasted.

Harpe didn't know if he'd wounded the shooter, but his adversary's reaction hadn't indicated any crippling weakness. As far as Harpe could tell, they were still on equal footing, except that the bastard had him outgunned.

Desperate measures, he thought. When a situation seemed hopeless, with nothing left to lose, a bold man could occasionally save himself with some constructive panic. Charging at the enemy seemed foolish, on its face, but Harpe was cut off from the stable's exit otherwise.

If he was tough enough, it just might work.

But first . . .

Slowly, working by feel and taking care to muffle any small metallic sounds, Harpe started to reload his six-shooter.

Price knew Harpe was up to something, but he couldn't put his finger on it. Rustling noises, clicking sounds, the background noise of horses—he absorbed it all, but could make nothing of it.

Harpe's shot from the dark had come close, taking a bite out of Price's hat brim. He'd returned fire on instinct, sighting on Harpe's muzzle flash, but without effect. Price knew the sound of death throes when he heard it, and the noise that emanated from the shadows now was something else.

But what?

To answer that, he'd have to go in search of Harpe, taking the stable one stall at a time. As he'd already seen, that game played into his enemy's hands and increased his own risk, but alternatives eluded him.

His right-hand pistol was empty after the last fusillade, and Price reloaded it as quickly as the darkness would allow. When all six chambers were replenished, he laid the gun in his lap and started on the other, replacing the three cartridges he'd fired so far. That job was still in progress when Price heard a sound his ears couldn't mistake—the grating of a wooden door across the stable's floorboards as Harpe opened one of the stalls.

Make that one of the *occupied* stalls, since the empties all seemed to be open and waiting for horses that hadn't arrived yet. Peering into the darkness, listening to more shuffling noises, Price wondered what Harpe had in mind.

If he thinks he can mount up and ride out of here—

As if conjured by thought, a drumming of hoofbeats resounded through the stable. Price thumbed the loading gate shut on his second revolver and cocked both weapons, rising to meet his enemy's charge through the darkness. Pistol shots slammed into the partition beside him, and Price answered in kind, pivoting to track the rider as he passed, still firing.

As the horse fled into outer darkness, Price ran after it, cursing, heedless to danger. He could hear the hoofbeats dwindling as the animal outran him, racing northward through the town and out of Agua Caliente. But as Price emerged from the stable, he found that the horse had left something behind.

Wiley Harpe knelt in the dust where he'd tumbled from his mount, some thirty feet in front of Price. He held a pistol in his right hand, while the left was pressed against his side, the fingers painted black by moonlight.

"You're damned quick," Harpe said. "I give you that."

"You give me nothing," Price replied. "Can you stand up?"

"I wouldn't be surprised."

"Your choice. The way you are makes it a shorter fall."

"And confident." Harpe flashed a crooked smile.

"Your choice," Price said again. "Get on with it."

"What was her name?" Harpe asked, surprising him.

"Why would you care?"

"I wouldn't, normally." The bandit struggled to his feet, groaning. "I'm curious, is all. What sort of woman makes you travel all this way and kill four men?"

"It's five," Price said.

"Not yet."

"Her name was Mary. If you have to ask about the rest of it, I can't explain it to you anyway."

"My loss, I suppose. The killing's easy for you, though."

"Sometimes."

"We have that much in common, then."

"You think so?"

"I'd bet money on it."

"You already bet your life."

"All right. Let's play it out."

Harpe's move was quick, but Price was faster. He shot Harpe in the chest, right handed, then put two more bullets in him as he fell. The outlaw's body jerked with each impact, but Price couldn't have sworn he felt the final shot.

Price moved to stand above him, studying the dead man's face. He'd hoped for warts or scars, some brand of evil on Harpe's countenance, but it was unremarkable. He would've passed Harpe on the street without a second glance.

The dead man's lips were drawn back from his teeth a bit. It might've been a grimace, but to Price it had the aspect of a final mocking smile.

Price cocked one of the Colts, and stooped to press its smoking muzzle flush against Harpe's forehead. *One more for the road,* he thought, then shook his head and eased the hammer down.

A muffled sound behind him made Price turn.

The street was filled with people, watching Price, eyeing the body at his feet.

He hadn't heard them coming, though there must've been a hundred in the street now, maybe more. Price checked the foremost ranks for weapons, but the hands that he could see were empty.

Not that it would matter if they rushed him, since he had no more than five shots left.

"All right, who's next?" he asked in English.

No one in the silent crowd replied.

Price didn't raise his pistols. He would fight if they came at him, but he saw no reason to provoke more killing if it was avoidable. There'd been enough to last him for a while, and if this was to be the end, he'd take it as it came.

"Maybe this fellow was a friend of yours," he said to no one in particular, "but we had business and it wouldn't wait. Somebody wants to fight for him, let's do it."

No response.

"All right," Price said at last. "If no one wants to fight, I'm leaving."

Holstering his guns, he took a forward step and then another. When he came within ten feet or so of the front rank, the crowd began to part for him. It could've been a trick, some kind of pincer movement to surround him, but Price didn't feel like standing in the middle of the street until his beard grew down around his knees.

If they were working up to something, let it come.

He passed among the silent watchers, and they turned away from him as he drew near. It seemed to Price that they were focused more on Harpe than on himself now. When the Mexicans began to move, it was away from him and toward the fallen outlaw's prostrate corpse.

Price almost turned when some of them began to kick and strike it, sounds of impact unmistakable, but there were some things that he simply didn't need to see.

Old scores, he thought, and moved on to the alley where he'd left his horse.

The animal was waiting for him, and it made a little welcome sound as he approached. "I'm glad to see you, too," Price said. "It took a little longer than I thought."

The blood against his ribs felt sticky as it dried.

Mounted, he thought about the Winchester he'd dropped in the cantina, and decided he could do without it. Getting out of town felt like the thing to do, but which way should he go?

Northward lay Texas, but he'd have to swing a wide loop to avoid La Strella and the *federales* who were doubtless hunting him by now. There were mountains to the west and ocean to the east, if he rode far enough.

And south?

The land was in turmoil, with rebels contesting a brutal government, while the peasants just tried to stay alive from day to day. Taking that road was doubly dangerous, maybe even suicidal. One gringo, more or less, would never be missed if he vanished in strife-ridden Mexico.

"South it is," he decided.

The horse gave him no argument, and seconds later they were on their way, speeding into the night.

THE EPIC WESTERN FROM THE AUTHOR OF
THE GUN

JUSTICE GUN

LIVE BY IT. DIE BY IT.

BY LYLE BRANDT

GUNMAN MATTHEW PRICE DID NOT THINK
HE WAS GOING TO MAKE IT OUT OF
REDEMPTION, TEXAS, ALIVE.
BUT AS HE STUMBLES OUT OF TOWN
GUT-SHOT AND DYING, HE IS RESCUED BY A
BLACK FAMILY PIONEERING THEIR WAY TO
FREEDOM. NOW, MATT MUST RETURN THE
FAVOR AND HELP THEM WHEN
TROUBLEMAKERS IN THEIR NEW SETTLEMENT
OFFER UP A NOT-SO-WARM WELCOME.

0-425-19094-3